Agatha Christie Crime Collection

Agatha Christie

CRIME COLLECTION

Peril at End House

The Body in the Library

Hercule Poirot's Christmas

HAMLYN · · · LONDON

Photoset by Petty & Sons Ltd, Leeds
SBN 6007 66 136

CONTENTS

Peril at End House

To

EDEN PHILLPOTTS

to whom I shall always be grateful for
his friendship and the encouragement
he gave me many years ago

1. *The Majestic Hotel*

NO SEASIDE TOWN in the south of England is, I think, as attractive as St. Loo. It is well named the Queeen of Watering Places and reminds one forcibly of the Riviera. The Cornish coast is to my mind every bit as fascinating as that of the south of France.

I remarked as much to my friend, Hercule Poirot.

'So it said on our menu in the restaurant car yesterday, *mon ami*. Your remark is not original.'

'But don't you agree?'

He was smiling to himself and did not at once answer my question. I repeated it.

'A thousand pardons, Hastings. My thoughts were wandering. Wandering indeed to that part of the world you mentioned just now.'

'The south of France?'

'Yes. I was thinking of that last winter that I spent there and of the events which occurred.'

I remembered. A murder had been committed on the Blue Train, and the mystery—a complicated and baffling one—had been solved by Poirot with his usual unerring acumen.

'How I wish I had been with you,' I said with deep regret.

'I too,' said Poirot. 'Your experience would have been invaluable to me.'

I looked at him sideways. As a result of long habit, I distrust his compliments, but he appeared perfectly serious. And after all, why not? I have a very long experience of the methods he employs.

'What I particularly missed was your vivid imagination, Hastings,' he went on dreamily. 'One needs a certain amount of light relief. My valet, Georges, an admirable man with whom I sometimes permitted myself to discuss a point, has no imagination whatever.'

This remark seemed to me quite irrelevant.

'Tell me, Poirot,' I said. 'Are you never tempted to renew your activities? This passive life——'

'Suits me admirably, my friend. To sit in the sun—what could be more charming? To step from your pedestal at the zenith of your fame—what could be a grander gesture? They say of me: *"That is Hercule Poirot!—The great—the unique!—There was never anyone like him, there never will be!" Eh bien*—I am satisfied. I ask no more. I am modest.'

I should not myself have used the word *modest*. It seemed to me that my little friend's egotism had certainly not declined with his years. He leaned back in his chair, caressing his moustache and almost purring with self-satisfaction.

We were sitting on one of the terraces of the Majestic Hotel. It is the biggest hotel in St. Loo and stands in its own grounds on a headland overlooking the sea. The gardens of the hotel lay below us freely interspersed with palm trees. The sea was of a deep and lovely blue, the sky clear and the sun shining with all the single-hearted fervour an August sun should (but in England so often does not) have. There was a vigorous humming of bees, a pleasant sound—and altogether nothing could have been more ideal.

We had only arrived last night, and this was the first morning of what we proposed should be a week's stay. If only these weather conditions continued, we should indeed have a perfect holiday.

I picked up the morning paper which had fallen from my hand and resumed my perusal of the morning's news. The political situation seemed unsatisfactory, but uninteresting, there was trouble in China, there was a long account of a rumoured City swindle, but on the whole there was no news of a very thrilling order.

'Curious thing this parrot disease,' I remarked, as I turned the sheet.

'Very curious.'

'Two more deaths at Leeds, I see.'

'Most regrettable.'

I turned a page.

'Still no news of that flying fellow, Seton, in his round-the-world flight. Pretty plucky, these fellows. That amphibian machine of his, the *Albatross*, must be a great invention. Too bad if he's gone west. Not that they've given up hope yet. He may have made one of the Pacific islands.'

'The Solomon islanders are still cannibals, are they not?' inquired Poirot pleasantly.

'Must be a fine fellow. That sort of thing makes one feel it's a good thing to be an Englishman after all.'

'It consoles for the defeats at Wimbledon,' said Poirot.

'I—I didn't mean,' I began.

My friend waved my attempted apology aside gracefully.

'Me,' he announced. 'I am not amphibian, like the machine of the poor Captain Seton, but I am cosmopolitan. And for the English I have always had, as you know, a great admiration. The thorough way, for instance, in which they read the daily paper.'

My attention had strayed to political news.

'They seem to be giving the Home Secretary a pretty bad time of it,' I remarked with a chuckle.

'The poor man. He has his troubles, that one. Ah! yes. So much so that he seeks for help in the most improbable quarters.'

I stared at him.

With a slight smile, Poirot drew from his pocket his morning's correspondence, neatly secured by a rubber band. From this he selected one letter which he tossed across to me.

'It must have missed us yesterday,' he said.

I read the letter with a pleasurable feeling of excitement.

'But, Poirot,' I cried. 'This is most flattering!'

'You think so, my friend?'

'He speaks in the warmest terms of your ability.'

'He is right,' said Poirot, modestly averting his eyes.

'He begs you to investigate this matter for him—puts it as a personal favour.'

'Quite so. It is unnecessary to repeat all this to me. You understand, my dear Hastings. I have read the letter myself.'

'It's too bad,' I cried. 'This will put an end to our holiday.'

'No, no, *calmez vous*—there is no question of that.'

'But the Home Secretary says the matter is urgent.'

'He may be right—or again he may not. These politicians they are easily excited. I have seen myself, in the Chambre des Deputés in Paris——'

'Yes, yes, but Poirot, surely we ought to be making arrangements? The express to London has gone—it leaves at twelve o'clock. The next——'

'Calm yourself, Hastings, calm yourself, I pray of you! Always the excitement, the agitation. We are not going to London to-day—nor yet to-morrow.'

'But this summons——'

'Does not concern me. I do not belong to your police force,

Hastings. I am asked to undertake a case as a private investigator. I refuse.'

'You *refuse?*'

'Certainly. I write with perfect politeness, tender my regrets, my apologies, explain that I am completely desolated—but what will you? I have retired—I am finished.'

'You are not finished,' I exclaimed warmly.

Poirot patted my knee.

'There speaks the good friend—the faithful dog. And you have reason, too. The grey cells, they still function—the order, the method—it is still there. But when I have retired, my friend, I have retired! It is finished! I am not a stage favourite who gives the world a dozen farewells. In all generosity I say: let the young men have a chance. They may possibly do something creditable. I doubt it, but they may. Anyway they will do well enough for this doubtless tiresome affair of the Home Secretary's.'

'But, Poirot, the compliment!'

'Me, I am above compliments. The Home Secretary, being a man of sense, realises that if he can only obtain my services all will be successful. What will you? He is unlucky. Hercule Poirot has solved his last case.'

I looked at him. In my heart of hearts I deplored his obstinacy. The solving of such a case as was indicated might add still further lustre to his already world-wide reputation. Nevertheless I could not but admire his unyielding attitude.

Suddenly a thought struck me and I smiled.

'I wonder,' I said, 'that you are not afraid. Such an emphatic pronouncement will surely tempt the gods.'

'Impossible,' he replied, 'that anyone should shake the decision of Hercule Poirot.'

'*Impossible*, Poirot?'

'You are right, *mon ami*, one should not use such a word. *Eh, ma foi*, I do not say that if a bullet should strike the wall by my head, I would not investigate the matter! One is human after all!'

I smiled. A little pebble had just struck the terrace beside us, and Poirot's fanciful analogy from it tickled my fancy. He stooped now and picked up the pebble as he went on.

'Yes—one is human. One is the sleeping dog—well and good, but the sleeping dog can be roused. There is a proverb in your language that says so.'

'In fact,' I said, 'if you find a dagger planted by your pillow to-morrow morning—let the criminal who put it there beware!'

He nodded, but rather absently.

Suddenly, to my surprise, he rose and descended the couple of steps that led from the terrace to the garden. As he did so, a girl came into sight hurrying up towards us.

I had just registered the impression that she was a decidedly pretty girl when my attention was drawn to Poirot who, not looking where he was going, had stumbled over a root and fallen heavily. He was just abreast of the girl at the time and she and I between us helped him to his feet. My attention was naturally on my friend, but I was conscious of an impression of dark hair, an impish face and big dark blue eyes.

'A thousand pardons,' stammered Poirot. 'Mademoiselle, you are most kind. I regret exceedingly—ouch!—my foot he pains me considerably. No, no, it is nothing really—the turned ankle, that is all. In a few minutes all will be well. But if you could help me, Hastings—you and Mademoiselle between you, if she will be so very kind. I am ashamed to ask it of her.'

With me on the one side and the girl on the other we soon got Poirot on to a chair on the terrace. I then suggested fetching a doctor, but this my friend negatived sharply.

'It is nothing, I tell you. The ankle turned, that is all. Painful for the moment, but soon over.' He made a grimace. 'See, in a little minute I shall have forgotten. Mademoiselle, I thank you a thousand times. You were most kind. Sit down, I beg of you.'

The girl took a chair.

'It's nothing,' she said. 'But I wish you would let it be seen to.'

'Mademoiselle, I assure you, it is a *bagatelle*! In the pleasure of your society the pain passes already.'

The girl laughed.

'That's good.'

'What about a cocktail?' I suggested. 'It's just about the time.'

'Well——' She hesitated. 'Thanks very much.'

'Martini?'

'Yes, please—dry Martini.'

I went off. On my return, after having ordered the drinks, I found Poirot and the girl engaged in animated conversation.

'Imagine, Hastings,' he said, 'that house—the one on the point—that we have admired so much, it belongs to Mademoiselle here.'

'Indeed?' I said, though I was unable to recall having expressed any admiration. In fact I had hardly noticed the house. 'It looks rather eerie and imposing standing there by itself far from anything.'

'It's called End House,' said the girl. 'I love it—but it's a tumble-down old place. Going to rack and ruin.'

'You are the last of an old family, Mademoiselle?'

'Oh! we're nothing important. But there have been Buckleys here for two or three hundred years. My brother died three years ago, so I'm the last of the family.'

'That is sad. You live there alone, Mademoiselle?'

'Oh! I'm away a good deal and when I'm at home there's usually a cheery crowd coming and going.'

'That is so modern. Me, I was picturing you in a dark mysterious mansion, haunted by a family curse.'

'How marvellous! What a picturesque imagination you must have. No, it's not haunted. Or if so, the ghost is a beneficent one. I've had three escapes from sudden death in as many days, so I must bear a charmed life.'

Poirot sat up alertly.

'Escapes from death? That sounds interesting, Mademoiselle.'

'Oh! they weren't very thrilling. Just accidents, you know.' She jerked her head sharply as a wasp flew past. 'Curse these wasps. There must be a nest of them round here.'

'The bees and the wasps—you do not like them, Mademoiselle? You have been stung—yes?'

'No—but I hate the way they come right past your face.'

'The bee in the bonnet,' said Poirot. 'Your English phrase.'

At that moment the cocktails arrived. We all held up our glasses and made the usual inane observations.

'I'm due in the hotel for cocktails, really,' said Miss Buckley. 'I expect they're wondering what has become of me.'

Poirot cleared his throat and set down his glass.

'Ah! for a cup of good rich chocolate,' he murmured. 'But in England they make it not. Still, in England you have some very pleasing customs. The young girls, their hats they come on and off —so prettily—so easily——'

The girl stared at him.

'What do you mean? Why shouldn't they?'

'You ask that because you are young—so young, Mademoiselle.

But to me the natural thing seems to have a coiffure high and rigid —so—and the hat attached with many hatpins—*là—là—là—et là.'*

He executed four vicious jabs in the air.

'But how frightfully uncomfortable!'

'Ah! I should think so,' said Poirot. No martyred lady could have spoken with more feeling. 'When the wind blew it was the agony—it gave you the *migraine*.'

Miss Buckley dragged off the simple wide-brimmed felt she was wearing and cast it down beside her.

'And now we do this,' she laughed.

'Which is sensible and charming,' said Poirot, with a little bow.

I looked at her with interest. Her dark hair was ruffled and gave her an elfin look. There was something elfin about her altogether. The small, vivid face, pansy-shaped, the enormous dark blue eyes, and something else—something haunting and arresting. Was it a hint of recklessness? There were dark shadows under the eyes.

The terrace on which we were sitting was a little used one. The main terrace where most people sat was just round the corner at a point where the cliff shelved directly down to the sea.

From round this corner now there appeared a man, a red-faced man with a rolling carriage who carried his hands half clenched by his side. There was something breezy and care-free about him—a typical sailor.

'I can't think where the girl's got to,' he was saying in tones that easily carried to where we sat. 'Nick—Nick.'

Miss Buckley rose.

'I knew they'd be getting in a state. Attaboy—George—here I am.'

'Freddie's frantic for a drink. Come on, girl.'

He cast a glance of frank curiosity at Poirot, who must have differed considerably from most of Nick's friends.

The girl performed a wave of introduction.

'This is Commander Challenger—er——'

But to my surprise Poirot did not supply the name for which she was waiting. Instead he rose, bowed very ceremoniously and murmured.

'Of the English Navy. I have a great regard for the English Navy.'

This type of remark is not one that an Englishman acclaims most readily. Commander Challenger flushed and Nick Buckley took command of the situation.

'Come on, George. Don't gape. Let's find Freddie and Jim.'

She smiled at Poirot.

'Thanks for the cocktail. I hope the ankle will be all right.'

With a nod to me she slipped her hand through the sailor's arm and they disappeared round the corner together.

'So that is one of Mademoiselle's friends,' murmured Poirot thoughtfully. 'One of her cheery crowd. What about him? Give me your expert judgment, Hastings. Is he what you call a good fellow —yes?'

Pausing for a moment to try and decide exactly what Poirot thought I should mean by a 'good fellow,' I gave a doubtful assent.

'He seems all right—yes,' I said. 'So far as one can tell by a cursory glance.'

'I wonder,' said Poirot.

The girl had left her hat behind. Poirot stooped to pick it up and twirled it round absent-mindedly on his finger.

'Has he a *tendresse* for her? What do you think, Hastings?'

'My dear Poirot! How *can* I tell? Here—give me that hat. The lady will want it. I'll take it to her.'

Poirot paid no attention to my request. He continued to revolve the hat slowly on his finger.

'Pas encore. Ça m'amuse.'

'Really, Poirot!'

'Yes, my friend, I grow old and childish, do I not?'

This was so exactly what I was feeling that I was somewhat disconcerted to have it put into words. Poirot gave a little chuckle, then leaning forward he laid a finger against the side of his nose.

'But no—I am not so completely imbecile as you think! We will return the hat—but assuredly—but later! We will return it to End House and thus we shall have the opportunity of seeing the charming Miss Nick again.'

'Poirot,' I said. 'I believe you have fallen in love.'

'She is a pretty girl—eh?'

'Well—you saw for yourself. Why ask me?'

'Because, alas! I cannot judge. To me, nowadays, anything young is beautiful. *Jeunesse—jeunesse*. . . . It is the tragedy of my years. But you—I appeal to you? Your judgment is not up to date, naturally, having lived in the Argentine so long. You admire the figure of five years ago, but you are at any rate more modern than I am. She is pretty—yes? She has the appeal to the sexes?'

'One sex is sufficient, Poirot. The answer, I should say, is very much in the affirmative. Why are you so interested in the lady?'

'Am I interested?'

'Well—look at what you've just been saying.'

'You are under a misapprehension, *mon ami*. I may be interested in the lady—yes—but I am much more interested in her hat.'

I stared at him, but he appeared perfectly serious.

He nodded his head at me.

'Yes, Hastings, this very hat.' He held it towards me. 'You see the reason for my interest?'

'It's a nice hat,' I said, bewildered. 'But quite an ordinary hat. Lots of girls have hats like it.'

'Not like this one.'

I looked at it more closely.

'You see, Hastings?'

'A perfectly plain fawn felt. Good style——'

'I did not ask you to describe the hat. It is plain that you do *not* see. Almost incredible, my poor Hastings, how you hardly ever *do* see! It amazes me every time anew! But regard, my dear old imbecile—it is not necessary to employ the grey cells—the eyes will do. Regard—regard——'

And then at last I saw to what he had been trying to draw my attention. The slowly turning hat was revolving on his finger, and that finger was stuck neatly through a hole in the brim of the hat. When he saw that I had realised his meaning, he drew his finger out and held the hat towards me. It was a small neat hole, quite round, and I could not imagine its purpose, if purpose it had.

'Did you observe the way Mademoiselle Nick flinched when a bee flew past? The bee in the bonnet—the hole in the hat.'

'But a bee couldn't make a hole like that.'

'Exactly, Hastings! What acumen! It could not. *But a bullet could, mon cher*!'

'A bullet?'

'*Mais oui!* A bullet like *this*."

He held out his hand with a small object in the palm of it.

'A spent bullet, *mon ami*. It was that which hit the terrace just now when we were talking. A spent bullet!'

'You mean——?'

'*I mean that one inch of difference and that hole would be not through the hat but through the head*. Now do you see why I am interested, Hastings? You were right, my friend, when you told me not to use the word "impossible." Yes—one is human! Ah! but he made a grave mistake, that would-be murderer, when he shot at his victim within a dozen yards of Hercule Poirot! For him, it is indeed *la mauvaise chance*. But you see now why we must make our entry into End House and get into touch with Mademoiselle? *Three near escapes from death in three days*. That is what she said. We must act quickly, Hastings. The peril is very close at hand.'

2. *End House*

'POIROT,' I SAID. 'I have been thinking.'

'An admirable exercise, my friend. Continue it.'

We were sitting facing each other at lunch at a small table in the window.

'This shot must have been fired quite close to us. And yet we did not hear it.'

'And you think that in the peaceful stillness, with the rippling waves the only sound, we should have done so?'

'Well, it's odd.'

'No, it is not odd. Some sounds—you get used to them so soon that you hardly notice they are there. All this morning, my friend, speedboats have been making trips in the bay. You complained at first—soon, you did not even notice. But, *ma foi*, you could fire a machine gun almost and not notice it when one of those boats is on the sea.'

'Yes, that's true.'

'Ah! *voilà*,' murmured Poirot. 'Mademoiselle and her friends. They are to lunch here, it seems. And therefore I must return the hat. But no matter. The affair is sufficiently serious to warrant a visit all on its own.'

He leaped up nimbly from his seat, hurried across the room, and presented the hat with a bow just as Miss Buckley and her companions were seating themselves at table.

They were a party of four, Nick Buckley, Commander Challenger, another man and another girl. From where we sat we had a very imperfect view of them. From time to time the naval man's laugh boomed out. He seemed a simple, likeable soul, and I had already taken a fancy to him.

My friend was silent and distrait during our meal. He crumbled his bread, made strange little ejaculations to himself and straightened everything on the table. I tried to talk, but meeting with no encouragement soon gave it up.

He continued to sit on at the table long after he had finished his cheese. As soon as the other party had left the room, however, he too rose to his feet. They were just settling themselves at a table in the lounge when Poirot marched up to them in his most military fashion, and addressed Nick directly.

'Mademoiselle, may I crave one little word with you.'

The girl frowned. I realised her feelings clearly enough. She was afraid that this queer little foreigner was going to be a nuisance. I could not but sympathise with her, knowing how it must appear in her eyes. Rather unwillingly, she moved a few steps aside.

Almost immediately I saw an expression of surprise pass over her face at the low hurried words Poirot was uttering.

In the meantime, I was feeling rather awkward and ill at ease. Challenger with ready tact came to my rescue, offering me a cigarette and making some commonplace observation. We had taken each other's measure and were inclined to be sympathetic to each other. I fancied that I was more his own kind than the man with whom he had been lunching. I now had the opportunity of observing the latter. A tall, fair, rather exquisite young man, with a rather fleshy nose and over-emphasised good-looks. He had a supercilious manner and a tired drawl. There was a sleekness about him that I especially disliked.

Then I looked at the woman. She was sitting straight opposite me in a big chair and had just thrown off her hat. She was an unusual type—a weary Madonna describes it best. She had fair, almost colourless hair, parted in the middle and drawn straight down over her ears to a knot in the neck. Her face was dead white and emaciated—yet curiously attractive. Her eyes were very light grey with large pupils. She had a curious look of detachment. She was staring at me. Suddenly she spoke.

'Sit down—till your friend has finished with Nick.'

She had an affected voice, languid and artificial—yet which had withal a curious attraction—a kind of resonant lingering beauty. She impressed me, I think, as the most tired person I had ever met. Tired in mind, not in body, as though she had found everything in the world to be empty and valueless.

'Miss Buckley very kindly helped my friend when he twisted his ankle this morning,' I explained, as I accepted her offer.

'So Nick said.' Her eyes considered me, still detachedly. 'Nothing wrong with his ankle now, is there?'

I felt myself blushing.

'Just a momentary sprain,' I explained.

'Oh! well—I'm glad to hear Nick didn't invent the whole thing. She's the most heaven-sent little liar that ever existed, you know. Amazing—it's quite a gift.'

I hardly knew what to say. My discomfiture seemed to amuse her.

'She's one of my oldest friends,' she said, 'and I always think loyalty's such a tiresome virtue, don't you? Principally practised by the Scots—like thrift and keeping the Sabbath. But Nick is a liar, isn't she, Jim? That marvellous story about the brakes of the car—and Jim says there was nothing in it at all.'

The fair man said in a soft, rich voice:

'I know something about cars.'

He half turned his head. Outside amongst other cars was a long, red car. It seemed longer and redder than any car could be. It had a long gleaming bonnet of polished metal. A super car!

'Is that your car?' I asked on a sudden impulse.

He nodded.

'Yes.'

I had an insane desire to say, 'It would be!'

Poirot rejoined us at that moment. I rose, he took me by the arm, gave a quick bow to the party, and drew me rapidly away.

'It is arranged, my friend. We are to call on Mademoiselle at End House at half-past six. She will be returned from the motoring by then. Yes, yes, surely she will have returned—in safety.'

His face was anxious and his tone was worried.

'What did you say to her?'

'I asked her to accord me an interview—as soon as possible. She was a little unwilling—naturally. She thinks—I can see the thoughts passing through her mind: "Who is he—this little man? Is he the bounder, the upstart, the Moving Picture director?" If she could have refused she would—but it is difficult—asked like that on the spur of the moment it is easier to consent. She admits that she will be back by six-thirty. *Ça y est?*'

I remarked that that seemed to be all right then, but my remark met with little favour. Indeed Poirot was as jumpy as the proverbial cat. He walked about our sitting-room all the afternoon, murmuring to himself and ceaselessly rearranging and straightening the ornaments. When I spoke to him, he waved his hands and shook his head. In the end we started out from the hotel at barely six o'clock.

'It seems incredible,' I remarked, as we descended the steps of the terrace. 'To attempt to shoot anyone in an hotel garden. Only a madman would do such a thing.'

'I disagree with you. Given one condition, it would be quite a reasonably safe affair. To begin with the garden is deserted. The people who come to hotels are like a flock of sheep. It is customary to sit on the terrace overlooking the bay—*eh bien*, so everyone sits on the terrace. Only, I who am an original, sit overlooking the garden. And even then, I *saw* nothing. There is plenty of cover, you observe—trees, groups of palms, flowering shrubs. Anyone could hide himself comfortably and be unobserved whilst he waited for Mademoiselle to pass this way. And she would come this way. To come round by the road from End House would be much longer. Mademoiselle Nick Buckley, she would be of those who are always late and taking the short cut!'

'All the same, the risk was enormous. He might have been seen—and you can't make shooting look like an accident.'

'Not like an *accident*—no.'

'What do you mean?'

'Nothing—a little idea. I may or may not be justified. Leaving it aside for a moment, there is what I mentioned just now—an essential *condition*.'

'Which is?'

'Surely you can tell me, Hastings.'

'I wouldn't like to deprive you of the pleasure of being clever at my expense!'

'Oh! the sarcasm! The irony! Well, what leaps to the eye is this: *the motive cannot be obvious*. If it *were*—why, then, truly the risk would indeed be too great to be taken! People would say: "I wonder if it were So-and-So. Where was So-and-So when the shot was fired?" No, the murderer—the would-be murderer, I should say—cannot be obvious. And that, Hastings, is why I am afraid! Yes, at this minute I am afraid. I reassure myself. I say: "There are four of them." I say: "Nothing can happen when they are all together." I say: "It would be madness!" And all the time I am afraid. These "accidents"—I want to hear about them!'

He turned back abruptly.

'It is still early. We will go the other way by the road. The garden has nothing to tell us. Let us inspect the orthodox approach to End House.'

Our way led out of the front gate of the hotel and up a sharp hill to the right. At the top of it was a small lane with a notice on the wall:

'TO END HOUSE ONLY.'

We followed it and after a few hundred yards the lane gave an abrupt turn and ended in a pair of dilapidated entrance gates, which would have been the better for a coat of paint.

Inside the gates, to the right, was a small lodge. This lodge presented a piquant contrast to the gates and to the condition of the grass-grown drive. The small garden round it was spick and span, the window frames and sashes had been lately painted and there were clean bright curtains at the windows.

Bending over a flower-bed was a man in a faded Norfolk jacket. He straightened up as the gate creaked and turned to look at us. He was a man of about sixty, six foot at least, with a powerful frame and a weather-beaten face. His head was almost completely bald. His eyes were a vivid blue and twinkled. He seemed a genial soul.

'Good-afternoon,' he observed as we passed.

I responded in kind, and as we went on up the drive I was conscious of those blue eyes raking our backs inquisitively.

'I wonder,' said Poirot, thoughtfully.

He left it at that without vouchsafing any explanation of what it was that he wondered.

The house itself was large and rather dreary-looking. It was shut in by trees, the branches of which actually touched the roof. It was clearly in bad repair. Poirot swept it with an appraising glance before ringing the bell—an old-fashioned bell that needed a Herculean pull to produce any effect and which once started, echoed mournfully on and on.

The door was opened by a middle-aged woman—'a decent woman in black'—so I felt she should be described. Very respectable, rather mournful, completely uninterested.

Miss Buckley, she said, had not yet returned. Poirot explained that we had an appointment. He had some little difficulty in gaining his point, she was the type that is apt to be suspicious of foreigners.

Indeed I flatter myself that it was *my* appearance which turned the scale. We were admitted and ushered into the drawing-room to await Miss Buckley's return.

There was no mournful note here. The room gave on the sea and was full of sunshine. It was shabby and betrayed conflicting styles—ultra modern of a cheap variety superimposed on solid Victorian. The curtains were of faded brocade, but the covers were new and gay and the cushions were positively hectic. On the walls were hung family portraits. Some of them, I thought, looked remarkably good. There was a gramophone and some records lying idly about. There was a portable wireless, practically no books, and one newspaper flung open on the end of the sofa. Poirot picked it up—then laid it down with a grimace. It was the St. Loo *Weekly Herald and Directory*. Something impelled him to pick it up a second time, and he was glancing at a column when the door opened and Nick Buckley came into the room.

'Bring the ice, Ellen,' she called over her shoulder, then addressed herself to us.

'Well, here I am—and I've shaken off the others. I'm devoured with curiosity. Am I the long-lost heroine that is badly wanted for the Talkies? You were so very solemn'—she addressed herself to Poirot—'that I feel it can't be anything else. Do make me a handsome offer.'

'Alas! Mademoiselle——' began Poirot.

'Don't say it's the opposite,' she begged him. 'Don't say you paint miniatures and want me to buy one. But no—with that moustache and staying at the Majestic, which has the nastiest food and the highest prices in England—no, it simply can't be.'

The woman who had opened the door to us came into the room with ice and a tray of bottles. Nick mixed cocktails expertly, continuing to talk. I think at last Poirot's silence (so unlike him) impressed itself upon her. She stopped in the very act of filling the glasses and said sharply:

'Well?'

'That is what I wish it to be—well, Mademoiselle.' He took the cocktail from her hand. 'To your good health, Mademoiselle—to your continued good health.'

The girl was no fool. The significance of his tone was not lost on her.

'Is—anything the matter?'

'Yes, Mademoiselle. This . . .'

He held out his hand to her with the bullet on the palm of it. She picked it up with a puzzled frown.

'You know what that is?'

'Yes, of course I know. It's a bullet.'

'Exactly. Mademoiselle—it was not a wasp that flew past your face this morning—it was this bullet.'

'Do you mean—was some criminal idiot shooting bullets in an hotel garden?'

'It would seem so.'

'Well, I'm damned,' said Nick frankly. 'I do seem to bear a charmed life. That's number four.'

'Yes,' said Poirot. 'That is number four. I want, Mademoiselle, to hear about the other three—accidents.'

She stared at him.

'I want to be very sure, Mademoiselle, that they were—*accidents*.'

'Why, of course! What else could they be?'

'Mademoiselle, prepare yourself, I beg, for a great shock. What if someone is attempting your life?'

All Nick's response to this was a burst of laughter. The idea seemed to amuse her hugely.

'What a marvellous idea! My dear man, who on earth do you think would attempt my life? I'm not the beautiful young heiress whose death releases millions. I wish somebody *was* trying to kill me—that *would* be a thrill, if you like—but I'm afraid there's not a hope!'

'Will you tell me, Mademoiselle, about those accidents?'

'Of course—but there's nothing in it. They were just stupid things. There's a heavy picture hangs over my bed. It fell in the night. Just by pure chance I had happened to hear a door banging somewhere in the house and went down to find it and shut it—and so I escaped. It would probably have bashed my head in. That's No. 1.'

Poirot did not smile.

'Continue, Mademoiselle. Let us pass to No. 2.'

'Oh, that's weaker still. There's a scrambly cliff path down to the sea. I go down that way to bathe. There's a rock you can dive off. A boulder got dislodged somehow and came roaring down just missing me. The third thing was quite different. Something went wrong with the brakes of the car—I don't know quite what—the garage man explained, but I didn't follow it. Anyway if I'd gone through the gate and down that hill, they wouldn't have held and I suppose I'd have gone slap into the Town Hall and there would have been the devil of a smash. Slight defacement of the Town Hall, complete obliteration of me. But owing to my *always* leaving something behind, I turned back and merely ran into the laurel hedge.'

'And you cannot tell me what the trouble was?'

'You can go and ask them at Mott's Garage. They'll know. It was something quite simple and mechanical that had been unscrewed, I think. I wondered if Ellen's boy (my stand-by who opened the door to you, has got a small boy) had tinkered with it. Boys do like messing about with cars. Of course Ellen swore he'd never been near the car. I think something must just have worked loose in spite of what Mott said.'

'Where is your garage, Mademoiselle?'

'Round the other side of the house.'

'Is it kept locked?'

Nick's eyes widened in surprise.

'Oh! *no*. Of course not.'

'Anyone could tamper with the car unobserved?'

'Well—yes—I suppose so. But it's so silly.'

'No, Mademoiselle. It is not silly. You do not understand. You are in danger—grave danger. I tell it to you. I! And you do not know who I am?'

'No?' said Nick, breathlessly.

'I am Hercule Poirot.'

'Oh!' said Nick, in rather a flat tone. 'Oh, yes.'

'You know my name, eh?'

'Oh, yes.'

She wriggled uncomfortably. A hunted look came into her eyes. Poirot observed her keenly.

'You are not at ease. That means, I suppose, that you have not read my books.'

'Well—no—not all of them. But I know the name,.of course.'

'Mademoiselle, you are a polite little liar.' (I started, remembering the words spoken at the Majestic Hotel that day after lunch.) 'I forget—you are only a child—you would not have heard. So quickly does fame pass. My friend there—he will tell you.'

Nick looked at me. I cleared my throat, somewhat embarrassed.

'Monsieur Poirot is—er—was—a great detective,' I explained.

'Ah! my friend,' cried Poirot. 'Is that all you can find to say? *Mais dis donc!* Say then to Mademoiselle that I am a detective unique, unsurpassed, the greatest that ever lived!'

'That is now unnecessary,' I said coldly. 'You have told her yourself.'

'Ah, yes, but it is more agreeable to have been able to preserve the modesty. One should not sing one's own praises.'

'One should not keep a dog and have to bark oneself,' agreed Nick, with mock sympathy. 'Who is the dog, by the way? Dr. Watson, I presume.'

'My name is Hastings,' I said coldly.

'Battle of—1066,' said Nick. 'Who said I wasn't educated? Well, this is all too, *too* marvellous! Do you think someone really wants to do away with me? It would be thrilling. But, of course, that sort of thing doesn't really happen. Only in books. I expect Monsieur Poirot is like a surgeon who's invented an operation or a doctor who's found an obscure disease and wants everyone to have it.'

'Sacré tonnerre!' thundered Poirot. 'Will you be serious? You young people of to-day, will nothing make you serious? It would not have been a joke, Mademoiselle, if you had been lying in the hotel garden a pretty little corpse with a nice little hole through your head instead of your hat. You would not have laughed then—eh?'

'Unearthly laughter heard at a *séance*,' said Nick. 'But seriously, M. Poirot—it's very kind of you and all that—but the whole thing *must* be an accident.'

'You are as obstinate as the devil!'

'That's where I got my name from. My grandfather was popularly supposed to have sold his soul to the devil. Everyone round here called him Old Nick. He was a wicked old man—but great fun. I adored him. I went everywhere with him and so they called us Old Nick and Young Nick. My real name is Magdala.'

'That is an uncommon name.'

'Yes, it's a kind of family one. There have been lots of Magdalas in the Buckley family. There's one up there.' She nodded at a picture on the wall.

'Ah!' said Poirot. Then looking at a portrait hanging over the mantelpiece, he said:

'Is that your grandfather, Mademoiselle?'

'Yes, rather an arresting portrait, isn't it? Jim Lazarus offered to buy it, but I wouldn't sell. I've got an affection for Old Nick.'

'Ah!' Poirot was silent for a minute, then he said very earnestly: '*Revenons à nos moutons*. Listen, Mademoiselle. I implore you to be serious. You are in danger. To-day, somebody shot at you with a Mauser pistol——'

'A Mauser pistol?'

For a moment she was startled.

'Yes, why? Do you know of anyone who has a Mauser pistol?'

She smiled.

'I've got one myself.'

'You have?'

'Yes—it was Dad's. He brought it back from the War. It's been knocking round here ever since. I saw it only the other day in that drawer.'

She indicated an old-fashioned bureau. Now, as though suddenly struck by an idea, she crossed to it and pulled the drawer open. She turned rather blankly. Her voice held a new note.

'Oh!' she said. 'It's—it's gone.'

3. *Accidents?*

IT WAS FROM THAT MOMENT that the conversation took on a different tone. Up to now, Poirot and the girl had been at cross-purposes. They were separated by a gulf of years. His fame and reputation meant nothing to her—she was of the generation that knows only the great names of the immediate moment. She was, therefore, unimpressed by his warnings. He was to her only a rather comic elderly foreigner with an amusingly melodramatic mind.

And this attitude baffled Poirot. To begin with, his vanity suffered. It was his constant dictum that all the world knew Hercule Poirot. Here was someone who did not. Very good for him, I could not but feel—but not precisely helpful to the object in view!

With the discovery of the missing pistol, however, the affair took on a new phase. Nick ceased to treat it as a mildly amusing joke. She still treated the matter lightly, because it was her habit and her creed to treat all occurrences lightly, but there was a distinct difference in her manner.

She came back and sat down on the arm of a chair, frowning thoughtfully.

'That's odd,' she said.

Poirot whirled round on me.

'You remember, Hastings, the little idea I mentioned? Well, it was correct, my little idea! Supposing Mademoiselle had been found shot lying in the hotel garden? She might not have been found for some hours—few people pass that way. And *beside her hand*—just fallen from it—*is her own pistol.* Doubtless the good Madame Ellen would identify it. There would be suggestions, no doubt, of worry or of sleeplessness——'

Nick moved uneasily.

'That's true. I have been worried to death. Everybody's been telling me I'm nervy. Yes—they'd say all that. . . .'

'And bring in a verdict of suicide. Mademoiselle's fingerprints conveniently on the pistol and nobody else's—but yes, it would be very simple and convincing.'

'How terribly amusing!' said Nick, but not, I was glad to note, as though she were terribly amused.

Poirot accepted her words in the conventional sense in which they were uttered.

'N'est ce pas? But you understand, Mademoiselle, there must be no more of this. Four failures—yes—but the fifth time there may be a success.'

'Bring out your rubber-tyred hearses,' murmured Nick.

'But we are here, my friend and I, to obviate all that!'

I felt grateful for the 'we.' Poirot has a habit of sometimes ignoring my existence.

'Yes,' I put in. 'You mustn't be alarmed, Miss Buckley. We will protect you.'

'How frightfully nice of you,' said Nick. 'I think the whole thing is perfectly marvellous. Too, too thrilling.'

She still preserved her airy detached manner, but her eyes, I thought, looked troubled.

'And the first thing to do,' said Poirot, 'is to have the consultation.'

He sat down and beamed upon her in a friendly manner.

'To begin with, Mademoiselle, a conventional question—but—have you any enemies?'

Nick shook her head rather regretfully.

'I'm afraid not,' she said, apologetically.

'*Bon*. We will dismiss that possibility then. And now we ask the question of the cinema, of the detective novel—Who profits by your death, Mademoiselle?'

'I can't imagine,' said Nick. 'That's why it all seems such nonsense. There's this beastly old barn, of course, but it's mortgaged up to the hilt, the roof leaks and there can't be a coal mine or anything exciting like that hidden in the cliff.'

'It is mortgaged—*hein*?'

'Yes. I had to mortgage it. You see there were two lots of death duties—quite soon after each other. First my grandfather died—just six years ago, and then my brother. That just about put the lid on the financial position.'

'And your father?'

'He was invalided home from the War, then got pneumonia and died in 1919. My mother died when I was a baby. I lived here with grandfather. He and Dad didn't get on (I don't wonder), so Dad found it convenient to park me and go roaming the world on his own account. Gerald—that was my brother—didn't get on with grandfather either. I dare say I shouldn't have got on with him if I'd been a boy. Being a girl saved me. Grandfather used to say I was a chip off the old block and had inherited his spirit.' She laughed. 'He was an awful old rip, I believe. But frightfully lucky. There was a saying round here that everything he touched turned to gold. He was a gambler, though, and gambled it away again. When he died he left hardly anything beside the house and land. I was sixteen when he died and Gerald was twenty-two. Gerald was killed in a motor accident just three years ago and the place came to me.'

'And after you, Mademoiselle? Who is your nearest relation?'

'My cousin, Charles. Charles Vyse. He's a lawyer down here. Quite good and worthy but very dull. He gives me good advice and tries to restrain my extravagant tastes.'

'He manages your affairs for you—eh?'

'Well—yes, if you like to put it that way. I haven't many affairs to manage. He arranged the mortgage for me and made me let the lodge.'

'Ah!—the lodge. I was going to ask you about that. It is let?'

'Yes—to some Australians. Croft their name is. Very hearty, you know—and all that sort of thing. Simply oppressively kind.

Always bringing up sticks of celery and early peas and things like that. They're shocked at the way I let the garden go. They're rather a nuisance, really—at least he is. Too terribly friendly for words. She's a cripple, poor thing, and lies on a sofa all day. Anyway they pay the rent and that's the great thing.'

'How long have they been here?'

'Oh! about six months.'

'I see. Now, beyond this cousin of yours—on your father's side or your mother's, by the way?'

'Mother's. My mother was Amy Vyse.'

'*Bien!* Now, beyond this cousin, as I was saying, have you any other relatives?'

'Some very distant cousins in Yorkshire—Buckleys.'

'No one else?'

'No.'

'That is lonely.'

Nick stared at him.

'Lonely? What a funny idea. I'm not down here much, you know. I'm usually in London. Relations are too devastating as a rule. They fuss and interfere. It's much more fun to be on one's own.'

'I will not waste the sympathy. You are a modern, I see, Mademoiselle. Now—your household.'

'How grand that sounds! Ellen's the household. And her husband, who's a sort of gardener—not a very good one. I pay them frightfully little because I let them have the child here. Ellen does for me when I'm down here and if I have a party we get in who and what we can to help. I'm giving a party on Monday. It's Regatta week, you know.'

'Monday—and to-day is Saturday. Yes. Yes. And now, Mademoiselle, your friends—the ones with whom you were lunching to-day, for instance?'

'Well, Freddie Rice—the fair girl—is practically my greatest friend. She's had a rotten life. Married to a beast—a man who drank and drugged and was altogether a queer of the worst description. She had to leave him a year or two ago. Since then she's drifted round. I wish to goodness she'd get a divorce and marry Jim Lazarus.'

'Lazarus? The art dealer in Bond Street?'

'Yes. Jim's the only son. Rolling in money, of course. Did you see that car of his? He's a Jew, of course, but a frightfully decent one. And he's devoted to Freddie. They go about everywhere together. They are staying at the Majestic over the week-end and are coming to me on Monday.'

'And Mrs. Rice's husband?'

'The mess? Oh! he's dropped out of everything. Nobody knows where he is. It makes it horribly awkward for Freddie. You can't divorce a man when you don't know where he is.'

'Évidément!'

'Poor Freddie,' said Nick, pensively. 'She's had rotten luck. The thing was all fixed once. She got hold of him and put it to him, and he said he was perfectly willing, but he simply hadn't got the cash to take a woman to a hotel. So the end of it all was she forked out—and he took it and off he went and has never been heard of from that day to this. Pretty mean, I call it.'

'Good heavens,' I exclaimed.

'My friend Hastings is shocked,' remarked Poirot. 'You must be more careful, Mademoiselle. He is out of date, you comprehend. He has just returned from those great clear open spaces, etc., and he has yet to learn the language of nowadays.'

'Well, there's nothing to get shocked about,' said Nick, opening her eyes very wide. 'I mean, everybody knows, don't they, that there are such people. But I call it a low-down trick all the same. Poor old Freddie was so damned hard up at the time that she didn't know where to turn.'

'Yes, yes, not a very pretty affair. And your other friend, Mademoiselle. The good Commander Challenger?'

'George? I've known George all my life—well, for the last five years anyway. He's a good scout, George.'

'He wishes you to marry him—eh?'

'He does mention it now and again. In the small hours of the morning or after the second glass of port.'

'But you remain hard-hearted.'

'What would be the use of George and me marrying one another? We've neither of us got a bean. And one would get terribly bored with George. That "playing for one's side," "good old school" manner. After all, he's forty if he's a day.'

The remark made me wince slightly.

'In fact he has one foot in the grave,' said Poirot. 'Oh! do not mind me, Mademoiselle. I am a grandpapa—a nobody. And now, tell me more about these accidents. The picture, for instance?'

'It's been hung up again—on a new cord. You can come and see it if you like.'

She led the way out of the room and we followed her. The picture in question was an oil painting in a heavy frame. It hung directly over the bed-head.

With a murmured, 'You permit, Mademoiselle,' Poirot removed his shoes and mounted upon the bed. He examined the picture and the cord, and gingerly tested the weight of the painting. With an elegant grimace he descended.

'To have that descend on one's head—no, it would not be pretty. The cord by which it was hung, Mademoiselle, was it, like this one, a wire cable?'

'Yes, but not so thick. I got a thicker one this time.'

'That is comprehensible. And you examined the break—the edges were frayed?'

'I think so—but I didn't notice particularly. Why should I?'

'Exactly. As you say, why should you? All the same, I should much like to look at that piece of wire. Is it about the house anywhere?'

'It was still on the picture. I expect the man who put the new wire on just threw the old one away.'

'A pity. I should like to have seen it.'

'You don't think it was just an accident after all? Surely it couldn't have been anything else.'

'It may have been an accident. It is impossible to say. But the damage to the brakes of your car—that was not an accident. And the stone that rolled down the cliff—I should like to see the spot where that accident occurred.'

Nick took us out in the garden and led us to the cliff edge. The sea glittered blue below us. A rough path led down the face of the rock. Nick described just where the accident occurred and Poirot nodded thoughtfully. Then he asked:

'How many ways are there into your garden, Mademoiselle?'

'There's the front way—past the lodge. And a tradesman's entrance—a door in the wall half-way up that lane. Then there's a gate just along here on the cliff edge. It leads out on to a zig-zag path that leads up from that beach to the Majestic Hotel. And then, of course, you can go straight through a gap in the hedge into the Majestic garden—that's the way I went this morning. To go through the Majestic garden is a short cut to the town anyway.'

'And your gardener—where does he usually work?'

'Well, he usually potters round the kitchen garden, or else he sits in the potting-shed and pretends to be sharpening the shears.'

'Round the other side of the house, that is to say?'

'So that if anyone were to come in here and dislodge a boulder he would be very unlikely to be noticed.'

Nick gave a sudden little shiver.

'Do you—do you really think that is what happened?' she asked, 'I can't believe it somehow. It seems so perfectly futile.'

Poirot drew the bullet from his pocket again and looked at it.

'That was not futile, Mademoiselle,' he said gently.

'It must have been some madman.'

'Possibly. It is an interesting subject of after-dinner conversation—are all criminals really madmen? There may be a malformation in their little grey cells—yes, it is very likely. That, it is the affair of the doctor. For me—I have different work to perform. I have the innocent to think of, not the guilty—the victim, not the criminal. It is you I am considering now, Mademoiselle, not your unknown assailant. You are young and beautiful, and the sun shines and the world is pleasant, and there is life and love ahead of you. It is all that of which I think, Mademoiselle. Tell me, these friends of yours, Mrs. Rice and Mr. Lazarus—they have been down here, how long?'

'Freddie came down on Wednesday to this part of the world. She stopped with some people near Tavistock for a couple of nights. She came on here yesterday. Jim has been touring round about, I believe.'

'And Commander Challenger?'

'He's at Devonport. He comes over in his car whenever he can—week-ends mostly.'

Poirot nodded. We were walking back to the house. There was a silence, and then he said suddenly:

'Have you a friend whom you can trust, Mademoiselle?'

'There's Freddie.'

'Other than Mrs. Rice.'

'Well, I don't know. I suppose I have. Why?'

'Because I want you to have a friend to stay with you—immediately.'

'Oh!'

Nick seemed rather taken aback. She was silent a moment or two, thinking. Then she said doubtfully:

'There's Maggie. I could get hold of her, I expect.'

'Who is Maggie?'

'One of my Yorkshire cousins. There's a large family of them. He's a clergyman, you know. Maggie's about my age, and I usually have her to stay sometime or other in the summer. She's no fun, though—one of those painfully pure girls, with the kind of hair that has just become fashionable by accident. I was hoping to get out of having her this year.'

'Not at all. Your cousin, Mademoiselle, will do admirably. Just the type of person I had in mind.'

'All right,' said Nick, with a sigh. 'I'll wire her. I certainly don't know who else I could get hold of just now. Everyone's fixed up. But if it isn't the Choirboys' Outing or the Mothers' Beanfeast she'll come all right. Though what you expect her to *do*. . . .'

'Could you arrange for her to sleep in your room?'

'I suppose so.'

'She would not think that an odd request?'

'Oh, no, Maggie never thinks. She just *does*—earnestly, you know. Christian works—with faith and perseverance. All right, I'll wire her to come on Monday.'

'Why not to-morrow?'

'With Sunday trains? She'll think I'm dying if I suggest that. No, I'll say Monday. Are you going to tell her about the awful fate hanging over me?'

'*Nous verrons*. You still make a jest of it? You have courage, I am glad to see.'

'It makes a diversion anyway,' said Nick.

Something in her tone struck me and I glanced at her curiously. I had a feeling that there was something she had left untold. We had re-entered the drawing-room. Poirot was fingering the newspaper on the sofa.

'You read this, Mademoiselle?' he asked, suddenly.

'The St. Loo *Herald*? Not seriously. I opened it to see the tides. It gives them every week.'

'I see. By the way, Mademoiselle, have you ever made a will?'

'Yes, I did. About six months ago. Just before my op.'

'*Qu'est ce que vous dites?* Your *op*?'

'Operation. For appendicitis. Someone said I ought to make a will, so I did. It made me feel quite important.'

'And the terms of that will?'

'I left End House to Charles. I hadn't much else to leave, but what there was I left to Freddie. I should think probably the—what do you call them—liabilities would have exceeded the assets, really.'

Poirot nodded absently.

'I will take my leave now. *Au revoir, Mademoiselle*. Be careful.'

'What of?' asked Nick.

'You are intelligent. Yes, that is the weak point—in which direction are you to be careful? Who can say? But have confidence, Mademoiselle. In a few days I shall have discovered the truth.'

'Until then beware of poison, bombs, revolver shots, motor accidents and arrows dipped in the secret poison of the South American Indians,' finished Nick glibly.

'Do not mock yourself, Mademoiselle,' said Poirot gravely.

He paused as he reached the door.

'By the way,' he said. 'What price did M. Lazarus offer you for the portrait of your grandfather?'

'Fifty pounds.'

'Ah!' said Poirot.

He looked earnestly back at the dark saturnine face above the mantelpiece.

'But, as I told you, I don't want to sell the old boy.'

'No,' said Poirot, thoughtfully. 'No, I understand.'

4. *There must be something!*

'POIROT,' I SAID, as soon as we were out upon the road. 'There is one thing I think you ought to know.'

'And what is that, *mon ami?*'

I told him of Mrs. Rice's version of the trouble with the motor.

'*Tiens! Ç'est interessant, ça*. There is, of course, a type, vain, hysterical, that seeks to make itself interesting by having marvellous escapes from death and which will recount to you surprising histories that never happened! Yes, it is well known, that type there. Such people will even do themselves grave bodily injury to sustain the fiction.'

'You don't think that——'

'That Mademoiselle Nick is of that type? No, indeed. You observed, Hastings, that we had great difficulty in convincing her of her danger. And right to the end she kept up the farce of a half-mocking disbelief. She is of her generation, that little one. All the same, it is interesting—what Madame Rice said. Why should she say it? Why say it even if it were true? It was unnecessary—almost *gauche*.'

'Yes,' I said. 'That's true. She dragged it into the conversation neck and crop—for no earthly reason that I could see.'

'That is curious. Yes, that is curious. The little facts that are curious, I like to see them appear. They are significant. They point the way.'

'The way—where?'

'You put your finger on the weak spot, my excellent Hastings. Where? Where indeed! Alas, we shall not know till we get there.'

'Tell me, Poirot,' I said. 'Why did you insist on her getting this cousin to stay?'

Poirot stopped and waved an excited forefinger at me.

'Consider,' he cried. 'Consider for one little moment, Hastings. How are we handicapped! How are our hands tied! To hunt down a murderer after a crime has been committed—*c'est tout simple!* Or at least it is simple to one of my ability. The murderer has, so to speak, signed his name by committing the crime. But here there is no crime—and what is more we do not want a crime. To detect a crime before it has been committed—that is indeed of a rare difficulty.

'What is our first aim? The safety of Mademoiselle. And that is not easy. No, it is not easy, Hastings. We cannot watch over her day and night—we cannot even send a policeman in big boots to watch over her. We cannot pass the night in a young lady's sleeping chamber. The affair bristles with difficulties.

'But we can do one thing. We can make it more difficult for our assassin. We can put Mademoiselle upon her guard and we can introduce a perfectly impartial witness. It will take a very clever man to get round those two circumstances.'

He paused, and then said in an entirely different tone of voice: 'But what I am afraid of, Hastings——'

'Yes?'

'What I am afraid of is—that he *is* a very clever man. And I am not easy in my mind. No, I am not easy at all.'

'Poirot,' I said. 'You're making me feel quite nervous.'

'So am I nervous. Listen, my friend, that paper, the St. Loo

Weekly Herald. It was open and folded back at—where do you think? A little paragraph which said, *"Among the guests staying at the Majestic Hotel are M. Hercule Poirot and Captain Hastings."* Supposing—just supposing that someone had read that paragraph. They know my name—everyone knows my name——'

'Miss Buckley didn't,' I said, with a grin.

'She is a scatterbrain—she does not count. A serious man—a criminal—would know my name. And he would be afraid! He would wonder! He would ask himself questions. Three times he has attempted the life of Mademoiselle and now Hercule Poirot arrives in the neighbourhood. "Is that coincidence?" he would ask himself. And he would fear that it might *not* be coincidence. What would he do then?'

'Lie low and hide his tracks,' I suggested.

'Yes—yes—or else—if he had real audacity, he would strike *quickly*—without loss of time. Before I had time to make the inquiries—*pouf*, Mademoiselle is dead. That is what a man of audacity would do.'

'But why do you think that somebody read that paragraph other than Miss Buckley?'

'It was not Miss Buckley who read that paragraph. When I mentioned my name it meant nothing to her. It was not even familiar. Her face did not change. Besides she told us—she opened the paper to look at the tides—nothing else. Well, there was no tide table on that page.'

'You think someone in the house——'

'Someone in the house or who had access to it. And that last is easy—the window stands open. Without doubt Miss Buckley's friends pass in and out.'

'Have you any idea? Any suspicion?'

Poirot flung out his hands.

'Nothing. Whatever the motive, it is, as I predicted, not an obvious one. That is the would-be murderer's security—that is why he could act so daringly this morning. On the face of it, no one seems to have any reason for desiring the little Nick's death. The property? End House? That passes to the cousin—but does he particularly want a heavily mortgaged and very dilapidated old house? It is not even a family place so far as he is concerned. He is not a Buckley, remember. We must see this M. Charles Vyse, certainly, but the idea seems fantastic.

'Then there is Madame—the bosom friend—with her strange eyes and her air of a lost Madonna——'

'You felt that too?' I asked, startled.

'What is her concern in the business? She tells you that her friend is a liar. *C'est gentille, ça!* Why does she tell you? Is she afraid of something that Nick may say? Is that something connected with the car? Or did she use that as an instance, and was her real fear of something else? Did anyone tamper with the car, and if so, who? And does she know about it?'

'Then the handsome blond, M. Lazarus. Where does he fit in? With his marvellous automobile and his money. Can he possibly be concerned in any way? Commander Challenger——'

'He's all right,' I put in quickly. 'I'm sure of that. A real pukka sahib.'

'Doubtless he has been to what you consider the right school. Happily, being a foreigner, I am free from these prejudices, and can make investigations unhampered by them. But I will admit that I find it hard to connect Commander Challenger with the case. In fact, I do not see that he can be so connected.'

'Of course he can't,' I said, warmly.

Poirot looked at me meditatively.

'You have an extraordinary effect on me, Hastings. You have so strongly the *flair* in the wrong direction that I am almost tempted to go by it! You are that wholly admirable type of man, honest, credulous, honourable, who is invariably taken in by any scoundrel. You are the type of man who invests in doubtful oil fields, and non-existent gold mines. From hundreds like you, the swindler makes his daily bread. Ah, well—I shall study this Commander Challenger. You have awakened my doubts.'

'My dear Poirot,' I cried, angrily. 'You are perfectly absurd. A man who has knocked about the world like I have——'

'Never learns,' said Poirot, sadly. 'It is amazing—but there it is.'

'Do you suppose I'd have made a success of my ranch out in the Argentine if I were the kind of credulous fool you make out?'

'Do not enrage yourself, *mon ami*. You have made a great success of it—you and your wife.'

'Bella,' I said, 'always goes by my judgment.'

'She is as wise as she is charming,' said Poirot. 'Let us not quarrel, my friend. See, there ahead of us, it says Mott's Garage. That, I think, is the garage mentioned by Mademoiselle Buckley. A few inquiries will soon give us the truth of that little matter.'

We duly entered the place and Poirot introduced himself by explaining that he had been recommended there by Miss Buckley. He made some inquiries about hiring a car for some afternoon drives and from there slid easily into the topic of the damage sustained by Miss Buckley's car not long ago.

Immediately the garage proprietor waxed voluble. Most extraordinary thing he'd ever seen. He proceeded to be technical. I, alas, am not mechanically minded. Poirot, I should imagine, is even less so. But certain facts did emerge unmistakable. The car had been tampered with. And the damage had been something quite easily done, occupying very little time.

'So that is that,' said Poirot, as we strolled away. 'The little Nick was right, and the rich M. Lazarus was wrong. Hastings, my friend, all this is very interesting.'

'What do we do now?'

'We visit the post office and send off a telegram if it is not too late.'

'A telegram?' I said hopefully.

'Yes,' said Poirot thoughtfully. 'A telegram.'

The post office was still open. Poirot wrote out his telegram and despatched it. He vouchsafed me no information as to its contents. Feeling that he wanted me to ask him, I carefully refrained from doing so.

'It is annoying that to-morrow is Sunday,' he remarked, as we strolled back to the hotel. 'We cannot now call upon M. Vyse till Monday morning.'

'You could get hold of him at his private address.'

'Naturally. But that is just what I am anxious not to do. I would prefer, in the first place, to consult him professionally and to form my judgment of him from that aspect.'

'Yes,' I said thoughtfully. 'I suppose that would be best.'

'The answer to one simple little question, for instance, might make a great difference. If M. Charles Vyse was in his office at twelve-thirty this morning, then it was not he who fired that shot in the garden of the Majestic Hotel.'

'Ought we not to examine the *alibis* of the three at the hotel?'

'That is much more difficult. It would be easy enough for one of them to leave the others for a few minutes, a hasty egress from one of the innumerable windows—lounge, smoking-room, drawing-room, writing-room, quickly under cover to the spot where the girl must pass—the shot fired and a rapid retreat. But as yet, *mon ami*, we are not even sure that we have arrived at all the *dramatis personæ* in the drama. There is the respectable Ellen—and her so far unseen husband. Both inmates of the house and possibly, for all we know, with a grudge against our little Mademoiselle. There are even the unknown Australians at the lodge. And there may be others, friends and intimates of Miss Buckley's whom she has no reason for suspecting and consequently has not mentioned. I cannot help feeling, Hastings, that there is something *behind* this—*something* that has not yet come to light. I have a little idea that Miss Buckley knows more than she told us.'

'You think she is keeping something back?'

'Yes.'

'Possibly with an idea of shielding whoever it is?'

Poirot shook his head with the utmost energy.

'No, no. As far as that goes, she gave me the impression of being utterly frank. I am convinced that as regards these attempts on her life, she was telling all she knew. But there is something else—something that she believes has nothing to do with that at all. And I should like to know what that something is. For I—I say it in all modesty—am a great deal more intelligent than *une petite comme ça*. I, Hercule Poirot, might see a connection where she sees none. It might give me the clue I am seeking. For I announce to you, Hastings, quite frankly and humbly, that I am as you express it, all on the sea. Until I can get some glimmering of the *reason* behind all this, I am in the dark. There must be *something*—some factor in the case that I do not grasp. What is it? *Je me demande ça sans cesse. Qu'est ce que c'est?*'

'You will find out,' I said, soothingly.

'So long,' he said sombrely, 'as I do not find out too late.'

5. *Mr. and Mrs. Croft*

THERE WAS DANCING that evening at the hotel. Nick Buckley dined there with her friends and waved a gay greeting to us.

She was dressed that evening in floating scarlet chiffon that dragged on the floor. Out of it rose her white neck and shoulders and her small impudent dark head.

'An engaging young devil,' I remarked.

'A contrast to her friend—eh?'

Frederica Rice was in white. She danced with a languorous weary grace that was as far removed from Nick's animation as anything could be.

'She is very beautiful,' said Poirot suddenly.

'Who? Our Nick?'

'No—the other. Is she evil? Is she good? Is she merely unhappy? One cannot tell. She is a mystery. She is, perhaps, nothing at all. But I tell you, my friend, she is an *allumeuse*.'

'What do you mean?' I asked curiously.

He shook his head, smiling.

'You will feel it sooner or later. Remember my words.'

Presently to my surprise, he rose. Nick was dancing with George Challenger. Frederica and Lazarus had just stopped and had sat down at their table. Then Lazarus got up and went away. Mrs. Rice was alone. Poirot went straight to her table. I followed him.

His methods were direct and to the point.

'You permit?' He laid a hand on the back of a chair then slid into it. 'I am anxious to have a word with you while your friend is dancing.'

'Yes?' Her voice sounded cool, uninterested.

'Madame, I do not know whether your friend has told you, If not, I will. To-day her life has been attempted.'

Her great grey eyes widened in horror and surprise. The pupils, dilated black pupils, widened too.

'What do you mean?'

'Mademoiselle Buckley was shot at in the garden of this hotel.'

She smiled suddenly—a gentle, pitying, incredulous smile.

'Did Nick tell you so?'

'No, Madame, I happened to see it with my own eyes. Here is the bullet.'

He held it out to her and she drew back a little.

'But, then—but, then——'

'It is no fantasy of Mademoiselle's imagination, you understand. I vouch for that. And there is more. Several very curious accidents have happened in the last few days. You will have heard—no, perhaps you will not. You only arrived yesterday, did you not?'

'Yes—yesterday.'

'Before that you were staying with friends, I understand. At Tavistock.'

'Yes.'

'I wonder, Madame, what were the names of the friends with whom you were staying.'

She raised her eyebrows.

'Is there any reason why I should tell you that?' she asked, coldly.

Poirot was immediately all innocent surprise.

'A thousand pardons, Madame. I was most *maladroit*. But I myself, having friends at Tavistock, fancied that you might have met them there. . . . Buchanan—that is the name of my friends.'

Mrs. Rice shook her head.

'I don't remember them. I don't think I can have met them.' Her tone now was quite cordial. 'Don't let us talk about boring people. Go on about Nick. Who shot at her? Why?'

'I do not know who—*as yet*,' said Poirot. 'But I shall find out. Oh! yes, I shall find out. I am, you know, a detective. Hercule Poirot is my name.'

'A very famous name.'

'Madame is too kind.'

She said slowly:

'What do you want me to do?'

I think she surprised us both there. We had not expected just that.

'I will ask you, Madame, to watch over your friend.'

'I will.'

'That is all.'

He got up, made a quick bow, and we returned to our own table.

'Poirot,' I said, 'aren't you showing your hand very plainly?'

'*Mon ami*, what else can I do? It lacks subtlety, perhaps, but it makes for safety. *I can take no chances*. At any rate one thing emerges plain to see.'

'What is that?'

'*Mrs. Rice was not at Tavistock*. Where was she? Ah! but I will find out. Impossible to keep information from Hercule Poirot. See—the handsome Lazarus has returned. She is telling him. He looks over at us. He is clever, that one. Note the shape of his head. Ah! I wish I knew——'

'What?' I asked, as he came to a stop.

'What I shall know on Monday,' he returned, ambiguously.

I looked at him but said nothing. He sighed.

'You have no longer the curiosity, my friend. In the old days——'

'There are some pleasures,' I said, coldly, 'that it is good for you to do without.'

'You mean——?'

'The pleasure of refusing to answer questions.'

'Ah c'est malin.'

'Quite so.'

'Ah, well, well,' murmured Poirot. 'The strong silent man beloved of novelists in the Edwardian age.'

His eyes twinkled with their old glint.

Nick passed our table shortly afterwards. She detached herself from her partner and swooped down on us like a gaily-coloured bird.

'Dancing on the edge of death,' she said lightly.

'It is a new sensation, Mademoiselle?'

'Yes. Rather fun.'

She was off again, with a wave of her hand.

'I wish she hadn't said that,' I said, slowly. 'Dancing on the edge of death. I don't like it.'

'I know. It is too near the truth. She has courage, that little one. Yes, she has courage. But unfortunately it is not courage that is needed at this moment. Caution, not courage—*voilà ce qu'il nous faut!*'

The following day was Sunday. We were sitting on the terrace in front of the hotel, and it was about half-past eleven when Poirot suddenly rose to his feet.

'Come, my friend. We will try a little experiment. I have ascertained that M. Lazarus and Madame have gone out in the car and Mademoiselle with them. The coast is clear.'

'Clear for what?'

'You shall see.'

We walked down the steps and across a short stretch of grass to where a gate gave on to the zig-zag path leading down to the sea. A couple of bathers were coming up it. They passed us laughing and talking.

When they had gone, Poirot walked to the point where an inconspicuous small gate, rather rusty on its hinges, bore the words in half obliterated letters, 'End House. Private.' There was no one in sight. We passed quietly through.

In another minute we came out on the stretch of lawn in front of the house. There was no one about. Poirot strolled to the edge of the cliff and looked over. Then he walked towards the house itself. The French windows on to the verandah were open and we passed straight into the drawing-room. Poirot wasted no time there. He opened the door and went out into the hall. From there he mounted the stairs, I at his heels. He went straight to Nick's bedroom—sat down on the edge of the bed and nodded to me with a twinkle.

'You see, my friend, how easy it is. No one has seen us come. No one will see us go. We could do any little affair we had to do in perfect safety. We could, for instance, fray through a picture wire so that it would be bound to snap before many hours had passed. And supposing that by chance anyone did happen to be in front of the house and see us coming. Then we would have a perfectly natural excuse—providing that we were known as friends of the house.'

'You mean that we can rule out a stranger?'

'That is what I mean, Hastings. It is no stray lunatic who is at the bottom of this. We must look nearer home than that.'

He turned to leave the room and I followed him. We neither of us spoke. We were both, I think, troubled in mind.

And then, at the bend of the staircase, we both stopped abruptly. A man was coming up.

He too stopped. His face was in shadow but his attitude was of one completely taken aback. He was the first to speak, in a loud, rather bullying, voice.

'What the hell are you doing here, I'd like to know?'

'Ah!' said Poirot. 'Monsieur—Croft, I think?'

'That's my name, but what——'

'Shall we go into the drawing-room to converse? It would be better, I think.'

The other gave way, turned abruptly and descended, we following close on his heels. In the drawing-room, with the door shut, Poirot made a little bow.

'I will introduce myself. Hercule Poirot, at your service.'

The other's face cleared a little.

'Oh!' he said slowly. 'You're the detective chap. I've read about you.'

'In the St. Loo *Herald*?'

'Eh? I've read about you way back in Australia. French, aren't you?'

'Belgian. It makes no matter. This is my friend, Captain Hastings.'

'Glad to meet you. But look what's the big idea? What are you doing here? Anything—wrong?'

'It depends what you call—wrong.'

The Australian nodded. He was a fine-looking man in spite of his bald head and advancing years. His physique was magnificent. He had a heavy, rather underhung face—a crude face, I called it to myself. The piercing blue of his eyes was the most noticeable thing about him.

'See here,' he said. 'I came round to bring little Miss Buckley a handful of tomatoes and a cucumber. That man of hers is no good—bone idle—doesn't grow a thing. Lazy hound. Mother and I—why, it makes us mad, and we feel it's only neighbourly to do what we can! We've got a lot more tomatoes than we can eat. Neighbours should be matey, don't you think? I came in, as usual, through the window and dumped the basket down. I was just going off again when I heard footsteps and men's voices overhead. That struck me as odd. We don't deal much in burglars round here—but after all it was possible. I thought I'd just make sure everything was all right. Then I met you two on the stairs coming down. It gave me a bit of a surprise. And now you tell me you're a bonza detective. What's it all about?'

'It is very simple,' said Poirot, smiling. 'Mademoiselle had a rather alarming experience the other night. A picture fell above her bed. She may have told you of it?'

'She did. A mighty fine escape.'

'To make all secure I promised to bring her some special chain—it will not do to repeat the occurrence, eh? She tells me she is going out this morning, but I may come and measure what amount of chain will be needed. *Voilà*—it is simple.'

He flung out his hands with a childlike simplicity and his most engaging smile.

Croft drew a deep breath.

'So that's all it is?'

'Yes—you have had the scare for nothing. We are very law-abiding citizens, my friend and I.'

'Didn't I see you yesterday?' said Croft, slowly. 'Yesterday evening it was. You passed our little place.'

'Ah! yes, you were working in the garden and were so polite as to say good-afternoon when we passed.'

'That's right. Well—well. And you're the Monsieur Hercule Poirot I've heard so much about. Tell me, are you busy, Mr. Poirot? Because if not, I wish you'd come back with me now—have a cup of morning tea, Australian fashion, and meet my old lady. She's read all about you in the newspapers.'

'You are too kind, M. Croft. We have nothing to do and shall be delighted.'

'That's fine.'

'You have the measurements correctly, Hastings?' asked Poirot, turning to me.

I assured him that I had the measurements correctly, and we accompanied our new friend.

Croft was a talker; we soon realised that. He told us of his home near Melbourne, of his early struggles, of his meeting with his wife, of their combined efforts and of his final good fortune and success.

'Right away we made up our minds to travel.' he said. 'We'd always wanted to come to the old country. Well, we did. We came down to this part of the world—tried to look up some of my wife's people—they came from round about here. But we couldn't trace any of them. Then we took a trip on the Continent—Paris, Rome, the Italian Lakes, Florence—all those places. It was while we were in Italy that we had the train accident. My poor wife was badly smashed up. Cruel, wasn't it? I've taken her to the best doctors and they all say the same—there's nothing for it but time—time and lying up. It's an injury to the spine.'

'What a misfortune!'

'Hard luck, isn't it? Well, there it was. And she'd only got one kind of fancy—to come down here. She kind of felt if we had a little place of our own—something small—it would make all the difference. We saw a lot of messy-looking shacks, and then by good luck we found this. Nice and quiet and tucked away—no cars passing, or gramophones next door. I took it right away.'

With the last words we had come to the lodge itself. He sent his voice echoing forth in a loud 'Cooee,' to which came an answering 'Cooee.'

'Come in,' said Mr. Croft. He passed through the open door and up the short flight of stairs to a pleasant bedroom. There, on a sofa, was a stout middle-aged woman with pretty grey hair and a very sweet smile.

'Who do you think this is, mother?' said Mr. Croft. 'The extra-special, world-celebrated detective, Mr. Hercule Poirot. I brought him right along to have a chat with you.'

'If that isn't too exciting for words,' cried Mrs. Croft, shaking Poirot warmly by the hand. 'Read about that Blue Train business, I did, and you just happening to be on it, and a lot about your other cases. Since this trouble with my back, I've read all the detective stories that ever were, I should think. Nothing else seems to pass the time away so quick. Bert, dear, call out to Edith to bring the tea along.'

'Right you are, mother.'

'She's a kind of nurse attendant, Edith is,' Mrs. Croft explained. 'She comes along each morning to fix me up. We're not bothering with servants. Bert's as good a cook and a house-parlourman as you'd find anywhere, and it gives him occupation—that and the garden.'

'Here we are,' cried Mr. Croft, reappearing with a tray. 'Here's the tea. This is a great day in our lives, mother.'

'I suppose you're staying down here, Mr. Poirot?' Mrs. Croft asked, as she leaned over a little and wielded the tea-pot.

'Why, yes, Madame, I take the holiday.'

'But surely I read that you had retired—that you'd taken a holiday for good and all.'

'Ah! Madame, you must not believe everything you read in the papers.'

'Well, that's true enough. So you still carry on business?'

'When I find a case that interests me.'

'Sure you're not down here on work?' inquired Mr. Croft, shrewdly. 'Calling it a holiday might be all part of the game.'

'You mustn't ask him embarrassing questions, Bert,' said Mrs. Croft. 'Or he won't come again. We're simple people, Mr. Poirot, and you're giving us a great treat coming here to-day—you and your friend. You really don't know the pleasure you're giving us.'

She was so natural and so frank in her gratification that my heart quite warmed to her.

'That was a bad business about that picture,' said Mr. Croft.

'That poor little girl might have been killed,' said Mrs. Croft, with deep feeling. 'She *is* a live wire. Livens the place up when she comes down here. Not much liked in the neighbourhood, so I've heard. But that's the way in these stuck English places. They don't like life and gaiety in a girl. I don't wonder she doesn't spend much time down here, and that long-nosed cousin of hers has no more chance of persuading her to settle down here for good and all than—than—well, I don't know what.'

'Don't gossip, Milly,' said her husband.

'Aha!' said Poirot. 'The wind is in that quarter. Trust the instinct of Madame! So M. Charles Vyse is in love with our little friend?'

'He's silly about her,' said Mrs. Croft. 'But she won't marry a country lawyer. And I don't blame her. He's a poor stick, anyway. I'd like her to marry that nice sailor—what's his name, Challenger. Many a smart marriage might be worse than that. He's older than she is, but what of that? Steadying—that's what she needs. Flying about all over the place, the Continent even, all alone or with that queer-looking Mrs. Rice. She's a sweet girl, Mr. Poirot—I know that well enough. But I'm worried about her. She's looked none too happy lately. She's had what I call a haunted kind of look. And it worries me! I've got my reasons for being interested in that girl, haven't I, Bert?'

Mr. Croft got up from his chair rather suddenly.

'No need to go into that, Milly,' he said. 'I wonder, Mr. Poirot, if you'd care to see some snapshots of Australia?'

The rest of our visit passed uneventfully. Ten minutes later we took our leave.

'Nice people,' I said. 'So simple and unassuming. Typical Australians.'

'You liked them?'

'Didn't you?'

'They were very pleasant—very friendly.'

'Well, what is it, then? There's something, I can see.'

'They were, perhaps, just a shade too "typical,"' said Poirot, thoughtfully. 'That cry of Cooee—that insistence on showing us snapshots—was it not playing a part just a little too thoroughly?'

'What a suspicious old devil you are!'

'You are right, *mon ami*. I am suspicious of everyone—of everything. I am afraid, Hastings—afraid.'

6. *A call upon Mr. Vyse*

POIROT CLUNG FIRMLY to the Continental breakfast. To see me consuming eggs and bacon upset and distressed him—so he always said. Consequently he breakfasted in bed upon coffee and rolls and I was free to start the day with the traditional Englishman's breakfast of bacon and eggs and marmalade.

I looked into his room on Monday morning as I went downstairs. He was sitting up in bed arrayed in a very marvellous dressing-gown.

'*Bon jour*, Hastings. I was just about to ring. This note that I have written, will you be so good as to get it taken over to End House and delivered to Mademoiselle at once.'

I held out my hand for it. Poirot looked at me and sighed.

'If only—if only, Hastings, you would part your hair in the middle instead of at the side! What a difference it would make to the symmetry of your appearance. And your moustache. If you *must* have a moustache, let it be a real moustache—a thing of beauty such as mine.'

Repressing a shudder at the thought, I took the note firmly from Poirot's hand and left the room.

I had rejoined him in our sitting-room when word was sent up to say Miss Buckley had called. Poirot gave the order for her to be shown up.

She came in gaily enough, but I fancied that the circles under her eyes were darker than usual. In her hand she held a telegram which she handed to Poirot.

'There,' she said. 'I hope that will please you!'

Poirot read it aloud.

'Arrive 5.30 to-day. Maggie.'

'My nurse and guardian!' said Nick. 'But you're wrong, you know. Maggie's got no kind of brains. Good works is about all she's fit for. That and never seeing the point of jokes. Freddie would be ten times better at spotting hidden assassins. And Jim Lazarus would be better still. I never feel one has got to the bottom of Jim.'

'And the Commander Challenger?'

'Oh! George! He'd never see anything till it was under his nose. But he'd let them have it when he did see. Very useful when it came to a show-down, George would be.'

She tossed off her hat and went on:

'I gave orders for the man you wrote about to be let in. It sounds mysterious. Is he installing a dictaphone or something like that?'

Poirot shook his head.

'No, no nothing scientific. A very simple little matter of opinion, Mademoiselle. Something I wanted to know.'

'Oh, well,' said Nick. 'It's all great fun, isn't it?'

'Is it, Mademoiselle?' asked Poirot, gently.

She stood for a minute with her back to us, looking out of the window. Then she turned. All the brave defiance had gone out of her face. It was childishly twisted awry, as she struggled to keep back the tears.

'No,' she said. 'It—it isn't, really. I'm afraid—I'm afraid. Hideously afraid. And I always thought I was brave.'

'So you are, *mon enfant*, so you are. Both Hastings and I, we have both admired your courage.'

'Yes, indeed,' I put in warmly.

'No,' said Nick, shaking her head. 'I'm not brave. It's—it's the *waiting*. Wondering the whole time if anything more's going to happen. And *how* it'll happen! And *expecting* it to happen.'

'Yes, yes—it is the strain.'

'Last night I pulled my bed out into the middle of the room. And I fastened my window and bolted my door. When I came here this morning, I came round by the road. I couldn't—I simply couldn't come through the garden. It's as though my nerve had gone all of a sudden. It's this thing coming on top of everything else.'

'What do you mean exactly by that, Mademoiselle? On top of everything else?'

There was a momentary pause before she replied.

'I don't mean anything particular. What the newspapers call "the strain of modern life," I suppose. Too many cocktails, too many cigarettes—all that sort of thing. It's just that I've got into a ridiculous—sort of—of state.'

She had sunk into a chair and was sitting there, her small fingers curling and uncurling themselves nervously.

'You are not being frank with me, Mademoiselle. There is something.'

'There isn't—there really isn't.'

'There is something you have not told me.'

'I've told you every single smallest thing.'

She spoke sincerely and earnestly.

'About these accidents—about the attacks upon you, yes.'

'Well—then?'

'But you have not told me everything that is in your heart—in your life. . . .'

She said slowly:

'Can anyone do that. . . ?'

'Ah! then,' said Poirot, with triumph. 'You admit it!'

She shook her head. He watched her keenly.

'Perhaps,' he suggested, shrewdly. 'It is not *your* secret?'

I thought I saw a momentary flicker of her eyelids. But almost immediately she jumped up.

'Really and truly, M. Poirot, I've told you every single thing I know about this stupid business. If you think I know something about someone else, or have suspicions, you are wrong. It's having *no* suspicions that's driving me mad! Because I'm not a fool. I can see that if those "accidents" weren't accidents, they must have been engineered by somebody very near at hand—somebody who—knows me. And that's what is so awful. Because I haven't the least idea—not the very least—who that somebody might be.'

She went over once more to the window and stood looking out. Poirot signed to me not to speak. I think he was hoping for some further revelation, now that the girl's self-control had broken down.

When she spoke, it was in a different tone of voice, a dreamy far-away voice.

'Do you know a queer wish I've always had? I love End House. I've always wanted to produce a play there. It's got an—an atmosphere of drama about it. I've seen all sorts of plays staged there in my mind. And now it's as though a drama were being acted there. Only I'm not producing it . . . I'm *in* it! I'm *right* in it! I am, perhaps, the person who—dies in the first act.'

Her voice broke.

'Now, now, Mademoiselle.' Poirot's voice was resolutely brisk and cheerful. 'This will not do. This is the hysteria.'

She turned and looked at him sharply.

'Did Freddie tell you I was hysterical?' she asked. 'She says I am, sometimes. But you mustn't always believe what Freddie says.

There are times, you know, when—when she isn't quite herself.'

There was a pause, then Poirot asked a totally irrelevant question:

'Tell me, Mademoiselle,' he said. 'Have you ever received an offer for End House?'

'To sell it, do you mean?'

'That is what I meant.'

'No.'

'Would you consider selling it if you got a good offer?'

Nick considered for a moment.

'No, I don't think so. Not, I mean, unless it was such a ridiculously good offer that it would be perfectly foolish not to.'

'*Précisément.*'

'I don't want to sell it, you know, because I'm fond of it.'

'Quite so. I understand.'

Nick moved slowly towards the door.

'By the way, there are fireworks to-night. Will you come? Dinner at eight o'clock. The fireworks begin at nine-thirty. You can see them splendidly from the garden where it overlooks the harbour.'

'I shall be enchanted.'

'Both of you, of course,' said Nick.

'Many thanks,' I said.

'Nothing like a party for reviving the drooping spirits,' remarked Nick. And with a little laugh she went out.

'*Pauvre enfant*,' said Poirot.

He reached for his hat and carefully flicked an infinitesimal speck of dust from its surface.

'We are going out?' I asked.

'*Mais oui*, we have legal business to transact, *mon ami*.'

'Of course. I understand.'

'One of your brilliant mentality could not fail to do so, Hastings.'

The offices of Messrs. Vyse, Trevannion & Wynnard were situated in the main street of the town. We mounted the stairs to the first floor and entered a room where three clerks were busily writing. Poirot asked to see Mr. Charles Vyse.

A clerk murmured a few words down a telephone, received, apparently, an affirmative reply, and remarking that Mr. Vyse would see us now, he led us across the passage, tapped on a door and stood aside for us to pass in.

From behind a large desk covered with legal papers, Mr. Vyse rose up to greet us.

He was a tall young man, rather pale, with impassive features. He was going a little bald on either temple and wore glasses. His colouring was fair and indeterminate.

Poirot had come prepared for the encounter. Fortunately he had with him an agreement, as yet unsigned, and on some technical points in connection with this, he wanted Mr. Vyse's advice.

Mr. Vyse, speaking carefully and correctly, was soon able to allay Poirot's alleged doubts, and to clear up some obscure points of the wording.

'I am very much obliged to you,' murmured Poirot. 'As a foreigner, you comprehend, these legal matters and phrasing are most difficult.'

It was then that Mr. Vyse asked who had sent Poirot to him.

'Miss Buckley,' said Poirot, promptly. 'Your cousin, is she not? A most charming young lady. I happened to mention that I was in perplexity and she told me to come to you. I tried to see you on Saturday morning—about half-past twelve—but you were out.'

'Yes, I remember. I left early on Saturday.'

'Mademoiselle your cousin must find that large house very lonely? She lives there alone, I understand.'

'Quite so.'

'Tell me, Mr. Vyse, if I may ask, is there any chance of that property being in the market?'

'Not the least, I should say.'

'You understand, I do not ask idly. I have a reason! I am in search, myself, of just such a property. The climate of St. Loo enchants me. It is true that the house appears to be in bad repair, there has not been, I gather, much money to spend upon it. Under those circumstances, is it not possible that Mademoiselle would consider an offer?'

'Not the least likelihood of it.' Charles Vyse shook his head with the utmost decision. 'My cousin is absolutely devoted to the place. Nothing would induce her to sell, I know. It is, you understand, a family place.'

'I comprehend that, but——'

'It is absolutely out of the question. I know my cousin. She has a fanatical devotion to the house.'

A few minutes later we were out in the street again.

'Well, my friend,' said Poirot. 'And what impression did this M. Charles Vyse make upon you?'

I considered.

'A very negative one,' I said at last. 'He is a curiously negative person.'

'Not a strong personality, you would say?'

'No, indeed. The kind of man you would never remember on meeting him again. A mediocre person.'

'His appearance is certainly not striking. Did you notice any discrepancy in the course of our conversation with him?'

'Yes,' I said slowly, 'I did. With regard to the selling of End House.'

'Exactly. Would you have described Mademoiselle Buckley's attitude towards End House as one of "fanatical devotion"?'

'It is a very strong term.'

'Yes—and Mr. Vyse is not given to using strong terms. His normal attitude—a legal attitude—is to under, rather than over, state. Yet he says that Mademoiselle has a fanatical devotion to the home of her ancestors.'

'She did not convey that impression this morning,' I said. 'She spoke about it very sensibly, I thought. She's obviously fond of the place—just as anyone in her position would be—but certainly nothing more.'

'So, in fact, one of the two is lying,' said Poirot, thoughtfully.

'One would not suspect Vyse of lying.'

'Clearly a great asset if one has any lying to do,' remarked Poirot. 'Yes, he has quite the air of a George Washington, that one. Did you notice another thing, Hastings?'

'What was that?'

'*He was not in his office at half-past twelve on Saturday.*'

7. Tragedy

THE FIRST PERSON WE SAW when we arrived at End House that evening was Nick. She was dancing about the hall wrapped in a marvellous kimono covered with dragons.

'Oh! it's only you!'

'Mademoiselle—I am desolated!'

'I know. It did sound rude. But you see, I'm waiting for my dress to arrive. They promised—the brutes—promised faithfully!'

'Ah! if it is a matter of *la toilette*! There is a dance to-night, is there not?'

'Yes. We are all going on to it after the fireworks. That is, I suppose we are.'

There was a sudden drop in her voice. But the next minute she was laughing.

'Never give in! That's my motto. Don't think of trouble and trouble won't come! I've got my nerve back to-night. I'm going to be gay and enjoy myself.'

There was a footfall on the stairs. Nick turned.

'Oh! here's Maggie. Maggie, here are the sleuths that are protecting me from the secret assassin. Take them into the drawing-room and let them tell you about it.'

In turn we shook hands with Maggie Buckley, and, as requested, she took us into the drawing-room. I formed an immediate favourable opinion of her.

It was, I think, her appearance of calm good sense that so attracted me. A quiet girl, pretty in the old-fashioned sense—certainly not smart. Her face was innocent of make-up and she wore a simple, rather shabby, black evening dress. She had frank blue eyes, and a pleasant slow voice.

'Nick has been telling me the most amazing things,' she said. 'Surely she must be exaggerating? Who ever would want to harm Nick? She can't have an enemy in the world.'

Incredulity showed strongly in her voice. She was looking at Poirot in a somewhat unflattering fashion. I realised that to a girl like Maggie Buckley, foreigners were always suspicious.

'Nevertheless, Miss Buckley, I assure you that it is the truth,' said Poirot quietly.

She made no reply, but her face remained unbelieving.

'Nick seems quite fey to-night,' she remarked. 'I don't know what's the matter with her. She seems in the wildest spirits.'

That word—fey! It sent a shiver through me. Also, something in the intonation of her voice had set me wondering.

'Are you Scotch, Miss Buckley?' I asked, abruptly.

'My mother was Scottish,' she explained.

She viewed me, I noticed with more approval than she viewed Poirot. I felt that my statement of the case would carry more weight with her than Poirot's would.

'Your cousin is behaving with great bravery,' I said. 'She's determined to carry on as usual.'

'It's the only way, isn't it?' said Maggie. 'I mean—whatever one's inward feelings are—it is no good making a fuss about them. That's only uncomfortable for everyone else.' She paused and then added in a soft voice. 'I'm very fond of Nick. She's been very good to me always.'

We could say nothing more for at that moment Frederica Rice drifted into the room. She was wearing a gown of Madonna blue and looked very fragile and ethereal. Lazarus soon followed her and then Nick danced in. She was wearing a black frock, and round her was wrapped a marvellous old Chinese shawl of vivid lacquer red.

'Hello, people,' she said. 'Cocktails?'

We all drank, and Lazarus raised his glass to her.

'That's a marvellous shawl, Nick,' he said. 'It's an old one, isn't it?'

'Yes—brought back by Great-Great-Great-Uncle Timothy from his travels.'

'It's a beauty—a real beauty. You wouldn't find another to match it if you tried.'

'It's warm,' said Nick. 'It'll be nice when we're watching the fireworks. And it's gay. I—I hate black.'

'Yes,' said Frederica. 'I don't believe I've ever seen you in a black dress before, Nick. Why did you get it?'

'Oh! I don't know.' The girl flung aside with a petulant gesture, but I had caught a curious curl of her lips as though of pain. 'Why does one do anything?'

We went in to dinner. A mysterious manservant had appeared—hired, I presume, for the occasion. The food was indifferent. The champagne, on the other hand, was good.

'George hasn't turned up,' said Nick. 'A nuisance his having to go back to Plymouth last night. He'll get over this evening sometime or other, I expect. In time for the dance, anyway. I've got a man for Maggie. Presentable, if not passionately interesting.'

A faint roaring sound drifted in through the window.

'Oh! curse that speedboat,' said Lazarus. 'I get so tired of it.'

'That's not the speedboat,' said Nick. 'That's a seaplane.'

'I believe you're right.'

'Of course I'm right. The sound's quite different.'

'When are you going to get your Moth, Nick?'

'When I can raise the money,' laughed Nick.

'And then, I suppose, you'll be off to Australia like that girl—what's her name?'

'I'd love to——'

'I admire her enormously,' said Mrs. Rice, in her tired voice. 'What marvellous nerve! All by herself too.'

'I admire all these flying people,' said Lazarus. 'If Michael Seton had succeeded in his flight round the world he'd have been the hero of the day—and rightly so. A thousand pities he's come to grief. He's the kind of man England can't afford to lose.'

'He may still be all right,' said Nick.

'Hardly. It's a thousand to one against by now. Poor Mad Seton.'

'They always called him Mad Seton, didn't they?' asked Frederica.

Lazarus nodded.

'He comes of rather a mad family,' he said. 'His uncle, Sir Matthew Seton who died about a week ago—he was as mad as a hatter.'

'He was the mad millionaire who ran bird sanctuaries, wasn't he?' asked Frederica.

'Yes. Used to buy up islands. He was a great woman-hater. Some girl chucked him once, I believe, and he took to Natural History by way of consoling himself.'

'Why do you say Michael Seton is dead?' persisted Nick. 'I don't see any reason for giving up hope—yet?'

'Of course, you knew him, didn't you?' said Lazarus. 'I forgot.'

'Freddie and I met him at Le Touquet last year,' said Nick. 'He was too marvellous, wasn't he, Freddie?'

'Don't ask me darling. He was your conquest, not mine. He took you up once, didn't he?'

'Yes—at Scarborough. It was simply too wonderful.'

'Have you done any flying, Captain Hastings?' Maggie asked of me in polite conversational tones.

I had to confess that a trip to Paris and back was the extent of my acquaintance with air travel.

Suddenly, with an exclamation, Nick sprang up.

'There's the telephone. Don't wait for me. It's getting late. And I've asked lots of people.'

She left the room. I glanced at my watch. It was just nine o'clock. Dessert was brought, and port. Poirot and Lazarus were talking Art. Pictures, Lazarus was saying, were a great drug in the market just now. They went on to discuss new ideas in furniture and decoration. I endeavoured to do my duty by talking to Maggie Buckley, but I had to admit that the girl was heavy in hand. She answered pleasantly, but without throwing the ball back. It was uphill work.

Frederica Rice sat dreamily silent, her elbows on the table and the smoke from her cigarette curling round her fair head. She looked like a meditative angel.

It was just twenty past nine when Nick put her head round the door.

'Come out of it, all of you! The animals are coming in two by two.'

We rose obediently. Nick was busy greeting arrivals. About a dozen people had been asked. Most of them were rather uninteresting. Nick, I noticed, made a good hostess. She sank her modernisms and made everyone welcome in an old-fashioned way. Among the guests I noticed Charles Vyse.

Presently we all moved out into the garden to a place overlooking the sea and the harbour. A few chairs had been placed there for the elderly people, but most of us stood. The first rocket flamed to heaven.

At that moment I heard a loud familiar voice, and turned my head to see Nick greeting Mr. Croft.

'It's too bad,' she was saying, 'that Mrs. Croft can't be here too. We ought to have carried her on a stretcher or something.'

'It's bad luck on poor mother altogether. But she never complains—that woman's got the sweetest nature—Ha! that's a good one.' This as a shower of golden rain showed up in the sky.

The night was a dark one—there was no moon—the new moon being due in three days' time. It was also, like most summer evenings, cold. Maggie Buckley, who was next me, shivered.

'I'll just run in and get a coat,' she murmured.

'Let me.'

'No, you wouldn't know where to find it.'

She turned towards the house. At that moment Frederica Rice's voice called:

'Oh, Maggie, get mine too. It's in my room.'

'She didn't hear,' said Nick. 'I'll get it, Freddie. I want my fur one—this shawl isn't nearly hot enough. It's this wind.'

There was, indeed, a sharp breeze blowing off the sea.

Some set pieces started down on the quay. I fell into conversation with an elderly young lady standing next me who put me through a rigorous catechism as to life, career, tastes and probable length of stay.

Bang! A shower of green stars filled the sky. They changed to blue, then red, then silver.

Another and yet another.

'"Oh!" and then "Ah!" that is what one says,' observed Poirot suddenly close to my ear. 'At the end it becomes monotonous, do you not find? Brrrr! The grass, it is damp to the feet! I shall suffer for this—a chill. And no possibility of obtaining a proper *tisane*!'

'A chill? On a lovely night like this?'

'A lovely night! A lovely night! You say that, because the rain it does not pour down in sheets! Always when the rain does not fall, it is a lovely night. But I tell you, my friend, if there were a little thermometer to consult you would see.'

'Well,' I admitted. 'I wouldn't mind putting on a coat myself.'

'You are very sensible. You have come from a hot climate.'

'I'll bring yours.'

Poirot lifted first one, then the other foot from the ground with a cat-like motion.

'It is the dampness of the feet I fear. Would it, think you, be possible to lay the hands on a pair of goloshes?'

I repressed a smile.

'Not a hope,' I said. 'You understand, Poirot, that it is no longer done.'

'Then I shall sit in the house,' he declared. 'Just for the Guy Fawkes show, shall I want only *enrhumer* myself? And catch, perhaps, a *fluxion de poitrine*?'

Poirot still murmuring indignantly, we bent our footsteps towards the house. Loud clapping drifted up to us from the quay below where another set piece was being shown—a ship, I believe, with *Welcome to Our Visitors* displayed across it.

'We are all children at heart,' said Poirot, thoughtfully. '*Les Feus D'Artifices*, the party, the games with balls—yes, and even the conjurer, the man who deceives the eye, however carefully it watches—*mais qu'est ce que vous avez?*'

I had caught him by the arm, and was clutching him with one hand, while with the other I pointed.

We were within a hundred yards of the house, and just in front of us, between us and the open French window, *there lay a huddled figure wrapped in a scarlet Chinese shawl. . . .*

'*Mon Dieu!*' whispered Poirot. '*Mon Dieu . . .*'

8. The fatal shawl

I SUPPOSE it was not more than forty seconds that we stood there, frozen with horror, unable to move, but it seemed like an hour. Then Poirot moved forward, shaking off my hand. He moved stiffly like an automaton.

'It has happened,' he murmured, and I can hardly describe the anguished bitterness of his voice. 'In spite of everything—in spite of my precautions, it has happened. Ah! miserable criminal that I am, why did I not guard her better. I should have foreseen—yes—I should have foreseen. Not for one instant should I have left her side.'

'You mustn't blame yourself,' I said.

My tongue stuck to the roof of my mouth, and I could hardly articulate.

Poirot only responded with a sorrowful shake of his head. He knelt down by the body.

And at that moment we received a second shock.

For Nick's voice rang out, clear and gay, and a moment later Nick appeared in the square of the window silhouetted against the lighted room behind.

'Sorry I've been so long, Maggie,' she said. 'But——'

Then she broke off—staring at the scene before her.

With a sharp exclamation, Poirot turned over the body on the lawn and I pressed forward to see.

I looked down into the dead face of Maggie Buckley.

In another minute Nick was beside us. She gave a sharp cry.

'Maggie—oh! Maggie—it—it can't——'

Poirot was still examining the girl's body. At last very slowly he rose to his feet.

'Is she—is——' Nick's voice broke off.'

'Yes, Mademoiselle. She is dead.'

'But why? But why? Who could have wanted to kill *her*?'

Poirot's reply came quickly and firmly.

'It was not her they meant to kill, Mademoiselle! It was *you*! They were misled by the shawl.'

A great cry broke from Nick.

'Why couldn't it have been me?' she wailed. 'Oh! why couldn't it have been me? I'd so much rather. I don't want to live—*now*. I'd be glad—willing—happy—to die.'

She flung up her arms wildly and then staggered slightly. I passed an arm round her quickly to support her.

'Take her into the house, Hastings,' said Poirot. 'Then ring up the police.'

'The police?'

'*Mais oui*! Tell them someone has been shot. And afterwards stay with Mademoiselle Nick. *On no account leave her*.'

I nodded comprehension of these instructions, and supporting the half-fainting girl, made my way through the drawing-room window. I laid the girl on the sofa there, with a cushion under her head, and then hurried out into the hall in search of the telephone.

I gave a slight start on almost running into Ellen. She was standing there with a most peculiar expression on her meek, respectable face. Her eyes were glittering and she was passing her tongue repeatedly over her dry lips. Her hands were trembling, as though with excitement. As soon as she saw me, she spoke.

'Has—has anything happened, sir?'

'Yes,' I said curtly. 'Where's the telephone?'

'Nothing—nothing wrong, sir?'

'There's been an accident,' I said evasively. 'Somebody hurt. I must telephone.'

'Who has been hurt, sir?'

There was a positive eagerness in her face.

'Miss Buckley. Miss Maggie Buckley.'

'Miss Maggie? Miss *Maggie*? Are you sure, sir—I mean are you sure that—that it's Miss Maggie?'

'I'm quite sure,' I said. 'Why?'

'Oh!—nothing. I—I thought it might be one of the other ladies. I thought perhaps it might be—Mrs. Rice.'

'Look here,' I said. 'Where's the telephone?'

'It's in the little room here, sir.' She opened the door for me and indicated the instrument.

'Thanks,' I said. And, as she seemed disposed to linger, I added: 'That's all I want, thank you.'

'If you want Dr. Graham——'

'No, no,' I said. 'That's all. Go please.'

She withdrew reluctantly, as slowly as she dared. In all probability she would listen outside the door, but I could not help that. After all, she would soon know all there was to be known.

I got the police station and made my report. Then, on my own initiative, I rang up the Dr. Graham Ellen had mentioned. I found his number in the book. Nick, at any rate, should have medical attention, I felt—even though a doctor could do nothing for that poor girl lying out there. He promised to come at once and I hung up the receiver and came out into the hall again.

If Ellen had been listening outside the door she had managed to disappear very swiftly. There was no one in sight when I came out. I went back into the drawing-room. Nick was trying to sit up.

'Do you think—could you get me—some brandy?'

'Of course.'

I hurried into the dining-room, found what I wanted and came back. A few sips of the spirit revived the girl. The colour began to come back into her cheeks. I rearranged the cushion for her head.

'It's all—so awful.' She shivered. 'Everything—everywhere.'

'I know, my dear, I know.'

'No, you don't! You can't. And it's all such a *waste*. If it only were me. It would be all over. . . .'

'You mustn't,' I said, 'be morbid.'

She only shook her head, reiterating: 'You don't know! You don't *know*!'

Then, suddenly she began to cry. A quiet, hopeless sobbing like a child. That, I thought, was probably the best thing for her, so I made no effort to stem her tears.

When their first violence had died down a little, I stole across to the window and looked out. I had heard an outcry of voices a few minutes before. They were all there by now, a semi-circle round the scene of the tragedy, with Poirot like a fantastical sentinel, keeping them back.

As I watched, two uniformed figures came striding across the grass. The police had arrived.

I went quietly back to my place by the sofa. Nick lifted her tear-stained face.

'Oughtn't I to be doing something?'

'No, my dear. Poirot will see to it. Leave it to him.'

Nick was silent for a minute or two, then she said:

'Poor Maggie. Poor dear old Maggie. Such a good sort who never harmed a soul in her life. That this should happen to *her*. I feel as though I'd killed her—bringing her down in the way that I did.'

I shook my head sadly. How little one can foresee the future. When Poirot insisted on Nick's inviting a friend, how little did he think that he was signing an unknown girl's death warrant.

We sat in silence. I longed to know what was going on outside, but I loyally fulfilled Poirot's instructions and stuck to my post.

It seemed hours later when the door opened and Poirot and a police inspector entered the room. With them came a man who was evidently Dr. Graham. He came over at once to Nick.

'And how are you feeling, Miss Buckley? This must have been a terrible shock.' His fingers were on her pulse. 'Not too bad.'

He turned to me.

'Has she had anything?'

'Some brandy,' I said.

'I'm all right,' said Nick, bravely.

'Able to answer a few questions, eh?'

'Of course.'

The police inspector moved forward with a preliminary cough. Nick greeted him with the ghost of a smile.

'Not impeding the traffic this time,' she said.

I gathered they were not strangers to each other.

'This is a terrible business, Miss Buckley,' said the inspector. 'I'm very sorry about it. Now Mr. Poirot here, whose name I'm very familiar with (and proud we are to have him with us, I'm sure), tells me that to the best of his belief you were shot at in the grounds of the Majestic Hotel the other morning?'

Nick nodded.

'I thought it was just a wasp,' she exclaimed. 'But it wasn't.'

'And you'd had some rather peculiar accidents before that?'

'Yes—at least it was odd their happening so close together.'

She gave a brief account of the various circumstances.

'Just so. Now how came it that your cousin was wearing your shawl to-night?'

'We came in to fetch her coat—it was rather cold watching the fireworks. I flung off the shawl on the sofa here. Then I went upstairs and put on the coat I'm wearing now—a light nutria one. I also got a wrap for my friend Mrs. Rice out of her room. There it is on the floor by the window. Then Maggie called out that she couldn't find her coat. I said it must be downstairs. She went down and called up she still couldn't find it. I said it must have been left in the car—it was a tweed coat she was looking for—she hasn't got an evening furry one—and I said I'd bring her down something of mine. But she said it didn't matter—she'd take my shawl if I didn't want it. And I said of course but would that be enough? And she said Oh, yes, because she really didn't feel it particularly cold after Yorkshire. She just wanted *something*. And I said all right, I'd be out in a minute. And when I did—did come out——'

She stopped, her voice breaking. . . .

'Now, don't distress yourself, Miss Buckley. Just tell me this. Did you hear a shot—or two shots?'

Nick shook her head.

'No—only just the fireworks popping and the squibs going off.'

'That's just it,' said the inspector. 'You'd never notice a shot with all that going on. It's no good asking you, I suppose, if you've any clue to who it is making these attacks upon you?'

'I haven't the least idea,' said Nick. 'I can't imagine.'

'And you wouldn't be likely to,' said the inspector. 'Some homicidal maniac—that's what it looks like to me. Nasty business. Well, I won't need to ask you any more questions to-night, miss. I'm more sorry about this than I can say.'

Dr. Graham stepped forward.

'I'm going to suggest, Miss Buckley, that you don't stay here. I've been talking it over with M. Poirot. I know of an excellent nursing home. You've had a shock, you know. What you need is complete rest——'

Nick was not looking at him. Her eyes had gone to Poirot.

'Is it—because of the shock?' she asked.

He came forward.

'I want you to feel safe, *mon enfant*. And *I* want to feel, too, that you *are* safe. There will be a nurse there—a nice practical unimaginative nurse. She will be near you all night. When you wake up and cry out—she will be there, close at hand. You understand?'

'Yes,' said Nick, 'I understand. But *you* don't. I'm not afraid any longer. I don't care one way or another. If any one wants to murder me, they can.'

'Hush, hush,' I said. 'You're over-strung.'

'You don't know. None of you know!'

'I really think M. Poirot's plan is a very good one,' the doctor broke in soothingly. 'I will take you in my car. And we will give you a little something to ensure a good night's rest. Now what do you say?'

'I don't mind,' said Nick. 'Anything you like. It doesn't matter.'

Poirot laid his hand on hers.

'I know, Mademoiselle. I know what you must feel. I stand before you ashamed and stricken to the heart. I, who promised protection, have not been able to protect. I have failed. I am a miserable. But believe me, Mademoiselle, my heart is in agony because of that failure. If you knew what I am suffering you would forgive, I am sure.'

'That's all right,' said Nick, still in the same dull voice. 'You mustn't blame yourself. I'm sure you did the best you could. Nobody could have helped it—or done more, I'm sure. Please don't be unhappy.'

'You are very generous, Mademoiselle.'

'No, I——'

There was an interruption. The door flew open and George Challenger rushed into the room.

'What's all this?' he cried. 'I've just arrived. To find a policeman at the gate and a rumour that somebody's dead. What is it all about? For God's sake, tell me. Is it—is it—Nick?'

The anguish in his tone was dreadful to hear. I suddenly realised that Poirot and the doctor between them completely blotted out Nick from his sight.

Before anyone had time to answer, he repeated his question.

'Tell me—it can't be true—Nick isn't *dead*?'

'No, *mon ami*,' said Poirot, gently. 'She is alive.'

And he drew back so that Challenger could see the little figure on the sofa.

For a moment or two Challenger stared at her incredulously. Then, staggering a little, like a drunken man, he muttered:

'Nick—Nick.'

And suddenly dropping on his knees beside the sofa and hiding his head in his hands, he cried in a muffled voice:

'Nick—my darling—I thought that you were dead.'

Nick tried to sit up.

'It's all right, George. Don't be an idiot. I'm quite safe.'

He raised his head and looked round wildly.

'But *somebody's* dead? The policeman said so.'

'Yes,' said Nick. 'Maggie. Poor old Maggie. Oh!——'

A spasm twisted her face. The doctor and Poirot came forward. Graham helped her to her feet. He and Poirot, one on each side, helped her from the room.

'The sooner you get to your bed the better,' remarked the doctor. I'll take you along at once in my car. I've asked Mrs. Rice to pack a few things ready for you to take.'

They disappeared through the door. Challenger caught my arm.

'I don't understand. Where are they taking her?'

I explained.

'Oh! I see. Now, then, Hastings, for God's sake give me the hang of this thing. What a ghastly tragedy! That poor girl.'

'Come and have a drink,' I said. 'You're all to pieces.'

'I don't mind if I do.'

We adjourned to the dining-room.

'You see,' he explained, as he put away a stiff whisky and soda. 'I thought it was Nick.'

There was very little doubt as to the feelings of Commander George Challenger. A more transparent lover never lived.

9. *A. to J.*

I DOUBT if I shall ever forget the night that followed. Poirot was a prey to such an agony of self-reproach that I was really alarmed. Ceaselessly he strode up and down the room heaping anathemas on his own head and deaf to my well-meant remonstrances.

'What it is to have too good an opinion of oneself. I am punished—yes, I am punished. I, Hercule Poirot. I was too sure of myself.'

'No, no,' I interpolated.

'But who would imagine—who could imagine—such unparalleled audacity? I had taken, as I thought, all possible precautions. I had warned the murderer——'

'Warned the murderer?'

'*Mais oui.* I had drawn attention to myself. I had let him see that I suspected—someone. I had made it, or so I thought, too dangerous for him to dare to repeat his attempts at murder. I had drawn a cordon round Mademoiselle. And he slips through it! Boldly—under our very eyes almost, he slips through it! In spite of us all—of everyone being on the alert, he achieves his object.'

'Only he doesn't,' I reminded him.

'That is the chance only! From my point of view, it is the same. A human life has been taken, Hastings—*whose* life is non-essential.'

'Of course,' I said. 'I didn't mean that.'

'But on the other hand, what you say is true. And that makes it worse—ten times worse. For the murderer is still as far as ever from achieving his object. Do you understand, my friend? The position is changed—for the worse. It may mean that not one life—but two—will be sacrificed.'

'Not while you're about,' I said stoutly.

He stopped and wrung my hand.

'*Merci, mon ami! Merci!* You still have confidence in the old one—you still have the faith. You put new courage into me. Hercule Poirot will not fail again. No second life shall be taken. I will rectify my error—for, see you, there must have been an error! Somewhere there has been a lack of order and method in my usually so well arranged ideas. I will start again. Yes, I will start at the beginning. And this time—I will not fail.'

'You really think, then,' I said, 'that Nick Buckley's life is still in danger?'

'My friend, for what other reason did I send her to this nursing home?'

'Then it wasn't the shock——'

'The shock! Pah! One can recover from shock as well in one's own home as in a nursing home—better, for that matter. It is not amusing there, the floors of green linoleum, the conversation of the nurses—the meals on trays, the ceaseless washing. No, no, it is for safety and safety only. I take the doctor into my confidence. He agrees. He will make all arrangements. No one, *mon ami, not even her dearest friend*, will be admitted to see Miss Buckley. You and I are the only ones permitted. *Pour les autres—eh bien!* "Doctor's orders," they will be told. A phrase very convenient and one not to be gainsaid.'

'Yes,' I said. 'Only——'

'Only what, Hastings?'

'That can't go on for ever.'

'A very true observation. But it gives us a little breathing space. And you realise, do you not, that the character of our operations has changed?'

'In what way?'

'Our original task was to ensure the safety of Mademoiselle. Our task now is a much simpler one—a task with which we are well acquainted. It is neither more nor less than the hunting down of a murderer.'

'You call that simpler?'

'Certainly it is simpler. The murderer has, as I said the other day, *signed his name to the crime*. He has come out into the open.'

'You don't think——' I hesitated, then went on. 'You don't think that the police are right? That this is the work of a madman, some wandering lunatic with homicidal mania?'

'I am more than ever convinced that such is not the case.'

'You really think that——'

I stopped. Poirot took up my sentence, speaking very gravely.

'That the murderer is someone in Mademoiselle's own circle? Yes, *mon ami*, I do.'

'But surely last night must almost rule out that possibility. We were all together and——'

He interrupted.

'Could you swear, Hastings, that any particular person had never left out little company there on the edge of the cliff? Is there any one person there whom you could swear you had seen *all* the time?'

'No,' I said slowly, struck by his words. 'I don't think I could. It was dark. We all moved about, more or less. On different occasions I noticed Mrs. Rice, Lazarus, you, Croft, Vyse—but all the time—no.'

Poirot nodded his head.

'Exactly. It would be a matter of a very few minutes. The two girls go to the house. The murderer slips away unnoticed, hides behind that sycamore tree in the middle of the lawn. Nick Buckley, or so he thinks, comes out of the window, passes within a foot of him, he fires three shots in rapid succession——'

'Three?' I interjected.

'Yes. He was taking no chances this time. We found three bullets in the body.'

'That was risky, wasn't it?'

'Less risky in all probability than one shot would have been. A Mauser pistol does not make a great deal of noise. It would resemble more or less the popping of the fireworks and blend in very well with the noise of them.'

'Did you find the pistol?' I asked.

'No. And there, Hastings, lies to my mind the indisputable proof that no stranger is responsible for this. We agree, do we not, that Miss Buckley's own pistol was taken in the first place for one reason only—to give her death the appearance of suicide.'

'Yes.'

'That is the only possible reason, is it not? But now, you observe, there is no pretence of suicide. *The murderer knows that we should not any longer be deceived by it.* He knows, in fact, what we know!'

I reflected, admitting to myself the logic of Poirot's deduction.

'What did he do with the pistol, do you think?'

Poirot shrugged his shoulders.

'For that, it is difficult to say. But the sea was exceedingly handy. A good toss of the arm, and the pistol sinks, never to be recovered. We cannot, of course, be absolutely sure—but that is what *I* should have done.'

His matter-of-fact tone made me shiver a little.

'Do you think—do you think he realised that he'd killed the wrong person?'

'I am quite sure he did not,' said Poirot, grimly. 'Yes, that must have been an unpleasant little surprise for him when he learnt the truth. To keep his face and betray nothing—it cannot have been easy.'

At that moment I bethought me of the strange attitude of the maid, Ellen. I gave Poirot an account of her peculiar demeanour. He seemed very interested.

'She betrayed surprise, did she, that it was Maggie who was dead?'

'Great surprise.'

'That is curious. And yet, the fact of a tragedy was clearly *not* a surprise to her. Yes, there is something there that must be looked into. Who is she, this Ellen? So quiet, so respectable in the English manner? Could it be she who——?' He broke off.

'If you're going to include the accidents,' I said, 'surely it would take a man to have rolled that heavy boulder down the cliff.'

'Not necessarily. It is very largely a question of leverage. Oh, yes, it could be done.'

He continued his slow pacing up and down of the room.

'Anyone who was at End House last night comes under suspicion. But those guests—no, I do not think it was one of them. For the most part, I should say, they were mere acquaintances. There was no intimacy between them and the young mistress of the house.'

'Charles Vyse was there,' I remarked.

'Yes, we must not forget him. He is, logically, our strongest suspect.' He made a gesture of despair and threw himself into a chair opposite mine. '*Voilà*—it is always that we come back to! Motive! We must find the motive if we are to understand this crime. And it is there, Hastings, that I am continually baffled. Who can possibly have a motive for doing away with Mademoiselle Nick? I have let myself go to the most absurd suppositions. I, Hercule Poirot, have descended to the most ignominious flights of fancy. I have adopted the mentality of the cheap thriller. The grandfather—the "Old Nick"—he who is supposed to have gambled his money away. Did he really do so, I have asked myself? Did he, on the contrary, hide it away? Is it hidden somewhere in End House? Buried somewhere in the grounds? With that end in view (I am ashamed to say it) I inquired of Mademoiselle Nick whether there had ever been any offers to buy the house.'

'Do you know, Poirot,' I said. 'I call that rather a bright idea. There may be something in it.'

Poirot groaned.

'You would say that! It would appeal, I knew, to your romantic but slightly mediocre mind. Buried treasure—yes, you would enjoy that idea.'

'Well—I don't see why not——'

'Because, my friend, the more prosaic explanation is nearly always the more probable. Then Mademoiselle's father—I have played with even more degrading ideas concerning him. He was a traveller. Supposing, I say to myself, that he has stolen a jewel—the eye of a God. Jealous priests are on his tracks. Yes, I Hercule Poirot, have descended to depths such as these.

'I have had other ideas concerning this father,' he went on. 'Ideas at once more dignified and more probable. Did he, in the course of his wanderings, contract a second marriage? Is there a nearer heir than M. Charles Vyse? But again, that leads nowhere, for we are up against the same difficulty—that there is really nothing of value to inherit.

'I have neglected no possibility. Even that chance reference of Mademoiselle Nick's to the offer made her by M. Lazarus. You remember? The offer to purchase her grandfather's portrait. I telegraphed on Saturday for an expert to come down and examine that picture. He was the man about whom I wrote to Mademoiselle this morning. Supposing, for instance, it were worth several thousand pounds?'

'You surely don't think a rich man like young Lazarus——?'

'Is he rich? Appearances are not everything. Even an old-established firm with palatial showrooms and every appearance of prosperity may rest on a rotten basis. And what does one do then? Does one run about crying out that times are hard? No, one buys a new and luxurious car. One spends a little more money than usual. One lives a little more ostentatiously. For credit, see you, is everything! But sometimes a monumental business has crashed—for no more than a few thousand pounds—*of ready money*.

'Oh! I know,' he continued, forestalling my protests. 'It is far-fetched—but it is not so bad as revengeful priests or buried treasure. It bears, at any rate, some relationship to things as they happen. And we can neglect nothing—nothing that might bring us nearer the truth.'

With careful fingers he straightened the objects on the table in front of him. When he spoke, his voice was grave and, for the first time, calm.

'*Motive!*' he said. 'Let us come back to that, and regard this problem calmly and methodically. To begin with, how many kinds of motive are there for murder? What are the motives which lead one human being to take another human being's life?

'We exclude for the moment homicidal mania. Because I am absolutely convinced that the solution of our problem does not lie there. We also exclude killing done on the spur of the moment under the impulse of an ungovernable temper. This is cold-blooded deliberate murder. What are the motives that actuate such a murder as that?

'There is, first, *Gain*. Who stood to gain by Mademoiselle Buckley's death? Directly, or indirectly. Well, we can put down Charles Vyse. He inherits a property that, from the financial point of view, is probably not worth inheriting. He might, perhaps, pay off the mortgage, build small villas on the land and eventually make a small profit. It is possible. The place might be worth something to him if he had any deeply cherished love of it—if, it were, for instance, a family place. That is, undoubtedly, an instinct very deeply implanted in some human beings, and it has, in cases I have known, actually led to crime. But I cannot see any such motive in M. Vyse's case.

'The only other person who would benefit at all by Mademoiselle Buckley's death is her friend, Madame Rice. But the amount would clearly be a very small one. Nobody else, as far as I can see, *gains* by Mademoiselle Buckley's death.

'What is another motive? Hate—or love that has turned to hate. The *crime passionnel*. Well, there again we have the word of the observant Madame Croft that both Charles Vyse and Commander Challenger are in love with the young lady.'

'I think we can say that we have observed the latter phenomenon for ourselves,' I remarked, with a smile.

'Yes—he tends to wear his heart on his sleeve, the honest sailor. For the other, we rely on the word of Madame Croft. Now, if Charles Vyse felt that he were supplanted, would he be so powerfully affected that he would kill his cousin rather than let her become the wife of another man?'

'It sounds very melodramatic,' I said, doubtfully.

'It sounds, you would say, un-English. I agree. But even the English have emotions. And a type, such as Charles Vyse, is the most likely to have them. He is a repressed young man. One who does not show his feelings easily. Such often have the most violent feelings. I would never suspect the Commander Challenger of murder for emotional reasons. No, no, he is not the type. But with Charles Vyse—yes, it is possible. But it does not entirely satisfy me.

'Another motive for crime—Jealousy. I separate it from the last, because jealousy may not, necessarily, be a sexual emotion. There is envy—envy of possession—of supremacy. Such a jealousy as drove the Iago of your great Shakespeare to one of the cleverest crimes (speaking from the professional point of view) that has ever been committed.'

'Why was it so clever?' I asked, momentarily diverted.

'*Parbleu*—because he got others to execute it. Imagine a criminal nowadays on whom one was unable to put the handcuffs because he had never done anything himself. But this is not the subject we were discussing. Can jealousy, of any kind, be responsible for this crime? Who has reason to envy Mademoiselle? Another woman? There is only Madame Rice, and as far as we can see, there was no rivalry between the two women. But again, that is only "as far as we can see." There may be something there.'

'Lastly—Fear. Does Mademoiselle Nick, by any chance, hold somebody's secret in her power? Does she know something which, if it were known, might ruin another life? If so, I think we can say very definitely, *that she herself is unaware of it*. But that might be, you know. That might be. And if so, it makes it very difficult. Because, whilst she holds the clue in her hands, she holds it unconsciously and will be quite unable to tell us what it is.'

'You really think that is possible?'

'It is a hypothesis. I am driven to it by the difficulty of finding a reasonable theory elsewhere. When you have eliminated other possibilities you turn to the one that is left and say—since the other is not—*this must be so. . . .*'

He was silent a long time.

At last, rousing himself from his absorption, he drew a sheet of paper towards him and began to write.

'What are you writing?' I asked, curiously.

'*Mon ami*, I am composing a list. It is a list of people surrounding Mademoiselle Buckley. Within that list, if my theory is correct, there must be the name of the murderer.'

He continued to write for perhaps twenty minutes—then shoved the sheets of paper across to me.

'*Voilà, mon ami*. See what you make of it.'

The following is a reproduction of the paper:

A. Ellen.
B. Her gardener husband.
C. Their child.
D. Mr. Croft.
E. Mrs. Croft.
F. Mrs. Rice.
G. Mr. Lazarus.
H. Commander Challenger.
I. Mr. Charles Vyse.
J.

Remarks:

A. *Ellen.*—Suspicious circumstances. Her attitude and words on hearing of the crime. Best opportunity of anyone to have staged accidents and to have known of pistol, *but* unlikely to have tampered with car, and general mentality of crime seems above her level.

Motive.—None—unless Hate arising out of some incident unknown.

Note.—Further inquiries as to her antecedents and general relations with N. B.

B. *Her Husband.*—Same as above. More likely to have tampered with car.

Note.—Should be interviewed.

C. *Child.*—Can be ruled out.

Note.—Should be interviewed. Might give valuable information.

D. *Mr. Croft.*—Only suspicious circumstance the fact that we met him mounting the stair to bedroom floor. Had a ready explanation which may be true. But it may not!
Nothing known of antecedents.

Motive.—None.

E. *Mrs. Croft.*—Suspicious circumstances. None.

Motive.—None.

F. *Mrs. Rice.*—Suspicious circumstances. Full opportunity. Asked N. B. to fetch wrap. Has deliberately tried to create impression that N. B. is a liar and her account of 'accidents' not to be relied on. Was not at Tavistock when accidents occurred. Where was she?

Motive.—*Gain?* Very slight. *Jealousy?* Possible, but nothing known. *Fear?* Also possible but nothing known.

Note.—Converse with N. B. on subject. See if any light is thrown upon matter. Possibly something to do with F. R.'s marriage.

G. *Mr. Lazarus.*—Suspicious circumstances. General opportunity. Offer to buy picture. Said brakes of car were quite all right (according to F. R.). May have been in neighbourhood prior to

Friday.

Motive.—None—unless profit on picture. *Fear?*—unlikely.

Note.—Find out where J. L. was before arriving at St. Loo. Find out financial position of Aaron Lazarus & Son.

H. *Commander Challenger*.—Suspicious circumstances. None. Was in neighbourhood all last week, so opportunity for 'accidents' good. Arrived half an hour after murder.

Motive.—None.

I. *Mr. Vyse*.—Suspicious circumstances. Was absent from office at time when shot was fired in garden of hotel. Opportunity good. Statement about selling of End House open to doubt. Of a repressed temperament. Would probably know about pistol.

Motive.—Gain? (slight). *Love or Hate?* Possible with one of his temperament. *Fear?* Unlikely.

Note.—Find out who held mortgage. Find out position of Vyse's firm.

J. ?.—There *could* be a J., *e.g.* an outsider. *But* with a link in the form of one of the foregoing. If so, probably connected with A. D. and E. or F. The existence of J. would explain (1) Ellen's lack of surprise at crime and her pleasurable satisfaction. (But that might be due to natural pleasurable excitement of her class over deaths.) (2) The reason for Croft and his wife coming to live in lodge. (3) Might supply motive for F. R.'s *fear* of secret being revealed or for *jealousy*.

Poirot watched me as I read.

'It is very English, is it not?' he remarked, with pride. 'I am more English when I write than when I speak.'

'It's an excellent piece of work,' I said, warmly. 'It sets all the possibilities out most clearly.'

'Yes,' he said, thoughtfully, as he took it back from me. 'And one name leaps to the eye, my friend. *Charles Vyse*. He has the best opportunities. We have given him the choice of two motives. *Ma foi*—if that was a list of racehorses, he would start favourite, *n'est ce pas?*'

'He is certainly the most likely suspect.'

'You have a tendency, Hastings, to prefer the least likely. That, no doubt, is from reading too many detective stories. In real life, nine times out of ten, it is the most likely and the most obvious person who commits the crime.'

'But you don't really think that is so this time?'

'There is only one thing that is against it. The boldness of the crime! That has stood out from the first. Because of that, as I say, the motive *cannot be obvious*.'

'Yes, that is what you said at first.'

'And that is what I say again.'

With a sudden brusque gesture he crumpled the sheets of paper and threw them on the floor.

'No,' he said, as I uttered an exclamation of protest. 'That list has been in vain. Still, it has cleared my mind. *Order and method!* That is the first stage. To arrange the facts with neatness and precision. The next stage——'

'Yes.'

'The next stage is that of the psychology. The correct employment of the little grey cells! I advise you, Hastings, to go to bed.'

'No,' I said. 'Not unless you do. I'm not going to leave you.'

'Most faithful of dogs! But see you, Hastings, you cannot assist me to think. That is all I am going to do—think.'

I still shook my head.

'You might want to discuss some point with me.'

'Well—well—you are a loyal friend. Take at least, I beg you, the easy-chair.'

That proposal I did accept. Presently the room began to swim and dip. The last thing I remember was seeing Poirot carefully retrieving the crumpled sheets of paper from the floor and putting them away tidily in the waste-paper basket.

Then I must have fallen asleep.

10. Nick's secret

IT WAS DAYLIGHT when I awoke.

Poirot was still sitting where he had been the night before. His attitude was the same, but in his face was a difference. His eyes were shining with that queer cat-like green light that I knew so well.

I struggled to an upright position, feeling very stiff and uncomfortable. Sleeping in a chair is a proceeding not to be recommended at my time of life. Yet one thing at least resulted from it—I awoke not in that pleasant state of lazy somnolence but with a mind and brain as active as when I fell asleep.

'Poirot,' I cried. 'You have thought of something.'

He nodded. He leaned forward, tapping the table in front of him.

'Tell me, Hastings, the answer to these three questions. *Why has Mademoiselle Nick been sleeping badly lately? Why did she buy a black evening dress—she never wears black? Why did she say last night, "I have nothing to live for—now"?'*

I stared. The questions seemed beside the point.

'Answer those questions, Hastings, answer them?'

'Well—as to the first—she said she had been worried lately.'

'Precisely. What has she been worried about?'

'And the black dress—well, everybody wants a change sometimes.'

'For a married man, you have very little appreciation of feminine psychology. If a woman thinks she does not look well in a colour, she refuses to wear it.'

'And the last—well, it was a natural thing to say after that awful shock.'

'No, *mon ami*, it was *not* a natural thing to say. To be horror-struck by her cousin's death, to reproach herself for it—yes, all that is natural enough. But the other, no. She spoke of life with weariness—as of a thing no longer dear to her. Never before had she displayed that attitude. She had been defiant—yes—she had snapped the fingers, yes—and then, when that broke down, she was afraid. Afraid, mark you, because life was sweet and she did not wish to die. But weary of life—no! That never! Even before dinner that was not so. We have there, Hastings, a *psychological change*. And that is interesting. What was it caused her point of view to change?'

'The shock of her cousin's death.'

'I wonder. It was the shock that loosed her tongue. But suppose the change was before that. Is there anything else could account for it?'

'I don't know of anything.'

'Think, Hastings. Use your little grey cells.'

'Really——'

'What was the last moment we had the opportunity of observing her?'

'Well, actually, I suppose, at dinner.'

'Exactly. After that, we only saw her receiving guests, making them welcome—purely a formal attitude. What happened at the end of dinner, Hastings?'

'She went to telephone,' I said, slowly.

'*À la bonheur*. You have got there at last. She went to telephone. And she was absent a long time. Twenty minutes at least. That is a long time for a telephone call. Who spoke to her over the telephone? What did they say? Did she really telephone? We have got to find out, Hastings, what happened in that twenty minutes. For there, or so I fully believe, we shall find the clue we seek.'

'You really think so?'

'*Mais oui, mais oui*! All along, Hastings, I have told you that Mademoiselle has been keeping something back. She doesn't think it has any connection with the murder—but I, Hercule Poirot, know better! It *must* have a connection. For all along, I have been conscious that there is a factor lacking. If there were not a factor lacking—why then, the whole thing would be plain to me! And as it is not plain to me—*eh bien*—then the missing factor is the keystone of the mystery! I know I am right, Hastings.

'I must know the answer to those three questions. And then—and then—I shall begin to *see*. . . .'

'Well,' I said, stretching my stiffened limbs, 'I think a bath and a shave are indicated.'

By the time I had had a bath and changed into day clothing I felt better. The stiffness and weariness of a night passed in uncomfortable conditions passed off. I arrived at the breakfast table feeling that one drink of hot coffee would restore me to my normal self.

I glanced at the paper, but there was little news in it beyond the fact that Michael Seton's death was now definitely confirmed. The intrepid airman had perished. I wondered whether, to-morrow, new headlines would have sprung into being: 'GIRL MURDERED DURING FIREWORK PARTY. MYSTERIOUS TRAGEDY.' Something like that.

I had just finished breakfast when Frederica Rice came up to my table. She was wearing a plain little frock of black marocain with a little soft pleated white collar. Her fairness was more evident than ever.

'I want to see M. Poirot, Captain Hastings. Is he up yet, do you know?'

'I will take you up with me now,' I said. 'We shall find him in the sitting-room.'

'Thank you.'

'I hope,' I said, as we left the dining-room together, 'that you didn't sleep too badly?'

'It was a shock,' she said, in a meditative voice. 'But, of course, I didn't know the poor girl. It's not as though it had been Nick.'

'I suppose you'd never met this girl before?'

'Once—at Scarborough. She came over to lunch with Nick.'

'It will be a terrible blow to her father and mother,' I said.

'Dreadful.'

But she said it very impersonally. She was, I fancied, an egoist. Nothing was very real to her that did not concern herself.

Poirot had finished his breakfast and was sitting reading the morning paper. He rose and greeted Frederica with all his customary Gallic politeness.

'Madame,' he said. *'Enchanté!'*

He drew forward a chair.

She thanked him with a very faint smile and sat down. Her two hands rested on the arms of the chair. She sat there very upright, looking straight in front of her. She did not rush into speech. There was something a little frightening about her stillness and aloofness.

'M. Poirot,' she said at last. 'I suppose there is no doubt that this—sad business last night was all part and parcel of the same thing? I mean—that the intended victim was really Nick?'

'I should say, Madame, that there was no doubt at all.'

Frederica frowned a little.

'Nick bears a charmed life,' she said.

There was some curious undercurrent in her voice that I could not understand.

'Luck, they say, goes in cycles,' remarked Poirot.

'Perhaps. It is certainly useless to fight against it.'

Now there was only weariness in her tone. After a moment or two, she went on.

'I must beg your pardon, M. Poirot. Nick's pardon, too. Up till last night I did not believe. I never dreamed that the danger was—serious.'

'Is that so, Madame?'

'I see now that everything will have to be gone into—carefully. And I imagine that Nick's immediate circle of friends will not be immune from suspicion. Ridiculous, of course, but there it is. Am I right, M. Poirot?'

'You are very intelligent, Madame.'

'You asked me some questions about Tavistock the other day, M. Poirot. As you will find out sooner or later, I might as well tell you the truth now. I was not at Tavistock.'

'No, Madame?'

'I motored down to this part of the world with Mr. Lazarus early last week. We did not wish to arouse more comment than necessary. We stayed at a little place called Shellacombe.'

'That is, I think, about seven miles from here, Madame?'

'About that—yes.'

Still that quiet far-away weariness.

'May I be impertinent, Madame?'

'Is there such a thing—in these days?'

'Perhaps you are right, Madame. How long have you and M. Lazarus been friends?'

'I met him six months ago.'

'And you—care for him, Madame?'

Frederica shrugged her shoulders.

'He is—rich.'

'Oh! *là là,*' cried Poirot. 'That is an ugly thing to say.'

She seemed faintly amused.

'Isn't it better to say it myself—than to have you say it for me?'

'Well—there is always that, of course. May I repeat, Madame, that you are *very* intelligent.'

'You will give me a diploma soon,' said Frederica, and rose.

'There is nothing more you wish to tell me, Madame?'

'I do not think so—no. I am going to take some flowers round to Nick and see how she is.'

'Ah, that is very *aimable* of you. Thank you, Madame, for your frankness.'

She glanced at him sharply, seemed about to speak, then thought better of it and went out of the room, smiling faintly at me as I held the door open for her.

'She is intelligent,' said Poirot. 'Yes, but so is Hercule Poirot!'

'What do you mean?'

'That it is all very well and very pretty to force the richness of M. Lazarus down my throat——'

'I must say that rather disgusted me.'

'*Mon cher*, always you have the right reaction in the wrong place. It is not, for the moment, a question of good taste or otherwise. If Madame Rice has a devoted friend who is rich and can give her all she needs—why then obviously Madame Rice would not need to murder her dearest friend for a mere pittance.'

'Oh!' I said.

'*Précisément!* "Oh!"'

'Why didn't you stop her going to the nursing home?'

'Why should I show my hand? Is it Hercule Poirot who prevents Mademoiselle Nick from seeing her friends? *Quelle idée!* It is the doctors and the nurses. Those tiresome nurses! So full of rules and regulations and "doctor's orders."'

'You're not afraid that they may let her in after all? Nick might insist.'

'Nobody will be let in, my dear Hastings, but you and me. And for that matter, the sooner we make our way there, the better.'

The sitting-room door flew open and George Challenger barged in. His tanned face was alive with indignation.

'Look here, M. Poirot,' he said. 'What's the meaning of this? I rang up that damned nursing home where Nick is. Asked how she was and what time I could come round and see her. And they say the doctor won't allow any visitors. I want to know the meaning of that? To put it plainly, is this your work? Or is Nick really ill from shock?'

'I assure you, Monsieur, that I do not lay down rules for nursing homes. I would not dare. Why not ring up the good doctor—what was his name now?—Ah, yes, Graham.'

'I have. He says she's going on as well as could be expected—usual stuff. But I know all the tricks—my uncle's a doctor. Harley Street. Nerve specialist. Psycho-analysis—all the rest of it. Putting relations and friends off with soothing words. I've heard about it all. I don't believe Nick isn't up to seeing anyone. I believe you're at the bottom of this, M. Poirot.'

Poirot smiled at him in a very kindly fashion. Indeed, I have always observed that Poirot has a kindly feeling for a lover.

'Now listen to me, *mon ami*,' he said. 'If one guest is admitted, others cannot be kept out. You comprehend? It must be all or none. We want Mademoiselle's safety, you and I, do we not? Exactly. Then, you understand—it must be *none*.'

'I get you,' said Challenger, slowly. 'But then——'

'Chut! We will say no more. We will forget even what we have said. The prudence, the extreme prudence, is what is needed at present.'

'I can hold my tongue,' said the sailor quietly.

He turned away to the door, pausing as he went out to say:

'No embargo on flowers, is there? So long as they are not white ones.'

Poirot smiled.

'And now,' he said, as the door shut behind the impetuous Challenger, 'whilst M. Challenger and Madame and perhaps M. Lazarus all encounter each other in the flower shop, you and I will drive quietly to our destination.'

'And ask for the answer to the three questions?' I said.

'Yes. We will ask. Though, as a matter of fact, I know the answer.'

'What?' I exclaimed.

'Yes.'

'But when did you find out?'

'Whilst I was eating my breakfast, Hastings. It stared me in the face.'

'Tell me.'

'No, I will leave you to hear it from Mademoiselle.'

Then, as if to distract my mind, he pushed an open letter across to me.

It was a report by the expert Poirot had sent to examine the picture of old Nicholas Buckley. It stated definitely that the picture was worth at most twenty pounds.

'So that is one matter cleared up,' said Poirot.

'No mouse in that mousehole,' I said, remembering a metaphor of Poirot's on one past occasion.

'Ah! you remember that? No, as you say, no mouse in that mousehole. Twenty pounds and M. Lazarus offered fifty. What an error of judgment for a seemingly astute young man. But there, there, we must start on our errand.'

The nursing home was set high on a hill overlooking the bay. A white-coated orderly received us. We were put into a little room downstairs and presently a brisk-looking nurse came to us.

One glance at Poirot seemed to be enough. She had clearly received her instructions from Dr. Graham together with a minute description of the little detective. She even concealed a smile.

'Miss Buckley has passed a very fair night,' she said. 'Come up, will you?'

In a pleasant room with the sun streaming into it, we found Nick. In the narrow iron bed, she looked like a tired child. Her face was white and her eyes were suspiciously red, and she seemed listless and weary.

'It's good of you to come,' she said in a flat voice.

Poirot took her hand in both of his.

'Courage, Mademoiselle. There is always something to live for.'

The words startled her. She looked up in his face.

'Oh!' she said. 'Oh!'

'Will you not tell me now, Mademoiselle, what it was that has been worrying you lately? Or shall I guess? And may I offer you, Mademoiselle, my very deepest sympathy.'

Her face flushed.

'So you know. Oh, well, it doesn't matter who knows now. Now that it's all over. Now that I shall never see him again.'

Her voice broke.

'Courage, Mademoiselle.'

'I haven't got any courage left. I've used up every bit in these last weeks. Hoping and hoping and—just lately—hoping against hope.'

I stared. I could not understand one word.

'Regard the poor Hastings,' said Poirot. 'He does not know what we are talking about.'

Her unhappy eyes met mine.

'Michael Seton, the airman,' she said. 'I was engaged to him—and he's dead.'

11. *The motive*

I WAS DUMBFOUNDED.

I turned on Poirot. 'Is this what you meant?'

'Yes, *mon ami*. This morning—I knew.'

'How did you know? How did you guess? You said it stared you in the face at breakfast.'

'So it did, my friend. From the front page of the newspaper. I remembered the conversation at dinner last night—and I saw everything.'

He turned to Nick again.

'You heard the news last night?'

'Yes. On the wireless. I made an excuse about the telephone. I wanted to hear the news alone—in case. . . .' She swallowed hard. 'And I heard it. . . .'

'I know. I know.'

He took her hand in both of his.

'It was—pretty ghastly. And all the people arriving. I don't know how I got through it. It all felt like a dream. I could see myself from outside—behaving just as usual. It was queer somehow.'

'Yes, yes, I understand.'

'And then, when I went to fetch Freddie's wrap—I broke down for a minute. I pulled myself together quite quickly. But Maggie kept calling up about her coat. And then at last she took my shawl and went, and I put on some powder and some rouge and followed her out. And there she was—dead. . . .'

'Yes, yes, it must have been a terrible shock.'

'You don't understand. I was angry! I wished it had been *me*! I wanted to be dead—and there I was—alive and perhaps to live for years! And Michael dead—drowned far away in the Pacific.'

'*Pauvre enfant*.'

'I don't want to be alive. I don't want to live, I tell you!' she cried, rebelliously.

'I know—I know. To all of us, Mademoiselle, there comes a time when death is preferable to life. But it passes—sorrow passes and grief. You cannot believe that now, I know. It is useless for an old man like me to talk. Idle words—that is what you think—idle words.'

'You think I'll forget—and marry someone else? Never!'

She looked rather lovely as she sat up in bed, her two hands clenched and her cheeks burning.

Poirot said gently:

'No, no. I am not thinking anything of the kind. You are very lucky, Mademoiselle. You have been loved by a brave man— a hero. How did you come to meet him?'

'It was at Le Touquet—last September. Nearly a year ago.'

'And you became engaged—when?'

'Just after Christmas. But it had to be a secret.'

'Why was that?'

'Michael's uncle—old Sir Matthew Seton. He loved birds and hated women.'

'Ah! ce n'est pas raisonable!'

'Well—I don't mean quite that. He was a complete crank. Thought women ruined a man's life. And Michael was absolutely dependent on him. He was frightfully proud of Michael and it was he who financed the building of the *Albatross* and the expenses of the round-the-world flight. It was the dearest dream of his life as well as of Michael's. If Michael had pulled it off—well, then he could have asked his uncle anything. And even if old Sir Matthew had still cut up rough, well, it wouldn't have really mattered. Michael would have been made—a kind of world hero. His uncle would have come round in the end.'

'Yes, yes, I see.'

'But Michael said it would be fatal if anything leaked out. We must keep it a dead secret. And I did. I never told anyone—not even Freddie.'

Poirot groaned.

'If only you had told me, Mademoiselle.'

Nick stared at him.

'But what difference would it have made? It couldn't have anything to do with these mysterious attacks on me? No, I'd promised Michael—and I kept my word. But it was awful—the anxiety, wondering and getting in a state the whole time. And everyone saying one was so nervy. And being unable to explain.'

'Yes, I comprehend all that.'

'He was missing once before, you know. Crossing the desert on the way to India. That was pretty awful, and then after all, it was all right. His machine was damaged, but it was put right, and he went on. And I kept saying to myself that it would be the same this time. Everyone said he must be dead—and I kept telling myself that he must be all right, really. And then—last night. . . .'

Her voice trailed away.

'You had hoped up till then?'

'I don't know. I think it was more that I refused to believe. It was awful never being able to talk to anyone.'

'Yes, I can imagine that. Were you never tempted to tell Madame Rice, for instance?'

'Sometimes I wanted to frightfully.'

'You do not think she—guessed?'

'I don't think so.' Nick considered the idea carefully. 'She never said anything. Of course she used to hint things sometimes. About our being great friends and all that.'

'You never considered telling her when M. Seton's uncle died? You know that he died about a week ago?'

'I know. He had an operation or something. I suppose I might have told anybody then. But it wouldn't have been a nice way of doing it, would it? I mean, it would have seemed rather boastful —to do it just then—when all the papers were full of Michael. And reporters would have come and interviewed me. It would all have been rather cheap. And Michael would have hated it.'

'I agree with you, Mademoiselle. You could not have announced it publicly. I only meant that you could have spoken of it privately to a friend.'

'I did sort of hint to one person,' said Nick. 'I—thought it was only fair. But I don't know how much he—the person took in.'

Poirot nodded.

'Are you on good terms with your cousin, M. Vyse?' he asked, with a rather abrupt change of subject.

'Charles? What put him into your head?'

'I was just wondering—that was all.'

'Charles means well,' said Nick. 'He's a frightful stick, of course. Never moves out of this place. He disapproves of me, I think.'

'Oh! Mademoiselle, Mademoiselle. And I hear that he has laid all his devotion at your feet!'

'Disapproving of a person doesn't keep you from having a pash for them. Charles thinks my mode of life is reprehensible and he disapproves of my cocktails, my complexion, my friends and my conversation. But he still feels my fatal fascination. He always hopes to reform me, I think.'

She paused and then said, with a ghost of a twinkle:

'Who have you been pumping to get the local information?'

'You must not give me away, Mademoiselle. I had a little conversation with the Australian lady, Madame Croft.'

'She's rather an old dear—when one has time for her. Terribly sentimental. Love and home and children—you know the sort of thing.'

'I am old-fashioned and sentimental myself, Mademoiselle.'

'Are you? I should have said that Captain Hastings was the sentimental one of you two.'

I blushed indignantly.

'He is furious,' said Poirot, eyeing my discomfiture with a good deal of pleasure. 'But you are right, Mademoiselle. Yes, you are right.'

'Not at all,' I said, angrily.

'Hastings has a singularly beautiful nature. It has been the greatest hindrance to me at times.'

'Don't be absurd, Poirot.'

'He is, to begin with, reluctant to see evil anywhere, and when he does see it his righteous indignation is so great that he is incapable of dissembling. Altogether a rare and beautiful nature. No, *mon ami*, I will not permit you to contradict me. It is as I say.'

'You've both been very kind to me,' said Nick, gently.

'*Là, là*, Mademoiselle. That is nothing. We have much more to do. To begin with, you will remain here. You will obey orders. You will do what I tell you. At this juncture I must not be hampered.'

Nick sighed wearily.

'I'll do anything you like. I don't care what I do.'

'You will see no friends for the present.'

'I don't care. I don't want to see anyone.'

'For you the passive part—for us the active one. Now, Mademoiselle, I am going to leave you. I will not intrude longer upon your sorrow.'

He moved towards the door, pausing with his hand on the handle to say over his shoulder:

'By the way, you once mentioned a will you made. Where is it, this will?'

'Oh! it's knocking round somewhere.'

'At End House?'

'Yes.'

'In a safe? Locked up in your desk?'

'Well, I really don't know. It's somewhere about.' She frowned. 'I'm frightfully untidy, you know. Papers and things like that would be mostly in the writing-table in the library. That's where most of the bills are. The will is probably with them. Or it might be in my bedroom.'

'You permit me to make the search—yes?'

'If you want to—yes. Look at anything you like.'

'*Merci,* Mademoiselle. I will avail myself of your permission.'

12. *Ellen*

POIROT SAID NO WORD till we had emerged from the nursing home into the outer air. Then he caught me by the arm.

'You see, Hastings? You see? Ah! *Sacré tonnerre!* I was right! I was right! Always I knew there was something lacking—some piece of the puzzle that was not there. And without that missing piece the whole thing was meaningless.'

His almost despairing triumph was double-Dutch to me. I could not see that anything very epoch-making had occurred.

'It was there all the time. And I could not see it. But how should I? To know there is *something*—that, yes—but to know what that something is. *Ah! Ça c'est bien plus difficile.'*

'Do you mean that this has some direct bearing on the crime?'

'*Ma foi*, do you not see?'

'As a matter of fact, I don't.'

'Is it possible? Why, it gives us what we have been looking for—the motive—the hidden obscure motive!'

'I may be very dense, but I can't see it. Do you mean jealousy of some kind?'

'Jealousy? No, no, my friend. The usual motive—the inevitable motive. Money, my friend, money!'

I stared. He went on, speaking more calmly.

'Listen, *mon ami*. Just over a week ago Sir Matthew Seton dies. And Sir Matthew Seton was a millionaire—one of the richest men in England.'

'Yes, but——'

'*Attendez*. One step at a time. He has a nephew whom he idolises and to whom, we may safely assume, he has left his vast fortune.'

'But——'

'*Mais oui*—legacies, yes, an endowment to do with his hobby, yes, but the bulk of the money would go to Michael Seton. Last Tuesday, Michael Seton is reported missing—*and on Wednesday the attacks on Mademoiselle's life begin.* Supposing, Hastings, that Michael Seton made a will before he started on this flight, and that in that will he left all he had to his fiancée.'

'That's pure supposition.'

'It is supposition—yes. *But it must be so.* Because, if it is not so, there is no meaning in anything that has happened. It is no paltry inheritance that is at stake. It is an enormous fortune.'

I was silent for some minutes, turning the matter over in my mind. It seemed to me that Poirot was leaping at conclusions in a most reckless manner, and yet I was secretly convinced that he was right. It was his extraordinary flair for being right that influenced me. Yet it seemed to me that there was a good deal to be proved still.

'But if nobody knew of the engagement,' I argued.

'Pah! Somebody *did* know. For the matter of that, somebody always *does* know. If they do not know, they guess. Madame Rice suspected. Mademoiselle Nick admitted as much. She may have had means of turning those suspicions into certainties.'

'How?'

'Well, for one thing, there must have been letters from Michael Seton to Mademoiselle Nick. They had been engaged some time. And her best friend could not call that young lady anything but careless. She leaves things here and there, and everywhere. I doubt if she has ever locked up anything in her life. Oh, yes, there would be means of making sure.'

'And Frederica Rice would know about the will that her friend had made?'

'Doubtless. Oh, yes, it narrows down now. You remember my list—a list of persons numbered from A. to J. It has narrowed down to only two persons. I dismiss the servants. I dismiss the Commander Challenger—even though he did take one hour and a half to reach here from Plymouth—and the distance is only thirty miles. I dismiss the long-nosed M. Lazarus who offered fifty pounds for a picture that was only worth twenty (it is odd, that, when you come to think of it. Most uncharacteristic of his race). I dismiss the Australians—so hearty and so pleasant. I keep two people on my list still.'

'One is Frederica Rice,' I said, slowly.

I had a vision of her face, the golden hair, the white fragility of the features.

'Yes. She is indicated very clearly. However carelessly worded Mademoiselle's will may have been, she would be plainly indicated as residuary legatee. Apart from End House, everything was to go to her. If Mademoiselle Nick instead of Mademoiselle Maggie had been shot last night, Madame Rice would be a rich woman to-day.'

'I can hardly believe it!'

'You mean that you can hardly believe that a beautiful woman can be a murderess? One often has a little difficulty with members of a jury on that account. But you may be right. There is still another suspect.'

'Who?'

'Charles Vyse.'

'But he only inherits the house.'

'Yes—but he may not know that. Did he make Mademoiselle's will for her? I think not. If so, it would be in his keeping, not 'knocking around somewhere,' or whatever the phrase was that Mademoiselle used. So, you see, Hastings, *it is quite probable that he knows nothing about that will.* He may believe that she has never made a will and that, in that case, he will inherit as next of kin.'

'You know,' I said, 'that really seems to me much more probable.'

'That is your romantic mind, Hastings. The wicked solicitor. A familiar figure in fiction. If as well as being a solicitor he has an impassive face, it makes the matter almost certain. It is true that, in some ways, he is more in the picture than Madame. He would be more likely to know about the pistol and more likely to use one.'

'And to send the boulder crashing down.'

'Perhaps. Though, as I have told you, much can be done by leverage. And the fact that the boulder was dislodged at the wrong minute, and consequently missed Mademoiselle, is more suggestive of feminine agency. The idea of tampering with the interior of a car seems masculine in conception—though many women are as good mechanics as men nowadays. On the other hand, there are one or two gaps in the theory against M. Vyse.'

'Such as——?'

'He is less likely to have known of the engagement than Madame. And there is another point. His action was rather precipitate.'

'What do you mean?'

'Well, until last night there was no *certitude* that Seton was dead. To act rashly, without due assurance, seems very uncharacteristic of the legal mind.'

'Yes,' I said. 'A woman would jump to conclusions.'

'Exactly. *Ce que femme veut, Dieu veut*. That is the attitude.'

'It's really amazing the way Nick has escaped. It seems almost incredible.'

And suddenly I remembered the tone in Frederica's voice as she had said: 'Nick bears a charmed life.'

I shivered a little.

'Yes,' said Poirot, thoughtfully. 'And I can take no credit to myself. Which is humiliating.'

'Providence,' I murmured.

'Ah! *mon ami*, I would not put on the shoulders of the good God the burden of men's wrongdoing. You say that in your Sunday morning voice of thankfulness—without reflecting that what you are really saying is that *le bon Dieu* has killed Miss Maggie Buckley.'

'Really, Poirot!'

'Really, my friend! But I will not sit back and say "*le bon Dieu* has arranged everything, I will not interfere." Because I am convinced that *le bon Dieu* created Hercule Poirot for the express purpose of interfering. It is my *métier*.'

We had been slowly ascending the zig-zag path up the cliff. It was at this juncture that we passed through the little gate into the grounds of End House.

'Pouf!' said Poirot. 'That ascent is a steep one. I am hot. My moustaches are limp. Yes, as I was saying just now, I am on the side of the innocent. I am on the side of Mademoiselle Nick because she was attacked. I am on the side of Mademoiselle Maggie because she has been killed.'

'And you are against Frederica Rice and Charles Vyse.'

'No, no, Hastings. I keep an open mind. I say only that at the moment one of those two is indicated. Chut!'

We had come out on the strip of lawn by the house, and a man was driving a mowing machine. He had a long, stupid face and lack-lustre eyes. Beside him was a small boy of about ten, ugly but intelligent-looking.

It crossed my mind that we had not heard the mowing machine in action, but I presumed that the gardener was not overworking himself. He had probably been resting from his labours, and had sprung into action on hearing our voices approaching.

'Good-morning,' said Poirot.

'Good-morning, sir.'

'You are the gardener, I suppose. The husband of Madame who works in the house.'

'He's my Dad,' said the small boy.

'That's right, sir,' said the man. 'You'll be the foreign gentleman, I take it, that's really a detective. Is there any news of the young mistress, sir?'

'I come from seeing her at the immediate moment. She has passed a satisfactory night.'

'We've had policemen here,' said the small boy. 'That's where the lady was killed. Here by the steps. I seen a pig killed once, haven't I, Dad?'

'Ah!' said his father, unemotionally.

'Dad used to kill pigs when he worked on a farm. Didn't you, Dad? I seen a pig killed. I liked it.'

'Young 'uns like to see pigs killed,' said the man, as though stating one of the unalterable facts of nature.

'Shot with a pistol, the lady was,' continued the boy. 'She didn't have her throat cut. No!'

We passed on to the house, and I felt thankful to get away from the ghoulish child.

Poirot entered the drawing-room, the windows of which were open and rang the bell. Ellen, neatly attired in black, came in answer to the bell. She showed no surprise at seeing us.

Poirot explained that we were here by permission of Miss Buckley to make a search of the house.

'Very good, sir.'

'The police have finished?'

'They said they had seen everything they wanted, sir. They've been about the garden since very early in the morning. I don't know whether they've found anything.'

She was about to leave the room when Poirot stopped her with a question.

'Were you very surprised last night when you heard Miss Buckley had been shot?'

'Yes, sir, very surprised. Miss Maggie was a nice young lady, sir. I can't imagine anyone being so wicked as to want to harm her.'

'If it had been anyone else, you would not have been so surprised—eh?'

'I don't know what you mean, sir?'

'When I came into the hall last night,' I said, 'you asked at once whether anyone had been hurt. Were you expecting anything of the kind?'

She was silent. Her fingers pleated a corner of her apron. She shook her head and murmured:

'You gentlemen wouldn't understand.'

'Yes, yes,' said Poirot, 'I would understand. However fantastic what you may say, I would understand.'

She looked at him doubtfully, then seemed to make up her mind to trust him.

'You see, sir,' she said, 'this isn't a good house.'

I was surprised and a little contemptuous. Poirot, however, seemed to find the remark not in the least unusual.

'You mean it is an old house.'

'Yes, sir, not a good house.'

'You have been here long?'

'Six years, sir. But I was here as a girl. In the kitchen as kitchen-maid. That was in the time of old Sir Nicholas. It was the same then.'

Poirot looked at her attentively.

'In an old house,' he said, 'there is sometimes an atmosphere of evil.'

'That's it, sir,' said Ellen, eagerly. 'Evil. Bad thoughts and bad deeds too. It's like dry rot in a house, sir, you can't get it out. It's a sort of feeling in the air. I always knew something bad would happen in this house, some day.'

'Well, you have been proved right.'

'Yes, sir.'

There was a very slight underlying satisfaction in her tone, the satisfaction of one whose gloomy prognostications have been shown to be correct.

'But you didn't think it would be Miss Maggie.'

'No, indeed, I didn't, sir. Nobody hated *her*—I'm sure of it.'

It seemed to me that in those words was a clue. I expected Poirot to follow it up, but to my surprise he shifted to quite a different subject.

'You didn't hear the shots fired?'

'I couldn't have told with the fireworks going on. Very noisy they were.'

'You weren't out watching them?'

'No, I hadn't finished clearing up dinner.'

'Was the waiter helping you?'

'No, sir, he'd gone out into the garden to have a look at the fireworks.'

'But you didn't go.'

'No, sir.'

'Why was that?'

'I wanted to get finished.'

'You don't care for fireworks?'

'Oh, yes, sir, it wasn't that. But you see, there's two nights of them, and William and I get the evening off to-morrow and go down into the town and see them from there.'

'I comprehend. And you heard Mademoiselle Maggie asking for her coat and unable to find it?'

'I heard Miss Nick run upstairs, sir, and Miss Buckley call up from the front hall saying she couldn't find something and I heard her say, "All right—I'll take the shawl——"'

'Pardon,' Poirot interrupted. 'You did not endeavour to search for the coat for her—or get it from the car where it had been left.'

'I had my work to do, sir.'

'Quite so—and doubtless neither of the two young ladies asked you because they thought you were out looking at the fireworks?'

'Yes, sir.'

'So that, other years, you *have* been out looking at the fireworks?'

A sudden flush came into her pale cheek.

'I don't know what you mean, sir. We're always allowed to go out into the garden. If I didn't feel like it this year, and would rather get on with my work and go to bed, well, that's my business, I imagine.'

'*Mais oui. Mais oui.* I did not intend to offend you. Why should you not do as you prefer. To make a change, it is pleasant.'

He paused and then added:

'Now another little matter in which I wonder whether you can help me. This is an old house. Are there, do you know, any secret chambers in it?'

'Well—there's a kind of sliding panel—in this very room. I remember being shown it as a girl. Only I can't remember just now where it is. Or was it in the library? I can't say, I'm sure.'

'Big enough for a person to hide in?'

'Oh, no, indeed, sir! A little cupboard place—a kind of niche. About a foot square, sir, not more that that.'

'Oh! that is not what I mean at all.'

The blush rose to her face again.

'If you think I was hiding anywhere—I wasn't! I heard Miss Nick run down the stairs and out and I heard her cry out—and I came into the hall to see if—if anything was the matter. And that's the gospel truth, sir. That's the gospel truth.'

13. *Letters*

HAVING SUCCESSFULLY got rid of Ellen, Poirot turned a somewhat thoughtful face towards me.

'I wonder now—did she hear those shots? I think she did. She heard them, she opened the kitchen door. She heard Nick rush down the stairs and out, and she herself came into the hall to find out what had happened. That is natural enough. But why did she not go out and watch the fireworks that evening? That is what I should like to know, Hastings.'

'What was your idea in asking about a secret hiding place?'

'A mere fanciful idea that, after all, we might not have disposed of J.'

'J?'

'Yes. The last person on my list. The problematical outsider. Supposing for some reason connected with Ellen, that J. had come to the house last night. He (I assume a he) conceals himself in a secret chamber in this room. A girl passes through whom he takes to be Nick. He follows her out—and shoots her. *Non—c'est idiot!* And anyway, we know that there is no hiding place. Ellen's decision to remain in the kitchen last night was a pure hazard. Come, let us search for the will of Mademoiselle Nick.'

There were no papers in the drawing-room. We adjourned to the library, a rather dark room looking out on the drive. Here there was a large old-fashioned walnut bureau-writing-table.

It took us some time to go through it. Everything was in complete confusion. Bills and receipts were mixed up together. Letters of invitation, letters pressing for payment of accounts, letters from friends.

'We will arrange these papers,' said Poirot, sternly, 'with order and method.'

He was as good as his word. Half an hour later, he sat back with a pleased expression on his face. Everything was neatly sorted, docketed and filed.

'*C'est bien, ça.* One thing is at least to the good. We have had to go through everything so thoroughly that there is no possibility of our having missed anything.'

'No, indeed. Not that there's been much to find.'

'Except possibly this.'

He tossed across a letter. It was written in large sprawling handwriting, almost indecipherable.

'DARLING,—Party was too too marvellous. Feel rather a worm to-day. You were wise not to touch that stuff—don't ever start, darling. It's too damned hard to give up. I'm writing the boy friend to hurry up the supply. What Hell life is!

'Yours,
'FREDDIE.'

'Dated last February,' said Poirot, thoughtfully. 'She takes drugs, of course, I knew that as soon as I looked at her.'

'Really? I never suspected such a thing.'

'It is fairly obvious. You have only to look at her eyes. And then there are her extraordinary variations of mood. Sometimes she is all on edge, strung up—sometimes she is lifeless—inert.'

'Drug-taking affects the moral sense, does it not?'

'Inevitably. But I do not think Madame Rice is a real addict. She is at the beginning—not the end.'

'And Nick?'

'There are no signs of it. She may have attended a dope party now and then for fun, but she is no taker of drugs.'

'I'm glad of that.'

I remembered suddenly what Nick had said about Frederica that she was not always herself. Poirot nodded and tapped the letter he held.

'This is what she was referring to, undoubtedly. Well, we have drawn the blank, as you say, here. Let us go up to Mademoiselle's room.'

There was a desk in Nick's room also, but comparatively little was kept in it. Here again, there was no sign of a will. We found the registration book of her car and a perfectly good dividend warrant of a month back. Otherwise there was nothing of importance.

Poirot sighed in an exasperated fashion.

'The young girls—they are not properly trained nowadays. The order, the method, it is left out of their bringing up. She is charming, Mademoiselle Nick, but she is a feather-head. Decidedly she is a feather-head.'

He was now going through the contents of a chest of drawers.

'Surely, Poirot,' I said, with some embarrassment, 'those are underclothes.'

He paused in surprise.

'And why not, my friend?'

'Don't you think—I mean—we can hardly——'

He broke into a roar of laughter.

'Decidedly, my poor Hastings, you belong to the Victorian era. Mademoiselle Nick would tell you so if she were here. In all probability she would say that you had the mind like the sink! Young ladies are not ashamed of their underclothes nowadays. The camisole, the cami-knicker, it is no longer a shameful secret. Every day, on the beach, all these garments will be discarded within a few feet of you. And why not?'

'I don't see any need for what you are doing.'

'*Écoutez*, my friend. Clearly, she does not lock up her treasures, Mademoiselle Nick. If she wished to hide anything from sight—where would she hide it? Underneath the stockings and the petticoats. Ah! what have we here?'

He held up a packet of letters tied with a faded pink ribbon.

'The love letters of M. Michael Seton, if I mistake not.'

Quite calmly he untied the ribbon and began to open out the letters.

'Poirot,' I cried, scandalised. 'You really can't do that. It isn't playing the game.'

'I am not playing a game, *mon ami*,' His voice rang out suddenly harsh and stern. 'I am hunting down a murderer.'

'Yes, but private letters——'

'May have nothing to tell me—on the other hand, they may. I must take every chance, my friend. Come, you might as well read them with me. Two pairs of eyes are no worse than one pair. Console yourself with the thought that the staunch Ellen probably knows them by heart.'

I did not like it. Still I realised that in Poirot's position he could not afford to be squeamish, and I consoled myself by the quibble that Nick's last word had been, 'Look at anything you like.'

The letters spread over several dates, beginning last winter.

New Year's Day.

'DARLING,—The New Year is in and I'm making good resolutions. It seems too wonderful to be true—that you should actually love me. You've made all the difference to my life. I believe we both knew—from the very first moment we met. Happy New Year, my lovely girl.

'Yours for ever,
'MICHAEL.'

February 8th.

'DEAREST LOVE,—How I wish I could see you more often. This is pretty rotten, isn't it? I hate all this beastly concealment, but I explained to you how things are. I know how much you hate lies and concealment. I do too. But honestly, it might upset the whole apple cart. Uncle Matthew has got an absolute bee in his bonnet about early marriages and the way they wreck a man's career. As though you could wreck mine, you dear angel!

'Cheer up, darling. Everything will come right.

'Yours,
'MICHAEL.'

March 2nd.

'I oughtn't to write to you two days running, I know. But I must. When I was up yesterday I thought of you. I flew over Scarborough. Blessed, blessed, blessed Scarborough—the most wonderful place in the world. Darling, you don't know how I love you!

'Yours,
'MICHAEL.'

April 18th.

'DEAREST,—The whole thing is fixed up. Definitely. If I pull this off (and I shall pull it off) I shall be able to take a firm line with Uncle Matthew—and if he doesn't like it—well, what do I care? It's adorable of you to be so interested in my long technical descriptions of the *Albatross*. How I long to take you up in her. Some day! Don't for goodness' sake, worry about me. The thing isn't half so risky as it sounds. I simply couldn't get killed now that I know you care for me. Everything will be all right, sweetheart. Trust your Michael.'

April 20th.

'YOU ANGEL,—Every word you say is true and I shall treasure that letter always. I'm not half good enough for you. You are so different from everybody else. I adore you.

'Your

'MICHAEL.'

The last was undated.

'DEAREST,—Well—I'm off to-morrow. Feeling tremendously keen and excited and absolutely certain of success. The old *Albatross* is all tuned up. She won't let me down.

'Cheer up, sweetheart, and don't worry. There's a risk, of course, but all life's risk really. By the way, somebody said I ought to make a will (tactful fellow—but he meant well), so I have—on a half sheet of notepaper—and sent it to old Whitfield. I'd no time to go round there. Somebody once told me that a man made a will of three words, "All to Mother," and it was legal all right. My will was rather like that—I remembered your name was really Magdala, which was clever of me! A couple of the fellows witnessed it.

'Don't take all this solemn talk about wills to heart, will you? (I didn't mean that pun. An accident.) I shall be as right as rain. I'll send you telegrams from India and Australia and so on. And keep up heart. *It's going to be all right.* See?

'Good-night and God bless you,

'MICHAEL.'

Poirot folded the letters together again.

'You see, Hastings? I had to read them—to make sure. It is as I told you.'

'Surely you could have found out some other way?'

'No, *mon cher*, that is just what I could not do. It had to be this way. We have now some very valuable evidence.'

'In what way?'

'We now know that the fact of Michael's having made a will in favour of Mademoiselle Nick is actually recorded in writing. Anyone who had read those letters would know the fact. And with letters carelessly hidden like that, anyone could read them.'

'Ellen?'

'Ellen, almost certainly, I should say. We will try a little experiment on her before passing out.'

'There is no sign of the will.'

'No, that is curious. But in all probability it is thrown on top of a bookcase, or inside a china jar. We must try to awaken Mademoiselle's memory on that point. At any rate, there is nothing more to be found here.'

Ellen was dusting the hall as we descended.

Poirot wished her good-morning very pleasantly as we passed. He turned back from the front door to say:

'You knew, I suppose, that Miss Buckley was engaged to the airman, Michael Seton?'

She stared.

'What? The one there's all the fuss in the papers about?'

'Yes.'

'Well, I never. To think of that. Engaged to Miss Nick.'

'Complete and absolute surprise registered very convincingly,' I remarked, as we got outside.

'Yes. It really seemed genuine.'

'Perhaps it was,' I suggested.

'And that packet of letters reclining for months under the *lingerie*? No, *mon ami*.'

'All very well,' I thought to myself. 'But we are not all Hercule Poirots. We do not all go nosing into what does not concern us.'

But I said nothing.

'This Ellen—she is an enigma,' said Poirot. 'I do not like it. There is something here that I do not understand.'

14. *The mystery of the missing Will*

WE WENT STRAIGHT BACK to the nursing home.

Nick looked rather surprised to see us.

'Yes, Mademoiselle,' said Poirot, answering her look. 'I am like the Jack in the Case. I pop up again. To begin with I will tell you that I have put the order in your affairs. Everything is now neatly arranged.'

'Well, I expect it was about time,' said Nick, unable to help smiling. 'Are you *very* tidy, M. Poirot?'

'Ask my friend Hastings here.'

The girl turned an inquiring gaze on me.

I detailed some of Poirot's minor peculiarities—toast that had to be made from a square loaf—eggs matching in size—his objection to golf as a game 'shapeless and haphazard,' whose only redeeming feature was the tee boxes! I ended by telling her the famous case which Poirot had solved by his habit of straightening ornaments on the mantelpiece.

Poirot sat by smiling.

'He makes the good tale of it, yes,' he said, when I had finished. 'But on the whole it is true. Figure to yourself, Mademoiselle, that I never cease trying to persuade Hastings to part his hair in the middle instead of on the side. See what an air, lop-sided and unsymmetrical, it gives him.'

'Then you must disapprove of me, M. Poirot,' said Nick. 'I wear a side parting. And you must approve of Freddie who parts her hair in the middle.'

'He was certainly admiring her the other evening,' I put in maliciously. 'Now I know the reason.'

'C'est assez,' said Poirot. 'I am here on serious business. Mademoiselle, this will of yours, I find it not.'

'Oh!' She wrinkled her brows. 'But does it matter so much? After all, I'm not dead. And wills aren't really important till you are dead, are they?'

'That is correct. All the same, I interest myself in this will of yours. I have various little ideas concerning it. Think, Mademoiselle. Try to remember where you placed it—where you saw it last.'

'I don't suppose I put it anywhere particular,' said Nick. 'I never do put things in places. I probably shoved it into a drawer.'

'You did not put it in the secret panel by any chance?'

'The secret *what?*'

'Your maid, Ellen, says that there is a secret panel in the drawing-room or the library.'

'Nonsense,' said Nick. 'I've never heard of such a thing. *Ellen* said so?'

'*Mais oui.* It seems she was in service at End House as a young girl. The cook showed it to her.'

'It's the first I've ever heard of it. I suppose Grandfather must have known about it, but, if so, he didn't tell me. And I'm sure he *would* have told me. M. Poirot, are you sure Ellen isn't making it all up?'

'No, Mademoiselle, I am not at all sure! *Il me semble* that there is something—odd about this Ellen of yours.'

'Oh! I wouldn't call her odd. William's a half-wit, and the child is a nasty little brute, but Ellen's all right. The essence of respectability.'

'Did you give her leave to go out and see the fireworks last night, Mademoiselle?'

'Of course. They always do. They clear up afterwards.'

'Yet she did not go out.'

'Oh, yes, she did.'

'How do you know, Mademoiselle?'

'Well—well—I suppose I don't know. I told her to go and she thanked me—and so, of course, I assumed that she did go.'

'On the contrary—she remained in the house.'

'But—how very odd!'

'You think it odd?'

'Yes, I do. I'm sure she's never done such a thing before. Did she say why?'

'She did not tell me the real reason—of that I am sure.'

Nick looked at him questioningly.

'Is it—important?'

Poirot flung out his hands.

'That is just what I cannot say, Mademoiselle. *C'est curieux*. I leave it like that.'

'This panel business too,' said Nick, reflectively. 'I can't help thinking that's frightfully queer—and unconvincing. Did she show you where it was?'

'She said she couldn't remember.'

'I don't believe there is such a thing.'

'It certainly looks like it.'

'She must be going batty, poor thing.'

'She certainly recounts the histories! She said also that End House was not a good house to live in.'

Nick gave a little shiver.

'Perhaps she's right there,' she said slowly. 'Sometimes I've felt that way myself. There's a queer feeling in that house. . . .'

Her eyes grew large and dark. They had a fated look. Poirot hastened to recall her to other topics.

'We have wandered from our subject, Mademoiselle. The will. The last will and testament of Magdala Buckley.'

'I put that,' said Nick, with some pride. 'I remember putting that, and I said pay all debts and testamentary expenses. I remembered that out of a book I'd read.'

'You did not use a will form, then?'

'No, there wasn't time for that. I was just going off to the nursing home, and besides Mr. Croft said will forms were very dangerous. It was better to make a simple will and not try to be too legal.'

'M. Croft? He was there?'

'Yes. It was he who asked me if I'd made one. I'd never have thought of it myself. He said if you died in—in——'

'Intestate,' I said.

'Yes, that's it. He said if you died intestate, the Crown pinched a lot and that would be a pity.'

'Very helpful, the excellent M. Croft!'

'Oh, he was,' said Nick warmly. 'He got Ellen in and her husband to witness it. Oh! of course! What an idiot I've been!'

We looked at her inquiringly.

'I've been a perfect idiot. Letting you hunt round End House. Charles has got it, of course! My cousin, Charles Vyse.'

'Ah! so that is the explanation.'

'Mr. Croft said a lawyer was the proper person to have charge of it.'

'Trés correcte, ce bon M. Croft.'

'Men are useful sometimes,' said Nick. 'A lawyer or the Bank—that's what he said. And I said Charles would be best. So we stuck it in an envelope and sent it off to him straight away.'

She lay back on her pillows with a sigh.

'I'm sorry I've been so frightfully stupid. But it is all right now. Charles has got it, and if you really want to see it, of course he'll show it to you.'

'Not without an authorisation from you,' said Poirot, smiling.

'How silly.'

'No, Mademoiselle. Merely prudent.'

'Well, I think it's silly.' She took a piece of paper from a little stack that lay beside her bed. 'What shall I say? Let the dog see the rabbit?'

'Comment?'

I laughed at his startled face.

He dictated a form of words, and Nick wrote obediently.

'Thank you, Mademoiselle,' said Poirot, as he took it.

'I'm sorry to have given you such a lot of trouble. But I really had forgotten. You know how one forgets things almost at once?'

'With order and method in the mind one does not forget.'

'I'll have to have a course of some kind,' said Nick. 'You're giving me quite an inferiority complex.'

'That is impossible. *Au revoir, Mademoiselle*.' He looked round the room. 'Your flowers are lovely.'

'Aren't they? The carnations are from Freddie and the roses from George and the lilies from Jim Lazarus. And look here——'

She pulled the wrapping from a large basket of hothouse grapes by her side.

Poirot's face changed. He stepped forward sharply.

'You have not eaten any of them?'

'No. Not yet.'

'Do not do so. You must eat nothing, Mademoiselle, that comes in from outside. *Nothing*. You comprehend?'

'Oh!'

She stared at him, the colour ebbing slowly from her face.

'I see. You think—you think it isn't over yet. You think that they're still trying?' she whispered.

He took her hand.

'Do not think of it. You are safe here. But remember—nothing that comes in from outside.'

I was conscious of that white frightened face on the pillow as we left the room.

Poirot looked at his watch.

'*Bon*. We have just time to catch M. Vyse at his office before he leaves it for lunch.'

On arrival we were shown into Charles Vyse's office after the briefest of delays.

The young lawyer rose to greet us. He was as formal and unemotional as ever.

'Good-morning, M. Poirot. What can I do for you?'

Without more ado Poirot presented the letter Nick had written. He took it and read it, then gazed over the top of it at us in a perplexed manner.

'I beg your pardon. I really am at a loss to understand?'

'Has not Mademoiselle Buckley made her meaning clear?'

'In this letter,' he tapped it with his finger-nail, 'she asks me to hand over to you a will made by her and entrusted to my keeping in February last.'

'Yes, Monsieur.'

'But, my dear sir, no will has been entrusted to my keeping!'

'*Comment?*'

'As far as I know my cousin never made a will. I certainly never made one for her.'

'She wrote this herself, I understand, on a sheet of notepaper and posted it to you.'

The lawyer shook his head.

'In that case all I can say is that I never received it.'

'Really, M. Vyse——'

'I never received anything of the kind, M. Poirot.'

There was a pause, then Poirot rose to his feet.

'In that case, M. Vyse, there is nothing more to be said. There must be some mistake.'

'Certainly there must be some mistake.'

He rose also.

'Good-day, M. Vyse.'

'Good-day. M. Poirot.'

'And that is that,' I remarked, when we were out in the street once more.

'*Précisément*.'

'Is he lying, do you think?'

'Impossible to tell. He has the good poker face, M. Vyse, besides looking as though he had swallowed one. One thing is clear, he will not budge from the position he has taken up. *He never received the will.* That is his point.'

'Surely Nick will have a written acknowledgment of its receipt.'

'*Cette petite*, she would never bother her head about a thing like that. She despatched it. It was off her mind. *Voilà*. Besides, on that very day, she went into a nursing home to have her appendix out. She had her emotions, in all probability.'

'Well, what do we do now?'

'*Parbleu*, we go and see M. Croft. Let us see what he can remember about this business. It seems to have been very much his doing.'

'He didn't profit by it in any way,' I said, thoughtfully.

'No. No, I cannot see anything in it from his point of view. He is probably merely the busybody—the man who likes to arrange his neighbour's affairs.'

Such an attitude was indeed typical of Mr. Croft, I felt. He was the kindly knowall who causes so much exasperation in this world of ours.

We found him busy in his shirt sleeves over a steaming pot in the kitchen. A most savoury smell pervaded the little lodge.

He relinquished his cookery with enthusiasm, being clearly eager to talk about the murder.

'Half a jiffy,' he said. 'Walk upstairs. Mother will want to be in on this. She'd never forgive us for talking down here. Cooee—Milly. Two friends coming up.'

Mrs. Croft greeted us warmly and was eager for news of Nick. I liked her much better than her husband.

'That poor dear girl,' she said. 'In a nursing home, you say? Had a complete breakdown, I shouldn't wonder. A dreadful business, M. Poirot—perfectly dreadful. An innocent young girl like that shot dead. It doesn't bear thinking about—it doesn't indeed. And no lawless wild part of the world either. Right here in the heart of the old country. Kept me awake all night, it did.'

'It's made me nervous about going out and leaving you, old lady,' said her husband, who had put on his coat and joined us. 'I don't like to think of your having been left all alone here yesterday evening. It gives me the shivers.'

'You're not going to leave me again, I can tell you,' said Mrs. Croft. 'Not after dark, anyway. And I'm thinking I'd like to leave this part of the world as soon as possible. I shall never feel the same about it. I shouldn't think poor Nicky Buckley could ever bear to sleep in that house again.'

It was a little difficult to reach the object of our visit. Both Mr. and Mrs. Croft talked so much and were so anxious to know all about everything. Were the poor dead girl's relations coming down? When was the funeral? Was there to be an inquest? What did the police think? Had they any clue yet? Was it true that a man had been arrested in Plymouth?

Then, having answered all these questions, they were insistent on offering us lunch. Only Poirot's mendacious statement that we were obliged to hurry back to lunch with the Chief Constable saved us.

At last a momentary pause occurred and Poirot got in the

question he had been waiting to ask.

'Why, of course,' said Mr. Croft. He pulled the blind cord up and down twice, frowning at it abstractedly. 'I remember all about it. Must have been when we first came here. I remember. Appendicitis—that's what the doctor said——'

'And probably not appendicitis at all,' interrupted Mrs. Croft. 'These doctors—they always like cutting you up if they can. It wasn't the kind you *have* to operate on anyhow. She'd had indigestion and one thing and another, and they'd X-rayed her and they said out it had better come. And there she was, poor little soul, just going off to one of those nasty Homes.'

'I just asked her,' said Mr. Croft, 'if she'd made a will. More as a joke than anything else.'

'Yes?'

'And she wrote it out then and there. Talked about getting a will form at the post office—but I advised her not to. Lot of trouble they cause sometimes, so a man told me. Anyway, her cousin is a lawyer. He could draw her out a proper one afterwards if everything was all right—as, of course, I knew it would be. This was just a precautionary matter.'

'Who witnessed it?'

'Oh! Ellen, the maid, and her husband.'

'And afterwards? What was done with it?'

'Oh! we posted it to Vyse. The lawyer, you know.'

'You know that it was posted?'

'My dear M. Poirot, I posted it myself. Right in this box here by the gate.'

'So if M. Vyse says he never got it——'

Croft stared.

'Do you mean that it got lost in the post? Oh! but surely that's impossible.'

'Anyway, you are certain that you posted it.'

'Certain sure,' said Mr. Croft, heartily. 'I'll take my oath on that any day.'

'Ah! well,' said Poirot. 'Fortunately it does not matter. Mademoiselle is not likely to die just yet awhile.'

'*Et voilà!*' said Poirot, when we were out of earshot and walking down to the hotel. 'Who is lying? M. Croft? Or M. Charles Vyse? I must confess I see no reason why M. Croft should be lying. To suppress the will would be of no advantage to him—especially when he had been instrumental in getting it made. No, his statement seems clear enough and tallies exactly with what was told us by Mademoiselle Nick. But all the same——'

'Yes?'

'All the same, I am glad that M. Croft was doing the cooking when we arrived. He left an excellent impression of a greasy thumb and first finger on a corner of the newspaper that covered the kitchen table. I managed to tear if off unseen by him. We will send it to our good friend Inspector Japp of Scotland Yard. There is just a chance that he might know something about it.'

'Yes?'

'You know, Hastings, I cannot help feeling that our genial M. Croft is a little too good to be genuine.'

'And now,' he added. '*Le déjeuner*. I faint with hunger.'

15. *Strange behaviour of Frederica*

POIROT'S INVENTIONS about the Chief Constable were proved not to have been so mendacious after all. Colonel Weston called upon us soon after lunch.

He was a tall man of military carriage with considerable good-looks. He had a suitable reverence for Poirot's achievements, with which he seemed to be well acquainted.

'Marvellous piece of luck for us having you down here, M. Poirot,' he said again and again.

His one fear was that he should be compelled to call in the assistance of Scotland Yard. He was anxious to solve the mystery and catch the criminal without their aid. Hence his delight at Poirot's presence in the neighbourhood.

Poirot, so far as I could judge, took him completely into his confidence.

'Deuced odd business,' said the Colonel. 'Never heard of anything like it. Well, the girl ought to be safe enough in a nursing home. Still, you can't keep her there for ever!'

'That, M. le Colonel, is just the difficulty. There is only one way of dealing with it.'

'And that is?'

'We must lay our hands on the person responsible.'

'If what you suspect is true, that isn't going to be so easy.'

'Ah! je le sais bien.'

'Evidence! Getting evidence is going to be the devil.'

He frowned abstractedly.

'Always difficult, these cases, where there's no routine work. If we could get hold of the pistol——'

'In all probability it is at the bottom of the sea. That is, if the murderer had any sense.'

'Ah!' said Colonel Weston. 'But often they haven't. You'd be surprised at the fool things people do. I'm not talking of murders—we don't have many murders down in these parts, I'm glad to say—but in ordinary police court cases. The sheer damn foolishness of these people would surprise you.'

'They are of a different mentality, though.'

'Yes—perhaps. If Vyse is the chap, well, we'll have our work cut out. He's a cautious man and a sound lawyer. He'll not give himself away. The woman—well, there would be more hope there. Ten to one she'll try again. Women have no patience.'

He rose.

'Inquest to-morrow morning. Coroner will work in with us and give away as little as possible. We want to keep things dark at present.'

He was turning towards the door when he suddenly came back.

'Upon my soul, I'd forgotten the very thing that will interest you most, and that I want your opinion about.'

Sitting down again, he drew from his pocket a torn scrap of paper with writing on it and handed it to Poirot.

'My police found this when they were searching the grounds. Not far from where you were all watching the fireworks. It's the only suggestive thing they did find.'

Poirot smoothed it out. The writing was large and straggling.

'. . . must have money at once. If not you . . . what will happen. I'm warning you.'

Poirot frowned. He read and re-read it.

'This is interesting,' he said. 'I may keep it?'

'Certainly. There are no fingerprints on it. I'll be glad if you can make anything of it.'

Colonel Weston got to his feet again.

'I really must be off. Inquest to-morrow, as I said. By the way, you are not being called as witness—only Captain Hastings. Don't want the newspaper people to get wise to your being on the job.'

'I comprehend. What of the relations of the poor young lady?'

'The father and mother are coming from Yorkshire to-day. They'll arrive about half-past five. Poor souls. I'm heartily sorry for them. They are taking the body back with them the following day.'

He shook his head.

'Unpleasant business. I'm not enjoying this, M. Poirot.'

'Who could, M. le Colonel? It is, as you say, an unpleasant business.'

When he had gone, Poirot examined the scrap of paper once more.

'An important clue?' I asked.

He shrugged his shoulders.

'How can one tell? There is a hint of blackmail about it! Someone of our party that night was being pressed for money in a very unpleasant way. Of course, it is possible that it was one of the strangers.'

He looked at the writing through a little magnifying glass.

'Does this writing look at all familiar to you, Hastings?'

'It reminds me a little of something—Ah! I have it—that note of Mrs. Rice's.'

'Yes,' said Poirot, slowly. 'There are resemblances. Decidedly there are resemblances. It is curious. Yet I do not think that this is the writing of Madame Rice. Come in,' he said, as a knock came at the door.

It was Commander Challenger.

'Just looked in,' he explained. 'Wanted to know if you were any further forward.'

'*Parbleu*,' said Poirot. 'At this moment I am feeling that I am considerably further back. I seem to progress *en reculant*.'

'That's bad. But I don't really believe it, M. Poirot. I've been hearing all about you and what a wonderful chap you are. Never had a failure, they say.'

'That is not true,' said Poirot. 'I had a bad failure in Belgium in 1893. You recollect, Hastings? I recounted it to you. The affair of the box of chocolates.'

'I remember,' I said.

And I smiled, for at the time that Poirot told me that tale, he had instructed me to say 'chocolate box' to him if ever I should fancy he was growing conceited! He was then bitterly offended when I used the magical words only a minute and a quarter later.

'Oh, well,' said Challenger, 'that is such a long time ago it hardly counts. Your are going to get to the bottom of this, aren't you?'

'That I swear. On the word of Hercule Poirot. I am the dog who stays on the scent and does not leave it.'

'Good. Got any ideas?'

'I have suspicions of two people.'

'I suppose I mustn't ask who they are?'

'I should not tell you! You see, I might possibly be in error.'

'*My alibi* is satisfactory, I trust,' said Challenger, with a faint twinkle.

Poirot smiled indulgently at the bronzed face in front of him. 'You left Devonport at a few minutes past 8.30. You arrived here at five minutes past ten—twenty minutes after the crime had been committed. But the distance from Devonport is only just over thirty miles, and you have often done it in an hour since the road is good. So, you see, your alibi is not good at all!'

'Well, I'm——'

'You comprehend, I inquire into everything. Your *alibi*, as I say, is not good. But there are other things besides alibis. You would like, I think, to marry Mademoiselle Nick?'

The sailor's face flushed.

'I've always wanted to marry her,' he said huskily.

'Precisely. *Eh bien*—Mademoiselle Nick was engaged to another man. A reason, perhaps, for killing the other man. But that is unnecessary—he dies the death of a hero.'

'So it *is* true—that Nick was engaged to Michael Seton? There's a rumour to that effect all over the town this morning.'

'Yes—it is interesting how soon news spreads. You never suspected it before?'

'I knew Nick was engaged to someone—she told me so two days ago. But she didn't give me a clue as to whom it was.'

'It was Michael Seton. *Entre nous*, he has left her, I fancy, a very pretty fortune. Ah! assuredly, it is not a moment for killing Mademoiselle Nick—from your point of view. She weeps for her lover now, but the heart consoles itself. She is young. And I think, Monsieur, that she is very fond of you. . . .'

Challenger was silent for a moment or two.

'If it should be. . . .' he murmured.

There was a tap on the door.

It was Frederica Rice.

'I've been looking for you,' she said to Challenger. 'They told me you were here. I wanted to know if you'd got my wrist-watch back yet.'

'Oh, yes, I called for it this morning.'

He took it from his pocket and handed it to her. It was a watch of rather an unusual shape—round, like a globe, set on a strap of plain black moiré. I remembered that I had seen one much the same shape on Nick Buckley's wrist.

'I hope it will keep better time now.'

'It's rather a bore. Something is always going wrong with it.'

'It is for beauty, Madame, and not for utility,' said Poirot.

'Can't one have both?' She looked from one to the other of us. 'Am I interrupting a conference?'

'No, indeed, Madame. We were talking the gossip—not the crime. We were saying how quickly news spreads—how that everyone now knows that Mademoiselle Nick was engaged to that brave airman who perished.'

'So Nick *was* engaged to Michael Seton!' exclaimed Frederica.

'It surprises you, Madame?'

'It does a little. I don't know why. Certainly I did think he was very taken with her last autumn. They went about a lot together. And then, after Christmas, they both seemed to cool off. As far as I know, they hardly met.'

'The secret, they kept it very well.'

'That was because of old Sir Matthew, I suppose. He was really a little off his head, I think.'

'You had no suspicion, Madame? And yet Mademoiselle was such an intimate friend.'

'Nick's a close little devil when she likes,' murmured Frederica. 'But I understand now why she's been so nervy lately. Oh! and I ought to have guessed from something she said only the other day.'

'Your little friend is very attractive, Madame.'

'Old Jim Lazarus used to think so at one time,' said Challenger, with his loud, rather tactless laugh.

'Oh! Jim——' She shrugged her shoulders, but I thought she was annoyed.

She turned to Poirot.

'Tell me, M. Poirot, did you——?'

She stopped. Her tall figure swayed and her face turned whiter still. Her eyes were fixed on the centre of the table.

'You are not well, Madame.'

I pushed forward a chair, helped her to sink into it. She shook her head, murmured, 'I'm all right,' and leaned forward, her face between her hands. We watched her awkwardly.

She sat up a minute.

'How absurd! George, darling, don't look so worried. Let's talk about murders. Something exciting. I want to know if M. Poirot is on the track.'

'It is early to say, Madame,' said Poirot, non-committally.

'But you have ideas—yes?'

'Perhaps. But I need a great deal more evidence.'

'Oh!' She sounded uncertain.

Suddenly she rose.

'I've got a head. I think I'll go and lie down. Perhaps to-morrow they'll let me see Nick.'

She left the room abruptly. Challenger frowned.

'You never know what that woman's up to. Nick may have been fond of her, but I don't believe she was fond of Nick. But there, you can't tell with women. It's darling—darling—darling—all the time—and "damn you" would probably express it much better. Are you going out, M. Poirot?' For Poirot had risen and was carefully brushing a speck off his hat.

'Yes, I am going into the town.'

'I've got nothing to do. May I come with you?'

'Assuredly. It will be a pleasure.'

We left the room. Poirot, with an apology, went back.

'My stick,' he explained, as he rejoined us.

Challenger winced slightly. And indeed the stick, with its embossed gold band, was somewhat ornate.

Poirot's first visit was to a florist.

'I must send some flowers to Mademoiselle Nick,' he explained.

He proved difficult to suit.

In the end he chose an ornate gold basket to be filled with orange carnations. The whole to be tied up with a large blue bow.

The shopwoman gave him a card and he wrote on it with a flourish: 'With the Compliments of Hercule Poirot.'

'I sent her some flowers this morning,' said Challenger. 'I might send her some fruit.'

'Inutile!' said Poirot.

'What?'

'I said it was useless. The eatables—it is not permitted.'

'Who says so?'

'I say so. I have made the rule. It has already been impressed on Mademoiselle Nick. She understands.'

'Good Lord!' said Challenger.

He looked thoroughly startled. He stared at Poirot curiously. 'So that's it, is it?' he said. 'You're still—afraid.'

16. *Interview with Mr. Whitfield*

THE INQUEST was a dry proceeding—mere bare bones. There was evidence of identification, then I gave evidence of the finding of the body. Medical evidence followed.

The inquest was adjourned for a week.

The St. Loo murder had jumped into prominence in the daily press. It had, in fact, succeeded 'Seton Still Missing. Unknown Fate of Missing Airman.'

Now that Seton was dead and due tribute had been paid to his memory, a new sensation was due. The St. Loo Mystery was a godsend to papers at their wits' end for news in the month of August.

After the inquest, having successfully dodged reporters, I met Poirot, and we had an interview with the Rev. Giles Buckley and his wife.

Maggie's father and mother were a charming pair, completely unworldly and unsophisticated.

Mrs. Buckley was a woman of character, tall and fair and showing very plainly her northern ancestry. Her husband was a small man, grey-headed, with a diffident appealing manner.

Poor souls, they were completely dazed by the misfortune that had overtaken them and robbed them of a well-beloved daughter. 'Our Maggie,' as they called her.

'I can scarcely realise it even now,' said Mr. Buckley. 'Such a dear child, M. Poirot. So quiet and unselfish—always thinking of others. Who could wish to harm her?'

'I could hardly understand the telegram,' said Mrs. Buckley. 'Why, it was only the morning before that we had seen her off.'

'In the midst of life we are in death,' murmured her husband.

'Colonel Weston has been very kind,' said Mrs. Buckley. 'He assures us that everything is being done to find the man who did this thing. He must be a madman. No other explanation is possible.'

'Madame, I cannot tell you how I sympathise with you in your loss—and how I admire your bravery!'

'Breaking down would not bring Maggie back to us,' said Mrs. Buckley, sadly.

'My wife is wonderful,' said the clergyman. 'Her faith and courage are greater than mine. It is all so—so bewildering, M. Poirot.'

'I know—I know, Monsieur.'

'You are a great detective, M. Poirot?' said Mrs. Buckley.

'It has been said, Madame.'

'Oh! I know. Even in our remote country village we have heard of you. You are going to find out the truth, M. Poirot?'

'I shall not rest until I do, Madame.'

'It will be revealed to you, M. Poirot,' quavered the clergyman. 'Evil cannot go unpunished.'

'Evil never goes unpunished, Monsieur. But the punishment is sometimes secret.'

'What do you mean by that, M. Poirot?'

Poirot only shook his head.

'Poor little Nick,' said Mrs. Buckley. 'I am really sorriest of all for her. I had a most pathetic letter. She says she feels she asked Maggie down here to her death.'

'That is morbid,' said Mr. Buckley.

'Yes, but I know how she feels. I wish they would let me see her. It seems so extraordinary not to let her own family visit her.'

'Doctors and nurses are very strict,' said Poirot, evasively. 'They make the rules—so—and nothing will change them. And doubtless they fear for her the emotion she would experience on seeing you.'

'Perhaps,' said Mrs. Buckley, doubtfully. 'But I don't hold with nursing homes. Nick would do much better if they let her come back with me—right away from this place.'

'It is possible—but I fear they will not agree. It is long since you have seen Mademoiselle Buckley?'

'I haven't seen her since last autumn. She was at Scarborough. Maggie went over and spent the day with her and then she came back and spent a night with us. She's a pretty creature—though I can't say I like her friends. And the life she leads—well, it's hardly her fault, poor child. She's had no upbringing of any kind.'

'It is a strange house—End House,' said Poirot, thoughtfully.

'I don't like it,' said Mrs. Buckley. 'I never have. There's something all wrong about that house. I disliked old Sir Nicholas intensely. He made me shiver.'

'Not a good man, I'm afraid,' said her husband. 'But he had a curious charm.'

'*I* never felt it,' said Mrs. Buckley. 'There's an evil feeling about that house. I wish we'd never let our Maggie go there.'

'Ah! wishing,' said Mr. Buckley, and shook his head.

'Well,' said Poirot. 'I must not intrude upon you any longer. I only wished to proffer to you my deep sympathy.'

'You have been very kind, M. Poirot. And we are indeed grateful for all you are doing.'

'You return to Yorkshire—when?'

'To-morrow. A sad journey. Good-bye, M. Poirot, and thank you again.'

'Very simple delightful people,' I said, after we had left.

Poirot nodded.

'It makes the heart ache, does it not, *mon ami*? A tragedy so useless—so purposeless. *Cette jeune fille*— Ah! but I reproach myself bitterly. I, Hercule Poirot, was on the spot and I did not prevent the crime!'

'Nobody could have prevented it.'

'You speak without reflection, Hastings. No ordinary person could have prevented it—but of what good is it to be Hercule Poirot with grey cells of a finer quality than other people's, if you do not manage to do what ordinary people cannot?'

'Well, of course,' I said. 'If you are going to put it like that——.'

'Yes, indeed. I am abashed, downhearted—completely abased.'

I reflected that Poirot's abasement was strangely like other people's conceit, but I prudently forebore from making any remark.

'And now,' he said, '*en avant. To London.*'

'London?'

'*Mais oui*. We shall catch the two o'clock train very comfortably. All is peaceful here. Mademoiselle is safe in the nursing home. No one can harm her. The watchdogs, therefore, can take leave of absence. There are one or two little pieces of information that I require.'

Our first proceeding on arriving in London was to call upon the late Captain Seton's solicitors, Messrs. Whitfield, Pargiter & Whitfield.

Poirot had arranged for an appointment beforehand, and although it was past six o'clock, we were soon closeted with Mr. Whitfield, the head of the firm.

He was a very urbane and impressive person. He had in front of him a letter from the Chief Constable and another from some high official at Scotland Yard.

'This is all very irregular and unusual, M.—ah—Poirot,' he said, as he polished his eyeglasses.

'Quite so, M. Whitfield. But then murder is also irregular—and, I am glad to say, sufficiently unusual.'

'True. True. But rather far-fetched—to make a connection between this murder and my late client's bequest—eh?'

'I think not.'

'Ah! you think not. Well—under the circumstances—and I must admit that Sir Henry puts it very strongly in his letter—I shall be—er—happy to do anything that is in my power.'

'You acted as legal adviser to the late Captain Seton?'

'To all the Seton family, my dear sir. We have done so—our firm have done so, I mean—for the last hundred years.'

'*Parfaitement*. The late Sir Matthew Seton made a will?'

'We made it for him.'

'And he left his fortune—how?'

'There were several bequests—one to the Natural History Museum—but the bulk of his large—his, I may say, *very* large fortune—he left to Captain Michael Seton absolutely. He had no other near relations.'

'A very large fortune, you say?'

'The late Sir Matthew was the second richest man in England,' replied Mr. Whitfield, composedly.

'He had somewhat peculiar views, had he not?'

Mr. Whitfield looked at him severely.

'A millionaire, M. Poirot, is allowed to be eccentric. It is almost expected of him.'

Poirot received this correction meekly and asked another question.

'His death was unexpected, I understand?'

'*Most* unexpected. Sir Matthew enjoyed remarkably good health. He had an internal growth, however, which no one had suspected. It reached a vital tissue and an immediate operation was necessary. The operation was, as always on these occasions, completely successful. But Sir Matthew died.'

'And his fortune passed to Captain Seton.'

'That is so.'

'Captain Seton had, I understand, made a will before leaving England?'

'If you can call it a will—yes,' said Mr. Whitfield, with strong distaste.

'It is legal?'

'It is perfectly legal. The intention of the testator is plain and it is properly witnessed. Oh, yes, it is legal.'

'But you do not approve of it?'

'May dear sir, what are *we* for?'

I had often wondered. Having once had occasion to make a perfectly simple will myself, I had been appalled at the length and verbiage that resulted from my solicitor's office.

'The truth of the matter was,' continued Mr. Whitfield, 'that at the time Captain Seton had little or nothing to leave. He was dependent on the allowance he received from his uncle. He felt, I suppose, that anything would do.'

And had thought correctly, I whispered to myself.

'And the terms of this will?' asked Poirot.

'He leaves everything of which he dies possessed to his affianced wife, Miss Magdala Buckley absolutely. He names me as his executor.'

'Then Miss Buckley inherits?'

'Certainly Miss Buckley inherits.'

'And if Miss Buckley had happened to die last Monday?'

'Captain Seton having predeceased her, the money would go to whoever she had named in her will as residuary legatee—or failing a will to her next of kin.'

'I may say,' added Mr. Whitfield with an air of enjoyment, 'that the death duties would have been enormous. Enormous! Three deaths, remember, in rapid succession.' He shook his head. "Enormous!"

'But there would have been something left?' murmured Poirot, meekly.

'My dear sir, as I told you, Sir Matthew was the second richest man in England.'

Poirot rose.

'Thank you, Mr. Whitfield, very much for the information that you have given me.'

'Not at all. Not at all. I may say that I shall be in communication with Miss Buckley—indeed, I believe the letter has already gone. I shall be happy to be of any service I can to her.'

'She is a young lady,' said Poirot, 'who could do with some sound legal advice.'

'There will be fortune hunters, I am afraid,' said Mr. Whitfield, shaking his head.

'It seems indicated,' agreed Poirot. 'Good-day, Monsieur.'

'Good-bye, M. Poirot. Glad to have been of service to you. Your name is—ah!—familiar to me.'

He said this kindly—with an air of one making a valuable admission.

'It is all exactly as you thought, Poirot,' I said, when we were outside.

'*Mon ami*, it was bound to be. *It could not be any other way*. We will go now to the Cheshire Cheese where Japp meets us for an early dinner.'

We found Inspector Japp of Scotland Yard awaiting us at the chosen rendezvous. He greeted Poirot with every sign of warmth.

'Years since I've seen you, Moosior Poirot? Thought you were growing vegetable marrows in the country.'

'I tried, Japp, I tried. But even when you grow vegetable marrows you cannot get away from murder.'

He sighed. I knew of what he was thinking—that strange affair at Fernley Park. How I regretted that I had been far away at that time.

'And Captain Hastings too,' said Japp. 'How are you, sir?'

'Very fit, thanks,' I said.

'And now there are more murders?' continued Japp, facetiously.

'As you say—more murders.'

'Well, you mustn't be depressed, old cock,' said Japp. 'Even if you can't see your way clear—well—you can't go about at your time of life and expect to have the success you used to do. We all of us get stale as the years go by. Got to give the young 'uns a chance, you know.'

'And yet the old dog is the one who knows the tricks,' murmured Poirot. 'He is cunning. He does not leave the scent.'

'Oh! well—we're talking about human beings, not dogs.'

'Is there so much difference?'

'Well, it depends how you look at things. But you're a caution, isn't he, Captain Hastings? Always was. Looks much the same—hair a bit thinner on top but the face fungus fuller than ever."

'Eh?' said Poirot. 'What is that?'

'He's congratulating you on your moustaches,' I said, soothingly.

'They are luxuriant, yes,' said Poirot, complacently caressing them.

Japp went off into a roar of laughter.

'Well,' he said, after a minute or two, 'I've done your bit of business. Those fingerprints you sent me——'

'Yes?' said Poirot, eagerly.

'Nothing doing. Whoever the gentleman may be—he hasn't passed through *our* hands. On the other hand, I wired to Melbourne and nobody of that description or name is known there.'

'Ah!'

'So there may be something fishy after all. But he's not one of the lads.'

'As to the other business,' went on Japp.

'Yes?'

'Lazarus and Son have a good reputation. Quite straight and honourable in their dealings. Sharp, of course—but that's another matter. You've got to be sharp in business. But they're all right. They're in a bad way, though—financially, I mean.'

'Oh!—is that so?'

'Yes—the slump in pictures has hit them badly. And antique furniture too. All this modern Continental stuff coming into fashion. They built new premises last year and—well—as I say, they're not far from Queer Street.'

'I am much obliged to you.'

'Not at all. That sort of thing isn't my line, as you know. But I made a point of finding out as you wanted to know. We can always get information.'

'My good Japp, what should I do without you?'

'Oh! that's all right. Always glad to oblige an old friend. I let you in on some pretty good cases in the old days, didn't I?'

This, I realised, was Japp's way of acknowledging indebtedness to Poirot, who had solved many a case which had baffled the Inspector.

'They were the good days—yes.'

'I wouldn't mind having a chat with you now and again even in these days. Your methods may be old-fashioned but you've got your head screwed on the right way, M. Poirot.'

'What about my other question. The Dr. MacAllister?'

'Oh, him! He's a woman's doctor. I don't mean a gynaecologist. I mean one of these nerve doctors—tell you to sleep in purple walls and an orange ceiling—talk to you about your libido, whatever that is—tell you to let it rip. He's a bit of a quack, if you ask me—but he gets the women all right. They flock to him. Goes abroad a good deal —does some kind of medical work in Paris, I believe.'

'Why Dr. MacAllister?' I asked, bewildered. I had never heard of the name. 'Where does he come in?'

'Dr. MacAllister is the uncle of Commander Challenger,' explained Poirot. 'You remember he referred to an uncle who was a doctor?'

'How thorough you are,' I said. 'Did you think he had operated on Sir Matthew?'

'He's not a surgeon,' said Japp.

'*Mon ami*,' said Poirot, 'I like to inquire into everything. Hercule Poirot is a good dog. The good dog follows the scent, and if, regrettably, there is no scent to follow, he noses around—seeking always something that is not very nice. So also, does Hercule Poirot. And often—oh! so often—does he find it!'

'It's not a nice profession, ours,' said Japp. 'Stilton, did you say? I don't mind if I do. No, it's not a nice profession. And yours is worse than mine—not official, you see, and therefore a lot more worming yourself into places in underhand ways.'

'I do not disguise myself, Japp. Never have I disguised myself.'

'You couldn't,' said Japp. 'You're unique. Once seen, never forgotten.'

Poirot looked at him rather doubtfully.

'Only my fun,' said Japp. 'Don't mind me. Glass of port? Well, if you say so.'

The evening became thoroughly harmonious. We were soon in the middle of reminiscences. This case, that case, and the other. I must say that I, too, enjoyed talking over the past. Those had been good days. How old and experienced I felt now!

Poor old Poirot. He was perplexed by this case—I could see that. His powers were not what they were. I had the feeling that he was going to fail—that the murderer of Maggie Buckley would never be brought to book.

'Courage, my friend,' said Poirot, slapping me on the shoulder. 'All is not lost. Do not pull the long face, I beg of you.'

'That's all right. I'm all right.'

'And so am I. And so is Japp.'

'We're all all right,' declared Japp, hilariously.

And on this pleasant note we parted.

The following morning we journeyed back to St. Loo. On arrival at the hotel Poirot rang up the nursing home and asked to speak to Nick.

Suddenly I saw his face change—he almost dropped the instrument.

'*Comment?* What is that? Say it again, I beg.'

'He waited for a minute or two listening. Then he said:

'Yes, yes, I will come at once.'

He turned a pale face to me.

'Why did I go away, Hastings? *Mon Dieu!* Why did I go away?'

'What has happened?'

'Mademoiselle Nick is dangerously ill. Cocaine poisoning. They have got at her after all. *Mon Dieu! Mon Dieu! why did I go away?*'

17. *A box of chocolates*

ALL THE WAY to the nursing home Poirot murmured and muttered to himself. He was full of self-reproach.

'I should have known,' he groaned. 'I should have known! And yet, what could I do? I took every precaution. It is impossible—impossible. *No one* could get to her! Who has disobeyed my orders?'

At the nursing home we were shown into a little room downstairs, and after a few minutes Dr. Graham came to us. He looked exhausted and white.

'She'll do,' he said. 'It's going to be all right. The trouble was knowing how much she'd taken of the damned stuff.'

'What was it?'

'Cocaine.'

'She will live?'

'Yes, yes, she'll live.'

'But how did it happen? How did they get at her? Who has been allowed in?' Poirot fairly danced with impotent excitement.

'Nobody has been allowed in.'

'Impossible.'

'It's true.'

'But then——'

'It was a box of chocolates.'

'Ah! *sacré*. And I told her to eat *nothing—nothing*—that came from outside.'

'I don't know about that. It's hard work keeping a girl from a box of chocolates. She only ate one, thank goodness.'

'Was there cocaine in all the chocolates?'

'No. The girl ate one. There were two others in the top layer. The rest were all right.'

'How was it done?'

'Quite clumsily. Chocolate cut in half—the cocaine mixed with the filling and the chocolate stuck together again. Amateurishly. What you might call a home-made job.'

Poirot groaned.

'Ah! if I knew—if I knew. Can I see Mademoiselle?'

'If you come back in an hour I think you can see her,' said the doctor. 'Pull yourself together, man. She isn't going to die.'

For another hour we walked the streets of St. Loo. I did my best to distract Poirot's mind—pointing out to him that all was well, that, after all, no mischief had been done.

But he only shook his head, and repeated at intervals:

'*I am afraid, Hastings, I am afraid. . . .*'

And the strange way he said it made me, too, feel afraid.

Once he caught me by the arm.

'Listen, my friend. *I am all wrong.* I have been all wrong from the beginning.'

'You mean it isn't the money——'

'No, no, I am right about that. Oh, yes. But those two—it is too simple—too easy, that. There is another twist still. Yes, there is something!'

And then in an outburst of indignation:

'*Ah! cette petite!* Did I not *forbid* her? Did I not say, "Do not touch anything from outside?" And she disobeys me—me, Hercule Poirot. Are not four escapes from death enough for her? Must she take a fifth chance? *Ah, c'est inoui!*'

At last we made our way back. After a brief wait we were conducted upstairs.

Nick was sitting up in bed. The pupils of her eyes were widely dilated. She looked feverish and her hands kept twitching violently.

'At it again,' she murmured.

Poirot experienced real emotion at the sight of her. He cleared his throat and took her hand in his.

'Ah! Mademoiselle—Mademoiselle.'

'I shouldn't care,' she said, defiantly, 'if they *had* got me this time. I'm sick of it all—sick of it!'

'*Pauvre petite!*'

'Something in me doesn't like to give them best!'

'That is the spirit—*le sport*—you must be the good sport, Mademoiselle.'

'Your old nursing home hasn't been so safe after all,' said Nick.

'If you had obeyed orders, Mademoiselle——'

She looked faintly astonished.

'But I have.'

'Did I not impress upon you that you were to eat nothing that came from outside?'

'No more I did.'

'But these chocolates——'

'Well, they were all right. *You* sent them.'

'What is that you say, Mademoiselle?'

'*You* sent them!'

'Me? Never. Never anything of the kind.'

'But you *did*. Your card was in the box.'

'What?'

Nick made a spasmodic gesture towards the table by the bed. The nurse came forward.

'You want the card that was in the box?'

'Yes, please, nurse.'

There was a moment's pause. The nurse returned to the room with it in her hand.

'Here it is.'

I gasped. So did Poirot. For on the card, in flourishing handwriting, was written the same words that I had seen Poirot inscribe on the card that accompanied the basket of flowers.

'With the Compliments of Hercule Poirot.'

'*Sacré tonnerre!*'

'You see,' said Nick, accusingly.

'I did not write this!' cried Poirot.

'What?'

'And yet,' murmured Poirot, 'and yet it is my handwriting.'

'I know. It's exactly the same as the card that came with the orange carnations. I never doubted that the chocolates came from you.'

Poirot shook his head.

'How should you doubt? Oh! the devil! The clever, cruel devil! To think of *that*! Ah! but he has genius, this man, genuis! '*With the Compliments of Hercule Poirot*.' So simple. Yes, but one had to think of it. And I—I did not *think*. I omitted to foresee this move.'

Nick moved restlessly.

'Do not agitate yourself, Mademoiselle. You are blameless—blameless. It is I that am to blame, miserable imbecile that I am! I should have foreseen this move. Yes, I should have foreseen it.'

His chin dropped on his breast. He looked the picture of misery.

'I really think——' said the nurse.

She had been hovering nearby, a disapproving expression on her face.

'Eh? Yes, yes, I will go. Courage Mademoiselle. This is the last mistake I will make. I am ashamed, desolated—I have been tricked, outwitted—as though I were a little schoolboy. *But it shall not happen again*. No. I promise you. Come, Hastings.'

Poirot's first proceeding was to interview the matron. She was, naturally, terribly upset over the whole business.

'It seems incredible to me, M. Poirot, absolutely incredible. That a thing like that should happen in my nursing home.'

Poirot was sympathetic and tactful. Having soothed her sufficiently, he began to inquire into the circumstance of the arrival of the fatal packet. Here, the matron declared, he would do best to interview the orderly who had been on duty at the time of its arrival.

The man in question, whose name was Hood, was a stupid but honest-looking young fellow of about twenty-two. He looked nervous and frightened. Poirot put him at his ease, however.

'No blame can be attached to you,' he said, kindly. 'But I want you to tell me exactly when and how this parcel arrived.'

The orderly looked puzzled.

'It's difficult to say, sir,' he said, slowly. 'Lots of people come and inquire and leave things for the different patients.'

'The nurse says this came last night,' I said. 'About six o'clock.'

The lad's face brightened.

'I do remember, now, sir. A gentleman brought it.'

'A thin-faced gentleman—fair-haired?'

'He was fair-haired—but I don't know about thin-faced.'

'Would Charles Vyse bring it himself?' I murmured to Poirot.

I had forgotten that the lad would know a local name.

'It wasn't Mr. Vyse,' he said. 'I know him. It was a bigger gentleman—handsome-looking—came in a big car.'

'Lazarus,' I exclaimed.

Poirot shot me a warning glance and I regretted my precipitance.

'He came in a large car and he left this parcel. It was addressed to Miss Buckley?'

'Yes, sir.'

'And what did you do with it?'

'I didn't touch it, sir. Nurse took it up.'

'Quite so, but you touched it when you took it from the gentleman, *n'est ce pas?*'

'Oh! that, yes, of course, sir. I took it from him and put it on the table.'

'Which table? Show me, if you please.'

The orderly led us into the hall. The front door was open. Close to it, in the hall, was a long marble-topped table on which lay letters and parcels.

'Everything that comes is put on here, sir. Then the nurses take things up to the patients.'

'Do you remember what time this parcel was left?'

'Must have been about five-thirty, or a little after. I know the post had just been, and that's usually at about half-past five. It was a pretty busy afternoon, a lot of people leaving flowers and coming to see patients.'

'Thank you. Now, I think, we will see the nurse who took up the parcel.'

This proved to be one of the probationers, a fluffy little person all agog with excitement. She remembered taking the parcel up at six o'clock when she came on duty.

'Six o'clock,' murmured Poirot. 'Then it must have been twenty minutes or so that the parcel was lying on the table downstairs.'

'Pardon?'

'Nothing, Mademoiselle. Continue. You took the parcel to Miss Buckley?'

'Yes, there were several things for her. There was this box and some flowers also—sweet peas—from a Mr. and Mrs. Croft, I think. I took them up at the same time. And there was a parcel that had come by post—and curiously enough *that* was a box of Fuller's chocolates also.'

'*Comment?* A second box?'

'Yes, rather a coincidence. Miss Buckley opened them both. She said: 'Oh! what a shame. I'm not allowed to eat them.' Then she opened the lids to look inside and see if they were both just the same, and your card was in one and she said, 'Take the other impure box away, nurse. I might get them mixed up.' Oh! dear, whoever would have thought of such a thing? Seems like an Edgar Wallace, doesn't it?'

Poirot cut short this flood of speech.

'Two boxes, you say? From whom was the other box?'

'There was no name inside.'

'And which was the one that came—that had the appearance of coming—from me? The one by post or the other?'

'I declare now—I can't remember. Shall I go up and ask Miss Buckley?'

'If you would be so amiable.'

She ran up the stairs.

'Two boxes,' murmured Poirot. 'There is confusion for you.'

The nurse returned breathless.

'Miss Buckley isn't sure. She unwrapped them both before she looked inside. But she thinks it wasn't the box that came by post.'

'Eh?' said Poirot, a little confused.

'The box from you was the one that didn't come by post. At least she thinks so, but she isn't quite sure.'

'*Diable!*' said Poirot, as we walked away. 'Is no one ever quite sure? In detective books—yes. But life—real life—is always full of muddle. Am I sure, myself, about anything at all? No, no—a thousand times, no.'

'Lazarus,' I said.

'Yes, that is a surprise, is it not?'

'Shall you say anything to him about it?'

'Assuredly. I shall be interested to see how he takes it. By the way, we might as well exaggerate the serious condition of Mademoiselle. It will do no harm to let it be assumed that she is at death's door. You comprehend? The solemn face—yes, admirable. You resemble closely an undertaker. *C'est tout à fait bien.*'

We were lucky in finding Lazarus. He was bending over the bonnet of his car outside the hotel.

Poirot went straight up to him.

'Yesterday evening, Monsieur Lazarus, you left a box of chocolates for Mademoiselle,' he began, without preamble.

Lazarus looked rather surprised.

'Yes?'

'That was very amiable of you.'

'As a matter of fact they were from Freddie, from Mrs. Rice. She asked me to get them.'

'Oh! I see.'

'I took them round there in the car.'

'I comprehend.'

He was silent for a minute or two and then said:

'Madame Rice, where is she?'

'I think she's in the lounge.'

We found Frederica having tea. She looked up at us with an anxious face.

'What is this I hear about Nick being taken ill?'

'It is a most mysterious affair, Madame. Tell me, did you send her a box of chocolates yesterday?'

'Yes. At least she asked me to get them for her.'

'*She* asked you to get them for her?'

'Yes.'

'But she was not allowed to see anyone. How did you see her?'

'I didn't. She telephoned.'

'Ah! And she said—what?'

'Would I get her a two-pound box of Fuller's chocolates.'

'How did her voice sound—weak?'

'No—not at all. Quite strong. But different somehow. I didn't realise it was she speaking at first.'

'Until she told you who she was?'

'Yes.'

'Are you sure, Madame, that it *was* your friend?'

Frederica looked startled.

'I—I—why, of course it was. Who else could it have been?'

'That is an interesting question, Madame.'

'You don't mean——'

'*Could you swear*, Madame, that it was your friend's voice—apart from what she said?'

'No.' said Frederica, slowly, 'I couldn't. Her voice was certainly different. I thought it was the phone—or perhaps being ill. . . .'

'If she had not told you who she was, you would not have recognised it?'

'No, no, I don't think I should. Who was it, M. Poirot? Who was it?'

'That is what I mean to know, Madame.'

The graveness of his face seemed to awaken her suspicions.

'Is Nick—has anything happened?' she asked, breathlessly.

Poirot nodded.

'She is ill—dangerously ill. Those chocolates, Madame—were poisoned.'

'The chocolates *I* sent her? But that's impossible—impossible!'

'Not impossible, Madame, since Mademoiselle is at death's door.'

'Oh, my God.' She hid her face in her hands, then raised it white and quivering. 'I don't understand—I don't understand. The other, yes, but not this. They couldn't be poisoned. Nobody ever touched them but me and Jim. You're making some dreadful mistake, M. Poirot.'

'It is not I that make a mistake—even though my name was in the box.'

She stared at him blankly.

'If Mademoiselle Nick dies——' he said, and made a threatening gesture with his hand.

She gave a low cry.

He turned away, and taking me by the arm, went up to the sitting-room.

He flung his hat on the table.

'I understand nothing—but nothing! I am in the dark. I am a little child. Who stands to gain by Mademoiselle's death? Madame Rice. Who buys the chocolates and admits it and tells a story of being rung up on the telephone that cannot hold water for a minute? Madame Rice. It is too simple—too stupid. And she is not stupid—no.'

'Well, then——'

'But she takes cocaine, Hastings. I am certain she takes cocaine. There is no mistaking it. And there was cocaine in those chocolates. And what does she mean when she said, '*The other, yes, but not this.*' It needs explaining, that! And the sleek M. Lazarus—what is *he* doing in all this? What does she know, Madame Rice? She knows something. But I cannot make her speak. She is not of those you can frighten into speech. But she knows something, Hastings. Is her tale of the telephone true, or did she invent it? If it is true, whose voice was it?

'I tell you, Hastings. This is all very black—very black.'

'Always darkest before dawn,' I said reassuringly.

He shook his head.

'Then the other box—that came by post. Can we rule that out? No, we cannot, because Mademoiselle is not sure. It is an annoyance, that!'

He groaned.

I was about to speak when he stopped me.

'No, no. Not another proverb. I cannot bear it. If you would be the good friend—the good helpful friend——'

'Yes,' I said, eagerly.

'Go out, I beg of you, and buy me some playing cards.'

I stared. 'Very well,' I said coldly.

I could not but suspect that he was making a deliberate excuse to get rid of me.

Here, however, I misjudged him. That night, when I came into the sitting-room about ten o'clock, I found Poirot carefully building card houses—and I remembered!

It was an old trick of his—soothing his nerves. He smiled at me.

'Yes—you remember. One needs the precision. One card on another—so—in exactly the right place and that supports the weight of the card on top and so on, up and up. Go to bed, Hastings. Leave me here, with my house of cards. I clear the mind.'

It was about five in the morning when I was shaken awake.

Poirot was standing by my bedside. He looked pleased and happy.

'It was very just what you said, *mon ami*. Oh! it was very just. More, it was *spirituel*!'

I blinked at him, being imperfectly awake.

'Always darkest before dawn—that is what you said. It has been very dark—and now it is dawn.'

I looked at the window. He was perfectly right.

'No, no, Hastings. In the head! The mind! The little grey cells!'

He paused and then said quietly:

'You see, Hastings, Mademoiselle is dead.'

'What?' I cried, suddenly wide awake.

'Hush—hush. It is as I say. Not really—*bien entendu*—but it can be arranged. Yes, for twenty-four hours it can be arranged. I arrange it with the doctor, with the nurses.

'You comprehend, Hastings? *The murderer has been successful*. Four times he has tried and failed. The fifth time he has succeeded.

'*And now, we shall see what happens next....*

'It will be very interesting.'

18. *The face at the window*

THE EVENTS OF THE NEXT DAY are completely hazy in my memory. I was unfortunate enough to awake with fever on me. I have been liable to these bouts of fever at inconvenient times ever since I once contracted malaria.

In consequence, the events of that day take on in my memory the semblance of a nightmare—with Poirot coming and going as a kind of fantastic clown, making a periodic appearance in a circus.

He was, I fancy, enjoying himself to the full. His pose of baffled despair was admirable. How he achieved the end he had in view and which he had disclosed to me in the early hours of the morning, I cannot say.

But achieve it he did.

It cannot have been easy. The amount of deception and subterfuge involved must have been colossal. The English character is averse to lying on a wholesale scale and that, no less, was what Poirot's plan required. He had, first, to get Dr. Graham converted to the scheme. With Dr. Graham on his side, he had to persuade the Matron and some members of the staff of the nursing home to conform to the plan. There again, the difficulties must have been immense. It was probably Dr. Graham's influence that turned the scale.

Then there was the Chief Constable and the police. Here, Poirot would be up against officialdom. Nevertheless he wrung at last an unwilling consent out of Colonel Weston. The Colonel made it clear that it was in no way his responsibility. Poirot and Poirot alone was responsible for the spreading abroad of these lying reports. Poirot agreed. He would have agreed to anything so long as he was permitted to carry out his plan.

I spent most of the day dozing in a large armchair with a rug over my knees. Every two or three hours or so, Poirot would burst in and report progress.

'*Comment ça va, mon ami?* How I commiserate you. But it is as well, perhaps. The farce, you do not play it as well as I do. I come this moment from ordering a wreath—a wreath immense—stupendous. Lilies, my friend—large quantities of lilies. *"With heartfelt regret. From Hercule Poirot."* Ah! what a comedy.'

He departed again.

'I come from a most poignant conversation with Madame Rice,' was his next piece of information. 'Very well dressed in the black, that one. Her poor friend—what a tragedy! I groan sympathetically. Nick, she says, was so joyous, so full of life. Impossible to think of her as dead. I agree. "It is, I say, the irony of death that it takes one like that. The old and useless are left." Oh! *là là*! I groan again.'

'How you are enjoying this,' I murmured, feebly.

'*Du tout.* It is part of my plan, that is all. To play the comedy successfully, you must put the heart into it. Well, then, the conventional expressions of regret over, Madame comes to matters nearer home. All night she has lain awake wondering about those sweets. It is impossible—impossible. "Madame", I say, "It is not impossible. You can see the analyst's report." Then she says, and her voice is far from steady, "It was—*cocaine*, you say?" I assent. And she says, "Oh, my God. I don't understand."'

'Perhaps that's true.'

'She understands well enough that she is in danger. She is intelligent. I told you that before. Yes, she is in danger, and she knows it.'

'And yet it seems to me that for the first time you don't believe her guilty.'

Poirot frowned. The excitement of his manner abated.

'It is profound what you say there, Hastings. No—it seems to me that—somehow—the facts no longer fit. These crimes—so far what has marked them most—the subtlety, is it not? And here is no subtlety at all—only the crudity, pure and simple. No, it does not fit.'

He sat down at the table.

'*Voilà*—let us examine the facts. There are three possibilities. There are the sweets bought by Madame and delivered by M. Lazarus. And in that case the guilt rests with one or the other or *both*. And the telephone call, supposedly from Madamoiselle Nick, that is an invention pure and simple. That is the straightforward—the obvious solution.

'Solution 2: The *other* box of sweets—that which came by post. Anyone may have sent those. Any of the suspects on our list from A. to J. (You remember? A very wide field.) But, if that were the guilty box, *what is the point of the telephone call?* Why complicate matters with a second box?'

I shook my head feebly. With a temperature of 102, any complication seemed to me quite unnecessary and absurd.

'Solution 3: A poisoned box was substituted for the innocent box bought by Madame. In that case the telephone call is ingenious and understandable. Madame is to be what you call the kitten's paw. She is to pull the roasting chestnuts out of the fire. So Solution 3 is the most logical—but, alas, it is also the most difficult. How be sure of substituting a box at the right moment? The orderly might take the box straight upstairs—a hundred and one possibilities might prevent the substitution being effected. No, it does not seem sense.'

'Unless it were Lazarus,' I said.

Poirot looked at me.

'You have the fever, my friend. It mounts, does it not?'

I nodded.

'Curious how a few degrees of heat should stimulate the intellect. You have uttered there an observation of profound simplicity. So simple, was it, that I had failed to consider it. But it would suppose a very curious state of affairs. M. Lazarus, the dear friend of Madame, doing his best to get her hanged. It opens up possibilities of a very curious nature. But complex—very complex.'

I closed my eyes. I was glad I had been brilliant, but I did not want to think of anything complex. I wanted to go to sleep.

Poirot, I think, went on talking, but I did not listen. His voice was vaguely soothing....

It was late afternoon when I saw him next.

'My little plan, it has made the fortune of the flower shops,' he announced. 'Everybody orders wreaths. M. Croft, M. Vyse, Commander Challenger——'

The last name awoke a chord of compunction in my mind.

'Look here, Poirot,' I said. 'You must let him in on this. Poor fellow, he will be distracted with grief. It isn't fair.'

'You have always the tenderness for him, Hastings.'

'I like him. He's a thoroughly decent chap. You've got to take him into the secret.'

Poirot shook his head.

'No, *mon ami*. I do not make the exceptions.'

'But you don't suspect him of having anything to do with it?'

'I do not make the exceptions.'

'Think how he must be suffering.'

'On the contrary, I prefer to think of what a joyful surprise I prepare for him. To think the loved one dead—and find her alive! It is a sensation unique—stupendous.'

'What a pig-headed old devil you are. He'd keep the secret all right.'

'I am not so sure.'

'He's the soul of honour. I'm certain of it.'

'That makes it all the more difficult to keep a secret. Keeping a secret is an art that requires many lies magnificently told, and a great aptitude for playing the comedy and enjoying it. Could he dissemble, the Commander Challenger? If he is what you say he is, he certainly could *not*.'

'Then you won't tell him?'

'I certainly refuse to imperil my little idea for the sake of the sentiment. It is life and death we play with, *mon cher*. Anyway, the suffering, it is good for the character. Many of your famous clergymen have said so—even a Bishop if I am not mistaken.'

I made no further attempt to shake his decision. His mind, I could see, was made up.

'I shall not dress for dinner,' he murmured. 'I am too much the broken old man. That is my part, you understand. All my self-confidence has crashed—I am broken. I have failed. I shall eat hardly any dinner—the food untasted on the plate. That is the attitude, I think. In my own apartment I will consume some brioches and some chocolate *éclairs* (so called) which I had the foresight to buy at a confectioners. *Et vous?*'

'Some more quinine, I think,' I said, sadly.

'Alas, my poor Hastings. But courage, all will be well to-morrow.'

'Very likely. These attacks often last only twenty-four hours.'

I did not hear him return to the room. I must have been asleep.

When I awoke, he was sitting at the table writing. In front of him was a crumpled sheet of paper smoothed out. I recognised it for the paper on which he had written that list of people—A. to J.—which he had afterwards crumpled up and thrown away.

He nodded in answer to my unspoken thought.

'Yes, my friend. I have resurrected it. I am at work upon it from a different angle. I compile a list of questions concerning each person. The questions may have no bearing on the crime—they are just things that I do not know—things that remain unexplained, and for which I seek to supply the answer from my own brain.'

'How far have you got?'

'I have finished. You would like to hear? You are strong enough?'

'Yes, as a matter of fact, I am feeling a great deal better.'

'*À la bonheur!* Very well, I will read them to you. Some of them, no doubt, you will consider puerile.'

He cleared his throat.

'A. *Ellen.*—Why did she remain in the house and not go out to see fireworks? (Unusual, as Mademoiselle's evidence and surprise make clear.) What did she think or suspect might happen? Did she admit anyone (J. for instance) to the house? Is she speaking the truth about the secret panel? If there is such a thing why is she unable to remember where it is? (Mademoiselle seems very certain there is no such thing—and she would surely know.) If she invented it, why did she invent it? Had she read Michael Seton's love letters or was her surprise at Mademoiselle Nick's engagement genuine?

'B. *Her Husband.*—Is he as stupid as he seems? Does he share Ellen's knowledge whatever it is, or does he not? Is he, in any respect, a mental case?

'C. *The Child.*—Is his delight in blood a natural instinct common to his age and development, or is it morbid, and is that morbidity inherited from either parent? Has he ever shot with a toy pistol?

'D. *Who is Mr. Croft?*—Where does he really come from? Did he post the will as he swears he did? What motive could he have in *not* posting it?

'E. *Same as above.*—Who *are* Mr. and Mrs. Croft? Are they in hiding for some reason—and if so, what reason? Have they any connection with the Buckley family?

'F. *Mrs. Rice.*—Was she really aware of the engagement between Nick and Michael Seton? Did she merely guess it, or had she actually read the letters which passed between them? (In that case she would know Mademoiselle was Seton's heir.) Did she know that she herself was Mademoiselle's residuary legatee? (This, I think, is likely. Mademoiselle would probably tell her so, adding perhaps that she would not get much out of it.) Is there any truth in Commander Challenger's suggestion that Lazarus was attracted by Mademoiselle Nick? (This might explain a certain lack of cordiality between the two friends which seems to have shown itself in the last few months.) Who is the 'boy friend' mentioned in her note as supplying the drug? *Could this possibly be J.?* Why did she turn faint one day in this room? Was it something that had been said—or was it something she *saw*? Is her account of the telephone message asking her to buy chocolates correct—or is it a deliberate lie? What did she mean by "I can understand the other—but not this?" If she is not herself guilty, what knowledge has she got that she is keeping to herself?'

'You perceive,' said Poirot, suddenly breaking off, "that the questions concerning Madame Rice are almost innumerable. From beginning to end, she is an enigma. And that forces me to a conclusion. Either Madame Rice is guilty—or she knows—or shall we say, thinks she knows—who *is* guilty. But is she right? Does she know or does she merely suspect? And how is it possible to make her speak?'

He sighed.

'Well, I will go on with my list of questions.

'G. *Mr. Lazarus.*—Curious—there are practically no questions to ask concerning him—except the crude one. Did he substitute the poisoned sweets? Otherwise I find only one totally irrelevant question. But I have put it down. Why did M. Lazarus offer fifty pounds for a picture that was only worth twenty?'

'He wanted to do Nick a good turn,' I suggested.

'He would not do it that way. He is a dealer. He does not buy to sell at a loss. If he wished to be amiable he would lend her money as a private individual.'

'It can't have any bearing on the crime, anyway.'

'No, that is true—but all the same, I should like to know. I am a student of the psychology, you understand.

'Now we come to H.

'H. *Commander Challenger.*—Why did Mademoiselle Nick tell him she was engaged to someone else? What necessitated her having to tell him that? She told no one else. Had he proposed to her? What are his relations with his uncle?'

'His uncle, Poirot?'

'Yes, the doctor. That rather questionable character. Did any private news of Michael Seton's death come through to the Admiralty before it was announced publicly?'

'I don't quite see what you're driving at, Poirot. Even if Challenger knew beforehand about Seton's death, it does not seem to get us anywhere. It provides no earthly motive for killing the girl he loved.'

'I quite agree. What you say is perfectly reasonable. But these are just things I should like to know. I am still the dog, you see, nosing about for the things that are not very nice!

'I. *M. Vyse.*—Why did he say what he did about his cousin's fanatical devotion to End House? What possible motive could he have in saying that? Did he, or did he not, receive the will? Is he, in fact, an honest man—or is he not an honest man?

'*And now J.—Eh bien*, J. is what I put down before—a giant question mark. Is there such a person, or is there not——

'*Mon Dieu!* my friend, what have you?'

I had started from my chair with a sudden shriek. With a shaking hand I pointed at the window.

'A face, Poirot!' I cried. 'A face pressed against the glass. A dreadful face! It's gone now—but I saw it.'

Poirot strode to the window and pushed it open. He leant out.

'There is no one there now,' he said, thoughtfully. 'You are sure you did not imagine it, Hastings?'

'Quite sure. It was a horrible face.'

'There is a balcony, of course. Anyone could reach there quite easily if they wanted to hear what we were saying. When you say a dreadful face, Hastings, just what do you mean?'

'A white, staring face, hardly human.'

'*Mon ami*, that is the fever. A face, yes. An unpleasant face, yes. But a face hardly human—*no*. What you saw was the effect of a face pressed closely against the glass—that allied to the shock of seeing it there at all.'

'It was a dreadful face,' I said, obstinately.

'It was not the face of—anyone you know?'

'No, indeed.'

'H'm—it might have been, though! I doubt if you would recognise it under these circumstances. I wonder now—yes, I very much wonder....'

He gathered up his papers thoughtfully.

'One thing at least is to the good. If the owner of that face overheard our conversation we did not mention that Mademoiselle Nick was alive and well. Whatever else our visitor may have heard, that at least escaped him.'

'But surely,' I said, 'the results of this—er—brilliant manœuvre of yours have been slightly disappointing up to date. Nick is dead and no startling developments have occurred!'

'I did not expect them yet awhile. Twenty-four hours, I said. *Mon ami*, to-morrow, if I am not mistaken, certain things will arise. Otherwise—otherwise I am wrong from start to finish. There is the post, you see. I have hopes of to-morrow's post.'

I awoke in the morning feeling weak but with the fever abated. I also felt hungry. Poirot and I had breakfast served in our sitting-room.

'Well?' I said, maliciously, as he sorted his letters. 'Has the post done what you expected of it?'

Poirot, who had just opened two envelopes which patently contained bills, did not reply. I thought he looked rather cast down and not his usual cock-a-hoop self.

I opened my own mail. The first was a notice of a spiritualist meeting.

'If all else fails, we must go to the spiritualists,' I remarked. 'I often wonder that more tests of this kind aren't made. The spirit of the victim comes back and names the murderer. That would be a proof.'

'It would hardly help us,' said Poirot, absently. 'I doubt if Maggie Buckley knew whose hand it was shot her down. Even if she could speak she would have nothing of value to tell us. *Tiens!* that is odd.'

'What is?'

'You talk of the dead speaking, and at that moment I open this letter.'

He tossed it across to me. It was from Mrs. Buckley and ran as follows:

'Langley Rectory.

'DEAR MONSIEUR POIROT,—On my return here I found a letter written by my poor child on her arrival at St. Loo. There is nothing in it of interest to you, I'm afraid, but I thought perhaps you would care to see it.

'Thanking you for your kindness,

'Yours sincerely,

'JEAN BUCKLEY.'

The enclosure brought a lump to my throat. It was so terribly commonplace and so completely untouched by any apprehension of tragedy:

'DEAR MOTHER,—I arrived safely. Quite a comfortable journey. Only two other people in the carriage all the way to Exeter.

'It is lovely weather here. Nick seems very well and gay—a little restless, perhaps, but I cannot see why she should have telegraphed for me in the way she did. Tuesday would have done just as well.

'No more now. We are going to have tea with some neighbours.

They are Australians and have rented the lodge. Nick says they are kind but rather awful. Mrs. Rice and Mr. Lazarus are coming to stay. He is the art dealer. I will post this in the box by the gate, then it will catch the post. Will write to-morrow.

'Your loving daughter,

'MAGGIE.

'P.S.—Nick says there *is* a reason for her wire. She will tell me after tea. She is very queer and jumpy.'

'The voice of the dead,' said Poirot, quietly. 'And it tells us—nothing.'

'The box by the gate,' I remarked idly. 'That's where Croft said he posted the will.'

'Said so—yes. I wonder. How I wonder!'

'There is nothing else of interest among your letters?'

'Nothing. Hastings, I am very unhappy. I am in the dark. Still in the dark. I comprehend nothing.'

At that moment the telephone rang. Poirot went to it.

Immediately I saw a change come over his face. His manner was very restrained, nevertheless he could not disguise from my eyes his intense excitement.

His own contributions to the conversation were entirely non-committal so that I could not gather what it was all about.

Presently, however, with a '*Tres bien. Je vous remercie,*' he put back the receiver and came back to where I was sitting. His eyes were sparkling with excitement. '*Mon ami*,' he said. '*What did I tell you?* Things have begun to happen.'

'What was it?'

That was M. Charles Vyse on the telephone. He informs me that this morning, through the post, he has received a will signed by his cousin, Miss Buckley, and dated the 25th of February last.'

'What? *The* will?'

'*Évidément*.'

'It has turned up?'

'Just at the right moment, *n'est ce pas?*'

'Do you think he is speaking the truth?'

'Or do I think he has had the will all along? Is that what you would say? Well, it is all a little curious. But one thing is certain; I told you that, if Mademoiselle Nick were supposed to be dead, we should have developments—and sure enough here they are!'

'Extraordinary,' I said. 'You were right. I suppose this is the will making Frederica Rice residuary legatee?'

'M. Vyse said nothing about the contents of the will. He was far too correct. But there seems very little reason to doubt that this is the same will. It is witnessed, he tells me, by Ellen Wilson and her husband.'

'So we are back at the old problem,' I said. 'Frederica Rice.'

'The enigma!'

'Frederica Rice,' I murmured, inconsequently. 'It's a pretty name.'

'Prettier than what her friends call her. Freddie'—he made a face—'*ce n'est pas jolie*—for a young lady.'

'There aren't many abbreviations of Frederica,' I said. 'It's not like Margaret where you can have half a dozen—Maggie, Margot, Madge, Peggie——'

'True. Well, Hastings, are you happier now? That things have begun to happen?'

'Yes, of course. Tell me—did you expect *this* to happen?'

'No—not exactly. I had formulated nothing very precise to myself. All I had said was that given a certain result, the causes of that result must make themselves evident.'

'Yes,' I said, respectfully.

'What was it that I was going to say just as that telephone rang?' mused Poirot. 'Oh, yes, that letter from Mademoiselle Maggie. I wanted to look at it once again. I have an idea in the back of my mind that something in it struck me as rather curious.'

I picked it up from where I had tossed it, and handed it to him.

He read it over to himself. I moved about the room, looking out of the window and observing the yachts racing on the bay.

Suddenly an exclamation startled me. I turned round. Poirot was holding his head in his hands and rocking himself to and fro, apparently in an agony of woe.

'Oh!' he groaned. 'But I have been blind—blind.'

'What's the matter?'

'Complex, I have said? Complicated? *Mais non.* Of a simplicity extreme—extreme. And miserable one that I am, I saw nothing—nothing.'

'Good gracious, Poirot, what is this light that has suddenly burst upon you?'

'Wait—wait—do not speak? I must arrange my ideas. Rearrange them in the light of this discovery so stupendous.'

Seizing his list of questions, he ran over them silently, his lips moving busily. Once or twice he nodded his head emphatically.

Then he laid them down and leaning back in his chair he shut his eyes. I thought at last that he had gone to sleep.

Suddenly he sighed and opened his eyes.

'But, yes!' he said. 'It all fits in! All the things that have puzzled me. All the things that have seemed to me a little unnatural. They all have their place.'

'You mean—you know everything?'

'Nearly everything. All that matters. In some respects I have been right in my deductions. In other ways ludicrously far from the truth. But now it is all clear. I shall send to-day a telegram asking two questions—but the answers to them I know already—I know *here*!' He tapped his forehead.

'And when you receive the answers?' I asked, curiously.

He sprang to his feet.

'My friend, do you remember that Mademoiselle Nick said she wanted to stage a play at End House? To-night, we stage such a play in End House. But it will be a play produced by Hercule Poirot. Mademoiselle Nick will have a part to play in it.' He grinned suddenly. 'You comprehend, Hastings, *there will be a ghost in this play*. Yes, a ghost. End House has never seen a ghost. It will have one to-night. No'—as I tried to ask a question—'I will say no more. To-night, Hastings, we will produce our comedy—and reveal the truth. But now, there is much to do—much to do.'

He hurried from the room.

19. *Poirot produces a Play*

IT WAS A CURIOUS GATHERING that met that night at End House.

I had hardly seen Poirot all day. He had been out for dinner but had left me a message that I was to be at End House at nine o'clock. Evening dress, he had added, was not necessary.

The whole thing was like a rather ridiculous dream.

On arrival I was ushered into the dining-room, and when I looked round I realised that every person on Poirot's list from A. to I. (J. was necessarily excluded, being in the Mrs. Harris-like position of 'there ain't no sich person') was present.

Even Mrs. Croft was there in a kind of invalid chair. She smiled and nodded at me.

'This is a surprise, isn't it?' she said, cheerfully. 'It makes a change for me, I must say. I think I shall try and get out now and again. All M. Poirot's idea. Come and sit by me, Captain Hastings. Somehow I feel this is rather a gruesome business—but Mr. Vyse made a point of it.'

'Mr. Vyse?' I said, rather surprised.

Charles Vyse was standing by the mantelpiece. Poirot was beside him talking earnestly to him in an undertone.

I looked round the room. Yes, they were all there. After showing me in (I had been a minute or two late) Ellen had taken her place on a chair just beside the door. On another chair, sitting painfully straight and breathing hard, was her husband. The child, Alfred, squirmed uneasily between his father and mother.

The rest sat round the dining-table. Frederica in her black dress, Lazarus beside her, George Challenger and Croft on the other side of the table. I sat a little away from it near Mrs. Croft. And now Charles Vyse, with a final nod of the head, took his place at the head of the table, and Poirot slipped unobtrusively into a seat next to Lazarus.

Clearly the producer, as Poirot had styled himself, did not propose to take a prominent part in the play. Charles Vyse was apparently in charge of the proceedings. I wondered what surprises Poirot had in store for him.

The young lawyer cleared his throat and stood up. He looked just the same as ever, impassive, formal and unemotional.

'This is rather an unconventional gathering we have here to-night,' he said. 'But the circumstances are very peculiar. I refer, of course, to the circumstances surrounding the death of my cousin, Miss Buckley. There will have, of course, to be an autopsy—there seems to be no doubt that she met her death by poison, and that that poison was administered with the intent to kill. This is police business and I need not go into it. The police would doubtless prefer me not to do so.

'In an ordinary case, the will of a deceased person is read after the funeral, but in deference to M. Poirot's especial wish, I am proposing to read it before the funeral takes place. In fact, I am proposing to read it here and now. That is why everyone has been asked to come here. As I said just now, the circumstances are unusual and justify a departure from precedent.

'The will itself came into my possession in a somewhat unusual manner. Although dated last February, it only reached me by post this morning. However, it is undoubtedly in the handwriting of my cousin—I have no doubt on that point, and though a most informal document, it is properly attested.'

He paused and cleared his throat once more.

Every eye was upon his face.

From a long envelope in his hand, he drew out an enclosure. It was, as we could see, an ordinary piece of End House notepaper with writing on it.

'It is quite short,' said Vyse. He made a suitable pause, then began to read:

'This is the last Will and Testament of Magdala Buckley. I direct that all my funeral expenses should be paid and I appoint my cousin Charles Vyse as my executor. I leave everything of which I die possessed to Mildred Croft in grateful recognition of the services rendered by her to my father, Philip Buckley, which services nothing can ever repay.

'Signed—MAGDALA BUCKLEY,
'Witnesses—ELLEN WILSON.
'WILLIAM WILSON.'

I was dumbfounded! So I think was everyone else. Only Mrs. Croft nodded her head in quiet understanding.

'It's true,' she said, quietly. 'Not that I ever meant to let on about it. Philip Buckley was out in Australia, and if it hadn't been for me—well, I'm not going into that. A secret it's been and a secret it had better remain. She knew about it, though. Nick did, I mean. Her father must have told her. We came down here because we wanted to have a look at the place. I'd always been curious about this End House Philip Buckley talked of. And that dear girl knew all about it, and couldn't do enough for us. Wanted us to come and live with her, she did. But we wouldn't do that. And so she insisted on our having the lodge—and not a penny of rent would she take. We pretended to pay it, of course, so as not to cause talk, but she handed it back to us. And now—this! Well, if anyone says there is no gratitude in the world, I'll tell them they're wrong. This proves it.'

There was still an amazed silence. Poirot looked at Vyse.

'Had you any idea of this?'

Vyse shook his head.

'I knew Philip Buckley had been in Australia. But I never heard any rumours of a scandal there.'

He looked inquiringly at Mrs. Croft.

She shook her head.

'No, you won't get a word out of me. I never have said a word and I never shall. The secret goes to the grave with me.'

Vyse said nothing. He sat quietly tapping the table with a pencil.

'I presume, M. Vyse'—Poirot leaned forward—'that as next of kin you could contest that will? There is, I understand, a vast fortune at stake which was not the case when the will was made.'

Vyse looked at him coldly.

'The will is perfectly valid. I should not dream of contesting my cousin's disposal of her property.'

'You're an honest fellow,' said Mrs. Croft, approvingly. 'And I'll see you don't lose by it.'

Charles shrank a little from this well-meant but slightly embarrassing remark.

'Well, Mother,' said Mr. Croft, with an elation he could not quite keep out of his voice. 'This *is* a surprise! Nick didn't tell *me* what she was doing.'

'The dear sweet girl,' murmured Mrs. Croft, putting her handkerchief to her eyes. 'I wish she could look down and see us now. Perhaps she does—who knows?'

'Perhaps,' agreed Poirot.

Suddenly an idea seemed to strike him. He looked round.

'An idea! We are all here seated round a table. Let us hold a *séance*.'

'A *séance*?' said Mrs. Croft, somewhat shocked. 'But surely——'

'Yes, yes, it will be most interesting. Hastings, here, has pronounced mediumistic powers.' (Why fix on *me*, I thought.) 'To get through a message from the other world—the opportunity is unique! I feel the conditions are propitious. You feel the same, Hastings.'

'Yes,' I said resolutely, playing up.

'Good. I knew it. Quick, the lights.'

In another minute he had risen and switched them off. The whole thing had been rushed on the company before they had had the energy to protest had they wanted to do so. As a matter of fact they were, I think, still dazed with astonishment over the will.

The room was not quite dark. The curtains were drawn back and the window was open for it was a hot night, and through those windows came a faint light. After a minute or two, as we sat in silence, I began to be able to make out the faint outlines of the furniture. I wondered very much what I was supposed to do and cursed Poirot heartily for not having given me my instructions beforehand.

However, I closed my eyes and breathed in a rather stertorous manner.

Presently Poirot rose and tiptoed to my chair. Then returning to his own, he murmured.

'Yes, he is already in a trance. Soon—things will begin to happen.'

There is something about sitting in the dark, waiting, that fills one with unbearable apprehension. I know that I myself was a prey to nerves and so, I was sure, was everyone else. And yet I had at least an idea of what was about to happen. I knew the one vital fact that no one else knew.

And yet, in spite of all that, my heart leapt into my mouth as I saw the dining-room door slowly opening.

It did so quite soundlessly (it must have been oiled) and the effect was horribly grisly. It swung slowly open and for a minute or two that was all. With its opening a cold blast of air seemed to enter the room. It was, I suppose, a common or garden draught owing to the open window, but it *felt* like the icy chill mentioned in all the ghost stories I have ever read.

And then we all saw it! Framed in the doorway was a white shadowy figure. Nick Buckley . . .

She advanced slowly and noiselessly—with a kind of floating ethereal motion that certainly conveyed the impression of nothing human. . . .

I realised then what an actress the world had missed. Nick had wanted to play a part at End House. Now she was playing it, and I felt convinced that she was enjoying herself to the core. She did it perfectly.

She floated forward into the room—and the silence was broken.

There was a gasping cry from the invalid chair beside me. A kind of gurgle from Mr. Croft. A startled oath from Challenger. Charles Vyse drew back his chair, I think. Lazarus leaned forward. Frederica alone made no sound or movement.

And then a scream rent the room. Ellen sprang up from her chair.

'It's her!' she shrieked. 'She's come back. She's walking! Them that's murdered always walks. It's her! It's her!'

And then, with a click the lights went on.

I saw Poirot standing by them, the smile of the ringmaster on his face. Nick stood in the middle of the room in her white draperies.

It was Frederica who spoke first. She stretched out an unbelieving hand—touched her friend.

'Nick,' she said. 'You're—you're *real*!'

It was almost a whisper.

Nick laughed. She advanced.

'Yes,' she said. 'I'm real enough. Thank you so much for what you did for my father, Mrs. Croft. But I'm afraid you won't be able to enjoy the benefit of that will just yet.'

'Oh, my God,' gasped Mrs. Croft. 'Oh, my God.' She twisted to and fro in her chair. 'Take me away, Bert. Take me away. It was all a joke, my dear—all a joke, that's all it was. Honest.'

'A queer sort of joke,' said Nick.

The door had opened again and a man had entered so quietly that I had not heard him. To my surprise I saw that it was Japp. He exchanged a quick nod with Poirot as though satisfying him of something. Then his face suddenly lit up and he took a step forward towards the squirming figure in the invalid chair.

'Hello-ello-ello,' he said. 'What's this? An old friend! Milly Merton, I declare! And at your old tricks again, my dear.'

He turned round in an explanatory way to the company, disregarding Mrs. Croft's shrill protests.

'Cleverest forger we've ever had, Milly Merton. We knew there had been an accident to the car they made their last getaway in. But there! Even an injury to the spine wouldn't keep Milly from her tricks. She's an artist, she is!'

'Was that will a forgery?' said Vyse.

He spoke in tones of amazement.

'Of course it was a forgery,' said Nick scornfully. 'You don't think I'd make a silly will like that, do you? I left you End House, Charles, and everything else to Frederica.'

She crossed as she spoke and stood by her friend, and just at that moment *it happened!*

A spurt of flame from the window and the hiss of a bullet. Then another and the sound of a groan and a fall outside. . . .

And Frederica on her feet with a thin trickle of blood running down her arm. . . .

20. J.

IT WAS ALL SO SUDDEN that for a moment no one knew what had happened.

Then, with a violent exclamation, Poirot ran to the window. Challenger was with him.

A moment later they reappeared, carrying with them the limp body of a man. As they lowered him carefully into a big leather armchair and his face came into view, I uttered a cry.

'The face—the face at the window. . . .'

It was the man I had seen looking in on us the previous evening. I recognised him at once. I realised that when I had said he was hardly human I had exaggerated as Poirot had accused me of doing.

Yet there was something about this face that justified my impression. It was a lost face—the face of one removed from ordinary humanity.

White, weak, depraved—it seemed a mere mask—as though the spirit within had fled long ago.

Down the side of it there trickled a stream of blood.

Frederica came slowly forward till she stood by the chair.

Poirot intercepted her. 'You are hurt, Madame?'

She shook her head. 'The bullet grazed my shoulder—that is all.'

She put him aside with a gentle hand and bent down.

The man's eyes opened and he saw her looking down at him.

'I've done for you this time, I hope,' he said in a low vicious snarl, and then, his voice changing suddenly till it sounded like a child's, 'Oh! Freddie, I didn't mean it. I didn't mean it. You've always been so decent to me. . . .'

'It's all right——'

She knelt down beside him.

'I didn't mean——"

His head dropped. The sentence was never finished.

Frederica looked up at Poirot.

'Yes, Madame, he is dead,' he said, gently.

She rose slowly from her knees and stood looking down at him. With one hand she touched his forehead—pitifully, it seemed. Then she sighed and turned to the rest of us.

'He was my husband,' she said, quietly.

'J.,' I murmured.

Poirot caught my remark, and nodded a quick assent.

'Yes,' he said softly. 'Always I felt that there was a J. I said so from the beginning, did I not?'

'He was my husband,' said Frederica again. Her voice was terribly tired. She sank into a chair that Lazarus brought for her. 'I might as well tell you everything—now.'

'He was—completely debased. He was a drug fiend. He taught me to take drugs. I have been fighting the habit ever since I left him. I think—at last—I am nearly cured. But it has been—difficult. Oh! so horribly difficult. Nobody knows how difficult!'

'I could never escape from him. He used to turn up and demand money—with threats. A kind of blackmail. If I did not give him money he would shoot himself. That was always his threat. Then he took to threatening to shoot *me*. He was not responsible. He was mad—crazy. . . .

'I suppose it was he who shot Maggie Buckley. He didn't mean to shoot her, of course. He must have thought it was me.

'I ought to have said, I suppose. But, after all, I wasn't *sure*. And those queer accidents Nick had—that made me feel that perhaps it wasn't him after all. It might have been someone quite different.

'And then—one day—I saw a bit of his handwriting on a torn piece of paper on M. Poirot's table. It was a part of a letter he had sent me. I knew then that M. Poirot was on the track.

'Since then I have felt that it was only a matter of time. . . .

'But I don't understand about the sweets. He wouldn't have wanted to poison *Nick*. And anyway, I don't see how he *could* have had anything to do with that. I've puzzled and puzzled.'

She put both hands to her face, then took them away and said with a queer pathetic finality:

'That's all. . . .'

21. *The person—K.*

LAZARUS came quickly to her side.

'My dear,' he said. 'My dear.'

Poirot went to the sideboard, poured out a glass of wine and brought it to her, standing over her while she drank it.

She handed the glass back to him and smiled.

'I'm all right now,' she said. 'What—what had we better do next?'

She looked at Japp, but the Inspector shook his head. 'I'm on a holiday, Mrs. Rice. Just obliging an old friend—that's all I'm doing. The St. Loo police are in charge of the case.'

She looked at Poirot.

'And M. Poirot is in charge of the St. Loo police?'

'Oh! *quelle idée, Madame!* I am a mere humble adviser.'

'M. Poirot,' said Nick. 'Can't we hush it up?'

'You wish that, Mademoiselle?'

'Yes. After all—I'm the person most concerned. And there will be no more attacks on me—now.'

'No, that is true. There will be no more attacks on you now.'

'You're thinking of Maggie. But, M. Poirot, nothing will bring Maggie back to life again? If you make all this public, you'll only bring a terrible lot of suffering and publicity on Frederica—and she hasn't deserved it.'

'You say she has not deserved it?'

'Of course she hasn't! I told you right at the beginning that she had a brute of a husband. You've seen to-night—what he was. Well, he's dead. Let that be the end of things. Let the police go on looking for the man who shot Maggie. They just won't find him, that's all.'

'So that is what you say, Mademoiselle? *Hush it all up.*'

'Yes. Please. Oh! *please.* Please, *dear* M. Poirot.'

Poirot looked slowly round.

'What do you all say?'

Each spoke in turn.

'I agree,' I said, as Poirot looked at me.

'I, too,' said Lazarus.

'Best thing to do,' from Challenger.

'Let's forget everything that's passed in this room to-night.' This very determinedly from Croft.

'You *would* say that!' interpolated Japp.

'Don't be hard on me, dearie,' his wife sniffed to Nick, who looked at her scornfully but made no reply.

'Ellen?'

'Me and William won't say a word, sir. Least said, soonest mended.'

'And you, M. Vyse?'

'A thing like this can't be hushed up,' said Charles Vyse. 'The facts must be made known in the proper quarter.'

'Charles!' cried Nick.

'I'm sorry, dear. I look at it from the legal aspect.'

Poirot gave a sudden laugh.

'So you are seven to one. The good Japp is neutral.'

'I'm on holiday,' said Japp, with a grin. 'I don't count.'

'Seven to one. Only M. Vyse holds out—on the side of law and order! You know, M. Vyse, you are a man of character!'

Vyse shrugged his shoulders.

'The position is quite clear. There is only one thing to do.

'Yes—you are an honest man. *Eh bien*—I, too, range myself on the side of the minority. *I, too, am for the truth.*'

'M. Poirot!' cried Nick.

'Mademoiselle—you dragged me into the case. I came into it at your wish. You cannot silence me now.'

He raised a threatening forefinger in a gesture that I knew well.

'Sit down—all of you, and I will tell you—the truth.'

Silenced by his imperious attitude, we sat down meekly and turned attentive faces towards him.

'*Écoutez!* I have a list here—a list of persons connected with the crime. I numbered them with the letters of the alphabet including the letter J. J. stood for a person unknown—linked to the crime by one of the others. I did not know who J. was until to-night, *but I knew that there was such a person.* The events of to-night have proved that I was right.

'But yesterday, I suddenly realised that I had made a grave error. I had made an omission. I added another letter to my list. The letter K.'

'Another person unknown?' asked Vyse, with a slight sneer.

'Not exactly. I adopted J. as the symbol for a person unknown. Another person unknown would be merely another J. K. has a different significance. *It stands for a person who should have been included in the original list, but who was overlooked.*'

He bent over Frederica.

'Reassure yourself, Madame. *Your husband was not guilty of murder.* It was the person K. who shot Mademoiselle Maggie.'

She stared.

'But who is K?'

Poirot nodded to Japp. He stepped forward and spoke in tones reminiscent of the days when he had given evidence in police courts.

'Acting on information received, I took up a position here early in the evening, having been introduced secretly into the house by M. Poirot. I was concealed behind the curtains in the drawing-room.

When everyone was assembled in this room, a young lady entered the drawing-room and switched on the light. She made her way to the fireplace and opened a small recess in the panelling that appeared to be operated with a spring. She took from the recess a pistol. With this in her hand she left the room. I followed her and opening the door a crack I was able to observe her further movements. Coats and wraps had been left in the hall by the visitors on arrival. The young lady carefully wiped the pistol with a handkerchief and then placed it in the pocket of a grey wrap, the property of Mrs. Rice——'

A cry burst from Nick.

'This is untrue—every word of it!'

Poirot pointed a hand at her.

'Voilà!' he said. *'The person K.! It was Mademoiselle Nick who shot her cousin, Maggie Buckley.'*

'Are you mad?' cried Nick. 'Why should I kill Maggie?'

'In order to inherit the money left to her by Michael Seton! Her name too was Magdala Buckley—and it was to her he was engaged—not you.'

'You—you——'

She stood there trembling—unable to speak. Poirot turned to Japp.

'You telephoned to the police?'

'Yes, they are waiting in the hall now. They've got the warrant.'

'You're all mad!' cried Nick, contemptuously. She moved swiftly to Frederica's side. 'Freddie, give me your wrist-watch as—as a souvenir, will you?'

Slowly Frederica unclasped the jewelled watch from her wrist and handed it to Nick.

'Thanks. And now—I suppose we must go through with this perfectly ridiculous comedy.'

'The comedy you planned and produced in End House. Yes—but you should not have given the star part to Hercule Poirot. That, Mademoiselle, was your mistake—your very grave mistake.'

22. *The end of the story*

'YOU WANT ME TO EXPLAIN?'

Poirot looked round with a gratified smile and the air of mock humility I knew so well.

We had moved into the drawing-room and our numbers had lessened. The domestics had withdrawn tactfully, and the Crofts had been asked to accompany the police. Frederica, Lazarus, Challenger, Vyse and I remained.

'*Eh bien*—I confess it—I was fooled—fooled completely and absolutely. The little Nick, she had me where she wanted me, as your idiom so well expresses it. Ah! Madame, when you said that your friend was a clever little liar—how right you were! How right!'

'Nick always told lies,' said Frederica, composedly. 'That's why I didn't really believe in these marvellous escapes of hers.'

'And I—imbecile that I was—did!'

'Didn't they really happen?' I asked. I was, I admit, still hopelessly confused.

'They were invented—very cleverly—to give just the impression they did.'

'What was that?'

'They gave the impression that Mademoiselle Nick's life was in danger. But I will begin earlier than that. I will tell you the story as I have pieced it out—not as it came to me imperfectly and in flashes.

'At the beginning of the business then, we have this girl, this Nick Buckley, young and beautiful, unscrupulous, and passionately and fanatically devoted to her home.'

Charles Vyse nodded.

'I told you that.'

'And you were right. Mademoiselle Nick loved End House. But she had no money. The house was mortgaged. She wanted money—she wanted it feverishly—and she could not get it. She met this young Seton at Le Touquet, he is attracted by her. She knows that in all probability he is his uncle's heir and that that uncle is worth millions. Good, her star is in the ascendant, she thinks. But he is not really seriously attracted. He thinks her good fun, that is all. They meet at Scarborough, he takes her up in his machine and then—the catastrophe occurs. He meets Maggie and falls in love with her at first sight.

'Mademoiselle Nick is dumbfounded. Her cousin Maggie whom she has never considered pretty! But to young Seton she is "different". The one girl in the world for him. They become secretly engaged. Only one person knows—has to know. That person is Mademoiselle Nick. The poor Maggie—she is glad that there is one person she can talk to. Doubtless she reads to her cousin parts of her fiancé's letters. So it is that Mademoiselle gets to hear of the will. She pays no attention to it at the time. But it remains in her mind.

'Then comes the sudden and unexpected death of Sir Matthew Seton, and hard upon that the rumours of Michael Seton's being missing. And straight away an outrageous plan comes into our young lady's head. Seton does not know that her name is Magdala also. He only knows her as Nick. His will is clearly quite informal—a mere mention of a name. But in the eyes of the world Seton is her friend! It is with *her* that his name has been coupled. If she were to claim to be engaged to him, no one would be surprised. *But to do that successfully Maggie must be out of the way*.

'Time is short. She arranges for Maggie to come and stay in a few days' time. Then she has her escapes from death. The picture whose cord she cuts through. The brake of the car that she tampers with. The boulder—that perhaps was natural and she merely invented the story of being underneath on the path.

'And then—she sees *my* name in the paper. (I told you, Hastings, everyone knew Hercule Poirot!) and she has the audacity to make *me* an accomplice! The bullet through the hat that falls at my feet. Oh! the pretty comedy. And I am taken in! I believe in the peril that menaces her! *Bon!* She has got a valuable witness on her side. I play into her hands by asking her to send for a friend.

'She seizes the chance and sends for Maggie to come a day earlier.

'How easy the crime is actually! She leaves us at the dinner table and after hearing on the wireless that Seton's death is a fact, she starts to put her plan into action. She has plenty of time, then, to take Seton's letters to Maggie—look through them and select the few that will answer her purpose. These she places in her own room. Then, later, she and Maggie leave the fireworks and go back to the house. She tells her cousin to put on her shawl. Then stealing out after her, she shoots her. Quick, into the house, the pistol concealed in the secret panel (of whose existence she thinks nobody knows). Then upstairs. There she waits till voices are heard. The body is discovered. It is her cue.

'Down she rushes and out through the window.

'How well she played her part! Magnificently! Oh, yes, she staged a fine drama here. The maid, Ellen, said this was an evil house. I am inclined to agree with her. It was from the house that Mademoiselle Nick took her inspiration.'

'But those poisoned sweets,' said Frederica. 'I still don't understand about that.'

'It was all part of the same scheme. Do you not see that if Nick's life was attempted *after* Maggie was dead that absolutely settled the question that Maggie's death had been a mistake.

'When she thought the time was ripe she rang up Madame Rice and asked her to get her a box of chocolates.'

'Then it *was* her voice?'

'But, yes! How often the simple explanation is the true one! *N'est ce pas?* She made her voice sound a little different—that was all. So that you might be in doubt when questioned. Then, when the box arrived—again how simple. She fills three of the chocolates with cocaine (she had cocaine with her, cleverly concealed), eats one of them and is ill—but not *too* ill. She knows very well how much cocaine to take and just what symptoms to exaggerate.

'And the card—*my* card! *Ah! Sapristi*—she has a nerve! It *was* my card—the one I sent with the flowers. Simple, was it not? Yes, but it had to be thought of....'

There was a pause.

Then Frederica asked:

'Why did she put the pistol in my coat?'

'I thought you would ask that, Madame. It was bound to occur to you in time. Tell me—had it ever entered your head that Mademoiselle Nick no longer liked you? Did you ever feel that she might—hate you?'

'It's difficult to say,' said Frederica, slowly. 'We lived an insincere life. She *used* to be fond of me.'

'Tell me, M. Lazarus—it is not a time for false modesty, you understand—was there ever anything between you and her?'

'No.' Lazarus shook his head. 'I was attracted to her at one time. And then—I don't know why—I went off her.'

'Ah!' said Poirot, nodding his head sagely. 'That was her tragedy. She attracted people—and then they "went off her." Instead of liking her better and better you fell in love with her friend. She began to hate Madame—Madame who had a rich friend behind her. Last winter when she made a will, she was fond of Madame. Later it was different.

'She remembered that will. She did not know that Croft had suppressed it—that it had never reached its destination. Madame (or so the world would say) had got a motive for desiring her death. So it was to Madame she telephoned asking her to get the chocolates. To-night, the will would have been read, naming Madame her residuary legatee—and then the pistol would be found in her coat—*the pistol with which Maggie Buckley was shot.* If Madame found it, she might incriminate herself by trying to get rid of it.'

'She must have hated me,' murmured Frederica.

'Yes, Madame. You had what she had not—the knack of winning love, and *keeping* it.'

'I'm rather dense,' said Challenger, 'but I haven't quite fathomed the will business yet?'

'No? That's a different business altogether—a very simple one. The Crofts are lying low down here. Mademoiselle Nick has to have an operation. She has made no will. The Crofts see a chance. They persuade her to make one and take charge of it for the post. Then, if anything happens to her—if she dies—they produce a cleverly forged will—leaving the money to Mrs. Croft with a reference to Australia and Philip Buckley whom they know once visited the country.

'But Mademoiselle Nick has her appendix removed quite satisfactorily so the forged will is no good. For the moment, that is. Then the attempts on her life begin. The Crofts are hopeful once more. Finally, I announce her death. The chance is too good to be missed. The forged will is immediately posted to M. Vyse. Of course, to begin with, they naturally thought her much richer than she is. They knew nothing about the mortgage.'

'What I really want to know, M. Poirot,' said Lazarus, 'is how you actually got wise to all this. When did you begin to suspect?'

'Ah! there I am ashamed. I was so long—so long. There were things that worried me—yes. Things that seemed not quite right. Discrepancies between what Mademoiselle Nick told me and what other people told me. Unfortunately, I always believed Mademoiselle Nick.

'And then, suddenly, I got a revelation. Mademoiselle Nick made one mistake. She was too clever. When I urged her to send for a friend she promised to do so—and suppressed the fact that she had already sent for Mademoiselle Maggie.'

'It seemed to her less suspicious—*but it was a mistake.*'

'For Maggie Buckley wrote a letter home immediately on arrival, and in it she used one innocent phrase that puzzled me: *"I don't see why Nick should have telegraphed for me the way she did. Tuesday would have done just as well."* What did that mention of Tuesday mean? *It could only mean one thing.* Maggie had been coming to stay on Tuesday anyway. But in that case Mademoiselle Nick had lied—or had at any rate suppressed the truth.

'And for the first time I looked at her in a different light. I criticised her statements. Instead of believing them, I said, "Suppose this were not true." I remembered the discrepancies. "How would it be if every time it was Mademoiselle Nick who was lying and not the other person?"

'I said to myself. Let us be simple. What has *really* happened?

'And I saw that what had really happened was that *Maggie Buckley* had been killed. Just that! But who could want Maggie Buckley dead?'

'And then I thought of something else—a few foolish remarks that Hastings had made not five minutes before. He had said that there were plenty of abbreviations for Margaret—Maggie, Margot, etc. And it suddenly occurred to me to wonder what was Mademoiselle Maggie's real name?

'Then, *tout d'un coup*, it came to me! Supposing her name was *Magdala*! It was a Buckley name, Mademoiselle Nick had told me so. Two Magdala Buckleys. Supposing . . .

'In my mind I ran over the letters of Michael Seton's that I had read. Yes—there was nothing impossible. There was a mention of Scarborough—but Maggie had been in Scarborough with Nick—her mother had told me so.

'And it explained one thing which had worried me. Why were there so *few* letters? If a girl keeps her love-letters at all, she keeps all of them. Why these select few? Was there any peculiarity about them?'

'And I remembered that there was no *name* mentioned in them. They all began differently—but they began with a term of endearment. Nowhere in them was there the name—*Nick*.

'And there was something else, something that I ought to have seen at once—that cried the truth aloud.'

'What was that?'

'Why—this. Mademoiselle Nick underwent an operation for

appendicitis on February 27th last. There is a letter of Michael Seton's dated March 2nd, and no mention of anxiety, of illness or anything unusual. That ought to have shown me that the letters were written to a *different person altogether*.

'Then I went through a list of questions that I had made. And I answered them in the light of my new idea.

'In all but a few isolated questions the result was simple and convincing. And I answered, too, another question which I had asked myself earlier. *Why did Mademoiselle Nick buy a black dress?* The answer was that she and her cousin had to be dressed alike, with the scarlet shawl as an additional touch. That was the true and convincing answer, *not* the other. A girl would not buy mourning before she knew her lover was dead. She would be unreal—unnatural.

'And so I, in turn, staged my little drama. And the thing I hoped for happened! Nick Buckley had been very vehement about the question of a secret panel. She had declared there was no such thing. But if there were—and I did not see why Ellen should have invented it—*Nick must know of it.* Why was she so vehement? Was it possible that she had hidden the pistol there? With the secret intention of using it to throw suspicion on somebody later?

'I let her see that appearances were very black against Madame. That was as she had planned. As I foresaw, she was unable to resist the crowning proof. Besides it was safer for herself. That secret panel might be found by Ellen and the pistol in it!

'We are all safely in here. She is waiting outside for her cue. It is absolutely safe, she thinks, to take the pistol from its hiding place and put it in Madame's coat. . . .

'And so—at the last—she failed. . . .'

Frederica shivered.

'All the same,' she said. 'I'm glad I gave her my watch.'

'Yes, Madame.'

She looked up at him quickly.

'You know that too?'

'What about Ellen?' I asked, breaking in. 'Did she know or suspect anything?'

'No. I asked her. She told me that she decided to stay in the house that night because in her own phrase she "thought something was up." Apparently Nick urged her to see the fireworks rather too decisively.

She had fathomed Nick's dislike of Madame. She told me

that "she felt in her bones something was going to happen," but she thought it was going to happen to Madame. She knew Miss Nick's temper, she said, and she was always a queer little girl.'

'Yes,' murmured Frederica. 'Yes, let us think of her like that. A queer little girl. A queer little girl who couldn't help herself. . . . I shall —anyway.'

Poirot took her hand and raised it gently to his lips.

Charles Vyse stirred uneasily.

'It's going to be a very unpleasant business,' he said, quietly. 'I must see about some kind of defence for her, I suppose.'

'There will be no need, I think,' said Poirot, gently. 'Not if I am correct in my assumptions.'

He turned suddenly on Challenger.

'That's where you put the stuff, isn't it?' he said. 'In those wrist-watches.'

'I—I——' The sailor stammered at a loss.

'Do not try and deceive me—with your hearty good-fellow manner. It has deceived Hastings—but it does not deceive *me*. You make a good thing out of it, do you not—the traffic in drugs—you and your uncle in Harley Street?'

'M. Poirot.'

Challenger rose to his feet.

My little friend blinked up at him placidly.

'You are the useful "boy friend." Deny it, if you like. But I advise you, if you do not want the facts put in the hands of the police—to go.'

And to my utter amazement, Challenger did go. He went from the room like a flash.

I stared after him open-mouthed.

Poirot laughed.

'I told you so, *mon ami*. Your instincts are always wrong. *C'est épatant!*'

'Cocaine was in the wrist-watch——' I began.

'Yes, yes. That is how Mademoiselle Nick had it with her so conveniently at the nursing home. And having finished her supply in the chocolate box she asked Madame just now for hers *which was full.*'

'You mean she can't do without it?'

'*Non, non.* Mademoiselle Nick is not an addict. Sometimes—for fun—that is all. But to-night she needed it for a different purpose. It will be a full dose this time.'

'You mean——?' I gasped.

'It is the best way. Better than the hangman's rope. But pst! We must not say so before M. Vyse who is all for law and order. Officially I know nothing. The contents of the wrist-watch—it is the merest guess on my part.'

'Your guesses are always right, M. Poirot,' said Frederica.

'I must be going,' said Charles Vyse, cold disapproval in his attitude as he left the room.

Poirot looked from Frederica to Lazarus.

'You are going to get married—eh?'

'As soon as we can.'

'And indeed, M. Poirot,' said Frederica. 'I am not the drug-taker you think. I have cut myself down to a tiny dose. I think now—with happiness in front of me—I shall not need a wrist-watch any more.'

'I hope you will have happiness, Madame,' said Poirot, gently. 'You have suffered a great deal. And in spite of everything you have suffered, you have still the quality of mercy in your heart. . . .'

'I will look after her,' said Lazarus. 'My business is in a bad way, but I believe I shall pull through. And if I don't—well, Frederica does not mind being poor—with me.'

She shook her head, smiling.

'It is late,' said Poirot, looking at the clock.

We all rose.

'We have spent a strange night in this strange house,' Poirot went on. 'It is, I think, as Ellen says, an evil house. . . .'

He looked up at the picture of old Sir Nicholas.

Then, with a sudden gesture, he drew Lazarus aside.

'I ask your pardon, but, of all my questions, there is one still unanswered. Tell me, why did you offer fifty pounds for that picture? It would give me much pleasure to know—so as, you comprehend, to leave nothing unanswered.'

Lazarus looked at him with an impassive face for a minute or two. Then he smiled.

'You see, M. Poirot,' he said. 'I am a dealer.'

'Exactly.'

'That picture is not worth a penny more than twenty pounds. I knew that if I offered Nick fifty, she would immediately suspect it was worth more and would get it valued elsewhere. Then she would find that I had offered her far more than it was worth. The next time I offered to buy a picture she would not have got it valued.'

'Yes, and then?'

'The picture on the far wall is worth at least five thousand pounds,' said Lazarus drily.

'Ah!' Poirot drew a long breath.

'Now I know everything,' he said, happily.

The Body in the Library

To my friend
NAN

CHAPTER I

1

MRS. BANTRY WAS DREAMING. Her sweet peas had just taken a First at the flower show. The vicar, dressed in cassock and surplice, was giving out the prizes in church. His wife wandered past, dressed in a bathing-suit, but as is the blessed habit of dreams this fact did not arouse the disapproval of the parish in the way it would assuredly have done in real life. . . .

Mrs. Bantry was enjoying her dream a good deal. She usually did enjoy those early-morning dreams that were terminated by the arrival of early-morning tea. Somewhere in her inner consciousness was an awareness of the usual early-morning noises of the household. The rattle of the curtain-rings on the stairs as the housemaid drew them, the noises of the second housemaid's dustpan and brush in the passage outside. In the distance the heavy noise of the front-door bolt being drawn back.

Another day was beginning. In the meantime she must extract as much pleasure as possible from the flower show—for already its dream-like quality was becoming apparent. . . .

Below her was the noise of the big wooden shutters in the drawing-room being opened. She heard it, yet did not hear it. For quite half an hour longer the usual household noises would go on, discreet, subdued, not disturbing because they were so familiar. They would culminate in a swift, controlled sound of footsteps along the passage, the rustle of a print dress, the subdued chink of tea-things as the tray was deposited on the table outside, then the soft knock and the entry of Mary to draw the curtains.

In her sleep Mrs. Bantry frowned. Something disturbing was penetrating through to the dream state, something out of its time. Footsteps along the passage, footsteps that were too hurried and too soon. Her ears listened unconsciously for the chink of china, but there was no chink of china.

The knock came at the door. Automatically from the depths of her dream Mrs. Bantry said: 'Come in.' The door opened—now there would be the chink of curtain-rings as the curtains were drawn back.

But there was no chink of curtain-rings. Out of the dim green light Mary's voice came—breathless, hysterical: 'Oh, m'am, oh, m'am, *there's a body in the library*.'

And then with a hysterical burst of sobs she rushed out of the room again.

2

Mrs. Bantry sat up in bed.

Either her dream had taken a very odd turn or else—or else Mary had really rushed into the room and had said (incredible! fantastic!) that there was a body in the library.

'Impossible,' said Mrs. Bantry to herself. 'I must have been dreaming.'

But even as she said it, she felt more and more certain that she had not been dreaming, that Mary, her superior self-controlled Mary, had actually uttered those fantastic words.

Mrs. Bantry reflected a minute and then applied an urgent conjugal elbow to her sleeping spouse.

'Arthur, Arthur, wake up.'

Colonel Bantry grunted, muttered, and rolled over on his side.

'Wake up, Arthur. Did you hear what she said?'

'Very likely,' said Colonel Bantry indistinctly. 'I quite agree with you, Dolly,' and promptly went to sleep again.

Mrs. Bantry shook him.

'You've got to listen. Mary came in and said that there was a body in the library.'

'Eh, what?'

'A *body* in the *library*.'

'Who said so?'

'Mary.'

Colonel Bantry collected his scattered faculties and proceeded to deal with the situation. He said:

'Nonsense, old girl; you've been dreaming.'

'No, I haven't. I thought so, too, at first. But I haven't. She really came in and said so.'

'Mary came in and said there was a body in the library?'

'Yes.'

'But there couldn't be,' said Colonel Bantry.

'No—no, I suppose not,' said Mrs. Bantry doubtfully.

Rallying, she went on:

'But then why did Mary say there was?'

'She can't have.'

'She did.'

'You must have imagined it.'

'I didn't imagine it.'

Colonel Bantry was by now thoroughly awake and prepared to deal with the situation on its merits. He said kindly:

'You've been dreaming, Dolly, that's what it is. It's that detective story you were reading—*The Clue of the Broken Match*. You know—Lord Edgbaston finds a beautiful blonde dead on the library hearthrug. Bodies are always being found in libaries in books. I've never known a case in real life.'

'Perhaps you will now,' said Mrs. Bantry. 'Anyway, Arthur, you've got to get up and see.'

'But really, Dolly, it *must* have been a dream. Dreams often do seem wonderfully vivid when you first wake up. You feel quite sure they're true.'

'I was having quite a different sort of dream—about a flower show and the vicar's wife in a bathing-dress—something like that.'

With a sudden burst of energy Mrs. Bantry jumped out of bed and pulled back the curtains. The light of a fine autumn day flooded the room.

'I did *not* dream it,' said Mrs. Bantry firmly. 'Get up at once, Arthur, and go downstairs and see about it.'

'You want me to go downstairs and ask it there's a body in the library? I shall look a damned fool.'

'You needn't ask anything,' said Mrs. Bantry. 'If there *is* a body—and of course it's just possible that Mary's gone mad and thinks she sees things that aren't there—well, somebody will tell you soon enough. *You* won't have to say a word.'

Grumbling, Colonel Bantry wrapped himself in his dressing-gown and left the room. He went along the passage and down the staircase. At the foot of it was a little knot of huddled servants, some of them were sobbing. The butler stepped forward impressively.

'I'm glad you have come, sir. I have directed that nothing should be done until you came. Will it be in order for me to ring up the police, sir?'

'Ring 'em up about what?'

The butler cast a reproachful glance over his shoulder at the tall young woman who was weeping hysterically on the cook's shoulder.

'I understood, sir, that Mary had already informed you. She said she had done so.'

Mary gasped out:

'I was so upset I don't know what I said. It all came over me again and my legs gave way and my inside turned over. Finding it like that—oh, oh, oh!'

She subsided again on to Mrs. Eccles, who said: 'There, there, my dear,' with some relish.

'Mary is naturally somewhat upset, sir, having been the one to make the gruesome discovery,' explained the butler. 'She went into the library as usual, to draw the curtains, and—and almost stumbled over the body.'

'Do you mean to tell me,' demanded Colonel Bantry, 'that there's a dead body in my library—*my* library?'

The butler coughed.

'Perhaps, sir, you would like to see for yourself.'

3

'Hallo, 'allo, 'allo. Police station here. Yes, who's speaking?'

Police-Constable Palk was buttoning up his tunic with one hand while the other held the receiver.

'Yes, yes, Gossington Hall. Yes? Oh, good-morning, sir.' Police-Constable Palk's tone underwent a slight modification. It became less impatiently official, recognizing the generous patron of the police sports and the principal magistrate of the district.

'Yes, sir? What can I do for you?—I'm sorry, sir, I didn't quite catch—a *body*, did you say?—yes?—yes, if you please, sir—that's right, sir—young woman not known to you, you say?—quite, sir. Yes, you can leave it all to me.'

Police-Constable Palk replaced the receiver, uttered a long-drawn whistle and proceeded to dial his superior officer's number.

Mrs. Palk looked in from the kitchen whence proceeded an appetizing smell of frying bacon.

'What is it?'

'Rummest thing you ever heard of,' replied her husband. 'Body of a young woman found up at the Hall. In the Colonel's library.'

'Murdered?'

'Strangled, so he says.'

'Who was she?'

'The Colonel says he doesn't know her from Adam.'

'Then what was she doing in 'is library?'

Police-Constable Palk silenced her with a reproachful glance and spoke officially into the telephone.

'Inspector Slack? Police-Constable Palk here. A report has just come in that the body of a young woman was discovered this morning at seven-fifteen——'

4

Miss Marple's telephone rang when she was dressing. The sound of it flurried her a little. It was an unusual hour for her telephone to ring. So well ordered was her prim spinster's life that unforeseen telephone calls were a source of vivid conjecture.

'Dear me,' said Miss Marple, surveying the ringing instrument with perplexity. 'I wonder who that can be?'

Nine o'clock to nine-thirty was the recognized time for the village to make friendly calls to neighbours. Plans for the day, invitations and so on were always issued then. The butcher had been known to ring up just before nine if some crisis in the meat trade had occurred. At intervals during the day spasmodic calls might occur, though it was considered bad form to ring up after nine-thirty at night. It was true that Miss Marple's nephew, a writer, and therefore erratic, had been known to ring up at the most peculiar times, once as late as ten minutes to midnight. But whatever Raymond West's eccentricities, early rising was not one of them. Neither he nor anyone of Miss Marple's acquaintance would be likely to ring up before eight in the morning. Actually a quarter to eight.

Too early even for a telegram, since the post office did not open until eight.

'It must be,' Miss Marple decided, 'a wrong number.'

Having decided this, she advanced to the impatient instrument and quelled its clamour by picking up the receiver. 'Yes?' she said.

'Is that you, Jane?'

Miss Marple was much surprised.

'Yes, it's Jane. You're up very early, Dolly.'

Mrs. Bantry's voice came breathless and agitated over the wires.

'The most awful thing has happened.'

'Oh, my dear.'

'We've just found a body in the library.'

For a moment Miss Marple thought her friend had gone mad.

'You've found a *what?*'

'I know. One doesn't believe it, does one? I mean, I thought they only happened in books. I had to argue for hours with Arthur this morning before he'd even go down and see.'

Miss Marple tried to collect herself. She demanded breathlessly: 'But whose body is it?'

'It's a blonde.'

'A what?'

'A blonde. A beautiful blonde—like books again. None of us have ever seen her before. She's just lying there in the library, dead. That's why you've got to come up at once.'

'You want *me* to come up?'

'Yes, I'm sending the car down for you.'

Miss Marple said doubtfully:

'Of course, dear, if you think I can be of any comfort to you——'

'Oh, I don't want comfort. But you're so good at bodies.'

'Oh no, indeed. My little successes have been mostly theoretical.'

'But you're very good at murders. She's been murdered, you see, strangled. What I feel is that if one has got to have a murder actually happening in one's house, one might as well enjoy it, if you know what I mean. That's why I want you to come and help me find out who did it and unravel the mystery and all that. It really *is* rather thrilling, isn't it?'

'Well, of course, my dear, if I can be of any *help* to you.'

'Splendid! Arthur's being rather difficult. He seems to think I shouldn't enjoy myself about it at all. Of course, I do know it's very sad and all that, but then I don't know the girl—and when you've seen her you'll understand what I mean when I say she doesn't look *real* at all.'

5

A little breathless, Miss Marple alighted from the Bantrys' car, the door of which was held open for her by the chauffeur.

Colonel Bantry came out on the steps, and looked a little surprised.

'Miss Marple?—er—very pleased to see you.'

'Your wife telephoned to me,' explained Miss Marple.

'Capital, capital. She ought to have someone with her. She'll crack up otherwise. She's putting a good face on things at the moment, but you know what it is——'

At this moment Mrs. Bantry appeared, and exclaimed:

'Do go back into the dining-room and eat your breakfast, Arthur. Your bacon will get cold.'

'I thought it might be the Inspector arriving,' explained Colonel Bantry.

'He'll be here soon enough,' said Mrs. Bantry. 'That's why it's important to get your breakfast first. You need it.'

'So do you. Much better come and eat something, Dolly——'

'I'll come in a minute,' said Mrs. Bantry. 'Go on, Arthur.'

Colonel Bantry was shooed back into the dining-room rather like a recalcitrant hen.

'*Now!*' said Mrs. Bantry with an intonation of triumph. 'Come on.'

She led the way rapidly along the long corridor to the east of the house. Outside the library door Constable Palk stood on guard. He intercepted Mrs. Bantry with a show of authority.

'I'm afraid nobody is allowed in, madam. Inspector's orders.'

'Nonsense, Palk,' said Mrs. Bantry. 'You know Miss Marple perfectly well.'

Constable Palk admitted to knowing Miss Marple.

'It's very important that she should see the body,' said Mrs. Bantry. 'Don't be stupid, Palk. After all, it's *my* library, isn't it?'

Constable Palk gave way. His habit of giving in to the gentry was lifelong. The Inspector, he reflected, need never know about it.

'Nothing must be touched or handled in any way,' he warned the ladies.

'Of course not,' said Mrs. Bantry impatiently. 'We know *that*. You can come in and watch, if you like.'

Constable Palk availed himself of this permission. It had been his intention, anyway.

Mrs. Bantry bore her friend triumphantly across the library to the big old-fashioned fireplace. She said, with a dramatic sense of climax: 'There!'

Miss Marple understood then just what her friend had meant when she said the dead girl wasn't real. The library was a room very typical of its owners. It was large and shabby and untidy. It had big sagging arm-chairs, and pipes and books and estate papers laid out on the big table. There were one or two good old family portraits on the walls, and some bad Victorian water-colours, and some would-be-funny hunting scenes. There was a big vase of Michaelmas daisies in the corner. The whole room was dim and mellow and casual. It spoke of long occupation and familiar use and of links with tradition.

And across the old bearskin hearthrug there was sprawled something new and crude and melodramatic.

The flamboyant figure of a girl. A girl with unnaturally fair hair dressed up off her face in elaborate curls and rings. Her thin body was dressed in a backless evening dress of white spangled satin. The face was heavily made up, the powder standing out grotesquely on its blue swollen surface, the mascara of the lashes lying thickly on the distorted cheeks, the scarlet of the lips looking like a gash. The fingernails were enamelled in a deep blood-red and so were the toenails in their cheap silver sandal shoes. It was a cheap, tawdry, flamboyant figure—most incongruous in the solid old-fashioned comfort of Colonel Bantry's library.

Mrs. Bantry said in a low voice:

'You see what I mean? It just isn't *true*!'

The old lady by her side nodded her head. She looked down long and thoughtfully at the huddled figure.

She said at last in a gentle voice:

'She's very young.'

'Yes—yes—I suppose she is.' Mrs. Bantry seemed almost surprised—like one making a discovery.

Miss Marple bent down. She did not touch the girl. She looked at the fingers that clutched frantically at the front of the girl's dress, as though she had clawed it in her last frantic struggle for breath.

There was the sound of a car scrunching on the gravel outside. Constable Palk said with urgency:

'That'll be the Inspector. . . .'

True to his ingrained belief that the gentry didn't let you down, Mrs. Bantry immediately moved to the door. Miss Marple followed her. Mrs. Bantry said:

'That'll be all right, Palk.'

Constable Palk was immensely relieved.

6

Hastily downing the last fragments of toast and marmalade with a drink of coffee, Colonel Bantry hurried out into the hall and was relieved to see Colonel Melchett, the Chief Constable of the county, descending from a car with Inspector Slack in attendance. Melchett was a friend of the Colonel's. Slack he had never much taken to—an energetic man who belied his name and who accompanied his bustling manner with a good deal of disregard for the feelings of any one he did not consider important.

'Morning, Bantry,' said the Chief Constable. 'Thought I'd better come along myself. This seems an extraordinary business.'

'It's—it's——' Colonel Bantry struggled to express himself. 'It's *incredible—fantastic*!'

'No idea who the woman is?'

'Not in the slightest. Never set eyes on her in my life.'

'Butler know anything?' asked Inspector Slack.

'Lorrimer is just as taken aback as I am.'

'Ah,' said Inspector Slack. 'I wonder.'

Colonel Bantry said:

'There's breakfast in the dining-room, Melchett, if you'd like anything?'

'No, no—better get on with the job. Haydock ought to be here any minute now—ah, here he is.'

Another car drew up and big, broad-shouldered Doctor Haydock, who was also the police surgeon, got out. A second police car had disgorged two plain-clothes men, one with a camera.

'All set—eh?' said the Chief Constable. 'Right. We'll go along. In the library, Slack tells me.'

Colonel Bantry groaned.

'It's incredible! You know, when my wife insisted this morning that the housemaid had come in and said there was a body in the library, I just wouldn't believe her.'

'No, no, I can quite understand that. Hope your missus isn't too badly upset by it all?'

'She's been wonderful—really wonderful. She's got old Miss Marple up here with her—from the village, you know.'

'Miss Marple?' The Chief Constable stiffened. 'Why did she send for her?'

'Oh, a woman wants another woman—don't you think so?'

Colonel Melchett said with a slight chuckle:

'If you ask me, your wife's going to try her hand at a little amateur detecting. Miss Marple's quite the local sleuth. Put it over us properly once, didn't she, Slack?'

Inspector Slack said: 'That was different.'

'Different from what?'

'That was a local case, that was, sir. The old lady knows everything that goes on in the village, that's true enough. But she'll be out of her depth here.'

Melchett said dryly: 'You don't know very much about it yourself yet, Slack.'

'Ah, you wait, sir. It won't take me long to get down to it.'

7

In the dining-room Mrs. Bantry and Miss Marple, in their turn, were partaking of breakfast.

After waiting on her guest, Mrs. Bantry said urgently:

'Well, Jane?'

Miss Marple looked up at her, slightly bewildered.

Mrs. Bantry said hopefully:

'Doesn't it *remind* you of anything?'

For Miss Marple had attained fame by her ability to link up trivial village happenings with graver problems in such a way as to throw light upon the latter.

'No,' said Miss Marple thoughtfully, 'I can't say that it does—not at the moment. I was reminded a little of Mrs. Chetty's youngest—Edie, you know—but I think that was just because this poor girl bit her nails and her front teeth stuck out a little. Nothing more than that. And, of course,' went on Miss Marple, pursuing the parallel further, 'Edie was fond of what I call cheap finery, too.'

'You mean her dress?' said Mrs. Bantry.

'Yes, a very tawdry satin—poor quality.'

Mrs. Bantry said:

'I know. One of those nasty little shops where everything is a guinea.' She went on hopefully:

'Let me see, what happened to Mrs. Chetty's Edie?'

'She's just gone into her second place—and doing very well, I believe.'

Mrs. Bantry felt slightly disappointed. The village parallel didn't seem to be exactly hopeful.

'What I can't make out,' said Mrs. Bantry, 'is what she could possibly be doing in Arthur's study. The window was forced, Palk tells me. She might have come down here with a burglar and then they quarrelled—but that seems such nonsense, doesn't it?'

'She was hardly dressed for burglary,' said Miss Marple thoughtfully.

'No, she was dressed for dancing—or a party of some kind. But there's nothing of that kind down here—or anywhere near.'

'N-n-o,' said Miss Marple doubtfully.

Mrs. Bantry pounced.

'Something's in your mind, Jane.'

'Well, I was just wondering——'

'Yes?'

'Basil Blake.'

Mrs. Bantry cried impulsively: 'Oh, no!' and added as though in explanation, 'I know his mother.'

The two women looked at each other.

Miss Marple sighed and shook her head.

'I quite understand how you feel about it.'

'Selina Blake is the nicest woman imaginable. Her herbaceous borders are simply marvellous—they make me green with envy. And she's frightfully generous with cuttings.'

Miss Marple, passing over these claims to consideration on the part of Mrs. Blake, said:

'All the same, you know, there has been a lot of *talk*.'

'Oh, I know—I know. And of course Arthur goes simply livid

when he hears Basil Blake mentioned. He was really *very* rude to Arthur, and since then Arthur won't hear a good word for him. He's got that silly slighting way of talking that these boys have nowadays—sneering at people sticking up for their school or the Empire or that sort of thing. And then, of course, the *clothes* he wears!

'People say,' continued Mrs. Bantry, 'that it doesn't matter what you wear in the country. I never heard such nonsense. It's just in the country that everyone notices.' She paused, and added wistfully: 'He was an adorable baby in his bath.'

'There was a lovely picture of the Cheviot murderer as a baby in the paper last Sunday,' said Miss Marple.

'Oh, but Jane, you don't think *he*——'

'No, no, dear. I didn't mean that at all. That would indeed be jumping to conclusions. I was just trying to account for the young woman's presence down here. St. Mary Mead is such an unlikely place. And then it seemed to me that the only possible explanation was Basil Blake. He *does* have parties. People came down from London and from the studios—you remember last July? Shouting and singing—the most *terrible* noise—every one very drunk, I'm afraid—and the mess and the broken glass next morning simply unbelievable—so old Mrs. Berry told me—and a young woman asleep in the bath with practically *nothing on*!'

Mrs. Bantry said indulgently:

'I suppose they were film people.'

'Very likely. And then—what I expect you've heard—several week-ends lately he's brought down a young woman with him—a platinum blonde.'

Mrs. Bantry exclaimed:

'You don't think it's *this* one?'

'Well—I wondered. Of course, I've never seen her close to—only just getting in and out of the car—and once in the cottage garden when she was sunbathing with just some shorts and a brassière. I never really saw her *face*. And all these girls with their make-up and their hair and their nails look so alike.'

'Yes. Still, it *might* be. It's an idea, Jane.'

CHAPTER II

1

IT WAS AN IDEA that was being at that moment discussed by Colonel Melchett and Colonel Bantry.

The Chief Constable, after viewing the body and seeing his subordinates set to work on their routine tasks, had adjourned with the master of the house to the study in the other wing of the house.

Colonel Melchett was an irascible-looking man with a habit of tugging at his short red moustache. He did so now, shooting a perplexed sideways glance at the other man. Finally, he rapped out:

'Look here, Bantry, got to get this off my chest. Is it a fact that you don't know from Adam who this girl is?'

The other's answer was explosive, but the Chief Constable interrupted him.

'Yes, yes, old man, but look at it like this. Might be deuced awkward for you. Married man—fond of your missus and all that. But just between ourselves—if you *were* tied up with this girl in any way, better say so *now*. Quite natural to want to suppress the fact—should feel the same myself. But it won't do. Murder case. Facts bound to come out. Dash it all, I'm not suggesting *you* strangled the girl—not the sort of thing you'd do—*I* know that. But, after all, she came here—to this house. Put it she broke in and was waiting to see you, and some bloke or other followed her down and did her in. Possible, you know. See what I mean?'

'Damn it all, Melchett, I tell you I've never set eyes on that girl in my life! I'm not that sort of man.'

'That's all right, then. Shouldn't blame you, you know. Man of the world. Still, if you say, so—— Question is, what was she doing down here? She doesn't come from these parts—that's quite certain.'

'The whole thing's a nightmare,' fumed the angry master of the house.

'The point is, old man, what was she doing in your library?'

'How should I know? *I* didn't ask her here.'

'No, no. But she *came* here, all the same. Looks as though she wanted to see you. You haven't had any odd letters or anything?'

'No, I haven't.'

Colonel Melchett inquired delicately:

'What were you doing yourself last night?'

'I went to the meeting of the Conservative Association. Nine o'clock, at Much Benham.'

'And you got home when?'

'I left Much Benham just after ten—had a bit of trouble on the way home, had to change a wheel. I got back at a quarter to twelve.'

'You didn't go into the library?'

'No.'

'Pity.'

'I was tired. I went straight up to bed.'

'Anyone waiting up for you?'

'No. I always take the latchkey. Lorrimer goes to bed at eleven unless I give orders to the contrary.'

'Who shuts up the library?'

'Lorrimer. Usually about seven-thirty this time of year.'

'Would he go in there again during the evening?'

'Not with my being out. He left the tray with whisky and glasses in the hall.'

'I see. What about your wife?'

'I don't know. She was in bed when I got home and fast asleep. She may have sat in the library yesterday evening or in the drawing-room. I forgot to ask her.'

'Oh well, we shall soon know all the details. Of course, it's possible one of the servants may be concerned, eh?'

Colonel Bantry shook his head.

'I don't believe it. They're all a most respectable lot. We've had 'em for years.'

Melchett agreed.

'Yes, it doesn't seem likely that they're mixed up in it. Looks more as though the girl came down from town—perhaps with some young fellow. Though why they wanted to break into this house——'

Bantry interrupted.

'London. That's more like it. We don't have goings on down here—at least——'

'Well, what is it?'

'Upon my word!' exploded Colonel Bantry. 'Basil Blake!'

'Who's he?'

'Young fellow connected with the film industry. Poisonous young brute. My wife sticks up for him because she was at school with his mother, but of all the decadent useless young jackanapes! Wants his behind kicked! He's taken that cottage on the Lansham Road—you know—ghastly modern bit of building. He has parties there, shrieking, noisy crowds, and he has girls down for the week-end.'

'Girls?'

'Yes, there was one last week—one of these platinum blondes——'

The Colonel's jaw dropped.

'A platinum blonde, eh?' said Melchett reflectively.

'Yes. I say, Melchett, you don't think——'

The Chief Constable said briskly:

It's a possibility. It accounts for a girl of this type being in St. Mary Mead. I think I'll run along and have a word with this young fellow—Braid—Blake—what did you say his name was?'

'Blake. Basil Blake?'

'Will he be at home, do you know?'

'Let me see. What's to-day—Saturday? Usually gets here some time Saturday morning.'

Melchett said grimly:

'We'll see if we can find him.'

2

Basil Blake's cottage, which consisted of all modern conveniences enclosed in a hideous shell of half timbering and sham Tudor, was known to the postal authorities, and to William Booker, builder, as 'Chatsworth'; to Basil and his friends as 'The Period Piece,' and to the village of St. Mary Mead at large as 'Mr. Booker's new house.'

It was little more than a quarter of a mile from the village proper, being situated on a new building estate that had been bought by the enterprising Mr. Booker just beyond the Blue Boar, with frontage on what had been a particularly unspoilt country lane. Gossington Hall was about a mile farther on along the same road.

Lively interest had been aroused in St. Mary Mead when news went round that 'Mr. Booker's new house' had been bought by a film star. Eager watch was kept for the first appearance of the legendary creature in the village, and it may be said that as far as appearances went Basil Blake was all that could be asked for. Little star—not even a film actor. He was a very junior person, rejoicing in the title of about fifteenth in the list of those responsible for Set Decorations at Lenville Studios, headquarters of British New Era Films. The village maidens lost interest, and the ruling class of censorious spinisters took exception to Basil Blake's way of life. Only the landlord of the Blue Boar continued to be enthusiastic about Basil and Basil's friends. The revenues of the Blue Boar had increased since the young man's arrival in the place.

The police car stopped outside the distorted rustic gate of Mr. Booker's fancy, and Colonel Melchett, with a glance of distaste at the excessive half timbering of Chatsworth, strode up to the front door and attacked it briskly with the knocker.

It was opened much more promptly than he had expected. A young man with straight, somewhat long, black hair, wearing orange corduroy trousers and a royal-blue shirt, snapped out: 'Well, what do you want?'

'Are you Mr. Basil Blake?'

'Of course I am.'

'I should be glad to have a few words with you, if I may, Mr. Blake?'

'Who are you?'

'I am Colonel Melchett, the Chief Constable of the County.'

Mr. Blake said insolently:

'You don't say so; how amusing!'

And Colonel Melchett, following the other in, understood what Colonel Bantry's reactions had been. The toe of his own boot itched.

Containing himself, however, he said with an attempt to speak pleasantly:

'You're an early riser, Mr. Blake.'

'Not at all. I haven't been to bed yet.'

'Indeed.'

'But I don't suppose you've come here to inquire into my hours of bedgoing—or if you have it's rather a waste of the county's time and money. What is it you want to speak to me about?'

Colonel Melchett cleared his throat.

"I understand, Mr. Blake, that last week-end you had a visitor—a—er—fair-haired young lady.'

Basil Blake stared, threw back his head and roared with laughter.

'Have the old cats been on to you from the village? About my morals? Damn it all, morals aren't a police matter. *You* know that.'

'As you say,' said Melchett dryly, 'your morals are no concern of mine. I have come to you because the body of a fair-haired young woman of slightly—er—exotic appearance has been found—murdered.'

'Strewth!' Blake stared at him. 'Where?'

'In the library at Gossington Hall.'

'At Gossington? At old Bantry's? I say, that's pretty rich. Old Bantry! The dirty old man!'

Colonel Melchett went very red in the face. He said sharply through the renewed mirth of the young man opposite him: 'Kindly control your tongue, sir. I came to ask you if you can throw any light on this business.'

'You've come round to ask me if I've missed a blonde? Is that it? Why should—hallo, 'allo, 'allo, what's this?'

A car had drawn up outside with a scream of brakes. Out of it tumbled a young woman dressed in flapping black-and-white pyjamas. She had scarlet lips, blackened eyelashes, and a platinum-blonde head. She strode up to the door, flung it open, and exclaimed angrily:

'Why did you run out on me, you brute?'

Basil Blake had risen.

'So there you are! Why shouldn't I leave you? I told you to clear out and you wouldn't.'

'Why the hell should I because you told me to? I was enjoying myself.'

'Yes—with that filthy brute Rosenberg. You know what *he's* like.'

'You were jealous, that's all.'

'Don't flatter yourself. I hate to see a girl I like who can't hold her drink and lets a disgusting Central European paw her about.'

'That's a damned lie. You were drinking pretty hard yourself—and going on with the black-haired Spanish bitch.'

'If I take you to a party I expect you to be able to behave yourself.'

'And I refuse to be dictated to, and that's that. You said we'd go to the party and come on down here afterwards. I'm not going to leave a party before I'm ready to leave it.'

'No—and that's why I left you flat. I was ready to come down here and I came. I don't hang round waiting for any fool of a woman.'

'Sweet, polite person you are!'

'You seem to have followed me down all right!'

'I wanted to tell you what I thought of you!'

'If you think you can boss me, my girl, you're wrong!'

'And if you think you can order me about, you can think again!'

They glared at each other.

It was at this moment that Colonel Melchett seized his opportunity, and cleared his throat loudly.

Basil Blake swung round on him.

'Hallo, I forgot you were here. About time you took yourself off, isn't it? Let me introduce you—Dinah Lee—Colonel Blimp of the County Police. And now, Colonel, that you've seen my blonde is alive and in good condition, perhaps you'll get on with the good work concerning old Bantry's little bit of fluff. Good-morning!'

Colonel Melchett said:

'I advise you to keep a civil tongue in your head, young man, or you'll let yourself in for trouble,' and stumped out, his face red and wrathful.

CHAPTER III

1

IN HIS OFFICE at Much Benham, Colonel Melchett received and scrutinized the reports of his subordinates.

'. . . so it all seems clear enough, sir,' Inspector Slack was concluding: 'Mrs. Bantry sat in the library after dinner and went to bed just before ten. She turned out the lights when she left the room and, presumably, no one entered the room afterwards. The servants went to bed at half-past ten and Lorrimer, after putting the drinks in the hall, went to bed at a quarter to eleven. Nobody heard anything out of the usual except the third housemaid, and she heard too much! Groans and a blood-curdling yell and sinister footsteps and I don't know what. The second housemaid who shares a room with her says the other girl slept all night through without a sound. It's those ones that make up things that cause us all the trouble.'

'What about the forced window?'

'Amateur job, Simmons says; done with a common chisel—ordinary pattern—wouldn't have made much noise. Ought to be a chisel about the house but nobody can find it. Still, that's common enough where tools are concerned.'

'Think any of the servants know anything?'

Rather unwillingly Inspector Slack replied:

'No, sir, I don't think they do. They all seemed very shocked and upset. I had my suspicions of Lorrimer—reticent, he was, if you know what I mean—but I don't think there's anything in it.'

Melchett nodded. He attached no importance to Lorrimer's reticence. The energetic Inspector Slack often produced that effect on people he interrogated.

The door opened and Dr. Haydock came in.

'Thought I'd look in and give you the rough gist of things.'

'Yes, yes, glad to see you. Well?'

'Nothing much. Just what you'd think. Death was due to strangulation. Satin waistband of her own dress, which was passed round the neck and crossed at the back. Quite easy and simple to do. Wouldn't have needed great strength—that is, if the girl were taken by surprise. There are no signs of a struggle.'

'What about time of death?'

'Say, between ten o'clock and midnight.'

'You can't get nearer than that?'

Haydock shook his head with a slight grin.

'I won't risk my professional reputation. Not earlier than ten and not later than midnight.'

'And your own fancy inclines to which time?'

'Depends. There was a fire in the grate—the room was warm—all that would delay rigor and cadaveric stiffening.'

'Anything more you can say about her?'

'Nothing much. She was young—about seventeen or eighteen, I should say. Rather immature in some ways but well developed muscularly. Quite a healthy specimen. She was virgo intacta, by the way.' And with a nod of his head the doctor left the room.

Melchett said to the Inspector:

'You're quite sure she'd never been seen before at Gossington?'

'The servants are positive of that. Quite indignant about it. They'd have remembered if they'd ever seen her about in the neighbourhood, they say.'

'I expect they would,' said Melchett. 'Anyone of that type sticks out a mile round here. Look at that young woman of Blake's.'

'Pity it wasn't her,' said Slack; 'then we should be able to get on a bit.'

'It seems to me this girl must have come down from London,' said the Chief Constable thoughtfully. 'Don't believe there will be any local leads. In that case, I suppose, we should do well to call in the Yard. It's a case for them, not for us.'

'Something must have brought her down here, though,' said Slack. He added tentatively: 'Seems to me, Colonel and Mrs. Bantry *must* know something—of course, I know they're friends of yours, sir——'

Colonel Melchett treated him to a cold stare.

He said stiffly:

'You may rest assured that I'm taking every possibility into account. *Every* possibility.' He went on: 'You've looked through the list of persons reported missing, I suppose?'

Slack nodded. He produced a typed sheet.

'Got 'em here. Mrs. Saunders, reported missing a week ago, dark-haired, blue eyed, thirty-six. 'Tisn't her—and, anyway, everyone knows except her husband that she's gone off with a fellow from Leeds—commercial. Mrs. Barnard—she's sixty-five. Pamela Reeves, sixteen, missing from her home last night, had attended Girl Guide rally, dark-brown hair in pigtail, five feet five——'

Melchett said irritably:

'Don't go on reading idiotic details, Slack. This wasn't a schoolgirl. In my opinion——'

He broke off as the telephone rang. 'Hallo—yes—yes, Much Benham Police Headquarters—what? Just a minute——'

He listened and wrote rapidly. Then he spoke again, a new tone in his voice:

'Ruby Keene, eighteen, occupation professional dancer, five feet four inches, slender, platinum-blonde hair, blue eyes, *retroussé* nose, believed to be wearing white diamante evening-dress, silver sandal shoes. Is that right? What? Yes, not a doubt of it, I should say. I'll send Slack over at once.'

He rang off and looked at his subordinate with rising excitement. 'We've got it, I think. That was the Glenshire Police (Glenshire was the adjoining county). Girl reported missing from the Majestic Hotel, Danemouth.'

'Danemouth,' said Inspector Slack. 'That's more like it.'

Danemouth was a large and fashionable watering-place on the coast not far away.

'It's only a matter of eighteen miles or so from here,' said the Chief Constable. 'The girl was a dance hostess or something at the Majestic. Didn't come on to do her turn last night and the management were very fed up about it. When she was still missing this morning one of the other girls got the wind up about her, or someone else did. It sounds a bit obscure. You'd better go over to Danemouth at once, Slack. Report there to Superintendent Harper, and co-operate with him.'

2

Activity was always to Inspector Slack's taste. To rush off in a car, to silence rudely those people who were anxious to tell him things, to cut short conversations on the plea of urgent necessity. All this was the breath of life to Slack.

In an incredibly short time, therefore, he had arrived at Danemouth, reported at police headquarters, had a brief interview with a distracted and apprehensive hotel manager, and, leaving the latter with the doubtful comfort of—'got to make sure it *is* the girl, first, before we start raising the wind'—was driving back to Much Benham in company with Ruby Keene's nearest relative.

He had put through a short call to Much Benham before leaving Danemouth, so the Chief Constable was prepared for his arrival, though not perhaps for the brief introduction of: 'This is Josie, sir.'

Colonel Melchett stared at his subordinate coldly. His feeling was that Slack had taken leave of his senses.

The young woman who had just got out of the car came to the rescue.

'That's what I'm known as professionally,' she explained with a momentary flash of large, handsome white teeth. 'Raymond and Josie, my partner and I call ourselves, and, of course, all the hotel know me as Josie. Josephine Turner's my real name.'

Colonel Melchett adjusted himself to the situation and invited

Miss Turner to sit down, meanwhile casting a swift, professional glance over her.

She was a good-looking young woman of perhaps nearer thirty than twenty, her looks depending more on skilful grooming than actual features. She looked competent and good-tempered, with plenty of common sense. She was not the type that would ever be described as glamorous, but she had nevertheless plenty of attraction. She was discreetly made up and wore a dark tailor-made suit. Though she looked anxious and upset she was not, the Colonel decided, particularly grief-stricken.

As she sat down she said: 'It seems too awful to be true. Do you really think it's Ruby?'

'That, I'm afraid, is what we've got to ask you to tell us. I'm afraid it may be rather unpleasant for you.'

Miss Turner said apprehensively:

'Does she—does she—look very terrible?'

'Well—I'm afraid it may be rather a shock to you.' He handed her his cigarette-case and she accepted one gratefully.

'Do—do you want me to look at her right away?'

'It would be best, I think, Miss Turner. You see, it's not much good asking you questions until we're sure. Best get it over, don't you think?'

'All right.'

They drove down to the mortuary.

When Josie came out after a brief visit, she looked rather sick.

'It's Ruby all right,' she said shakily. 'Poor kid! Goodness, I do feel queer. There isn't'—she looked round wistfully—'any gin?'

Gin was not available, but brandy was, and after gulping a little down Miss Turner regained her composure. She said frankly:

'It gives you a turn, doesn't it, seeing anything like that? Poor little Rube! What swine men are, aren't they?'

'You believe it was a man?'

Josie looked slightly taken aback.

'Wasn't it? Well, I mean—I naturally thought——'

'Any special man you were thinking of?'

She shook her head vigorously.

'No—not me. I haven't the least idea. Naturally Ruby wouldn't have let on to me if——'

'If what?'

Josie hesitated.

'Well—if she'd been—going about with anyone.'

Melchett shot her a keen glance. He said no more until they were back at his office. Then he began:

'Now, Miss Turner, I want all the information you can give me.'

'Yes, of course. Where shall I begin?'

'I'd like the girl's full name and address, her relationship to you and all you know about her.'

Josephine Turner nodded. Melchett was confirmed in his opinion that she felt no particular grief. She was shocked and distressed but no more. She spoke readily enough.

'Her name was Ruby Keene—her professional name, that is. Her real name was Rosy Legge. Her mother was my mother's cousin. I've known her all my life, but not particularly well, if you know what I mean. I've got a lot of cousins—some in business, some on the stage. Ruby was more or less training for a dancer. She had some good engagements last year in panto and that sort of thing. Not really classy, but good provincial companies. Since then she's been engaged as one of the dancing partners at the Palais de Danse in Brixwell—South London. It's a nice respectable place and they look after the girls well, but there isn't much money in it.' She paused.

Colonel Melchett nodded.

'Now this is where I come in. I've been dance and bridge hostess at the Majestic in Danemouth for three years. It's a good job, well paid and pleasant to do. You look after people when they arrive—size them up, of course—some like to be left alone and others are lonely and want to get into the swing of things. You try to get the right people together for bridge and all that, and get the young people dancing with each other. It needs a bit of tact and experience.'

Again Melchett nodded. He thought that this girl would be good at her job; she had a pleasant, friendly way with her and was, he thought, shrewd without being in the least intellectual.

'Besides that,' continued Josie, 'I do a couple of exhibition dances every evening with Raymond. Raymond Starr—he's the tennis and dancing pro. Well, as it happens, this summer I slipped on the rocks bathing one day and gave my ankle a nasty turn.'

Melchett had noticed that she walked with a slight limp.

'Naturally that put the stop to dancing for a bit and it was rather awkward. I didn't want the hotel to get someone else in my place. That's always a danger'—for a minute her good-natured blue eyes were hard and sharp; she was the female fighting for existence—'that they may queer your pitch, you see. So I thought of Ruby and suggested to the manager that I should get her down. I'd carry on with the hostess business and the bridge and all that. Ruby would just take on the dancing. Keep it in the family, if you see what I mean?'

Melchett said he saw.

'Well, they agreed, and I wired to Ruby and she came down. Rather a chance for her. Much better class than anything she'd ever done before. That was about a month ago.'

Colonel Melchett said:

'I understand. And she was a success?'

'Oh, yes,' Josie said carelessly, 'she went down quite well. She doesn't dance as well as I do, but Raymond's clever and carried her through, and she was quite nice-looking, you know—slim and fair and baby-looking. Overdid the make-up a bit—I was always on at her about that. But you know what girls are. She was only eighteen, and at that age they always go and overdo it. It doesn't do for a good-class place like the Majestic. I was always ticking her off about it and getting her to tone it down.'

Melchett asked: 'People liked her?'

'Oh, yes. Mind you, Ruby hadn't got much comeback. She was a bit dumb. She went down better with the older men than with the young ones.'

'Had she got any special friend?'

The girl's eyes met his with complete understanding.

'Not in the way *you* mean. Or, at any rate, not that *I* knew about. But then, you see, she wouldn't tell me.'

Just for a moment Melchett wondered why not—Josie did not give the impression of being a strict disciplinarian. But he only said: 'Will you describe to me now when you last saw your cousin.'

'Last night. She and Raymond do two exhibition dances—one at 10.30 and the other at midnight. They finished the first one. After it, I noticed Ruby dancing with one of the young men staying in the hotel. I was playing bridge with some people in the lounge. There's a glass panel between the lounge and the ballroom. That's the last time I saw her. Just after midnight Raymond came up in a terrible taking, said where was Ruby, she hadn't turned up, and it was time to begin? I *was* vexed, I can tell you! That's the sort of silly things girls do and get the management's backs up and then they get the sack! I went up with him to her room, but she wasn't there. I noticed that she'd changed. The dress she'd been dancing in—a sort of pink, foamy thing with full skirts—was lying over a chair. Usually she kept the same dress on unless it was the special dance night—Wednesdays, that is.

'I'd no idea where she'd got to. We got the band to play one more foxtrot—still no Ruby, so I said to Raymond *I*'d do the exhibition dance with him. We chose one that was easy on my ankle and made it short—but it played up my ankle pretty badly all the same. It's all swollen this morning. Still Ruby didn't show up. We sat about waiting up for her until two o'clock. Furious with her, I was.

Her voice vibrated slightly. Melchett caught the note of real anger in it. Just for a moment he wondered. The reaction seemed a little more intense than was justified by the facts. He had a feeling of something deliberately left unsaid. He said:

'And this morning, when Ruby Keene had not returned and her bed had not been slept in, you went to the police?'

He knew from Slack's brief telephone message from Danemouth that that was not the case. But he wanted to hear what Josephine Turner would say.

She did not hesitate. She said: 'No, *I* didn't.'

'Why not, Miss Turner?'

Her eyes met his frankly. She said:

'*You* wouldn't—in my place!'

'You think not?'

Josie said:

'I've got my job to think about. The one thing a hotel doesn't want is scandal—especially anything that brings in the police. I didn't think anything had happened to Ruby. Not for a minute! I thought she's just made a fool of herself about some young man. I thought she'd turn up all right—and I was going to give her a good dressing down when she did! Girls of eighteen are such fools.'

Melchett pretended to glance through his notes.

'Ah, yes, I see it was a Mr. Jefferson who went to the police. One of the guests staying at the hotel?'

Josephine Turner said shortly:

'Yes.'

Colonel Melchett asked:

'What made this Mr. Jefferson do that?'

Josie was stroking the cuff of her jacket. There was a constraint in her manner. Again Colonel Melchett had a feeling that something was being withheld. She said rather sullenly:

'He's an invalid. He—he gets all het up rather easily. Being an invalid, I mean.'

Melchett passed on from that. He asked:

'Who was the young man with whom you last saw your cousin dancing?'

'His name's Bartlett. He'd been there about ten days.'

'Were they on very friendly terms?'

'Not specially, I should say. Not that *I* knew, anyway.'

Again a curious note of anger in her voice.

'What does he have to say?'

'Said that after their dance Ruby went upstairs to powder her nose.'

'That was when she changed her dress?'

'I suppose so.'

'And that is the last thing you know? After that she just——'

'Vanished,' said Josie. 'That's right.'

'Did Miss Keene know anybody in St. Mary Mead? Or in this neighbourhood?'

'I don't know. She may have done. You see, quite a lot of young men come into Danemouth to the Majestic from all round about. I wouldn't know where they lived unless they happened to mention it.'

'Did you ever hear your cousin mention Gossington?'

'Gossington?' Josie looked patently puzzled.

'Gossington Hall.'

She shook her head.

'Never heard of it.' Her tone carried conviction. There was curiosity in it too.

'Gossington Hall,' explained Colonel Melchett, 'is where her body was found.'

'Gossington Hall?' She stared. 'How extraordinary!'

Melchett thought to himself: 'Extraordinary's the word!' Aloud he said:

'Do you know a Colonel or Mrs. Bantry?'

Again Josie shook her head.

'Or a Mr. Basil Blake?'

She frowned slightly.

'I think I've heard that name. Yes, I'm sure I have—but I don't remember anything about him.'

The diligent Inspector Slack slid across to his superior officer a page torn from his note-book. On it was pencilled:

'*Col. Bantry dined at Majestic last week.*'

Melchett looked up and met the Inspector's eye. The Chief Constable flushed. Slack was an industrious and zealous officer and Melchett disliked him a good deal. But he could not disregard the challenge. The Inspector was tacitly accusing him of favouring his own class—of shielding an 'old school tie.'

He turned to Josie.

'Miss Turner, I should like you, if you do not mind, to accompany me to Gossington Hall.'

Coldly, defiantly, almost ignoring Josie's murmur of assent, Melchett's eyes met Slack's.

CHAPTER IV

1

ST. MARY MEAD was having the most exciting morning it had known for a long time.

Miss Wetherby, a long-nosed, acidulated spinster, was the first to spread the intoxicating information. She dropped in upon her friend and neighbour Miss Hartnell.

'Forgive me coming so early, dear, but I thought, perhaps, you mightn't have heard the *news*.'

'What news?' demanded Miss Hartnell. She had a deep bass voice and visited the poor indefatigably, however hard they tried to avoid her ministrations.

'About the body in Colonel Bantry's library—a *woman's* body——'

'In Colonel Bantry's *library*?'

'Yes. Isn't it *terrible*?'

'His *poor* wife.' Miss Hartnell tried to disguise her deep and ardent pleasure.

'Yes, indeed. I don't suppose she had any idea.'

Miss Hartnell observed censoriously:

'She thought too much about her garden, and not enough about her husband. You've got to keep an eye on a man—all the time—all the time,' repeated Miss Hartnell fiercely.

'I know. I know. It's really too dreadful.

'I wonder what Jane Marple will say. Do you think she knew anything about it? She's so sharp about these things.'

'Jane Marple has gone up to Gossington.'

'What? This morning?'

'Very early. Before breakfast.

'But really! I do think! Well, I mean, I think that is carrying things *too* far. We all know Jane likes to poke her nose into things—but I call this—indecent!'

'Oh, but Mrs. Bantry sent for her.'

'Mrs. Bantry *sent* for her?'

'Well, the car came—with Muswell driving it.'

'Dear me! How very peculiar. . . .'

They were silent a minute or two digesting the news.

'Whose body?' demanded Miss Hartnell.

'You know that dreadful woman who comes down with Basil Blake?'

'That terrible peroxide blonde?' Miss Hartnell was slightly behind the times. She had not yet advanced from peroxide to platinum. 'The one who lies about in the garden with practically nothing on?'

'Yes, my dear. There she was—on the hearthrug—*strangled*!'

'But what do you mean—at *Gossington*?'

Miss Wetherby nodded with infinite meaning.

'Then—Colonel Bantry *too*——?'

Again Miss Wetherby nodded.

'Oh!'

There was a pause as the ladies savoured this new addition to village scandal.

'What a wicked woman!' trumpeted Miss Hartnell with righteous wrath.

'Quite, quite abandoned, I'm afraid!'

'And Colonel Bantry—such a nice quiet man——'

Miss Wetherby said zestfully:

'Those quiet ones are often the worst. Jane Marple always says so.'

2

Mrs. Price Ridley was among the last to hear the news.

A rich and dictatorial widow, she lived in a large house next door to the vicarage. Her informant was her little maid Clara.

'A *woman*, you say, Clara? *Found dead on Colonel Bantry's hearthrug.*'

'Yes, mum. And they say, mum, as she hadn't anything on at all, mum, not a stitch!'

'That will do, Clara. It is not necessary to go into details.'

'No, mum, and they say, mum, that at first they thought it was Mr. Blake's young lady—what comes down for the week-ends with 'im to Mr. Booker's new 'ouse. But now they say it's quite a different young lady. And the fishmonger's young man, he says he'd never have believed it of Colonel Bantry—not with him handing round the plate on Sundays and all.'

'There is a lot of wickedness in the world, Clara,' said Mrs. Price Ridley. 'Let this be a warning to you.'

'Yes, mum. Mother, she never *will* let me take a place where there's a gentleman in the 'ouse.'

'That will *do*, Clara,' said Mrs. Price Ridley.

3

It was only a step from Mrs. Price Ridley's house to the vicarage.

Mrs. Price Ridley was fortunate enough to find the vicar in his study.

The vicar, a gentle, middle-aged man, was always the last to hear anything.

'Such a *terrible* thing,' said Mrs. Price Ridley, panting a little, because she had come rather fast. 'I felt I must have your advice, your counsel about it, dear vicar.'

Mr. Clement looked mildly alarmed. He said:

'Has anything happened?'

'Has anything *happened*?' Mrs. Price Ridley repeated the question dramatically. 'The most terrible scandal! None of us had any idea of it. An abandoned woman, completely unclothed, strangled on Colonel Bantry's hearthrug.'

The vicar stared. He said:

'You—you are feeling quite well?'

'No wonder you can't believe it! *I* couldn't at first. The hypocrisy of the man! All these years!'

'Please tell me exactly what all this is about.'

Mrs. Price Ridley plunged into a full-swing narrative. When she had finished Mr. Clement said mildly:

'But there is nothing, is there, to point to Colonel Bantry's being involved in this?'

'Oh, dear vicar, you are so unworldly! But I must tell you a little story. Last Thursday—or was it the Thursday before? Well, it doesn't matter—I was going up to London by the cheap day train. Colonel Bantry was in the same carriage. He looked, I thought, very abstracted. And nearly the whole way he buried himself behind *The Times*. As though, you know, he didn't want to *talk*.'

The vicar nodded with complete comprehension and possible sympathy.

'At Paddington I said good-bye. He had offered to get me a taxi, but I was taking the bus down to Oxford Street—but he got into one, and I distinctly heard him tell the driver to go to—*where do you think?*'

Mr. Clement looked inquiring.

'An address in *St. John's Wood*!'

Mrs. Price Ridley paused triumphantly.

The vicar remained completely unenlightened.

'That, I consider, *proves* it,' said Mrs. Price Ridley.

4

At Gossington, Mrs. Bantry and Miss Marple were sitting in the drawing-room.

'You know,' said Mrs. Bantry, 'I can't help feeling glad they've taken the body away. It's not *nice* to have a body in one's house.'

Miss Marple nodded. 'I know, dear. I know just how you feel.'

'You can't,' said Mrs. Bantry; 'not until you've had one. I know you had one next door once, but that's not the same thing. I only hope,' she went on, 'that Arthur won't take a dislike to the library. We sit there so much. What are you doing, Jane?'

For Miss Marple, with a glance at her watch, was rising to her feet.

'Well, I was thinking I'd go home. If there's nothing more I can do for you?'

'Don't go yet,' said Mrs. Bantry. 'The finger-print men and the photographers and most of the police have gone, I know, but I still feel something might happen. You don't want to miss anything.'

The telephone rang and she went off to answer. She returned with a beaming face.

'I told you more things would happen. That was Colonel Melchett. He's bringing the poor girl's cousin along.'

'I wonder why,' said Miss Marple.

'Oh, I suppose, to see where it happened and all that.'

'More than that, I expect,' said Miss Marple.

'What do you mean, Jane?'

'Well, I think—perhaps—he might want her to meet Colonel Bantry.'

Mrs. Bantry said sharply:

'To see if she recognizes him? I suppose—oh yes, I suppose they're bound to suspect Arthur.'

'I'm afraid so.'

'As though Arthur could have anything to do with it!'

Miss Marple was silent.

Mrs. Bantry turned on her accusingly.

'And don't quote old General Henderson—or some frightful old man who kept his housemaid—at me. Arthur isn't like that.'

'No, no, of course not.'

'No, but he *really* isn't. He's just—sometimes—a little bit silly about pretty girls who come to tennis. You know—rather fatuous and avuncular. There's no harm in it. And why shouldn't he? After all,' finished Mrs. Bantry rather obscurely, 'I've got the garden.'

Miss Marple smiled.

'You must not worry, Dolly,' she said.

'No, I don't mean to. But all the same I do a little. So does Arthur. It's upset him. All these policemen prowling about. He's gone down to the farm. Looking at pigs and things always soothes him if he's been upset. Hallo, here they are.'

The Chief Constable's car drew up outside.

Colonel Melchett came in accompanied by a smartly dressed young woman.

'This is Miss Turner, Mrs. Bantry. The cousin of the—er—victim.'

'How do you do,' said Mrs. Bantry, advancing with outstretched hand. 'All this must be rather awful for you.'

Josephine Turner said frankly: 'Oh, it is. None of it seems *real*, somehow. It's like a bad dream.'

Mrs. Bantry introduced Miss Marple.

Melchett said casually: 'Your good man about?'

'He had to go down to one of the farms. He'll be back soon.'

'Oh——' Melchett seemed rather at a loss.

Mrs. Bantry said to Josie: 'Would you like to see where—where it happened? Or would you rather not?'

Josephine said after a moment's pause:

'I think I'd like to see.'

Mrs. Bantry led her to her library with Miss Marple and Melchett following behind.

'She was there,' said Mrs. Bantry, pointing dramatically; 'on the hearthrug.'

'Oh!' Josie shuddered. But she also looked perplexed. She said, her brow creased: 'I just *can't* understand it! I *can't*!'

'Well, *we* certainly can't,' said Mrs. Bantry.

Josie said slowly:

'It isn't the sort of place——' and broke off.

Miss Marple nodded her head gently in agreement with the unfinished sentiment.

'That,' she murmured, 'is what makes it so very interesting.'

'Come now, Miss Marple,' said Colonel Melchett good-humouredly, 'haven't you got an explanation?'

'Oh yes, I've got an *explanation*,' said Miss Marple. 'Quite a feasible one. But of course it's only my own *idea*. Tommy Bond,' she continued, 'and Mrs. Martin, our new schoolmistress. She went to wind up the clock and a frog jumped out.'

Josephine Turner looked puzzled. As they all went out of the room she murmured to Mrs. Bantry: 'Is the old lady a bit funny in the head?'

'Not at all,' said Mrs. Bantry indignantly.

Josie said: 'Sorry; I thought perhaps she thought she *was* a frog or something.'

Colonel Bantry was just coming in through the side door. Melchett hailed him, and watched Josephine Turner as he introduced them to each other. But there was no sign of interest or recognition in her face. Melchett breathed a sigh of relief. Curse Slack and his insinuations!

In answer to Mrs. Bantry's questions Josie was pouring out the story of Ruby Keene's disappearance.

'Frightfully worrying for you, my dear,' said Mrs. Bantry.

'I was more angry than worried,' said Josie. 'You see, I didn't know then that anything had happened to her.'

'And yet,' said Miss Marple, 'you went to the police. Wasn't that—excuse me—rather *premature*?'

Josie said eagerly:

'Oh, but I didn't. That was Mr. Jefferson——'

Mrs. Bantry said: 'Jefferson?'

'Yes, he's an invalid.'

'Not *Conway* Jefferson? But I know him well. He's an old friend of ours. Arthur, listen—Conway Jefferson. He's staying at the Majestic, and it was he who went to the police! Isn't that a coincidence?'

Josephine Turner said:

'Mr. Jefferson was here last summer too.'

'Fancy! And we never knew. I haven't seen him for a long time.' She turned to Josie. 'How—how is he, nowadays?'

Josie considered.

'I think he's wonderful, really—quite wonderful. Considering, I mean. He's always cheerful—always got a joke.'

'Are the family there with him?'

'Mr. Gaskell, you mean? And young Mrs. Jefferson? And Peter? Oh, yes.'

There was something inhibiting Josephine Turner's usual attractive frankness of manner. When she spoke of the Jeffersons there was something not quite natural in her voice.

Mrs. Bantry said: 'They're both very nice, aren't they? The young ones, I mean.'

Josie said rather uncertainly:

'Oh yes—yes, they are. I—we—yes, they are, *really*.'

5

'And what,' demanded Mrs. Bantry as she looked through the window at the retreating car of the Chief Constable, 'did she mean by that? "They are, *really*." Don't you think, Jane, that there's something——'

Miss Marple fell upon the words eagerly.

'Oh, I do—indeed I do. It's quite *unmistakable*! Her manner changed *at once* when the Jeffersons were mentioned. She had seemed quite natural up to then.'

'But what do you think it *is*, Jane?'

'Well, my dear, *you* know them. All I feel is that there is *something*, as you say, about them which is worrying that young woman. Another thing, did you notice that when you asked her if she wasn't anxious about the girl being missing, she said that she was *angry*! And she *looked* angry—*really* angry! That strikes me as *interesting*, you know. I have a feeling—perhaps I'm wrong—that that's her main reaction to the fact of the girl's death. She didn't care for her, I'm sure. She's not grieving in any way. But I do think, very definitely, that the thought of that girl, Ruby Keene, makes her *angry*. And the interesting point is—*why?*'

'We'll find out!' said Mrs. Bantry. 'We'll go over to Danemouth and stay at the Majestic—yes, Jane, you too. I need a change for my nerves after what has happened here. A few days at the Majestic—that's what we need. And you'll meet Conway Jefferson. He's a dear—a perfect dear. It's the saddest story imaginable. Had a son and a daughter, both of whom he loved dearly. They were both married, but they still spent a lot of time at home. His wife, too, was the sweetest woman, and he was devoted to her. They were flying home one year from France and there was an accident. They were all killed: the pilot, Mrs. Jefferson, Rosamund and Frank. Conway had both legs so badly injured they had to be amputated. And he's been wonderful—his courage, his pluck! He was a very active man and now he's a helpless cripple, but he never complains. His daughter-in-law lives with him—she was a widow when Frank Jefferson married her and she had a son by her first marriage—Peter Carmody. They both live with Conway. And Mark Gaskell, Rosamund's husband, is there too most of the time. The whole thing was the most awful tragedy.'

'And now,' said Miss Marple, 'there's another tragedy——'

Mrs. Bantry said: 'Oh yes—yes—but it's nothing to do with the Jeffersons.'

'Isn't it?' said Miss Marple. 'It was Mr. Jefferson who went to the police.'

'So he did. . . . You know, Jane, that *is* curious. . . .'

CHAPTER V

1

COLONEL MELCHETT was facing a much annoyed hotel manager. With him was Superintendent Harper of the Glenshire Police and the inevitable Inspector Slack—the latter rather disgruntled at the Chief Constable's wilful usurpation of the case.

Superintendent Harper was inclined to be soothing with the almost tearful Mr. Prestcott—Colonel Melchett tended towards a blunt brutality.

'No good crying over spilt milk,' he said sharply. 'The girl's dead—strangled. You're lucky that she wasn't strangled in your hotel. This puts the inquiry in a different county and lets your establishment down extremely lightly. But certain inquiries have got to be made, and the sooner we get on with it the better. You can trust us to be discreet and tactful. So I suggest you cut the cackle and come to the horses. Just what exactly do you know about the girl?'

'I knew nothing of her—nothing at all. Josie brought her here.'

'Josie's been here some time?'

'Two years—no, three.'

'And you like her?'

'Yes, Josie's a good girl—a nice girl. Competent. She gets on with people, and smoothes over differences—bridge, you know, is a touchy sort of game——' Colonel Melchett nodded feelingly. His wife was a keen but an extremely bad bridge player. Mr. Prestcott went on: 'Josie was very good at calming down unpleasantnesses. She could handle people well—sort of bright and firm, if you know what I mean.'

Again Melchett nodded. He knew now what it was Miss Josephine Turner had reminded him of. In spite of the make-up and the smart turnout there was a distinct touch of the nursery governess about her.

'I depend upon her,' went on Mr. Prestcott. His manner became aggrieved. 'What does she want to go playing about on slippery rocks in that damn fool way? We've got a nice beach here. Why couldn't she bathe from that? Slipping and falling and breaking her ankle. It wasn't fair on *me*! I pay her to dance and play bridge and keep people happy and amused—not to go bathing off rocks and breaking her ankle. Dancers ought to be careful of their ankles—not take risks. I was very annoyed about it. It wasn't fair to the hotel.'

Melchett cut the recital short.

'And then she suggested this girl—her cousin—coming down?'

Prestcott assented grudgingly.

'That's right. It sounded quite a good idea. Mind you, I wasn't going to pay anything extra. The girl could have her keep; but as for salary, that would have to be fixed up between her and Josie. That's the way it was arranged. *I* didn't know anything about the girl.'

'But she turned out all right?'

'Oh yes, there wasn't anything wrong with her—not to look at, anyway. She was very young, of course—rather cheap in style, perhaps, for a place of this kind, but nice manners—quiet and well-behaved. Danced well. People liked her.'

'Pretty?'

It had been a question hard to answer from a view of the blue swollen face.

Mr. Prestcott considered.

'Fair to middling. Bit weaselly, if you know what I mean. Wouldn't have been much without make-up. As it was she managed to look quite attractive.'

'Many young men hanging about after her?'

'I know what you're trying to get at, sir.' Mr. Prestcott became excited. '*I* never saw anything. Nothing special. One or two of the boys hung around a bit—but all in the day's work, so to speak. Nothing in the strangling line, I'd say. She got on well with the older people, too—had a kind of prattling way with her—seemed quite a kid, if you know what I mean. It amused them.'

Superintendent Harper said in a deep melancholy voice:

'Mr. Jefferson, for instance?'

The manager agreed.

'Yes, Mr. Jefferson was the one I had in mind. She used to sit with him and his family a lot. He used to take her out for drives sometimes. Mr. Jefferson's very fond of young people and very good to them. I don't want to have any misunderstanding. Mr. Jefferson's a cripple; he can't get about much—only where his wheel-chair will take him. But he's always keen on seeing young people enjoy themselves—watches the tennis and the bathing and all that—and gives parties for young people here. He likes youth—and there's nothing bitter about him as there well might be. A very popular gentleman and, I'd say, a very fine character.

Melchett asked:

'And he took an interest in Ruby Keene?'

'Her talk amused him, I think.'

'Did his family share his liking for her?'

'They were always very pleasant to her.'

Harper said:

'And it was he who reported the fact of her being missing to the police?'

He contrived to put into the words a significance and a reproach to which the manager instantly responded.

'Put yourself in my place, Mr. Harper. *I* didn't dream for a minute anything was wrong. Mr. Jefferson came along to my office, storming, and all worked up. The girl hadn't slept in her room. She hadn't appeared in her dance last night. She must have gone for a drive and had an accident, perhaps. The police must be informed at once! Inquiries made! In a state, he was, and quite high-handed. He rang up the police station then and there.'

'Without consulting Miss Turner?'

'Josie didn't like it much. I could see that. She was very annoyed about the whole thing—annoyed with Ruby, I mean. But what could she say?'

'I think,' said Melchett, 'we'd better see Mr. Jefferson. Eh, Harper?'

Superintendent Harper agreed.

2

Mr. Prestcott went up with them to Conway Jefferson's suite. It was on the first floor, overlooking the sea. Melchett said carelessly:

'Does himself pretty well, eh? Rich man?'

'Very well off indeed, I believe. Nothing's ever stinted when he comes here. Best rooms reserved—food usually *à la carte*, expensive wines—best of everything.'

Melchett nodded.

Mr. Prestcott tapped on the outer door and a woman's voice said: 'Come in.'

The manager entered, the others behind him.

Mr. Prestcott's manner was apologetic as he spoke to the woman who turned her head at their entrance from her seat by the window.

'I am so sorry to disturb you, Mrs. Jefferson, but these gentlemen are—from the police. They are very anxious to have a word with Mr. Jefferson. Er—Colonel Melchett—Superintendent Harper, Inspector—er—Slack—Mrs. Jefferson.'

Mrs. Jefferson acknowledged the introduction by bending her head.

A plain woman, was Melchett's first impression. Then, as a slight smile came to her lips and she spoke, he changed his opinion. She had a singularly charming and sympathetic voice and her eyes, clear hazel eyes, were beautiful. She was quietly but not unbecomingly dressed and was, he judged, about thirty-five years of age.

She said:

'My father-in-law is asleep. He is not strong at all, and this affair has been a terrible shock to him. We had to have the doctor, and the doctor gave him a sedative. As soon as he wakes he will, I know, want to see you. In the meantime, perhaps I can help you? Won't you sit down?'

Mr. Prestcott, anxious to escape, said to Colonel Melchett: 'Well—er—if that's all I can do for you?' and thankfully received permission to depart.

With his closing of the door behind him, the atmosphere took on a mellow and more social quality. Adelaide Jefferson had the power of creating a restful atmosphere. She was a woman who never seemed to say anything remarkable but who succeeded in stimulating other people to talk and in setting them at their ease. She struck now the right note when she said:

'This business has shocked us all very much. We saw quite a lot of the poor girl, you know. It seems quite unbelievable. My father-in-law is terribly upset. He was very fond of Ruby.'

Colonel Melchett said:

'It was Mr. Jefferson, I understand, who reported her disappearance to the police?'

He wanted to see exactly how she would react to that. There was a flicker—just a flicker—of—annoyance? concern?—he could not say what exactly, but there was *something*, and it seemed to him she had definitely to brace herself, as though to an unpleasant task, before going on.

She said:

'Yes, that is so. Being an invalid, he gets easily upset and worried. We tried to persuade him that it was all right, that there was some natural explanation, and that the girl herself would not like the police being notified. He insisted. Well'—she made a slight gesture—'he was right and we were wrong.'

Melchett asked: 'Exactly how well did you know Ruby Keene, Mrs. Jefferson?'

She considered.

'It's difficult to say. My father-in-law is very fond of young people and likes to have them round him. Ruby was a new type to him—he was amused and interested by her chatter. She sat with us a good deal in the hotel and my father-in-law took her out for drives in the car.'

Her voice was quite non-committal. Melchett thought to himself: 'She could say more if she chose.'

He said: 'Will you tell me what you can of the course of events last night?'

'Certainly, but there is very little that will be useful, I'm afraid. After dinner Ruby came and sat with us in the lounge. She remained even after the dancing had started. We had arranged to play bridge later, but we were waiting for Mark, that is Mark Gaskell, my brother-in-law—he married Mr. Jefferson's daughter, you know—who had some important letters to write, and also for Josie. She was going to make a fourth with us.'

'Did that often happen?'

'Quite frequently. She's a first-class player, of course, and very nice. My father-in-law is a keen bridge player and whenever possible liked to get hold of Josie to make the fourth instead of an outsider. Naturally, as she has to arrange the fours, she can't always play with us, but she does whenever she can, and as'—her eyes smiled a little—'my father-in-law spends a lot of money in the hotel, the management are quite pleased for Josie to favour us.'

Melchett asked:

'You like Josie?'

'Yes, I do. She's always good-humoured and cheerful, works hard and seems to enjoy her job. She's shrewd, though not well educated, and—well—never pretends about anything. She's natural and unaffected.'

'Please go on, Mrs. Jefferson.'

'As I say, Josie had to get her bridge fours arranged and Mark was writing, so Ruby sat and talked with us a little longer than usual. Then Josie came along, and Ruby went off to do her first solo dance with Raymond—he's the dance and tennis professional. She came back to us afterwards just as Mark joined us. Then she went off to dance with a young man and we four started our bridge.'

She stopped, and made a slight insignificant gesture of helplessness.

'And that's all I know! I just caught a glimpse of her once dancing, but bridge is an absorbing game and I hardly glanced through the glass partition at the ballroom. Then, at midnight, Raymond came along to Josie very upset and asked where Ruby was. Josie, naturally, tried to shut him up but——'

Superintendent Harper interrupted. He said in his quiet voice:

'Why "*naturally*," Mrs. Jefferson?'

'Well'—she hesitated, looked, Melchett thought, a little put out—'Josie didn't want the girl's absence made too much of. She considered herself responsible for her in a way. She said Ruby was probably up in her bedroom, said the girl had talked about having a headache earlier—I don't think that was true, by the way; Josie just said it by way of excuse. Raymond went off and telephoned up to Ruby's room, but apparently there was no answer, and he came back rather in a state—temperamental, you know. Josie went off with him and tried to soothe him down, and in the end she danced with him instead of Ruby. Rather plucky of her, because you could see afterwards it had hurt her ankle. She came back to us when the dance was over and tried to calm down Mr. Jefferson. He had got worked up by then. We persuaded him in the end to go to bed, told him Ruby had probably gone for a spin in a car and that they'd had a puncture. He went to bed worried, and this morning he began to agitate at once.' She paused. 'The rest you know.'

'Thank you, Mrs. Jefferson. Now I'm going to ask you if you've any idea who could have done this thing?'

She said immediately: 'No idea whatever. I'm afraid I can't help you in the slightest.'

He pressed her. 'The girl never said anything? Nothing about jealousy? About some man she was afraid of? Or intimate with?'

Adelaide Jefferson shook her head to each query.

There seemed nothing more that she could tell them.

The Superintendent suggested that they should interview young George Bartlett and return to see Mr. Jefferson later. Colonel Melchett agreed, and the three men went out, Mrs. Jefferson promising to send word as soon as Mr. Jefferson was awake.

'Nice woman,' said the Colonel, as they closed the door behind them.

'A very nice lady indeed,' said Superintendent Harper.

3

George Bartlett was a thin, lanky youth with a prominent Adam's apple and an immense difficulty in saying what he meant. He was in such a state of dither that it was hard to get a calm statement from him.

'I say, it is awful, isn't it? Sort of thing one reads about in the Sunday papers—but one doesn't feel it really happens, don't you know?'

'Unfortunately there is no doubt about it, Mr. Bartlett,' said the Superintendent.

'No, no, of course not. But it seems so rum somehow. And miles from here and everything—in some country house, wasn't it? Awfully county and all that. Created a bit of a stir in the neighbourhood—what?'

Colonel Melchett took charge.

'How well did you know the dead girl, Mr. Bartlett?'

George Bartlett looked alarmed.

'Oh, n-n-n-ot well at all, s-s-sir. No, hardly at all—if you know what I mean. Danced with her once or twice—passed the time of day—bit of tennis—*you* know.'

'You were, I think, the last person to see her alive last night?'

'I suppose I was—doesn't it sound awful? I mean, she was perfectly all right when I saw her—absolutely.'

'What time was that, Mr. Bartlett?'

'Well, you know, I never know about time—wasn't very late, if you know what I mean.'

'You danced with her?'

'Yes—as a matter of fact—well, yes, I did. Early on in the evening, though. Tell you what, it was just after her exhibition dance with the pro. fellow. Must have been ten, half-past, eleven, I don't know.'

'Never mind the time. We can fix that. Please tell us exactly what happened.'

'Well, we danced, don't you know. Not that *I'm* much of a dancer.'

'How you dance is not really relevant, Mr. Bartlett.'

George Bartlett cast an alarmed eye on the Colonel and stammered:

'No—er—n-n-n-o, I suppose it isn't. Well, as I say, we danced, round and round, and I talked, but Ruby didn't say very much and she yawned a bit. As I say, I don't dance awfully well, and so girls—well—incline to give it a miss, if you know what I mean. She said she had a headache—I know where I get off, so I said righty ho, and that was that.'

'What was the last you saw of her?'

'She went off upstairs.'

'She said nothing about meeting anyone? Or going for a drive? Or—or—having a date?' The Colonel used the colloquial expression with a slight effort.

Bartlett shook his head.

'Not to me.' He looked rather mournful. 'Just gave me the push.'

'What was her manner? Did she seem anxious, abstracted, anything on her mind?'

George Bartlett considered. Then he shook his head.

'Seemed a bit bored. Yawned, as I said. Nothing more.'

Colonel Melchett said:

'And what did you do, Mr. Bartlett?'

'Eh?'

'What did you do when Ruby Keene left you?'

George Bartlett gaped at him.

'Let's see now—what *did* I do?'

'We're waiting for you to tell us.'

'Yes, yes—of course. Jolly difficult, remembering things, what? Let me see. Shouldn't be surprised if I went into the bar and had a drink.'

'*Did* you go into the bar and have a drink?'

'That's just it. I *did* have a drink. Don't think it was just then. Have an idea I wandered out, don't you know? Bit of air. Rather stuffy for September. Very nice outside. Yes, that's it. I strolled around a bit, then I came in and had a drink and then I strolled back to the ballroom. Wasn't much doing. Noticed what's-her-name—Josie—was dancing again. With the tennis fellow. She'd been on the sick list—twisted ankle or something.'

'That fixes the time of your return at midnight. Do you intend us to understand that you spent over an hour walking about outside?'

'Well, I had a drink, you know. I was—well, I was thinking of things.'

This statement received more incredulity than any other.

Colonel Melchett said sharply:

'What were you thinking about?'

'Oh, I don't know. Things,' said Mr. Bartlett vaguely.

'You have a car, Mr. Bartlett?'

'Oh, yes, I've got a car.'

'Where was it, in the hotel garage?'

'No, it was in the courtyard, as a matter of fact. Thought I might go for a spin, you see.'

'Perhaps you did go for a spin?'

'No—no, I didn't. Swear I didn't.'

'You didn't, for instance, take Miss Keene for a spin?'

'Oh, I say. Look here, what are you getting at? I didn't—I swear I didn't. Really, now.'

'Thank you, Mr. Bartlett, I don't think there is anything more at present. *At present*,' repeated Colonel Melchett with a good deal of emphasis on the words.

They left Mr. Bartlett looking after them with a ludicrous expression of alarm on his unintellectual face.

'Brainless young ass,' said Colonel Melchett. 'Or isn't he?'

Superintendent Harper shook his head.

'We've got a long way to go,' he said.

CHAPTER VI

1

NEITHER THE NIGHT PORTER nor the barman proved helpful. The night porter remembered ringing up to Miss Keene's room just after midnight and getting no reply. He had not noticed Mr. Bartlett leaving or entering the hotel. A lot of gentlemen and ladies were strolling in and out, the night being fine. And there were side doors off the corridor as well as the one in the main hall. He was fairly certain Miss Keene had not gone out by the main door, but if she had come down from her room, which was on the first floor, there was a staircase next to it and a door out at the end of the corridor, leading on to the side terrace. She could have gone out of that unseen easily enough. It was not locked until the dancing was over at two o'clock.

The barman remembered Mr. Bartlett being in the bar the preceding evening but could not say when. Somewhere about the middle of the evening, he thought. Mr. Bartlett had sat against the wall and was looking rather melancholy. He did not know how long he was there. There were a lot of outside guests coming and going in the bar. He had noticed Mr. Bartlett but he couldn't fix the time in any way.

2

As they left the bar, they were accosted by a small boy of about nine years old. He burst immediately into excited speech.

'I say, are you the detectives? I'm Peter Carmody. It was my grandfather, Mr. Jefferson, who rang up the police about Ruby. Are you from Scotland Yard? You don't mind my speaking to you, do you?'

Colonel Melchett looked as though he were about to return a short answer, but Superintendent Harper intervened. He spoke benignly and heartily.

'That's all right, my son. Naturally interests you, I expect?'

'You bet it does. Do you like detective stories? I do. I read them all, and I've got autographs from Dorothy Sayers and Agatha Christie and Dickson Carr and H. C. Bailey. Will the murder be in the papers?'

'It'll be in the papers all right,' said Superintendent Harper grimly.

'You see, I'm going back to school next week and I shall tell them all that I knew her—really knew her *well*.'

'What did you think of her, eh?'

Peter considered.

'Well, I didn't like her much. I think she was rather a stupid sort of girl. Mum and Uncle Mark didn't like her much either. Only Grandfather. Grandfather wants to see you, by the way. Edwards is looking for you.'

Superintendent Harper murmured encouragingly:

'So your mother and your Uncle Mark didn't like Ruby Keene much? Why was that?'

'Oh, I don't know. She was always butting in. And they didn't like Grandfather making such a fuss of her. I expect,' said Peter cheerfully, 'that they're glad she's dead.'

Superintendent Harper looked at him thoughtfully. He said: 'Did you hear them—er—say so?'

'Well, not exactly. Uncle Mark said: "Well, it's one way out, anyway," and Mums said: "Yes, but such a horrible one," and Uncle Mark said it was no good being hypocritcal.'

The men exchanged glances. At that moment a respectable, clean-shaven man, neatly dressed in blue serge, came up to them.

'Excuse me, gentlemen. I am Mr. Jefferson's valet. He is awake now and sent me to find you, as he is very anxious to see you.'

Once more they went up to Conway Jefferson's suite. In the sitting-room Adelaide Jefferson was talking to a tall, restless man who was prowling nervously about the room. He swung round sharply to view the newcomers.

'Oh, yes. Glad you've come. My father-in-law's been asking for you. He's awake now. Keep him as calm as you can, won't you? His health's not too good. It's a wonder, really, that this shock didn't do for him.'

Harper said:

'I'd no idea his health was as bad as that.'

'He doesn't know it himself,' said Mark Gaskell. 'It's his heart, you see. The doctor warned Addie that he mustn't be over-excited or startled. He more or less hinted that the end might come any time, didn't he, Addie?'

Mrs. Jefferson nodded. She said:

'It's incredible that he's rallied the way he has.'

Melchett said dryly:

'Murder isn't exactly a soothing incident. We'll be as careful as we can.'

He was sizing up Mark Gaskell as he spoke. He didn't much care for the fellow. A bold, unscrupulous, hawk-like face. One of those men who usually get their own way and whom women frequently admire.

'But not the sort of fellow I'd trust,' the Colonel thought to himself.

Unscrupulous—that was the word for him.

The sort of fellow who wouldn't stick at anything. . . .

3

In the big bedroom overlooking the sea, Conway Jefferson was sitting in his wheeled-chair by the window.

No sooner were you in the room with him than you felt the power and magnetism of the man. It was as though the injuries which had left him a cripple had resulted in concentrating the vitality of his shattered body into a narrower and more intense focus.

He had a fine head, the red of the hair slightly grizzled. The face was rugged and powerful, deeply sun-tanned, and the eyes were a startling blue. There was no sign of illness or feebleness about him. The deep lines on his face were the lines of suffering, not the lines of weakness. Here was a man who would never rail against fate but accept it and pass on to victory.

He said: 'I'm glad you've come.' His quick eyes took them in. He said to Melchett: 'You're the Chief Constable of Radfordshire? Right. And you're Superintendent Harper? Sit down. Cigarettes on the table beside you.'

They thanked him and sat down. Melchett said:

'I understand, Mr. Jefferson, that you were interested in the dead girl?'

A quick, twisted smile flashed across the lined face.

'Yes—they'll all have told you that! Well, it's no secret. How much has my family said to you?'

He looked quickly from one to the other as he asked the question.

It was Melchett who answered.

'Mrs. Jefferson told us very little beyond the fact that the girl's chatter amused you and that she was by way of being a protégée. We have only exchanged half a dozen words with Mr. Gaskell.'

Conway Jefferson smiled.

'Addie's a discreet creature, bless her. Mark would probably have been more outspoken. I think, Melchett, that I'd better tell you some facts rather fully. It's important, in order that you should understand my attitude. And, to begin with, it's necessary that I go back to the big tragedy of my life. Eight years ago I lost my wife, my son and my daughter in an aeroplane accident. Since then I've been like a man who's lost half himself—and I'm not speaking of my physical plight! I was a family man. My daughter-in-law and my son-in-law have been very good to me. They've done all they can to take the place of my flesh and blood. But I've realized—especially of late—that they have, after all, their own lives to live.

'So you must understand that, essentially, I'm a lonely man. I like young people. I enjoy them. Once or twice I've played with the idea of adopting some girl or boy. During the last month I got very friendly with the child who's been killed. She was absolutely natural—completely naïve. She chattered on about her life and her experiences—in pantomime, with touring companies, with Mum and Dad as a child in cheap lodgings. Such a different life from any I've known! Never complaining, never seeing it as sordid. Just a natural, uncomplaining, hard-working child, unspoilt and charming. Not a lady, perhaps, but, thank God, neither vulgar nor—abominable word—"lady-like".

'I got more and more fond of Ruby. I decided, gentlemen, to adopt her legally. She would become—by law—my daughter. That,

I hope, explains my concern for her and the steps I took when I heard of her unaccountable disappearance.'

There was a pause. Then Superintendent Harper, his unemotional voice robbing the question of any offence, asked: 'May I ask what your son-in-law and daughter-in-law said to that?'

Jefferson's answer came back quickly:

'What could they say? They didn't, perhaps, like it very much. It's the sort of thing that arouses prejudice. But they behaved very well—yes, very well. It's not as though, you see, they were dependent on me. When my son Frank married I turned over half my worldly goods to him then and there. I believe in that. Don't let your children wait until you're dead. They want the money when they're young, not when they're middle-aged. In the same way when my daughter Rosamund insisted on marrying a poor man, I settled a big sum of money on her. That sum passed to him at her death. So, you see, that simplified the matter from the financial angle.'

'I see, Mr. Jefferson,' said Superintendent Harper.

But there was a certain reserve in his tone. Conway Jefferson pounced upon it.

'But you don't agree, eh?'

'It's not for me to say, sir, but families, in my experience, don't always act reasonably.'

'I dare say you're right, Superintendent, but you must remember that Mr. Gaskell and Mrs. Jefferson aren't, strictly speaking, my *family*. They're not blood relations.'

'That, of course, makes a difference,' admitted the Superintendent.

For a moment Conway Jefferson's eyes twinkled. He said: 'That's not to say that they didn't think me an old fool! That *would* be the average person's reaction. But I wasn't being a fool. I know character. With education and polishing, Ruby Keene could have taken her place anywhere.'

Melchett said:

'I'm afraid we're being rather impertinent and inquisitive, but it's important that we should get at all the facts. You proposed to make full provision for the girl—that is, settle money upon her, but you hadn't already done so?'

Jefferson said:

'I understand what you're driving at—the possibility of someone's benefiting by the girl's death? But nobody could. The necessary formalities for legal adoption were under way, but they hadn't yet been completed.'

Melchett said slowly: 'Then, if anything happened to you——?'

He left the sentence unfinished, as a query. Conway Jefferson was quick to respond.

'Nothing's likely to happen to me! I'm a cripple, but I'm not an invalid. Although doctors *do* like to pull long faces and give advice about not overdoing things. Not overdoing things! I'm as strong as a horse! Still, I'm quite aware of the fatalities of life—my God, I've good reason to be! Sudden death comes to the strongest man—especially in these days of road casualties. But I'd provided for that. I made a new will about ten days ago.'

'Yes?' Superintendent Harper leaned forward.

'I left the sum of fifty thousand pounds to be held in trust for Ruby Keene until she was twenty-five, when she would come into the principal.'

Superintendent Harper's eyes opened. So did Colonel Melchett's. Harper said in an almost awed voice:

'That's a very large sum of money, Mr. Jefferson.'

'In these days, yes, it is.'

'And you were leaving it to a girl you had only known a few weeks?'

Anger flashed into the vivid blue eyes.

'Must I go on repeating the same thing over and over again? I've no flesh and blood of my own—no nieces or nephews or distant cousins, even! I might have left it to charity. I prefer to leave it to an individual.' He laughed. 'Cinderella turned into a princess overnight! A fairy-godfather instead of a fairy-godmother. Why not? It's *my* money. *I* made it.'

Colonel Melchett asked: 'Any other bequests?'

'A small legacy to Edwards, my valet—and the remainder to Mark and Addie in equal shares.'

'Would—excuse me—the residue amount to a large sum?'

'Probably not. It's difficult to say exactly, investments fluctuate all the time. The sum involved, after death duties and expenses had been paid, would probably have come to something between five and ten thousand pounds net.'

'I see.'

'And you needn't think I was treating them shabbily. As I said, I divided up my estate at the time my children married. I left myself, actually, a very small sum. But after—after the tragedy—

I wanted something to occupy my mind. I flung myself into business. At my house in London I had a private line put in connecting my bedroom with my office. I worked hard—it helped me not to think, and it made me feel that my—my mutilation had not vanquished me. I threw myself into work'—his voice took on a deeper note, he spoke more to himself than to his audience—'and, by some subtle irony, everything I did prospered! My wildest speculations succeeded. If I gambled, I won. Everything I touched turned to gold. Fate's ironic way of righting the balance, I suppose.'

The lines of suffering stood out on his face again.

Recollecting himself, he smiled wryly at them.

'So you see, the sum of money I left Ruby was indisputably mine to do with as my fancy dictated.'

Melchett said quickly:

'Undoubtedly, my dear fellow, we are not questioning that for a moment.'

Conway Jefferson said: 'Good. Now I want to ask some questions in my turn, if I may. I want to hear—more about this terrible business. All I know is that she—that little Ruby was found strangled in a house some twenty miles from here.'

'That is correct. At Gossington Hall.'

Jefferson frowned.

'Gossington? But that's——'

'Colonel Bantry's house.'

'Bantry! *Arthur Bantry?* But I know him. Know him and his wife! Met them abroad some years ago. I didn't realize they lived in this part of the world. Why, it's——'

He broke off. Superintendent Harper slipped in smoothly:

'Colonel Bantry was dining in the hotel here Tuesday of last week. You didn't see him?'

'Tuesday? Tuesday? No, we were back late. Went over to Harden Head and had dinner on the way back.'

Melchett said:

'Ruby Keene never mentioned the Bantrys to you?'

Jefferson shook his head.

'Never. Don't believe she knew them. Sure she didn't. She didn't know anybody but theatrical folk and that sort of thing.' He paused and then asked abruptly:

'What's Bantry got to say about it?'

'He can't account for it in the least. He was out at a Conservative meeting last night. The body was discovered this morning. He says he's never seen the girl in his life.'

Jefferson nodded. He said:

'It certainly seems fantastic.'

Superintendent Harper cleared his throat. He said:

'Have you any idea at all, sir, who can have done this?'

'Good God, I wish I had!' The veins stood out on his forehead. It's incredible, unimaginable! I'd say it couldn't have happened, if it hadn't happened!'

'There's no friend of hers—from her past life—no man hanging about—or threatening her?'

'I'm sure there isn't. She'd have told me if so. She's never had a regular "boy friend." She told me so herself.'

Superintendent Harper thought:

'Yes, I dare say that's what *she* told you! But that's as my be!'

Conway Jefferson went on:

'Josie would know better than anyone if there had been some man hanging about Ruby or pestering her. Can't she help?'

'She says not.'

Jefferson said, frowning:

'I can't help feeling it must be the work of some maniac—the brutality of the method—breaking into a country house—the whole thing so unconnected and senseless. There are men of that type, men outwardly sane, but who decoy girls—sometimes children—away and kill them. Sexual crimes really, I suppose.'

Harper said:

'Oh, yes, there are such cases, but we've no knowledge of anyone of that kind operating in this neighbourhood.'

Jefferson went on:

'I've thought over all the various men I've seen with Ruby. Guests here and outsiders—men she'd danced with. They all seem harmless enough—the usual type. She had no special friend of any kind.'

Superintendent Harper's face remained quite impassive, but unseen by Conway Jefferson there was still a speculative glint in his eye.

It was quite possible, he thought, that Ruby Keene might have had a special friend even though Conway Jefferson did not know about it.

He said nothing, however. The Chief Constable gave him a glance of inquiry and then rose to his feet. He said:

'Thank you, Mr. Jefferson. That's all we need for the present.'

Jefferson said:

'You'll keep me informed of your progress?'

'Yes, yes, we'll keep in touch with you.'

The two men went out.

Conway Jefferson leaned back in his chair.

His eyelids came down and veiled the fierce blue of his eyes. He looked suddenly a very tired man.

Then, after a minute or two, the lids flickered. He called: 'Edwards?'

From the next room the valet appeared promptly. Edwards knew his master as no one else did. Others, even his nearest, knew only his strength. Edwards knew his weakness. He had seen Conway Jefferson tired, discouraged, weary of life, momentarily defeated by infirmity and loneliness.

'Yes, sir?'

Jefferson said:

'Get on to Sir Henry Clithering. He's at Melborne Abbas. Ask him, from me, to get here to-day if he can, instead of to-morrow. Tell him it's urgent.'

CHAPTER VII

1

WHEN THEY WERE outside Jefferson's door, Superintendent Harper said:

'Well, for what it's worth, we've got a motive, sir.'

'H'm,' said Melchett. 'Fifty thousand pounds, eh?'

'Yes, sir. Murder's been done for a good deal less than that.'

'Yes, but——'

Colonel Melchett left the sentence unfinished. Harper, however, understood him.

'You don't think it's likely in this case? Well, I don't either, as far as that goes. But it's got to be gone into, all the same.'

'Oh, of course.'

Harper went on:

'If, as Mr. Jefferson says, Mr. Gaskell and Mrs. Jefferson are already well provided for and in receipt of a comfortable income, well, it's not likely they'd set out to do a brutal murder.'

'Quite so. Their financial standing will have to be investigated, of course. Can't say I like the appearance of Gaskell much—looks a sharp, unscrupulous sort of fellow—but that's a long way from making him out a murderer.'

'Oh, yes, sir, as I say, I don't think it's *likely* to be either of them, and from what Josie said I don't see how it would have been humanly possible. They were both playing bridge from twenty minutes to eleven until midnight. No, to my mind there's another possibility much more likely.'

Melchett said: 'Boy friend of Ruby Keene's?'

'That's it, sir. Some disgruntled young fellow—not too strong in the head, perhaps. Someone, I'd say, she knew before she came here. This adoption scheme, if he got wise to it, may just have put the lid on things. He saw himself losing her, saw her being removed to a different sphere of life altogether, and he went mad and blind with rage. He got her to come out and meet him last night, had a row with her over it, lost his head completely and did her in.'

'And how did she come to be in Bantry's library?'

'I think that's feasible. They were out, say, in his car at the time. He came to himself, realized what he'd done, and his first thought was how to get rid of the body. Say they were near the gates of a big house at the time. The idea comes to him that if she's found there the hue and cry will centre round the house and its occupants and will leave him comfortably out of it. She's a little bit of a thing. He could easily carry her. He's got a chisel in the car. He forces a window and plops her down on the hearthrug. Being a strangling case, there's no blood or mess to give him away in the car. See what I mean, sir?'

'Oh, yes, Harper, it's all perfectly possible. But there's still one thing to be done. *Cherchez l'homme.*'

'What? Oh, very good, sir.'

Superintendent Harper tactfully applauded his superior's joke, although, owing to the excellence of Melchett's French accent he almost missed the sense of the words.

2

'Oh—er—I say—er—c-c-could I speak to you a minute?'

It was George Bartlett who thus waylaid the two men.

Colonel Melchett, who was not attracted to Mr. Bartlett and who was anxious to see how Slack had got on with the investigation of the girl's room and the questioning of the chambermaids, barked sharply:

'Well, what is it—what is it?'

Young Mr. Bartlett retreated a step or two, opening and shutting his mouth and giving an unconscious imitation of a fish in a tank.

'Well—er—probably isn't important, don't you know—thought I ought to tell you. Matter of fact, can't find my car.'

'What do you mean, can't find your car?'

Stammering a good deal, Mr. Bartlett explained that what he meant was that he couldn't find his car.

Superintendent Harper said:

'Do you mean it's been stolen?'

George Bartlett turned gracefully to the more placid voice.

'Well, that's just it, you know. I mean, one can't tell, can one? I mean someone may just have buzzed off in it, not meaning any harm, if you know what I mean.'

'When did you last see it, Mr. Bartlett?'

'Well, I was tryin' to remember. Funny how difficult it is to remember anything, isn't it?'

Colonel Melchett said coldly:

'Not, I should think, to a normal intelligence. I understood you to say just now that it was in the courtyard of the hotel last night——'

Mr. Bartlett was bold enough to interrupt. He said:

'That's just it—was it?'

'What do you mean by "was it"? You said it *was*.'

'Well—I mean I *thought* it was. I mean—well, I didn't go out and look, don't you see?'

Colonel Melchett sighed. He summoned all his patience. He said:

'Let's get this quite clear. When was the last time you saw—actually *saw* your car? What make is it, by the way?'

'Minoan 14.'

'And you last saw it—when?'

George Bartlett's Adam's apple jerked convulsively up and down.

'Been trying to think. Had it before lunch yesterday. Was going for a spin in the afternoon. But somehow, you know how it is, went to sleep instead. Then, after tea, had a game of squash and all that, and a bathe afterwards.'

'And the car was then in the courtyard of the hotel?'

'Suppose so, I mean, that's where I'd put it. Thought, you see, I'd take someone for a spin. After dinner, I mean. But it wasn't my lucky evening. Nothing doing. Never took the old bus out after all.'

Harper said:

'But, as far as you knew, the car was still in the courtyard?'

'Well, naturally. I mean, I'd put it there—what?'

'Would you have noticed if it had *not* been there?'

Mr. Bartlett shook his head.

'Don't think so, you know. Lot of cars going and coming and all that. Plenty of Minoans.'

Superintendent Harper nodded. He had just cast a casual glance out of the window. There were at that moment no fewer than eight Minoan 14s in the courtyard—it was the popular cheap car of the year.

'Aren't you in the habit of putting your car away at night?' asked Colonel Melchett.

'Don't usually bother,' said Mr. Bartlett. 'Fine weather and all that, you know. Such a fag putting a car away in a garage.'

Glancing at Colonel Melchett, Superintendent Harper said: 'I'll join you upstairs, sir. I'll just get hold of Sergeant Higgins and he can take down particulars from Mr. Bartlett.'

'Right, Harper.'

Mr. Bartlett murmured wistfully:

'Thought I ought to let you know, you know. Might be important, what?'

3

Mr. Prestcott had supplied his additional dancer with board and lodging. Whatever the board, the lodging was the poorest the hotel possessed.

Josephine Turner and Ruby Keene had occupied rooms at the extreme end of a mean and dingy little corridor. The rooms were small, faced north on to a portion of the cliff that backed the hotel, and were furnished with the odds and ends of suites that had once, some thirty years ago, represented luxury and magnificence in the best suites. Now, when the hotel had been modernized and the bedrooms supplied with built-in receptacles for clothes, these large Victorian oak and mahogany wardrobes were relegated to those rooms occupied by the hotel's resident staff, or given to guests in the height of the season when all the rest of the hotel was full.

As Melchett saw at once, the position of Ruby Keene's room was ideal for the purpose of leaving the hotel without being observed, and was particularly unfortunate from the point of view of throwing light on the circumstances of that departure.

At the end of the corridor was a small staircase which led down to an equally obscure corridor on the ground floor. Here there was a glass door which led out on to the side terrace of the hotel, an unfrequented terrace with no view. You could go from it to the main terrace in front, or you could go down a winding path and come out in a lane that eventually rejoined the cliff road farther along. Its surface being bad, it was seldom used.

Inspector Slack had been busy harrying chambermaids and examining Ruby's room for clues. He had been lucky enough to find the room exactly as it had been left the night before.

Ruby Keene had not been in the habit of rising early. Her usual procedure, Slack discovered, was to sleep until about ten or half-past and then ring for breakfast. Consequently, since Conway Jefferson had begun his representations to the manager very early, the police had taken charge of things before the chambermaids had touched the room. They had actually not been down that corridor at all. The other rooms there, at this season of the year, were only opened and dusted once a week.

'That's all to the good as far as it goes,' Slack explained gloomily. 'It means that if there *were* anything to find we'd find it, but there isn't anything.'

The Glenshire police had already been over the room for finger-prints, but there were none unaccounted for. Ruby's own, Josie's, and the two chambermaids—one on the morning and one on the evening shift. There were also a couple of prints made by Raymond Starr, but these were accounted for by his story that he had come up with Josie to look for Ruby when she did not appear for the midnight exhibition dance.

There had been a heap of letters and general rubbish in the pigeon-holes of the massive mahogany desk in the corner. Slack had just been carefully sorting through them. But he had found nothing of a suggestive nature. Bills, receipts, theatre programmes, cinema stubs, newspaper cuttings, beauty hints torn from magazines. Of the letters there were some from 'Lil,' apparently a friend from the Palais de Danse, recounting various affairs and gossip, saying they 'missed Rube a lot. Mr. Findeison asked after you ever so often! Quite put out, he is! Young Reg has taken up with May now you've gone. Barny asks after you now and then. Things going much as usual. Old Grouser still as mean as ever with us girls. He ticked off Ada for going about with a fellow.'

Slack had carefully noted all the names mentioned. Inquiries would be made—and it was possible some useful information might come to light. To this Colonel Melchett agreed; so did Superintendent Harper, who had joined them. Otherwise the room had little to yield in the way of information.

Across a chair in the middle of the room was the foamy pink dance frock Ruby had worn early in the evening with a pair of pink satin high-heeled shoes kicked off carelessly on the floor. Two sheer silk stockings were rolled into a ball and flung down. One had a ladder in it. Melchett recalled that the dead girl had had bare feet and legs. This, Slacked learned, was her custom. She used make-up on her legs instead of stockings and only sometimes wore stockings for dancing, by this means saving expense. The wardrobe door was open and showed a variety of rather flashy evening dresses and a row of shoes below. There was some soiled underwear in the clothes-basket, some nail-parings, soiled face-cleaning tissue and bits of cotton wool stained with rouge and nail-polish in the waste-paper basket—in fact, nothing out of the ordinary! The facts seemed plain to read. Ruby Keene had hurried upstairs, changed her clothes and hurried off again—*where?*

Josephine Turner, who might be supposed to know most of Ruby's life and friends, had proved unable to help. But this, as Inspector Slack pointed out, might be natural.

'If what you tell me is true, sir—about this adoption business, I mean—well, Josie would be all for Ruby breaking with any old friends she might have and who might queer the pitch, so to speak. As I see it, this invalid gentleman gets all worked up about Ruby Keene being such a sweet, innocent, childish little piece of goods.

Now, supposing Ruby's got a tough boy friend—that won't go down so well with the old boy. So it's Ruby's business to keep that dark. Josie doesn't know much about the girl anyway—not about her friends and all that. But one thing she wouldn't stand for—Ruby's messing up things by carrying on with some undesirable fellow. So it stands to reason that Ruby (who, as I see it, was a sly little piece!) would keep very dark about seeing any old friend. She wouldn't let on to Josie anything about it—otherwise Josie would say "No, you don't, my girl." But you know what girls are—especially young ones—always ready to make a fool of themselves over a tough guy. Ruby wants to see him. He comes down here, cuts up rough about the whole business, and wrings the girl's neck.'

'I expect you're right, Slack,' said Colonel Melchett disguising his usual repugnance for the unpleasant way Slack had of putting things. 'If so, we ought to be able to discover this tough friend's identity fairly easily.'

'You leave it to me, sir,' said Slack with his usual confidence. 'I'll get hold of this "Lil" girl at that Palais de Danse place and turn her right inside out. We'll soon get at the truth.'

Colonel Melchett wondered if they would. Slack's energy and activity always made him feel tired.

'There's one other person you might be able to get a tip from, sir,' went on Slack, 'and that's the dance and tennis pro. fellow. He must have seen a lot of her and he'd know more than Josie would. Likely enough she'd loosen her tongue a bit to him.'

'I have already discussed that point with Superintendent Harper.'

'Good, sir. *I*'ve done the chambermaids pretty thoroughly! They don't know a thing. Looked down on these two, as far as I can make out. Scamped the service as much as they dared. Chambermaid was in here last at seven o'clock last night, when she turned down the bed and drew the curtains and cleared up a bit. There's a bathroom next door, if you'd like to see it?'

The bathroom was situated between Ruby's room and the slightly larger room occupied by Josie. It was unilluminating. Colonel Melchett silently marvelled at the amounts of aids to beauty that women could use. Rows of jars of face cream, cleansing cream, vanishing cream, skin-feeding cream! Boxes of different shades of powder. An untidy heap of every variety of lipstick. Hair lotions and 'brightening' applications. Eyelash black, mascara, blue stain for under the eyes, at least twelve different shades of nail varnish, face tissues, bits of cotton wool, dirty powder-puffs. Bottles of lotions—astringent, tonic, soothing, etc.

'Do you mean to say,' he murmured feebly, 'that women use all these things?'

Inspector Slack, who always knew everything, kindly enlightened him.

'In private life, sir, so to speak, a lady keeps to one or two distinct shades, one for evening, one for day. They know what suits them and they keep to it. But these professional girls, they have to ring a change, so to speak. They do exhibition dances, and one night it's a tango and the next a crinoline Victorian dance and then a kind of Apache dance and then just ordinary ball-room, and, of course, the make-up varies a good bit.'

'Good Lord!' said the Colonel. 'No wonder the people who turn out these creams and messes make a fortune.'

'Easy money, that's what it is,' said Slack. 'Easy money. Got to spend a bit in advertisement, of course.'

Colonel Melchett jerked his mind away from the fascinating and age-long problem of woman's adornments. He said to Harper, who had just joined them:

'There's still this dancing fellow. Your pigeon, Superintendent?'

'I suppose so, sir.'

As they went downstairs Harper asked:

'What did you think of Mr. Bartlett's story, sir?'

'About his car? I think, Harper, that that young man wants watching. It's a fishy story. Supposing that he did take Ruby Keene out in that car last night, after all?'

4

Superintendent Harper's manner was slow and pleasant and absolutely non-committal. These cases where the police of two counties had to collaborate were always difficult. He liked Colonel Melchett and considered him an able Chief Constable, but he was nevertheless glad to be tackling the present interview by himself. Never do too much at once, was Superintendent Harper's rule. Bare routine inquiry for the first time. That left the persons you were interviewing relieved and predisposed them to be more unguarded in the next interview you had with them.

Harper already knew Raymond Starr by sight. A fine-looking specimen, tall, lithe and good-looking, with very white teeth in a deeply-bronzed face. He was dark and graceful. He had a pleasant, friendly manner and was very popular in the hotel.

'I'm afraid I can't help you much, Superintendent. I knew Ruby quite well, of course. She'd been here over a month and we had practised our dances together and all that. But there's really very little to say. She was quite a pleasant and rather stupid girl.'

'It's her friendships we're particularly anxious to know about. Her friendships with men.'

'So I suppose. Well, *I* don't know anything! She'd got a few young men in tow in the hotel, but nothing special. You see, she was nearly always monopolized by the Jefferson family.

'Yes, the Jefferson family.' Harper paused meditatively. He shot a shrewd glance at the young man. 'What did you think of that business, Mr. Starr?'

Raymond Starr said coolly: 'What business?'

Harper said: 'Did you know that Mr. Jefferson was proposing to adopt Ruby Keene legally?'

This appeared to be news to Starr. He pursed up his lips and whistled. He said:

'The clever little devil! Oh, well, there's no fool like an old fool.'

'That's how it strikes you, is it?'

'Well—what else can one say? If the old boy wanted to adopt someone, why didn't he pick upon a girl of his own class?'

'Ruby Keene never mentioned the matter to you?'

'No, she didn't. I knew she was elated about something, but I didn't know what it was.'

'And Josie?'

'Oh, I think Josie must have known what was in the wind. Probably she was the one who planned the whole thing. Josie's no fool. She's got a head on her, that girl.'

Harper nodded. It was Josie who had sent for Ruby Keene. Josie, no doubt, who had encouraged the intimacy. No wonder she had been upset when Ruby had failed to show up for her dance that night and Conway Jefferson had begun to panic. She was envisaging her plans going awry.

He asked:

'Could Ruby keep a secret, do you think?'

'As well as most. She didn't talk about her own affairs much.'

'Did she ever say anything—anything at all—about some friend of hers—someone from her former life who was coming to see her here, or whom she had had difficulty with—you know the sort of thing I mean, no doubt.'

'I know perfectly. Well, as far as I'm aware, there was no one of the kind. Not by anything she ever said.'

'Thank you, Mr. Starr. Now will you just tell me in your own words exactly what happened last night?'

'Certainly. Ruby and I did our ten-thirty dance together——'

'No signs of anything unusual about her then?'

Raymond considered.

'I don't think so. I didn't notice what happened afterwards. I had my own partners to look after. I do remember noticing she wasn't in the ball-room. At midnight she hadn't turned up. I was very annoyed and went to Josie about it. Josie was playing bridge with the Jeffersons. She hadn't any idea where Ruby was, and I think she got a bit of a jolt. I noticed her shoot a quick, anxious glance at Mr. Jefferson. I persuaded the band to play another dance and I went to the office and got them to ring up to Ruby's room. There wasn't any answer. I went back to Josie. She suggested that Ruby was perhaps asleep in her room. Idiotic suggestion really, but it was meant for the Jeffersons, of course! She came away with me and said we'd go up together.'

'Yes, Mr. Starr. And what did she say when she was alone with you?'

'As far as I can remember, she looked very angry and said: "Damned little fool. She can't do this sort of thing. It will ruin all her chances. Who's she with, do you know?"

'I said that I hadn't the least idea. The last I'd seen of her was dancing with young Bartlett. Josie said: "She wouldn't be with *him*. What *can* she be up to? She isn't with that film man, is she?"'

Harper said sharply: '*Film man?* Who was he?'

Raymond said: 'I don't know his name. He's never stayed here. Rather an unusual-looking chap—black hair and theatrical-looking. He has something to do with the film industry, I believe—or so he told Ruby. He came over to dine here once or twice and danced with Ruby afterwards, but I don't think she knew him at all well. That's why I was surprised when Josie mentioned him. I said I didn't think he'd been here to-night. Josie said: "Well, she must be out with *someone*. What on earth am I going to say to the Jeffersons?" I said what did it matter to the Jeffersons? And Josie said it *did* matter. And she said, too, that she'd never forgive Ruby if she went and messed things up.

'We'd got to Ruby's room by then. She wasn't there, of course, but she'd been there, because the dress she had been wearing was lying across a chair. Josie looked in the wardrobe and said she thought she'd put on her old white dress. Normally she'd have changed into a black velvet dress for our Spanish dance. I was pretty angry by this time at the way Ruby had let me down. Josie did her best to soothe me and said she'd dance herself so that old Prestcott shouldn't get after us all. She went away and changed her dress and we went down and did a tango—exaggerated style and quite showy but not really too exhausting upon the ankles. Josie was very plucky about it—for it hurt her, I could see. After that she asked me to help her soothe the Jeffersons down. She said it was important. So, of course, I did what I could.'

Superintendent Harper nodded. He said:

'Thank you, Mr. Starr.'

To himself he thought: 'It was important, all right! Fifty thousand pounds!'

He watched Raymond Starr as the latter moved gracefully away. He went down the steps of the terrace, picking up a bag of tennis balls and a racket on the way. Mrs. Jefferson, also carrying a racket, joined him and they went towards the tennis courts.

'Excuse me, sir.'

Sergeant Higgins, rather breathless, stood at Harper's side.

The Superintendent, jerked from the train of thought he was following, looked startled.

'Message just come through for you from headquarters, sir. Labourer reported this morning saw glare as of fire. Half an hour ago they found a burnt-out car in a quarry. Venn's Quarry—about two miles from here. Traces of a charred body inside.'

A flush came over Harper's heavy features. He said:

'What's come to Glenshire? An epidemic of violence? Don't tell me we're going to have a Rouse case now!'

He asked: 'Could they get the number of the car?'

'No, sir. But we'll be able to identify it, of course, by the engine number. A Minoan 14, they think it is.'

CHAPTER VIII

1

SIR HENRY CLITHERING, as he passed through the lounge of the Majestic, hardly glanced at its occupants. His mind was preoccupied. Nevertheless, as is the way of life, something registered in his subconscious. It waited its time patiently.

Sir Henry was wondering as he went upstairs just what had induced the sudden urgency of his friend's message. Conway Jefferson was not the type of man who sent urgent summonses to anyone. Something quite out of the usual must have occurred, decided Sir Henry.

Jefferson wasted no time in beating about the bush. He said:

'Glad you've come. Edwards, get Sir Henry a drink. Sit down, man. You've not heard anything, I suppose? Nothing in the papers yet?'

Sir Henry shook his head, his curiosity aroused.

'What's the matter?'

'Murder's the matter. I'm concerned in it and so are your friends the Bantrys.'

'Arthur and Dolly Bantry?' Clithering sounded incredulous.

'Yes, you see, the body was found in their house.'

Clearly and succinctly Conway Jefferson ran through the facts. Sir Henry listened without interrupting. Both men were accustomed to grasping the gist of a matter. Sir Henry, during his term as Commissioner of the Metropolitan Police, had been renowned for his quick grip on essentials.

'It's an extraordinary business,' he commented when the other had finished. 'How do the Bantrys come into it, do you think?'

'That's what worries me. You see, Henry, it looks to me as though possibly the fact that I know them might have a bearing on the case. That's the only connection I can find. Neither of them, I gather, ever saw the girl before. That's what they say, and there's no reason to disbelieve them. It's most unlikely they *should* know her. Then isn't it possible that she was decoyed away and her body deliberately left in the house of friends of mine?'

Clithering said:

'I think that's far fetched.'

'It's possible, though,' persisted the other.

'Yes, but unlikely. What do you want *me* to do?'

Conway Jefferson said bitterly:

'I'm an invalid. I disguise the fact—refuse to face it—but now it comes home to me. I can't go about as I'd like to, asking questions, looking into things. I've got to stay here meekly grateful for such scraps of information as the police are kind enough to dole out to me. Do you happen to know Melchett, by the way, the Chief Constable of Radfordshire?'

'Yes, I've met him.'

Something stirred in Sir Henry's brain. A face and figure noted unseeingly as he passed through the lounge. A straight-backed old lady whose face was familiar. It linked up with the last time he had seen Melchett. . . .

He said:

'Do you mean you want me to be a kind of amateur sleuth? That's not my line.'

Jefferson said:

'You're *not* an amateur, that's just it.'

"I'm not a professional any more. I'm on the retired list now.'

Jefferson said: 'That simplifies matters.'

'You mean that if I were still at Scotland Yard I couldn't butt in? That's perfectly true.'

'As it is,' said Jefferson, 'your experience qualifies you to take an interest in the case, and any co-operation you offer will be welcomed.'

Clithering said slowly:

'Etiquette permits, I agree. But what do you really want, Conway? To find out who killed this girl?'

'Just that.'

'You've no idea yourself?'

'None whatever.'

Sir Henry said slowly:

'You probably won't believe me, but you've got an expert at solving mysteries sitting downstairs in the lounge at this minute. Someone who's better than I am at it, and who in all probability *may* have some local dope.'

'What are you talking about?'

'Downstairs in the lounge, by the third pillar from the left, there sits an old lady with a sweet, placid, spinsterish face, and a mind that has plumbed the depths of human iniquity and taken it as all in the day's work. Her name's Miss Marple. She comes from the village of St. Mary Mead, which is a mile and a half from Gossington, she's a friend of the Bantrys—and where crime is concerned she's the goods, Conway.'

Jefferson stared at him with thick, puckered brows. He said heavily:

'You're joking.'

'No, I'm not. You spoke of Melchett just now. The last time I saw Melchett there was a village tragedy. Girl supposed to have drowned herself. Police quite rightly suspected that it wasn't suicide, but murder. They thought they knew who did it. Along to me comes old Miss Marple, fluttering and dithering. She's afraid, she says, they'll hang the wrong person. She's got no evidence, but she knows who did do it. Hands me a piece of paper with a name written on it. And, by God, Jefferson, she was right!'

Conway Jefferson's brows came down lower than ever. He grunted disbelievingly:

'Woman's intuition, I suppose,' he said sceptically.

'No, she doesn't call it that. Specialised knowledge is her claim.'

'And what does that mean?'

'Well, you know, Jefferson, *we* use it in police work. We get a burglary and we usually know pretty well who did it—of the regular crowd, that is. We know the sort of burglar who acts in a particular sort of way. Miss Marple has an interesting, though occasionally trivial, series of parallels from village life.'

Jefferson said sceptically:

'What is she likely to know about a girl who's been brought up in a theatrical milieu and probably never been in a village in her life?'

'I think,' said Sir Henry Clithering firmly, 'that she might have ideas.'

2

Miss Marple flushed with pleasure as Sir Henry bore down upon her.

'Oh, Sir Henry, this is indeed a great piece of luck meeting you here.'

Sir Henry was gallant. He said:

'To me it is a great pleasure.'

Miss Marple murmured, flushing: 'So kind of you.'

'Are you staying here?'

'Well, as a matter of fact, we are.'

'We?'

'Mrs. Bantry's here too.' She looked at him sharply. 'Have you heard yet? Yes, I can see you have. It is terrible, is it not?'

'What's Dolly Bantry doing here? Is her husband here too?'

'No. Naturally, they both reacted quite differently. Colonel Bantry, poor man, just shuts himself up in his study, or goes down to one of the farms, when anything like this happens. Like tortoises, you know, they draw their heads in and hope nobody will notice them. Dolly, of course, is *quite* different.'

'Dolly, in fact,' said Sir Henry, who knew his old friend fairly well, 'is almost enjoying herself, eh?'

'Well—er—yes. Poor dear.'

'And she's brought you along to produce the rabbits out of the hat for her?'

Miss Marple said composedly:

'Dolly thought that a change of scene would be a good thing and she didn't want to come alone.' She met his eye and her own gently twinkled. 'But, of course, your way of describing it is quite true. It's rather embarrassing for me, because, of course. I am no use at all.'

'No ideas? No village parallels?'

'I don't know very much about it all yet.'

'I can remedy that, I think. I'm going to call you into consultation, Miss Marple.'

He gave a brief recital of the course of events. Miss Marple listened with keen interest.

'Poor Mr. Jefferson,' she said. 'What a very sad story. These terrible accidents. To leave him alive, crippled, seems more cruel than if he had been killed too.'

'Yes, indeed. That's why all his friends admire him so much for the resolute way he's gone on, conquering pain and grief and physical disabilities.'

'Yes, it is splendid.'

'The only thing I can't understand is this sudden outpouring of affection for this girl. She may, of course, have had some remarkable qualities.'

'Probably not,' said Miss Marple placidly.

'You don't think so?'

'I don't think her qualities entered into it.'

Sir Henry said:

'He isn't just a nasty old man, you know.'

'Oh, no, no!' Miss Marple got quite pink. 'I wasn't implying that for a minute. What I was trying to say was—very badly, I know—that he was just looking for a nice bright girl to take his dead daughter's place—and then this girl saw her opportunity and played it for all she was worth! That sounds rather uncharitable, I know, but I have seen so many cases of the kind. The young maid-servant at Mr. Harbottle's, for instance. A *very* ordinary girl, but quiet with nice manners. His sister was called away to nurse a dying relative and when she got back she found the girl completely above herself, sitting down in the drawing-room laughing and talking and not wearing her cap or apron. Miss Harbottle spoke to her very sharply and the girl was impertinent, and then old Mr. Harbottle left her quite dumbfounded by saying that he thought she had kept house for him long enough and that he was making other arrangements.

'Such a scandal as it created in the village, but poor Miss Harbottle had to go and live *most* uncomfortably in rooms in Eastbourne. People *said* things, of course, but I believe there was no familiarity of any kind—it was simply that the old man found it much pleasanter to have a young, cheerful girl telling him how clever and amusing he was than to have his sister continually pointing out his faults to him, even if she *was* a good economical manager.'

There was a moment's pause, and then Miss Marple resumed.

'And there was Mr. Badger who had the chemist's shop. Made a lot of fuss over the young lady who worked in his toilet section. Told his wife they must look on her as a daughter and have her to live in the house. Mrs. Badger didn't see it that way at all.'

Sir Henry said: 'If she'd only been a girl in his own rank of life—a friend's child——'

Miss Marple interrupted him.

'Oh! but that wouldn't have been nearly as satisfactory from his point of view. It's like King Cophetua and the beggar maid. If you're really rather a lonely, tired old man, and if, perhaps, your own family have been neglecting you'—she paused for a second—'well, to befriend someone who will be overwhelmed with your magnificence—(to put it rather melodramatically, but I hope you see what I mean)—well, that's much more interesting. It makes you feel a much greater person—a beneficent monarch! The recipient is more likely to be dazzled, and that, of course, is a pleasant feeling for you.' She paused and said: 'Mr. Badger, you know, bought the girl in his shop some really fantastic presents, a diamond bracelet and a most expensive radio-gramophone. Took out a lot of his savings to do it. However, Mrs.

Badger, who was a much more astute woman than poor Miss Harbottle (marriage, of course, *helps*), took the trouble to find out a few things. And when Mr. Badger discovered that the girl was carrying on with a *very* undesirable young man connected with the racecourses, and had actually pawned the bracelet to give him the money—well, he was completely disgusted and the affair passed over quite safely. And he gave Mrs. Badger a diamond ring the following Christmas.'

Her pleasant, shrewd eyes met Sir Henry's. He wondered if what she had been saying was intended as a hint. He said:

'Are you suggesting that if there had been a young man in Ruby Keene's life, my friend's attitude towards her might have altered?'

'It probably would, you know. I dare say, in a year or two, he might have liked to arrange for her marriage himself—though more likely he wouldn't—gentlemen are usually rather selfish. But I certainly think that if Ruby Keene had had a young man she'd have been careful to keep very quiet about it.'

'And the young man might have resented that?'

'I suppose that *is* the most plausible solution. It struck me, you know, that her cousin, the young woman who was at Gossington this morning, looked definitely *angry* with the dead girl. What you've told me explains *why*. No doubt she was looking forward to doing very well out of the business.'

'Rather a cold-blooded character, in fact?'

'That's too harsh a judgment, perhaps. The poor thing has had to earn her living, and you can't expect her to sentimentalize because a well-to-do man and woman—as you have described Mr. Gaskell and Mrs. Jefferson—are going to be done out of a further large sum of money to which they have really no particular moral right. I should say Miss Turner was a hard-headed, ambitious young woman, with a good temper and considerable *joie de vivre*. A little,' added Miss Marple, 'like Jessie Golden, the baker's daughter.'

'What happened to her?' asked Sir Henry.

'She trained as a nursery governess and married the son of the house, who was home on leave from India. Made him a very good wife, I believe.'

Sir Henry pulled himself clear of these fascinating side issues. He said:

'Is there any reason, do you think, why my friend Conway Jefferson should suddenly have developed this "Cophetua complex," if you like to call it that?'

'There might have been.'

'In what way?'

Miss Marple said, hesitating a little:

'I should think—it's only a suggestion, of course—that perhaps his son-in-law and daughter-in-law *might* have wanted to get married again.'

'Surely he couldn't have objected to that?'

'Oh, no, not *objected*. But, you see, you must look at it from *his* point of view. He had a terrible shock and loss—so had they. The three bereaved people live together and the *link* between them is the loss they have all sustained. But Time, as my dear mother used to say, is a great healer. Mr. Gaskell and Mrs. Jefferson are young. Without knowing it themselves, they may have begun to feel restless, to resent the bonds that tied them to their past sorrow. And so, feeling like that, old Mr. Jefferson would have become conscious of a sudden lack of sympathy without knowing its cause. It's usually that. Gentlemen so *easily* feel neglected. With Mr. Harbottle it was Miss Harbottle going away. And With the Badgers it was Mrs. Badger taking such an interest in Spiritualism and always going out to séances.'

'I must say,' said Sir Henry ruefully, 'that I do dislike the way you reduce us all to a General Common Denominator.'

Miss Marple shook her head sadly.

'Human nature is very much the same anywhere, Sir Henry.'

Sir Henry said distastefully:

'Mr. Harbottle! Mr. Badger! And poor Conway! I hate to intrude the personal note, but have you any parallel for *my* humble self in your village?'

'Well, of course, there is Briggs.'

'Who's Briggs?'

'He was the head gardener up at Old Hall. *Quite* the best man they ever had. Knew *exactly* when the under-gardeners were slacking off—quite uncanny it was! He managed with only three men and a boy and the place was kept better than it had been with six. And took several firsts with his sweet peas. He's retired now.'

'Like me,' said Sir Henry.

'But he still does a little jobbing—if he likes the people.'

'Ah,' said Sir Henry. 'Again like me. That's what I'm doing now—jobbing—to help an old friend.'

'Two old friends.'

'Two?' Sir Henry looked a little puzzled.

Miss Marple said:

'I suppose you meant Mr. Jefferson. But I wasn't thinking of him. I was thinking of Colonel and Mrs. Bantry.'

'Yes—yes—I see——' He asked sharply: 'Was that why you alluded to Dolly Bantry as "poor dear" at the beginning of our conversation?'

'Yes. She hasn't begun to realize things yet. *I* know because I've had more experience. You see, Sir Henry, it seems to me that there's a great possibility of this crime being the kind of crime that never *does* get solved. Like the Brighton trunk murders. But if that happens it will be absolutely disastrous for the Bantrys. Colonel Bantry, like nearly all retired military men, is really *abnormally* sensitive. He reacts very quickly to public opinion. He won't notice it for some time, and then it will begin to go home to him. A slight here, and a snub there, and invitations that are refused, and excuses that are made—and then, little by little, it will dawn upon him and he'll retire into his shell and get terribly morbid and miserable.'

'Let me be sure I understand you rightly, Miss Marple. You mean that, because the body was found in his house, people will think that *he* had something to do with it?'

'Of course they will! I've no doubt they're saying so already. They'll say so more and more. And people will cold shoulder the Bantrys and avoid them. That's why the truth has got to be found out and why I was willing to come here with Mrs. Bantry. An open accusation is one thing—and quite easy for a soldier to meet. He's indignant and he has a chance of fighting. But this other *whispering* business will break him—will break them both. So you see, Sir Henry, we've *got* to find out the truth.'

Sir Henry said:

'Any ideas as to why the body should have been found in his house? There must be an explanation of that. Some connection.'

'Oh, of course.'

'The girl was last seen here about twenty minutes to eleven. By midnight, according to the medical evidence, she was dead. Gossington's about eighteen miles from here. Good road for sixteen of those miles until one turns off the main road. A powerful car could do it in well under half an hour. Practically *any* car could average thirty-five. But why anyone should either kill her here and take her body out to Gossington or should take her out to Gossington and strangle her there, I don't know.'

'Of course you don't, because it didn't happen.'

'Do you mean that she was strangled by some fellow who took her out in a car and he then decided to push her into the first likely house in the neighbourhood?'

'I don't think anything of the kind. I think there was a very careful plan made. What happened was that the plan went wrong.'

Sir Henry stared at her.

'Why did the plan go wrong?'

Miss Marple said rather apologetically:

'Such curious things happen, don't they? If I were to say that this particular plan went wrong because human beings are so much more vulnerable and sensitive than anyone thinks, it wouldn't sound sensible, would it? But that's what I believe—and——'

She broke off. 'Here's Mrs. Bantry now.'

CHAPTER IX

MRS. BANTRY was with Adelaide Jefferson. The former came up to Sir Henry and exclaimed: '*You?*'

'I, myself.' He took both her hands and pressed them warmly. 'I can't tell you how distressed I am at all this, Mrs. B.'

Mrs. Bantry said mechanically:

'*Don't call me Mrs. B!*' and went on: 'Arthur isn't here. He's taking it all rather seriously. Miss Marple and I have come here to sleuth. Do you know Mrs. Jefferson?'

'Yes, of course.'

He shook hands. Adelaide Jefferson said:

'Have you seen my father-in-law?'

'Yes, I have.'

'I'm glad. We're anxious about him. It was a terrible shock.'

Mrs. Bantry said:

'Let's go out on the terrace and have drinks and talk about it all.'

The four of them went out and joined Mark Gaskell, who was sitting at the extreme end of the terrace by himself.

After a few desultory remarks and the arrival of the drinks Mrs. Bantry plunged straight into the subject with her usual zest for direct action.

'We can talk about it, can't we?' she said. 'I mean, we're all old friends—except Miss Marple and she knows all about crime. And she wants to help.'

Mark Gaskell looked at Miss Marple in a somewhat puzzled fashion. He said doubtfully:

'Do you—er—write detective stories?'

The most unlikely people, he knew, wrote detective stories. And Miss Marple, in her old-fashioned spinster's clothes, looked a singularly unlikely person.

'Oh no, I'm not clever enough for *that*.'

'She's wonderful,' said Mrs. Bantry impatiently. 'I can't explain now, but she is. Now, Addie, I want to know all about things. What was she really like, this girl?'

'Well——' Adelaide Jefferson paused, glanced across at Mark, and half laughed. She said: 'You're so direct.'

'Did you like her?'

'No, of course I didn't.'

'What was she really like?' Mrs. Bantry shifted her inquiry to Mark Gaskell. Mark said deliberately:

'Common or garden gold-digger. And she knew her stuff. She'd got her hooks into Jeff all right.'

Both of them called their father-in-law Jeff.

Sir Henry thought, looking disapprovingly at Mark:

'Indiscreet fellow. Shouldn't be so outspoken.'

He had always disapproved a little of Mark Gaskell. The man had charm but he was unreliable—talked too much, was occasionally boastful—not quite to be trusted, Sir Henry thought. He had sometimes wondered if Conway Jefferson thought so too.

'But couldn't you *do* something about it?' demanded Mrs. Bantry.

Mark said dryly:

'We might have—if we'd realized it in time.'

He shot a glance at Adelaide and she coloured faintly. There had been reproach in that glance.

She said:

'Mark thinks I ought to have seen what was coming.'

'You left the old boy alone too much, Addie. Tennis lessons and all the rest of it.'

'Well, I had to have some exercise.' She spoke apologetically. 'Anyway, I never dreamed——'

'No,' said Mark, 'neither of us ever dreamed. Jeff has always been such a sensible, level-headed old boy.'

Miss Marple made a contribution to the conversation.

'Gentlemen,' she said with her old-maid's way of referring to the opposite sex as though it were a species of wild animal, 'are frequently not as level-headed as they seem.'

'I'll say you're right,' said Mark. 'Unfortunately, Miss Marple, we didn't realize that. We wondered what the old boy saw in that rather insipid and meretricious little bag of tricks. But we were pleased for him to be kept happy and amused. We thought there was no harm in her. No harm in her! I wish I'd wrung her neck!'

'Mark,' said Addie, 'you really *must* be careful what you say.'

He grinned at her engagingly.

'I suppose I must. Otherwise people will think I actually *did* wring her neck. Oh well, I suppose I'm under suspicion, anyway. If anyone had an interest in seeing that girl dead it was Addie and myself.'

'Mark,' cried Mrs. Jefferson, half laughing and half angry, 'you really *mustn't*!'

'All right, all right,' said Mark Gaskell pacifically. 'But I do like speaking my mind. Fifty thousand pounds our esteemed father-in-law was proposing to settle upon that half-baked nitwitted little slypuss.'

'Mark, you mustn't—she's dead.'

'Yes, she's dead, poor little devil. And after all, why shouldn't she use the weapons that Nature gave her? Who am I to judge? Done plenty of rotten things myself in my life. No, let's say Ruby was entitled to plot and scheme and we were mugs not to have tumbled to her game sooner.'

Sir Henry said:

'What did you say when Conway told you he proposed to adopt the girl?'

Mark thrust out his hands.

'What could we say? Addie, always the little lady, retained her self-control admirably. Put a brave face upon it. I endeavoured to follow her example.'

'*I* should have made a fuss!' said Mrs. Bantry.

'Well, frankly speaking, we weren't entitled to make a fuss. It was Jeff's money. We weren't his flesh and blood. He'd always been damned good to us. There was nothing for it but to bite on the bullet.' He added reflectively: 'But we didn't love little Ruby.'

Adelaide Jefferson said:

'If only it had been some other kind of girl. Jeff had two godchildren, you know. If it had been one of them—well, one would have *understood* it.' She added, with a shade of resentment: 'And Jeff's always seemed so fond of Peter.'

'Of course,' said Mrs. Bantry. 'I always have known Peter was your first husband's child—but I'd quite forgotten it. I've always thought of him as Mr. Jefferson's grandson.'

'So have I,' said Adelaide. Her voice held a note that made Miss Marple turn in her chair and look at her.

'It was Josie's fault,' said Mark. 'Josie brought her here.'

Adelaide said:

'Oh, but surely you don't think it was deliberate, do you? Why, you've always liked Josie so much.'

'Yes, I did like her. I thought she was a good sport.'

'It was sheer accident her bringing the girl down.'

'Josie's got a good head on her shoulders, my girl.'

'Yes, but she couldn't foresee——'

Mark said:

'No, she couldn't. I admit it. I'm not really accusing her of planning the whole thing. But I've no doubt she saw which way the wind was blowing long before we did and kept very quiet about it.'

Adelaide said with a sigh:

'I suppose one can't blame her for that.'

Mark said:

'Oh, we can't blame anyone for anything!'

Mrs. Bantry asked:

'Was Ruby Keene very pretty?'

Mark stared at her. 'I thought you'd seen——'

Mrs. Bantry said hastily:

'Oh yes, I saw her—her body. But she'd been strangled, you know, and one couldn't tell——' She shivered.

Mark said, thoughtfully:

'I don't think she was really pretty at all. She certainly wouldn't have been without any make-up. A thin ferrety little face, not much chin, teeth running down her throat, nondescript sort of nose——'

'It sounds revolting,' said Mrs. Bantry.

'Oh no, she wasn't. As I say, with make-up she managed to give quite an effect of good looks, don't you think so, Addie?'

'Yes, rather chocolate-box, pink and white business. She had nice blue eyes.'

'Yes, innocent baby stare, and the heavily-blacked lashes brought out the blueness. Her hair was bleached, of course. It's true, when I come to think of it, that in colouring—artificial colouring, anyway—she had a kind of spurious resemblance to Rosamund—my wife, you know. I dare say that's what attracted the old man's attention to her.'

He sighed.

'Well, it's a bad business. The awful thing is that Addie and I can't help being glad, really, that she's dead——'

He quelled a protest from his sister-in-law.

'It's no good, Addie; I know what you feel. I feel the same. And I'm not going to pretend! But, at the same time, if you know what I mean, I really am most awfully concerned for Jeff about the whole business. It's hit him very hard. I——'

He stopped, and stared towards the doors leading out of the lounge on to the terrace.

'Well, well—see who's here. What an unscrupulous woman you are, Addie.'

Mrs. Jefferson looked over her shoulder, uttered an exclamation and got up, a slight colour rising in her face. She walked quickly along the terrace and went up to a tall middle-aged man with a thin brown face, who was looking uncertainly about him.

Mrs. Bantry said: 'Isn't that Hugo McLean?'

Mark Gaskell said:

'Hugo McLean it is. Alias William Dobbin.'

Mrs. Bantry murmured:

'He's very faithful, isn't he?'

'Dog-like devotion,' said Mark. 'Addie's only got to whistle and Hugo comes trotting from any odd corner of the globe. Always hopes that some day she'll marry him. I dare say she will.'

Miss Marple looked beamingly after them. She said:

'I see. A romance?'

'One of the good old-fashioned kind,' Mark assured her. 'It's been going on for years. Addie's that kind of woman.'

He added meditatively: 'I suppose Addie telephoned him this morning. She didn't tell me she had.'

Edwards came discreetly along the terrace and paused at Mark's elbow.

'Excuse me, sir. Mr. Jefferson would like you to come up.'

'I'll come at once.' Mark sprang up.

He nodded to them, said: 'See you later,' and went off.

Sir Henry leant forward to Miss Marple. He said:

'Well, what do you think of the principal beneficiaries of the crime?'

Miss Marple said thoughtfully, looking at Adelaide Jefferson as she stood talking to her old friend:

'I should think, you know, that she was a very devoted mother.'

'Oh, she is,' said Mrs. Bantry. 'She's simply devoted to Peter.'

'She's the kind of woman,' said Miss Marple, 'that everyone likes. The kind of woman that could go on getting married again and again. I don't mean a *man's* woman—that's quite different.'

'I know what you mean,' said Sir Henry.

'What you both mean,' said Mrs. Bantry, 'is that she's a good listener.'

Sir Henry laughed. He said:

'And Mark Gaskell?'

'Ah,' said Miss Marple, 'he's a downy fellow.'

'Village parallel, please?'

'Mr. Cargill, the builder. He bluffed a lot of people into having things done to their houses they never meant to do. And how he charged them for it! But he could always explain his bill away plausibly. A downy fellow. He married money. So did Mr. Gaskell, I understand.'

'You don't like him.'

'Yes, I do. Most women would. But he can't take me in. He's a very attractive person, I think. But a little unwise, perhaps, to *talk* as much as he does.'

'Unwise is the word,' said Sir Henry. 'Mark will get himself into trouble if he doesn't look out.'

A tall dark young man in white flannels came up the steps to the terrace and paused just for a minute, watching Adelaide Jefferson and Hugo McLean.

'And that,' said Sir Henry obligingly, 'is X, whom we might describe as an interested party. He is the tennis and dancing pro.—Raymond Starr, Ruby Keene's partner.'

Miss Marple looked at him with interest. She said:

'He's very nice looking, isn't he?'

'I suppose so.'

'Don't be absurd, Sir Henry,' said Mrs. Bantry, 'there's no supposing about it. He *is* good looking.'

Miss Marple murmured:

'Mrs. Jefferson has been taking tennis lessons, I think she said.'

'Do you mean anything by that, Jane, or don't you?'

Miss Marple had no chance of replying to this downright question. Young Peter Carmody came across the terrace and joined them. He addressed himself to Sir Henry:

'I say, are you a detective, too? I saw you talking to the Superintendent—the fat one is a superintendent, isn't he?'

'Quite right, my son.'

'And somebody told me you were a frightfully important detective from London. The head of Scotland Yard or something like that.'

'The head of Scotland Yard is usually a complete dud in books, isn't he?'

'Oh no, not nowadays. Making fun of the police is very old-fashioned. Do you know who did the murder yet?'

'Not yet, I'm afraid.'

'Are you enjoying this very much, Peter?' asked Mrs. Bantry.

'Well, I am, rather. It makes a change, doesn't it? I've been hunting round to see if I could find any clues, but I haven't been lucky. I've got a souvenir, though. Would you like to see it? Fancy, mother wanted me to throw it away. I do think one's parents are rather trying sometimes.'

He produced from his pocket a small matchbox. Pushing it open, he disclosed the precious contents.

'See, *it's a fingernail. Her fingernail!* I'm going to label it *Fingernail of the Murdered Woman* and take it back to school. It's a good souvenir, don't you think?'

'Where did you get it?' asked Miss Marple.

'Well, it was a bit of luck, really. Because, of course, I didn't know she was going to be murdered *then.* It was before dinner last night. Ruby caught her nail in Josie's shawl and it tore it. Mums cut it off for her and gave it to me and said put it in the wastepaper basket, and I meant to, but I put it in my pocket instead, and this morning I remembered and looked to see if it was still there and it was, so now I've got it as a souvenir.'

'Disgusting,' said Mrs. Bantry.

Peter said politely: 'Oh, do you think so?'

'Got any other souvenirs?' asked Sir Henry.

'Well, I don't know. I've got something that might be.'

'Explain yourself, young man.'

Peter looked at him thoughtfully. Then he pulled out an envelope. From the inside of it he extracted a piece of brown tapey substance.

'It's a bit of that chap George Bartlett's shoe-lace,' he explained. 'I saw his shoes outside the door this morning and I bagged a bit just in case.'

'In case what?'

'In case he should be the murderer, of course. He was the last person to see her and that's always frightfully suspicious, you know. Is it nearly dinner-time, do you think? I'm frightfully hungry. It always seems such a long time between tea and dinner. Hallo, there's Uncle Hugo. I didn't know mums had asked *him* to come down. I suppose she sent for him. She always does if she's in a jam. Here's Josie coming. Hi, Josie!'

Josephine Turner, coming along the terrace, stopped and looked rather startled to see Mrs. Bantry and Miss Marple.

Mrs. Bantry said pleasantly:

'How d'you do, Miss Turner. We've come to do a bit of sleuthing!'

Josie cast a guilty glance round. She said, lowering her voice:

'It's awful. Nobody knows yet. I mean, it isn't in the papers yet. I suppose everyone will be asking me questions and it's so awkward. I don't know what I ought to say.'

Her glance went rather wistfully towards Miss Marple, who said: 'Yes, it will be a very difficult situation for you, I'm afraid.'

Josie warmed to this sympathy.

'You see, Mr. Prestcott said to me: "Don't talk about it." And that's all very well, but everyone is sure to ask me, and you can't offend people, can you? Mr. Prestcott said he hoped I'd feel able to carry on as usual—and he wasn't very nice about it, so of course I want to do my best. And I really don't see why it should all be blamed on me.'

Sir Henry said:

'Do you mind me asking you a frank question, Miss Turner?'

'Oh, do ask me anything you like,' said Josie, a little insincerely.

'Has there been any unpleasantness between you and Mrs. Jefferson and Mr. Gaskell over all this?'

'Over the murder, do you mean?'

'No, I don't mean the murder.'

Josie stood twisting her fingers together. She said rather sullenly:

'Well, there has and there hasn't, if you know what I mean. Neither of them have *said* anything. But I think they blamed it on me—Mr. Jefferson taking such a fancy to Ruby, I mean. It wasn't my fault, though, was it? These things happen, and I never dreamt of such a thing happening beforehand, not for a moment. I—I was quite dumbfounded.'

Her words rang out with what seemed undeniable sincerity.

Sir Henry said kindly:

'I'm quite sure you were. But once it *had* happened?'

Josie's chin went up.

'Well, it was a piece of luck, wasn't it? Everyone's got the right to have a piece of luck sometimes.'

She looked from one to the other of them in a slightly defiant questioning manner and then went on across the terrace and into the hotel.

Peter said judicially:

'I don't think *she* did it.'

Miss Marple murmured:

'It's interesting, that piece of fingernail. It had been worrying me, you know—how to account for her nails.'

'Nails?' asked Sir Henry.

'The dead girl's nails,' explained Mrs. Bantry. 'They were quite *short*, and now that Jane says so, of course it *was* a little unlikely. A girl like that usually has absolute talons.'

Miss Marple said:

'But of course if she tore one off, then she might clip the others close, so as to match. Did they find nail parings in her room, I wonder?'

Sir Henry looked at her curiously. He said:

'I'll ask Superintendent Harper when he gets back.'

'Back from where?' asked Mrs. Bantry. 'He hasn't gone over to Gossington, has he?'

Sir Henry said gravely:

'No. There's been another tragedy. Blazing car in a quarry——'

Miss Marple caught her breath.

'Was there someone in the car?'

'I'm afraid so—yes.'

Miss Marple said thoughtfully:

'I expect that will be the Girl Guide who's missing—Patience—no, Pamela Reeves.'

Sir Henry stared at her.

'Now why on earth do you think that, Miss Marple?'

Miss Marple got rather pink.

'Well, it was given out on the wireless that she was missing from her home—since last night. And her home was Daneleigh Vale; that's not very far from here. And she was last seen at the Girl-Guide Rally up on Danebury Downs. That's very close indeed. In fact, she'd have to pass through Danemouth to get home. So it does rather fit in, doesn't it? I mean, it looks as though she might have seen—or perhaps heard—something that no one was supposed to see and hear. If so, of course, she'd be a source of danger to the murderer and she'd have to be—removed. Two things like that *must* be connected, don't you think?'

Sir Henry said, his voice dropping a little:

'You think—a second murder?'

'Why not?' Her quiet placid gaze met his. 'When anyone has committed one murder, they don't shrink from another, do they? Nor even from a third.'

'A third? You don't think there will be a *third* murder?'

'I think it's just possible. . . . Yes, I think it's highly possible.'

'Miss Marple,' said Sir Henry, 'you frighten me. Do you know who is going to be murdered?'

Miss Marple said: 'I've a very good idea.'

CHAPTER X

1

SUPERINTENDENT HARPER stood looking at the charred and twisted heap of metal. A burnt-up car was always a revolting object, even without the additional gruesome burden of a charred and blackened corpse.

Venn's Quarry was a remote spot, far from any human habitation. Though actually only two miles as the crow flies from Danemouth, the approach to it was by one of those narrow, twisted, rutted roads, little more than a cart track, and which led nowhere except to the quarry itself. It was a long time now since the quarry had been worked, and the only people who came along the lane were the casual visitors in search of blackberries. As a spot to dispose of a car it was ideal. The car need not have been found for weeks but for the accident of the glow in the sky having been seen by Albert Biggs, a labourer, on his way to work.

Albert Biggs was still on the scene, though all he had to tell had been heard some time ago, but he continued to repeat the thrilling story with such embellishments as occurred to him.

'Why, dang my eyes, I said, whatever be that? Proper glow it was, up in the sky. Might be a bonfire, I says, but who's be having bonfire over to Venn's Quarry? No, I says, 'tis some mighty big fire, to be sure. But whatever would it be, I says? There's no house or farm to that direction. 'Tis over by Venn's, I says, that's where it is, to be sure. Didn't rightly know what I ought to do about it, but seeing as Constable Gregg comes along just then on his bicycle, I tells him about it. 'Twas all died down by then, but I tells him just where 'twere. 'Tis over that direction, I says. Big glare in the sky, I says. Mayhap as it's a rick, I says. One of them tramps, as likely as not, set alight of it. But I did never think as how it might be a car—far less as someone was being burnt up alive in it. 'Tis a terrible tragedy, to be sure.'

The Glenshire police had been busy. Cameras had clicked and the position of the charred body had been carefully noted before the police surgeon had started his own investigation.

The latter came over now to Harper, dusting black ash off his hands, his lips set grimly together.

'A pretty thorough job,' he said. 'Part of one foot and the shoe are about all that has escaped. Personally I myself couldn't say if the body was a man's or a woman's at the moment, though we'll get some indication from the bones, I expect. But the shoe is one of the black strapped affairs—the kind schoolgirls wear.'

'There's a schoolgirl missing from the next county,' said Harper; 'quite close to here. Girl of sixteen or so.'

'Then it's probably her,' said the doctor. 'Poor kid.'

Harper said uneasily: 'She wasn't alive when——'

'No, no, I don't think so. No signs of her having tried to get out. Body was just slumped down on the seat—with the foot sticking out.

She was dead when she was put there, I should say. Then the car was set fire to in order to try and get rid of the evidence.'

He paused, and asked:

'Want me any longer?'

'I don't think so, thank you.'

'Right, I'll be off.'

He strode away to his car. Harper went over to where one of his sergeants, a man who specialized in car cases, was busy.

The latter looked up.

'Quite a clear case, sir. Petrol poured over the car and the whole thing deliberately set light to. There are three empty cans in the hedge over there.'

A little farther away another man was carefully arranging small objects picked out of the wreckage. There was a scorched black leather shoe and with it some scraps of scorched and blackened material. As Harper approached, his subordinate looked up and exclaimed:

'Look at this, sir. This seems to clinch it.'

Harper took the small object in his hand. He said:

'Button from a Girl Guide's uniform?'

'Yes, sir.'

'Yes,' said Harper, 'that does seem to settle it.'

A decent, kindly man, he felt slightly sick. First Ruby Keene and now this child, Pamela Reeves.

He said to himself, as he had said before:

'What's come to Glenshire?'

His next move was first to ring up his own Chief Constable, and afterwards to get in touch with Colonel Melchett. The disappeance of Pamela Reeves had taken place in Radfordshire though her body had been found in Glenshire.

The next task set him was not a pleasant one. He had to break the news to Pamela Reeves's father and mother. . . .

2

Superintendent Harper looked up consideringly at the façade of Braeside as he rang the front door bell.

Neat little villa, nice garden of about an acre and a half. The sort of place that had been built fairly freely all over the countryside in the last twenty years. Retired Army men, retired Civil Servants—that type. Nice decent folk; the worst you could say of them was that they might be a bit dull. Spent as much money as they could afford on their children's education. Not the kind of people you associated with tragedy. And now tragedy had come to them. He sighed.

He was shown at once into a lounge where a stiff man with a grey moustache and a woman whose eyes were red with weeping both sprang up. Mrs. Reeves cried out eagerly:

'You have some news of Pamela?'

Then she shrank back, as though the Superintendent's commiserating glance had been a blow.

Harper said:

'I'm afraid you must prepare yourself for bad news.'

'Pamela——' faltered the woman.

Major Reeves said sharply:

'Something's happened—to the child?'

'Yes, sir.'

'Do you mean she's dead?'

Mrs. Reeves burst out:

'Oh no, no,' and broke into a storm of weeping. Major Reeves put his arm round his wife and drew her to him. His lips trembled but he looked inquiringly at Harper, who bent his head.

'An accident?'

'Not exactly, Major Reeves. She was found in a burnt-out car which had been abandoned in a quarry.'

'In a car? In a quarry?'

His astonishment was evident.

Mrs. Reeves broke down altogether and sank down on the sofa, sobbing violently.

Superintendent Harper said:

'If you'd like me to wait a few minutes?'

Major Reeves said sharply:

'What does this mean? Foul play?'

'That's what it looks like, sir. That's why I'd like to ask you some questions if it isn't too trying for you.'

'No, no, you're quite right. No time must be lost if what you suggest is true. But I can't believe it. Who would want to harm a child like Pamela?'

Harper said stolidly:

'You've already reported to your local police the circumstances of your daughter's disappearance. She left here to attend a Guides' rally and you expected her home for supper. That is right?'

'Yes.'

'She was to return by bus?'

'Yes.'

'I understand that, according to the story of her fellow Guides, when the rally was over Pamela said she was going into Danemouth to Woolworth's, and would catch a later bus home. That strikes you as quite a normal proceeding?'

'Oh yes, Pamela was very fond of going to Woolworth's. She often went into Danemouth to shop. The bus goes from the main road, only about a quarter of a mile from here.'

'And she had no other plans, so far as you know?'

'None.'

'She was not meeting anybody in Danemouth?'

'No, I'm sure she wasn't. She would have mentioned it if so. We expected her back for supper. That's why, when it got so late and she hadn't turned up, we rang up the police. It wasn't like her not to come home.'

'Your daughter had no undesirable friends—that is, friends that you didn't approve of?'

'No, there was never any trouble of that kind.'

Mrs. Reeves said tearfully:

'Pam was just a child. She was very young for her age. She liked games and all that. She wasn't precocious in any way.'

'Do you know a Mr. George Bartlett who is staying at the Majestic Hotel in Danemouth?'

Major Reeves stared.

'Never heard of him.'

'You don't think your daugther knew him?'

'I'm quite sure she didn't.'

He added sharply: 'How does he come into it?'

'He's the owner of the Minoan 14 car in which your daughter's body was found.'

Mrs. Reeves cried: 'But then he must——'

Harper said quickly:

'He reported his car missing early to-day. It was in the courtyard of the Majestic Hotel at lunch time yesterday. Anybody might have taken the car.'

'But didn't someone see who took it?'

The Superintendent shook his head.

'Dozens of cars going in and out all day. And a Minoan 14 is one of the commonest makes.'

Mrs. Reeves cried:

'But aren't you doing something? Aren't you trying to find the—the devil who did this? My little girl—oh, my little girl! She wasn't burnt alive, was she? Oh, Pam, Pam . . . !'

'She didn't suffer, Mrs. Reeves. I assure you she was already dead when the car was set alight.'

Reeves asked stiffly:

'How was she killed?'

Harper gave him a significant glance.

'We don't know. The fire has destroyed all evidence of that kind.'

He turned to the distraught woman on the sofa.

'Believe me, Mrs. Reeves, we're doing everything we can. It's a matter of checking up. Sooner or later we shall find someone who saw your daughter in Danemouth yesterday, and saw whom she was with. It all takes time, you know. We shall have dozens, hundreds of reports coming in about a Girl Guide who was seen here, there, and everywhere. It's a matter of selection and of patience—but we shall find out the truth in the end, never you fear.'

Mrs. Reeves asked:

'Where—where is she? Can I go to her?'

Again Superintendent Harper caught the husband's eye. He said:

'The medical officer is attending to all that. I'd suggest that your husband comes with me now and attends to all the formalities. In the meantime, try and recollect anything Pamela may have said—something, perhaps, that you didn't pay attention to at the time but which might throw some light upon things. You know what I mean—just some chance word or phrase. That's the best way you can help us.'

As the two men went towards the door, Reeves said, pointing to a photograph:

'There she is.'

Harper looked at it attentively. It was a hockey group. Reeves pointed out Pamela in the centre of the team.

'A nice kid,' Harper thought, as he looked at the earnest face of the pigtailed girl.

His mouth set in a grim line as he thought of the charred body in the car.

He vowed to himself that the murder of Pamela Reeves should not remain one of Glenshire's unsolved mysteries.

Ruby Keene, so he admitted privately, might have asked for what was coming to her, but Pamela Reeves was quite another story. A nice kid, if he ever saw one. He'd not rest until he'd hunted down the man or woman who'd killed her.

CHAPTER XI

A DAY OR TWO LATER Colonel Melchett and Superintendent Harper looked at each other across the former's big desk. Harper had come over to Much Benham for a consultation.

Melchett said gloomily:

'Well, we know where we are—or rather where we aren't!'

'Where we aren't expresses it better, sir.'

'We've got two deaths to take into account,' said Melchett. 'Two murders. Ruby Keene and the child Pamela Reeves. Not much to identify her by, poor kid, but enough. That shoe that escaped burning has been identified positively as hers by her father, and there's this button from her Girl Guide uniform. A fiendish business, Superintendent.'

Superintendent Harper said very quietly:

'I'll say you're right, sir.'

'I'm glad it's quite certain she was dead before the car was set on fire. The way she was lying, thrown across the seat, shows that. Probably knocked on the head, poor kid.'

'Or strangled, perhaps,' said Harper.

Melchett looked at him sharply.

'You think so?'

'Well, sir, there are murderers like that.'

'I know. I've seen the parents—the poor girl's mother is beside herself. Damned painful, the whole thing. The point for us to settle is—are the two murders connected?'

'I'd say definitely yes.'

'So would I.'

The Superintendent ticked off the points on his fingers.

'Pamela Reeves attended rally of Girl Guides on Danebury

Downs. Stated by companions to be normal and cheerful. Did not return with three companions by the bus to Medchester. Said to them that she was going into Danemouth to Woolworth's and would take the bus home from there. The main road into Danemouth from the downs does a big round inland. Pamela Reeves took a short-cut over two fields and a footpath and lane which would bring her into Danemouth near the Majestic Hotel. The lane, in fact, actually passes the hotel on the west side. It's possible, therefore, that she overheard or saw something—something concerning Ruby Keene—which would have proved dangerous to the murderer—say, for instance, that she heard him arranging to meet Ruby Keene at eleven that evening. He realizes that this schoolgirl has overheard, and he has to silence her.'

Colonel Melchett said:

'That's presuming, Harper, that the Ruby Keene crime was premeditated—not spontaneous.'

Superintendent Harper agreed.

'I believe it was, sir. It looks as though it would be the other way—sudden violence, a fit of passion or jealousy—but I'm beginning to think that that's not so. I don't see otherwise how you can account for the death of the Reeves child. If she was a witness of the actual crime, it would be late at night, round about eleven p.m., and what would she be doing round about the Majestic at that time? Why, at nine o'clock her parents were getting anxious because she hadn't returned.'

'The alternative is that she went to meet someone in Danemouth unknown to her family and friends, and that her death is quite unconnected with the other death.'

'Yes, sir, and I don't believe that's so. Look how even the old lady, old Miss Marple, tumbled to it at once that there was a connection. She asked at once if the body in the burnt car was the body of the missing Girl Guide. Very smart old lady, that. These old ladies are sometimes. Shrewd, you know. Put their fingers on the vital spot.'

'Miss Marple has done that more than once,' said Colonel Melchett dryly.

'And besides, sir, there's the car. That seems to me to link up her death definitely with the Majestic Hotel. It was Mr. George Bartlett's car.'

Again the eyes of the two men met. Melchett said:

'George Bartlett? Could be! What do you think?'

Again Harper methodically recited various points.

'Ruby Keene was last seen with George Bartlett. He says she went to her room (borne out by the dress she was wearing being found there), but did she go to her room and change *in order to go out with him?* Had they made a date to go out together earlier—discussed it, say, before dinner, and did Pamela Reeves happen to overhear?'

Melchett said: 'He didn't report the loss of his car until the following morning, and he was extremely vague about it then, pretended he couldn't remember exactly when he had last noticed it.'

'That might be cleverness, sir. As I see it, he's either a very clever gentleman pretending to be a silly ass, or else—well, he is a silly ass.'

'What we want,' said Melchett, 'is motive. As it stands, he had no motive whatever for killing Ruby Keene.'

'Yes—that's where we're stuck every time. Motive. All the reports from the Palais de Danse at Brixwell are negative, I understand?'

'Absolutely! Ruby Keene had no special boy friend. Slack's been into the matter thoroughly—give Slack his due, he *is* thorough.'

'That's right, sir. Thorough's the word.'

'If there was anything to ferret out, he'd have ferreted it out. But there's nothing there. He got a list of her most frequent dancing partners—all vetted and found correct. Harmless fellows, and all able to produce alibis for that night.'

'Ah,' said Superintendent Harper. 'Alibis. That's what we're up against.'

Melchett looked at him sharply. 'Think so? I've left that side of the investigation to you.'

'Yes, sir. It's been gone into—very thoroughly. We applied to London for help over it.'

'Well?'

'Mr. Conway Jefferson may think that Mr. Gaskell and young Mrs. Jefferson are comfortably off, but that is not the case. They're both extremely hard up.'

'Is that true?'

'Quite true, sir. It's as Mr. Conway Jefferson said, he made over considerable sums of money to his son and daughter when they married. That was over ten years ago, though. Mr. Frank Jefferson fancied himself as knowing good investments. He didn't invest in anything absolutely wildcat, but he was unlucky and showed poor judgment more than once. His holdings have gone steadily down. I should say the widow found it difficult to make both ends meet and send her son to a good school.'

'But she hasn't applied to her father-in-law for help?'

'No, sir. As far as I can make out she lives with him, and consequently has no household expenses.'

'And his health is such that he wasn't expected to live long?'

'That's right, sir. Now for Mr. Mark Gaskell. He's a gambler, pure and simple. Got through his wife's money very soon. Has got himself tangled up rather critically just at present. He needs money badly—and a good deal of it.'

'Can't say I liked the looks of him much,' said Colonel Melchett. 'Wild-looking sort of fellow—what? And he's got a motive all right. Twenty-five thousand pounds it meant to him getting that girl out of the way. Yes, it's a motive all right.'

'They both had a motive.'

'I am not considering Mrs. Jefferson.'

'No, sir, I know you're not. And, anyway, the alibi holds for both of them. They *couldn't* have done it. Just that.'

'You've got a detailed statement of their movements that evening?'

'Yes, I have. Take Mr. Gaskell first. He dined with his father-in-law and Mrs. Jefferson, had coffee with them afterwards when Ruby Keene joined them. Then he said he had to write letters and left them. Actually he took his car and went for a spin down to the front. He told me quite frankly he couldn't stick playing bridge for a whole evening. The old boy's mad on it. So he made letters an excuse. Ruby Keene remained with the others. Mark Gaskell returned when she was dancing with Raymond. After the dance Ruby came and had a drink with them, then she went off with young Bartlett, and Gaskell and the others cut for partners and started their bridge. That was at twenty minutes to eleven—and he didn't leave the table until after midnight. That's quite certain, sir. Everyone says so. The family, the waiters, everyone. Therefore *he* couldn't have done it. And Mrs. Jefferson's alibi is the same. She, too, didn't leave the table. They're out, both of them—out.'

Colonel Melchett leaned back, tapping the table with a paper cutter.

Superintendent Harper said:

'That is, assuming the girl was killed before midnight.'

'Haydock said she was. He's a very sound fellow in police work. If he says a thing, it's so.'

'There might be reasons—health, physical idiosyncrasy, or something.'

'I'll put it to him.' Melchett glanced at his watch, picked up the telephone receiver and asked for a number. He said: 'Haydock ought to be at home at this time. Now, assuming that she was killed *after* midnight?'

Harper said:

'Then there might be a chance. There was some coming and going afterwards. Let's assume that Gaskell had asked the girl to meet him outside somewhere—say at twenty-past twelve. He slips away for a minute or two, strangles her, comes back and disposes of the body later—in the early hours of the morning.'

Melchett said:

'Takes her by car thirty-odd miles to put her in Bantry's library? Dash it all, it's not a likely story.'

'No, it isn't,' the Superintendent admitted at once.

The telephone rang. Melchett picked up the receiver.

'Hallo, Haydock, is that you? Ruby Keene. Would it be possible for her to have been killed *after* midnight?'

'I told you she was killed between ten and midnight.'

'Yes, I know, but one could stretch it a bit—what?'

'No, you couldn't stretch it. When I say she was killed before midnight I mean before midnight, and don't try to tamper with the medical evidence.'

'Yes, but couldn't there be some physiological whatnot? You know what I mean.'

'I know that you don't know what you're talking about. The girl was perfectly healthy and not abnormal in any way—and I'm not going to say she was just to help you fit a rope round the neck of some wretched fellow whom you police wallahs have got your knife into. Now don't protest. I know your ways. And, by the way, the girl wasn't strangled willingly—that is to say, she was drugged first. Powerful narcotic. She died of strangulation but she was drugged first.' Haydock rang off.

Melchett said gloomily: 'Well, that's that.'

Harper said:

'Thought I'd found another likely starter—but it petered out.'

'What's that? Who?'

'Strictly speaking, he's your pigeon, sir. Name of Basil Blake. Lives near Gossington Hall.'

'Impudent young jackanapes!' The Colonel's brow darkened as he remembered Basil Blake's outrageous rudeness. 'How's he mixed up in it?'

'Seems he knew Ruby Keene. Dined over at the Majestic quite often—danced with the girl. Do you remember what Josie said to Raymond when Ruby was discovered to be missing? "She's not with that film fellow, is she?" I've found out it was Blake she meant. He's employed with the Lemville Studios, you know. Josie has nothing to go upon except a belief that Ruby was rather keen on him.'

'Very promising, Harper, very promising.'

'Not so good as it sounds, sir. Basil Blake was at a party at the studios that night. You know the sort of thing. Starts at eight with cocktails and goes on and on until the air's too thick to see through and everyone passes out. According to Inspector Slack, who's questioned him, he left the show round about midnight. At midnight Ruby Keene was dead.'

'Anyone bear out his statement?'

'Most of them, I gather, sir, were rather—er—far gone. The—er—young woman now at the bungalow—Miss Dinah Lee—says his statement is correct.'

'Doesn't mean a thing!'

'No, sir, probably not. Statements taken from other members of the party bear Mr. Blake's statement out on the whole, though ideas as to time are somewhat vague.'

'Where are these studios?'

'Lemville, sir, thirty miles south-west of London.'

'H'm—about the same distance from here?'

'Yes, sir.'

Colonel Melchett rubbed his nose. He said in a rather dissatisfied tone:

'Well, it looks as though we could wash him out.'

'I think so, sir. There is no evidence that he was seriously attracted by Ruby Keene. In fact'—the Superintendent coughed primly—'he seems fully occupied with his own young lady.'

Melchett said:

'Well, we are left with "X", an unknown murderer—so unknown Slack can't find a trace of him! Or Jefferson's son-in-law, who might have wanted to kill the girl—but didn't have a chance to do so. Daughter-in-law ditto. Or George Bartlett, who has no alibi—but unfortunately no motive either. Or with young Blake, who has an alibi and no motive. And that's the lot! No, stop, I suppose we ought to consider the dancing fellow—Raymond Starr. After all, he saw a lot of the girl.'

Harper said slowly:

'Can't believe he took much interest in her—or else he's a thundering good actor. And, for all practical purposes, he's got an alibi too. He was more or less in view from twenty minutes to eleven until midnight, dancing with various partners. I don't see that we can make a case against him.'

'In fact,' said Colonel Melchett, 'we can't make a case against anybody.'

'George Bartlett's our best hope. If we could only hit on a motive.'

'You've had him looked up?'

'Yes, sir. Only child. Coddled by his mother. Came into a good deal of money on her death a year ago. Getting through it fast. Weak rather than vicious.'

'May be mental,' said Melchett hopefully.

Superintendent Harper nodded. He said:

'Has it struck you, sir—that that may be the explanation of the whole case?'

'Criminal lunatic, you mean?'

'Yes, sir. One of those fellows who go about strangling young girls. Doctors have a long name for it.'

'That would solve all our difficulties,' said Melchett.

'There's only one thing I don't like about it,' said Superintendent Harper.

'What?'

'It's too easy.'

'H'm—yes—perhaps. So, as I said at the beginning, where are we?'

'Nowhere, sir,' said Superintendent Harper.

CHAPTER XII

1

CONWAY JEFFERSON stirred in his sleep and stretched. His arms were flung out, long, powerful arms into which all the strength of his body seemed to be concentrated since his accident.

Through the curtains the morning light glowed softly.

Conway Jefferson smiled to himself. Always, after a night of rest, he woke like this, happy, refreshed, his deep vitality renewed. Another day!

So for a minute he lay. Then he pressed the special bell by his hand. And suddenly a wave of remembrance swept over him.

Even as Edwards, deft and quiet-footed, entered the room, a groan was wrung from his master.

Edwards paused with his hand on the curtains. He said: 'You're not in pain, sir?'

Conway Jefferson said harshly:

'No. Go on, pull 'em.'

The clear light flooded the room. Edwards, understanding, did not glance at his master.

His face grim, Conway Jefferson lay remembering and thinking. Before his eyes he saw again the pretty, vapid face of Ruby. Only in his mind he did not use the adjective vapid. Last night he would have said innocent. A naïve, innocent child! And now?

A great weariness came over Conway Jefferson. He closed his eyes. He murmured below his breath:

'Margaret . . .'

It was the name of his dead wife. . . .

2

'I like your friend,' said Adelaide Jefferson to Mrs. Bantry.

The two women were sitting on the terrace.

'Jane Marple's a very remarkable woman,' said Mrs. Bantry.

'She's nice too,' said Addie smiling.

'People call her a scandalmonger,' said Mrs. Bantry, 'but she isn't really.'

'Just a low opinion of human nature?'

'You could call it that.'

'It's rather refreshing,' said Adelaide Jefferson, 'after having had too much of the other thing.'

Mrs. Bantry looked at her sharply.

Addie explained herself.

'So much high-thinking—idealization of an unworthy object!'

'You mean Ruby Keene?'

Addie nodded.

'I don't want to be horrid about her. There wasn't any harm in her. Poor little rat, she had to fight for what she wanted. She wasn't bad. Common and rather silly and quite good-natured, but a decided little gold-digger. I don't think she schemed or planned. It was just that she was quick to take advantage of a possibility. And she knew just how to appeal to an elderly man who was—lonely.'

'I suppose,' said Mrs. Bantry thoughtfully, 'that Conway *was* lonely?'

Addie moved restlessly. She said:

'He was—this summer.' She paused and then burst out: 'Mark will have it that it was all my fault. Perhaps it was, I don't know.'

She was silent for a minute, then, impelled by some need to talk, she went on speaking in a difficult, almost reluctant way.

'I—I've had such an odd sort of life. Mike Carmody, my first husband, died so soon after we were married—it—it knocked me out. Peter, as you know, was born after his death. Frank Jefferson was Mike's great friend. So I came to see a lot of him. He was Peter's godfather—Mike had wanted that. I got very fond of him—and—oh! sorry for him too.'

'Sorry?' queried Mrs. Bantry with interest.

'Yes, just that. It sounds odd. Frank had always had everything he wanted. His father and his mother couldn't have been nicer to him. And yet—how can I say it?—you see, old Mr. Jefferson's personality is so strong. If you live with it, you can't somehow have a personality of your own. Frank felt that.

'When we were married he was very happy—wonderfully so. Mr. Jefferson was very generous. He settled a large sum of money on Frank—said he wanted his children to be independent and not have to wait for his death. It was so nice of him—so generous. But it was much too sudden. He ought really to have accustomed Frank to independence little by little.

'It went to Frank's head. He wanted to be as good a man as his father, as clever about money and business, as far-seeing and successful. And, of course, he wasn't. He didn't exactly speculate with the money, but he invested in the wrong things at the wrong time. It's frightening, you know, how soon money goes if you're not clever about it. The more Frank dropped, the more eager he was to get it back by some clever deal. So things went from bad to worse.'

'But, my dear,' said Mrs. Bantry, 'couldn't Conway have advised him?'

'He didn't want to be advised. The one thing he wanted was to do well on his own. That's why we never let Mr. Jefferson know. When Frank died there was very little left—only a tiny income for me. And I—I didn't let his father know either. You see——'

She turned abruptly.

'It would have felt like betraying Frank to him. Frank would have hated it so. Mr. Jefferson was ill for a long time. When he got well he assumed that I was a very-well-off widow. I've never undeceived him. It's been a point of honour. He knows I'm very careful about money—but he approves of that, thinks I'm a thrifty sort of woman. And, of course, Peter and I have lived with him practically ever since, and he's paid for all our living expenses. So I've never had to worry.'

She said slowly:

'We've been like a family all these years—only—only—you see (or don't you see?) I've never been Frank's *widow* to him—I've been Frank's *wife*.'

Mrs. Bantry grasped the implication.

'You mean he's never accepted their deaths?'

'No. He's been wonderful. But he's conquered his own terrible tragedy by refusing to recognize death. Mark is Rosamund's husband and I'm Frank's wife—and though Frank and Rosamund aren't exactly here with us—they are still existent.'

Mrs. Bantry said softly:

'It's a wonderful triumph of faith.'

'I know. We've gone on, year after year. But suddenly—this summer—something went wrong in me. I felt—I felt rebellious. It's an awful thing to say, but I didn't want to think of Frank any more! All that was over—my love and companionship with him, and my grief when he died. It was something that had been and wasn't any longer.

'It's awfully hard to describe. It's like wanting to wipe the slate clean and start again. I wanted to be me—Addie, still reasonably young and strong and able to play games and swim and dance—just a *person*. Even Hugo—(you know Hugo McLean?) he's a dear and wants to marry me, but, of course, I've never really thought of it—but this summer I *did* begin to think of it—not seriously—only vaguely . . .'

She stopped and shook her head.

'And so I suppose it's true. *I neglected Jeff.* I don't mean *really* neglected him, but my mind and thoughts weren't with him. When Ruby, as I saw, amused him, I was rather glad. It left me freer to go and do my own things. I never dreamed—of course I never dreamed—that he would be so—so—*infatuated* by her!'

Mrs. Bantry asked:

'And when you did find out?'

'I was dumbfounded—absolutely dumbfounded! And, I'm afraid, angry too.'

'*I*'d have been angry,' said Mrs. Bantry.

'There was Peter, you see. Peter's whole future depends on Jeff. Jeff practically looked on him as a grandson, or so I thought, but, of course, he wasn't a grandson. He was no relation at all. And to think that he was going to be—disinherited!' Her firm, well-shaped hands shook a little where they lay in her lap. 'For that's what it felt like—and for a vulgar, gold-digging little simpleton——Oh! I could have killed her!'

She stopped, stricken. Her beautiful hazel eyes met Mrs. Bantry's in a pleading horror. She said:

'*What an awful thing to say!*'

Hugo McLean, coming quietly up behind them, asked:

'What's an awful thing to say?'

'Sit down, Hugo. You know Mrs. Bantry, don't you?'

McLean had already greeted the older lady. He said now in a slow, persevering way:

'What was an awful thing to say?'

Addie Jefferson said:

'That I'd like to have killed Ruby Keene.'

Hugo McLean reflected a minute or two. Then he said:

'No, I wouldn't say that if I were you. Might be misunderstood.'

His eyes—steady, reflective, grey eyes—looked at her meaningly. He said:

'You've got to watch your step, Addie.'

There was a warning in his voice.

3

When Miss Marple came out of the hotel and joined Mrs. Bantry a few minutes later, Hugo McLean and Adelaide Jefferson were walking down the path to the sea together.

Seating herself, Miss Marple remarked:

'He seems very devoted.'

'He's been devoted for years! One of those men.'

'I know. Like Major Bury. He hung round an Anglo-Indian widow for quite ten years. A joke among her friends! In the end she gave in—but unfortunately ten days before they were to have been married she ran away with the chauffeur! Such a nice woman, too, and usually so well balanced.'

'People do do very odd things,' agreed Mrs. Bantry.

'I wish you'd been here just now, Jane. Addie Jefferson was telling me all about herself—how her husband went through all his money but they never let Mr. Jefferson know. And then, this summer, things felt different to her——'

Miss Marple nodded.

'Yes. She rebelled, I suppose, against being made to live in the past? After all, there's a time for everything. You can't sit in the house with the blinds down for ever. I suppose Mrs. Jefferson just pulled them up and took off her widow's weeds, and her father-in-law, of course, didn't like it. Felt left out in the cold, though I don't suppose for a minute he realized who put her up to it. Still, he certainly wouldn't like it. And so, of course, like old Mr. Badger when his wife took up Spiritualism, he was just ripe for what happened. Any fairly nice-looking young girl who listened prettily would have done.'

'Do you think,' said Mrs. Bantry, 'that that cousin, Josie, got her down here deliberately—that it was a family plot?'

Miss Marple shook her head.

'No, I don't think so at all. I don't think Josie has the kind of mind that could foresee people's reactions. She's rather dense in that way. She's got one of those shrewd, limited, practical minds that never do foresee the future and are usually astonished by it.'

'It seems to have taken everyone by surprise,' said Mrs. Bantry. 'Addie—and Mark Gaskell too, apparently.'

Miss Marple smiled.

'I dare say he had his own fish to fry. A bold fellow with a roving eye! Not the man to go on being a sorrowing widower for years, no matter how fond he may have been of his wife. I should think they were both restless under old Mr. Jefferson's yoke of perpetual remembrance.'

'Only,' added Miss Marple cynically, 'it's easier for gentlemen, of course.'

4

At that very moment Mark was confirming this judgment on himself in a talk with Sir Henry Clithering.

With characteristic candour Mark had gone straight to the heart of things.

'It's just dawned on me,' he said, 'that I'm Favourite Suspect No. 1 to the police! They've been delving into my financial troubles. I'm broke, you know, or very nearly. If dear old Jeff dies according to schedule in a month or two, and Addie and I divide the dibs also according to schedule, all will be well. Matter of fact, I owe rather a lot. . . . If the crash comes it will be a big one! If I can stave it off, it will be the other way round—I shall come out on top and be a very rich man.'

Sir Henry Clithering said:

'You're a gambler, Mark.'

'Always have been. Risk everything—that's my motto! Yes, it's a lucky thing for me that somebody strangled that poor kind. I didn't do it. I'm not a strangler. I don't really think I could ever murder anybody. I'm too easy going. But I don't suppose I can ask the police to believe *that*! I must look to them like the answer to the criminal investigator's prayer! I had a motive, was on the spot, I am not burdened with high moral scruples! I can't imagine why I'm not in jug already! That Superintendent's got a very nasty eye.'

'You've got that useful thing, an alibi.'

'An alibi is the fishiest thing on God's earth! No innocent person ever has an alibi! Besides, it all depends on the time of death, or something like that, and you may be sure if three doctors say the girl was killed at midnight, at least six will be found who will swear positively that she was killed at five in the morning—and where's my alibi then?'

'At any rate, you are able to joke about it.'

'Damned bad taste, isn't it?' said Mark cheerfully. 'Actually, I'm rather scared. One is—with murder! And don't think I'm not sorry for old Jeff. I am. But it's better this way—bad as the shock was—than if he'd found her out.'

'What do you mean, found her out?'

Mark winked.

'Where did she go off to last night? I'll lay you any odds you like she went to meet a man. Jeff wouldn't have liked that. He wouldn't have liked it at all. If he'd found she was deceiving him—that she wasn't the prattling little innocent she seemed—well—my father-in-law is an odd man. He's a man of great self-control, but that self-control can snap. And then—look out!'

Sir Henry glanced at him curiously.

'Are you fond of him or not?'

'I'm very fond of him—and at the same time I resent him. I'll try and explain. Conway Jefferson is a man who likes to control his surroundings. He's a benevolent despot, kind, generous, and affectionate—but his is the tune, and the others dance to his piping.'

Mark Gaskell paused.

'I loved my wife. I shall never feel the same for anyone else. Rosamund was sunshine and laughter and flowers, and when she was killed I felt just like a man in the ring who's had a knock-out blow. But the referee's been counting a good long time now. I'm a man, after all. I like women. I don't want to marry again—not in the least. Well, that's all right. I've had to be discreet—but I've had my good times all right. Poor Addie hasn't. Addie's a really nice woman. She's the kind of woman men want to marry, not to sleep with. Give her half a chance and she would marry again—and be very happy and make the chap happy too. But old Jeff saw her always as Frank's wife—and hypnotized her into seeing herself like that. He doesn't know it, but we've been in prison. I broke out, on the quiet, a long time ago. Addie broke out this summer—and it gave him a shock. It split up his world. Result—Ruby Keene.'

Irrepressibly he sang:

> *"But she is dead and in her grave,*
> *And, oh, the difference to me!*

'Come and have a drink, Clithering.'

It was hardly surprising, Sir Henry reflected, that Mark Gaskell should be an object of suspicion to the police.

CHAPTER XIII

1

DR. METCALF was one of the best-known physicians in Danemouth. He had no aggressive bedside manner, but his presence in the sick room had an invariably cheering effect. He was middle-aged, with a quiet pleasant voice.

He listened carefully to Superintendent Harper and replied to his questions with gentle precision.

Harper said:

'Then I can take it, Doctor Metcalf, that what I was told by Mrs. Jefferson was substantially correct?'

'Yes, Mr. Jefferson's health is in a precarious state. For several years now the man has been driving himself ruthlessly. In his determination to live like other men, he has lived at a far greater pace than the normal man of his age. He has refused to rest, to take things easy, to go slow—or any of the other phrases with which I and his other medical advisers have tendered our opinion. The result is that the man is an overworked engine. Heart, lungs, blood pressure—they're all overstrained.'

'You say Mr. Jefferson has absolutely refused to listen?'

'Yes. I don't know that I blame him. It's not what I say to my patients, Superintendent, but a man may as well wear out as rust out. A lot of my colleagues do that, and take it from me it's not a bad way. In a place like Danemouth one sees most of the other thing: invalids clinging to life, terrified of over-exerting themselves, terrified of a breath of draughty air, of a stray germ, of an injudicious meal!'

'I expect that's true enough,' said Superintendent Harper. 'What it amounts to, then, is this: Conway Jefferson is strong enough, physically speaking—or, I suppose I mean, muscularly speaking. Just what can he do in the active line, by the way?'

'He has immense strength in his arms and shoulders. He was a powerful man before his accident. He is extremely dexterous in his handling of his wheeled chair, and with the aid of crutches he can move himself about a room—from his bed to the chair, for instance.'

'Isn't it possible for a man injured as Mr. Jefferson was to have artificial legs?'

'Not in his case. There was a spine injury.'

'I see. Let me sum up again. Jefferson is strong and fit in the muscular sense. He feels well and all that?'

Metcalf nodded.

'But his heart is in a bad condition. Any overstrain or exertion, or a shock or a sudden fright, and he might pop off. Is that it?'

'More or less. Over-exertion is killing him slowly, because he won't give in when he feels tired. That aggravates the cardiac condition. It is unlikely that exertion would kill him suddenly. But a sudden shock or fright might easily do so. That is why I expressly warned his family.'

Superintendent Harper said slowly:

'But in actual fact a shock *didn't* kill him. I mean, doctor, that there couldn't have been a much worse shock than this business, and he's still alive?'

Dr. Metcalf shrugged his shoulders.

'I know. But if you'd had my experience, Superintendent, you'd know that case history shows the impossibility of prognosticating accurately. People who *ought* to die of shock and exposure *don't* die of shock and exposure, etc., etc. The human frame is tougher than one can imagine possible. Moreover, in my experience, a *physical* shock is more often fatal than a *mental* shock. In plain language, a door banging suddenly would be more likely to kill Mr. Jefferson than the discovery that a girl he was fond of had died in a particularly horrible manner.'

'Why is that, I wonder?'

'The breaking of a piece of bad news nearly always sets up a defence reaction. It numbs the recipient. They are unable—at first—

to take it in. Full realization takes a little time. But the banged door, someone jumping out of a cupboard, the sudden onslaught of a motor as you cross a road—all those things are immediate in their action. The heart gives a terrified leap—to put it in layman's language.'

Superintendent Harper said slowly:

'But as far as anyone would know, Mr. Jefferson's death might easily have been caused by the shock of the girl's death?'

'Oh, easily.' The doctor looked curiously at the other. 'You don't think——'

'I don't know what I think,' said Superintendent Harper vexedly.

2

'But you'll admit, sir, that the two things would fit in very prettily together,' he said a little later to Sir Henry Clithering. 'Kill two birds with one stone. First the girl—and the fact of her death takes off Mr. Jefferson too—before he's had any opportunity of altering his will.'

'Do you think he will alter it?'

'You'd be more likely to know that, sir, than I would. What do you say?'

'I don't know. Before Ruby Keene came on the scene I happen to know that he had left his money between Mark Gaskell and Mrs. Jefferson. I don't see why he should now change his mind about that. But of course he might do so. Might leave it to a Cats' Home, or to subsidize young professional dancers.'

Superintendent Harper agreed.

'You never know what bee a man is going to get in his bonnet—especially when he doesn't feel there's any moral obligation in the disposal of his fortune. No blood relations in this case.'

Sir Henry said:

'He is fond of the boy—of young Peter.'

'D'you think he regards him as a grandson? You'd know that better than I would, sir.'

Sir Henry said slowly:

'No, I don't think so.'

'There's another thing I'd like to ask you, sir. It's a thing I can't judge for myself. But they're friends of yours and so you'd know. I'd like very much to know just how fond Mr. Jefferson is of Mr. Gaskell and young Mrs. Jefferson.'

Sir Henry frowned.

'I'm not sure if I understand you, Superintendent?'

'Well, it's this way, sir. How fond is he of them as *persons*—apart from his relationship to them?'

'Ah, I see what you mean.'

'Yes, sir. Nobody doubts that he was very attached to them both—but he was attached to them, as I see it, because they were, respectively, the husband and the wife of his daughter and his son. But supposing, for instance, one of them had married again?'

Sir Henry reflected. He said:

'It's an interesting point you raise there. I don't know. I'm inclined to suspect—this is a mere opinion—that it would have altered his attitude a good deal. He would have wished them well, borne no rancour, but I think, yes, I rather think that he would have taken very little more interest in them.'

'In both cases, sir?'

'I think so, yes. In Mr. Gaskell's, almost certainly, and I rather think in Mrs. Jefferson's also, but that's not nearly so certain. I think he *was* fond of her for her own sake.'

'Sex would have something to do with that,' said Superintendent Harper sapiently. 'Easier for him to look on her as a daughter than to look on Mr. Gaskell as a son. It works both ways. Women accept a son-in-law as one of the family easily enough, but there aren't many times when a woman looks on her son's wife as a daughter.'

Superintendent Harper went on:

'Mind if we walk along this path, sir, to the tennis court? I see Miss Marple's sitting there. I want to ask her to do something for me. As a matter of fact I want to rope you both in.'

'In what way, Superintendent?'

'To get at stuff that I can't get at myself. I want you to tackle Edwards for me, sir.'

'Edwards? What do you want from him?'

'Everything you can think of! Everything he knows and what he thinks! About the relations between the various members of the family, his angle on the Ruby Keene business. Inside stuff. He knows better than anyone the state of affairs—you be he does!

And he wouldn't tell *me*. But he'll tell *you*. Because you're a gentleman and a friend of Mr. Jefferson's. And something *might* turn up from it. That is, of course, if you don't object?'

Sir Henry said grimly:

'I don't object. I've been sent for, urgently, to get at the truth. I mean to do my utmost.'

He added:

'How do you want Miss Marple to help you?'

'With some girls. Some of those Girl Guides. We've rounded up half a dozen or so, the ones who were most friendly with Pamela Reeves. It's possible that they may know something. You see, I've been thinking. It seems to me that if that girl was really going to Woolworth's she would have tried to persuade one of the other girls to go with her. Girls usually like to shop with someone.'

'Yes, I think that's true.'

'So I think it's possible that Woolworth's was only an excuse. I want to know where the girl was really going. She may have let slip something. If so, I feel Miss Marple's the person to get it out of these girls. I'd say she knows a thing or two about girls—more than I do. And, anyway, they'd be scared of the police.'

'It sounds to me the kind of village domestic problem that is right up Miss Marple's street. She's very sharp, you know.'

The Superintendent smiled. He said:

'I'll say you're right. Nothing much gets past her.'

Miss Marple looked up at their approach and welcomed them eagerly. She listened to the Superintendent's request and at once acquiesced.

'I should like to help you very much, Superintendent, and I think that perhaps I *could* be of some use. What with the Sunday School, you know, and the Brownies, and our Guides, and the Orphanage quite near—I'm on the committee, you know, and often run in to have a little talk with Matron—and then *servants*—I usually have very young maids. Oh, yes, I've quite a lot of experience in when a girl is speaking the truth and when she is holding something back.'

'In fact, you're an expert,' said Sir Henry.

Miss Marple flashed him a reproachful glance and said:

'Oh, *please* don't laugh at me, Sir Henry.'

'I shouldn't dream of laughing at you. You've had the laugh of me too many times.'

'One does see so much evil in a village,' murmured Miss Marple in an explanatory voice.

'By the way,' said Sir Henry, 'I've cleared up one point you asked me about. The Superintendent tells me that there were nail clippings in Ruby's wastepaper-basket.'

Miss Marple said thoughtfully:

'There were? Then that's that. . . '

'Why did you want to know, Miss Marple?' asked the Superintendent.

Miss Marple said:

'It was one of the things that—well, that seemed *wrong* when I looked at the body. The hands were wrong, somehow, and I couldn't at first think *why*. Then I realized that girls who are very much made-up, and all that, usually have very long fingernails. Of course, I know that girls everywhere do bite their nails—it's one of those habits that are very hard to break oneself off. But vanity often does a lot to help. Still, I presumed that this girl *hadn't* cured herself. And then the little boy—Peter, you know—he said something which showed that her nails *had* been long, only she caught one and broke it. So then, of course, she might have trimmed off the rest to make an even appearance, and I asked about clippings and Sir Henry said he'd find out.'

Sir Henry remarked:

'You said just now, "*one* of the things that seemed wrong when you looked at the body." Was there something else?'

Miss Marple nodded vigorously.

'Oh yes!' she said. 'There was the dress. The dress was *all* wrong.'

Both men looked at her curiously.

'Now why?' said Sir Henry.

'Well, you see, it was an old dress. Josie said so, definitely, and I could see for myself that it was shabby and rather worn. Now that's all wrong.'

'I don't see why?'

Miss Marple got a little pink.

'Well, the idea is, isn't it, that Ruby Keene changed her dress and went off to meet someone on whom she presumably had what my young nephews call a "crush"?'

The Superintendent's eyes twinkled a little.

'That's the theory. She'd got a date with someone—a boy friend, as the saying goes.'

'Then why,' demanded Miss Marple, 'was she wearing an old dress?'

The Superintendent scratched his head thoughtfully. He said:

'I see your point. You think she'd wear a new one?'

'I think she'd wear her best dress. Girls do.'

Sir Henry interposed.

'Yes, but look here, Miss Marple. Suppose she was going outside to this *rendezvous*. Going in an open car, perhaps, or walking in some rough going. Then she'd not want to risk messing a new frock and she'd put on an old one.'

'That would be the sensible thing to do,' agreed the Superintendent.

Miss Marple turned on him. She spoke with animation.

'The sensible thing to do would be to change into trousers and a pullover, or into tweeds. That, of course (I don't want to be snobbish, but I'm afraid it's unavoidable), that's what a girl of—of our class would do.

'A well-bred girl,' continued Miss Marple, warming to her subject, 'is always very particular to wear the right clothes for the right occasion. I mean, however hot the day was, a well-bred girl would never turn up at a point-to-point in a silk flowered frock.'

'And the correct wear to meet a lover?' demanded Sir Henry.

'If she were meeting him inside the hotel or somewhere where evening dress was worn, she'd wear her best evening frock, of course —but *outside* she'd feel she'd look ridiculous in evening dress and she'd wear her most attractive sports wear.'

'Granted, Fashion Queen, but the girl Ruby——'

Miss Marple said:

'Ruby, of course, wasn't—well, to put it bluntly—Ruby *wasn't* a lady. She belonged to the class that wear their best clothes however unsuitable to the occasion. Last year, you know, we had a picnic outing at Scrantor Rocks. You'd be surprised at the unsuitable clothes the girls wore. Foulard dresses and patent shoes and quite elaborate hats, some of them. For climbing about over rocks and in gorse and heather. And the young men in their best suits. Of course, hiking's different again. That's practically a uniform—and girls don't seem to realize that shorts are very unbecoming unless they are very slender.'

The Superintendent said slowly:

'And you think that Ruby Keene——'

'I think that she'd have kept on the frock she was wearing—her best pink one. She'd only have changed it if she'd had something newer still.'

Superintendent Harper said:

'And what's your explanation, Miss Marple?'

Miss Marple said:

'I haven't got one—yet. But I can't help feeling that it's important. . . .'

3

Inside the wire cage, the tennis lesson that Raymond Starr was giving had come to an end.

A stout middle-aged woman uttered a few appreciative squeaks, picked up a sky-blue cardigan and went off towards the hotel.

Raymond called out a few gay words after her.

Then he turned towards the bench where the three onlookers were sitting. The balls dangled in a net in his hand, his racket was under one arm. The gay, laughing expression on his face was wiped off as though by a sponge from a slate. He looked tired and worried.

Coming towards them, he said: '*That's* over.'

Then the smile broke out again, that charming, boyish, expressive smile that went so harmoniously with his sun-tanned face and dark lithe grace.

Sir Henry found himself wondering how old the man was. Twenty-five, thirty, thirty-five? It was impossible to say.

Raymond said, shaking his head a little:

'*She*'ll never be able to play, you know.'

'All this must be very boring for you,' said Miss Marple.

Raymond said simply:

'It is, sometimes. Especially at the end of the summer. For a time the thought of the pay buoys you up, but even that fails to stimulate imagination in the end!'

Superintendent Harper got up. He said abruptly:

'I'll call for you in half an hour's time, Miss Marple, if that will be all right?'

'Perfectly, thank you. I shall be ready.'

Harper went off. Raymond stood looking after him. Then he said: 'Mind if I sit here for a bit?'

'Do,' said Sir Henry. 'Have a cigarette?' He offered his case, wondering as he did so why he had a slight feeling of prejudice against Raymond Starr. Was it simply because he was a professional tennis coach and dancer? If so, it wasn't the tennis—it was the dancing. The English, Sir Henry decided, had a distrust for any man who danced too well! This fellow moved with too much grace! Ramon—Raymond—which was his name? Abruptly, he asked the question.

The other seemed amused.

'Ramon was my original professional name. Ramon and Josie—Spanish effect, you know. Then there was rather a prejudice against foreigners—so I became Raymond—very British——'

Miss Marple said:

'And is your real name something quite different?'

He smiled at her.

'Actually my real name is Ramon. I had an Argentine grandmother, you see——' (And that accounts for that swing from the hips, thought Sir Henry parenthetically.) 'But my first name is Thomas. Painfully prosaic.'

He turned to Sir Henry.

'You come from Devonshire, don't you, sir? From Stane? My people lived down that way. At Alsmonston.'

Sir Henry's face lit up.

'Are you one of the Alsmonston Starrs? I didn't realize that.'

'No—I don't suppose you would.'

There was a slight bitterness in his voice.

Sir Henry said awkwardly:

'Bad luck—er—all that.'

'The place being sold up after it had been in the family for three hundred years? Yes, it was rather. Still, our kind have to go, I suppose. We've outlived our usefulness. My elder brother went to New York. He's in publishing—doing well. The rest of us are scattered up and down the earth. I'll say it's hard to get a job nowadays when you've nothing to say for yourself except that you've had a public-school education! Sometimes, if you're lucky, you get taken on as a reception clerk at an hotel. The tie and the manner are an asset there. The only job I could get was showman in a plumbing establishment. Selling superb peach and lemon-coloured porcelain baths. Enormous showrooms, but as I never knew the price of the damned things or how soon we could deliver them—I got fired.

'The only things I *could* do were dance and play tennis. I got taken on at an hotel on the Riviera. Good pickings there. I suppose I was doing well. Then I overheard an old Colonel, real old Colonel, incredibly ancient, British to the backbone and always talking about Poona. He went up to the manager and said at the top of his voice:

'"Where's the *gigolo?* I want to get hold of the *gigolo.* My wife and daughter want to dance, yer know. Where is the feller? What does he sting yer for? It's the *gigolo* I want."'

Raymond went on:

'Silly to mind—but I did. I chucked it. Came here. Less pay but pleasanter work. Mostly teaching tennis to rotund women who will never, never, never be able to play. That and dancing with the neglected wallflower daughters of rich clients. Oh well, it's life, I suppose. Excuse to-day's hard-luck story!'

He laughed. His teeth flashed out white, his eyes crinkled up at the corners. He looked suddenly healthy and happy and very much alive.

Sir Henry said:

'I'm glad to have a chat with you. I've been wanting to talk with you.'

'About Ruby Keene? I can't help you, you know. I don't know who killed her. I knew very little about her. She didn't confide in me.'

Miss Marple said: 'Did you like her?'

'Not particularly. I didn't dislike her.'

His voice was careless, uninterested.

Sir Henry said: 'So you've no suggestions to offer?'

'I'm afraid not. . . . I'd have told Harper if I had. It just seems to me one of those things! Petty, sordid little crime—no clues, no motive.'

'Two people had a motive,' said Miss Marple.

Sir Henry looked at her sharply.

'Really?' Raymond looked surprised.

Miss Marple looked insistently at Sir Henry and he said rather unwillingly:

'Her death probably benefits Mrs. Jefferson and Mr. Gaskell to the amount of fifty thousand pounds.'

'What?' Raymond looked really startled—more than startled—upset. 'Oh, but that's absurd—absolutely absurd—Mrs. Jefferson—neither of them—could have had anything to do with it. It would be incredible to think of such a thing.'

Miss Marple coughed.

She said gently:

'I'm afraid, you know, you're rather an idealist.'

'I?' he laughed. 'Not me! I'm a hard-boiled cynic.'

'Money,' said Miss Marple, 'is a very powerful motive.'

'Perhaps,' Raymond said hotly. 'But that either of those two would strangle a girl in cold blood——' He shook his head.

Then he got up.

'Here's Mrs. Jefferson now. Come for her lesson. She's late.' His voice sounded amused. 'Ten minutes late!'

Adelaide Jefferson and Hugo McLean were walking rapidly down the path towards them.

With a smiling apology for her lateness, Addie Jefferson went on to the court. McLean sat down on the bench. After a polite inquiry whether Miss Marple minded a pipe, he lit it and puffed for some minutes in silence, watching critically the two white figures about the tennis court.

He said at last:

'Can't see what Addie wants to have lessons for. Have a game, yes. No one enjoys it better than I do. But why *lessons*?'

'Wants to improve her game,' said Sir Henry.

'She's not a bad player,' said Hugo. 'Good enough, at all events. Dash it all, she isn't aiming to play at Wimbledon.'

He was silent for a minute or two. Then he said:

'Who *is* this Raymond fellow. Where do they come from, these pros.? Fellow looks like a dago to me.'

'He's one of the Devonshire Starrs,' said Sir Henry.

'What? Not really?'

Sir Henry nodded. It was clear that this news was unpleasing to Hugo McLean. He scowled more than ever.

He said: 'Don't know why Addie sent for *me*. She seems not to have turned a hair over this business! Never looked better. Why send for me?'

Sir Henry asked with some curiosity:

'When did she send for you?'

'Oh—er—when all this happened.'

'How did you hear? Telephone or telegram?'

'Telegram.'

'As a matter of curiosity, when was it sent off?'

'Well—I don't know exactly.'

'What time did you receive it?'

'I didn't exactly receive it. It was telephoned on to me—as a matter of fact.'

'Why, where were you?'

'Fact is, I'd left London the afternoon before. I was staying at Danebury Head.'

'What—quite near here?'

'Yes, rather funny, wasn't it? Got the message when I got in from a round of golf and came over here at once.'

Miss Marple gazed at him thoughtfully. He looked hot and uncomfortable. She said: 'I've heard it's very pleasant at Danebury Head, and not very expensive.'

'No, it's not expensive. I couldn't afford it if it was. It's a nice little place.'

'We must drive over there one day,' said Miss Marple.

'Eh? What? Oh—er—yes, I should.' He got up. 'Better take some exercise—get an appetite.'

He walked away stiffly.

'Women,' said Sir Henry, 'treat their devoted admirers very badly.'

Miss Marple smiled but made no answer.

'Does he strike you as rather a dull dog?' asked Sir Henry. 'I'd be interested to know.'

'A little limited in his ideas, perhaps,' said Miss Marple. 'But with possibilities, I think—oh, definitely possibilities.'

Sir Henry in his turn got up.

'It's time for me to go and do my stuff. I see Mrs. Bantry is on her way to keep you company.'

4

Mrs. Bantry arrived breathless and sat down with a gasp.

She said:

'I've been talking to chambermaids. But it isn't any good. I haven't found out a thing more! Do you think that girl can really have been carrying on with someone without everybody in the hotel knowing all about it?'

'That's a very interesting point, dear. I should say, definitely *not*. *Somebody* knows, depend upon it, if it's true! But she must have been very clever about it.'

Mrs. Bantry's attention had strayed to the tennis court. She said approvingly:

'Addie's tennis is coming on a lot. Attractive young man, that tennis pro. Addie's looking quite nice looking. She's still a very attractive woman—I shouldn't be at all surprised if she married again.'

'She'll be a rich woman, too, when Mr. Jefferson dies,' said Miss Marple.

'Oh, don't always have such a nasty mind, Jane! Why haven't you solved this mystery yet? We don't seem to be getting on at all. I thought you'd know *at once*.' Mrs. Bantry's tone held reproach.

'No, no, dear. I didn't know at once—not for some time.'

Mrs. Bantry turned startled and incredulous eyes on her.

'You mean you know *now* who killed Ruby Keene?'

'Oh yes,' said Miss Marple, 'I know *that*!'

'But Jane, who is it? Tell me at once.'

Miss Marple shook her head very firmly and pursed up her lips.

'I'm sorry, Dolly, but that wouldn't do at all.'

'Why wouldn't it do?'

'Because you're so indiscreet. You would go round telling everyone—or, if you didn't tell, you'd *hint*.'

'No, I wouldn't. I wouldn't tell a soul.'

'People who use that phrase are always the last to live up to it. It's no good, dear. There's a long way to go yet. A great many things that are quite obscure. You remember when I was so against letting Mrs. Partridge collect for the Red Cross, and I couldn't say *why*. The reason was that her nose had twitched in just the same way that that maid of mine, Alice, twitched *her* nose when I sent her out to pay the books. Always paid them a shilling or so short, and said, "it could go on to the next week's account," which of course, was *exactly* what Mrs. Partridge did, only on a much larger scale. Seventy-five pounds it was *she* embezzled.'

'Never mind Mrs. Partridge,' said Mrs. Bantry.

'But I had to explain to you. And if you care I'll give you a *hint*.

The trouble in this case is that everybody has been much too *credulous* and *believing*. You simply cannot *afford* to believe everything that people tell you. When there's anything fishy about, I never believe anyone at all! You see, I know human nature so well.'

Mrs. Bantry was silent for a minute or two. Then she said in a different tone of voice:

'I told you, didn't I, that I didn't see why I shouldn't enjoy myself over this case. A real murder in my own house! The sort of thing that will never happen again.'

'I hope not,' said Miss Marple.

'Well, so do I, really. Once is enough. But it's *my* murder, Jane; I want to enjoy myself over it.'

Miss Marple shot a glance at her.

Mrs. Bantry said belligerently:

'Don't you believe that?'

Miss Marple said sweetly:

'Of course, Dolly, if you tell me so.'

'Yes, but you never believe what people tell you, do you? You've just said so. Well, you're quite right.' Mrs. Bantry's voice took on a sudden bitter note. She said: 'I'm not altogether a fool. You may think, Jane, that I don't know what they're saying all over St. Mary Mead—all over the county! They're saying, one and all, that there's no smoke without fire, that if the girl was found in Arthur's library, then Arthur must know something about it. They're saying that the girl was Arthur's mistress—that she was his illegitimate daughter—that she was blackmailing him. They're saying anything that comes into their damned heads! And it will go on like that! Arthur won't realize it at first—he won't know what's wrong. He's such a dear old stupid that he'd never believe people would think things like that about him. He'll be cold-shouldered and looked at askance (whatever *that* means!) and it will dawn on him little by little and suddenly he'll be horrified and cut to the soul, and he'll fasten up like a clam and just *endure*, day after day, in misery.

'It's because of all that's going to happen to him that I've come here to ferret out every single thing about it that I can! This murder's *got* to be solved! If it isn't, then Arthur's whole life will be wrecked—and I won't have that happen. I won't! I won't! I won't!'

She paused for a minute and said:

'I *won't* have the dear old boy go through hell for something he didn't do. That's the only reason I came to Danemouth and left him alone at home—to find out the truth.'

'I know, dear,' said Miss Marple. 'That's why I'm here too.'

CHAPTER XIV

1

IN A QUIET HOTEL ROOM Edwards was listening deferentially to Sir Henry Clithering.

'There are certain questions I would like to ask you, Edwards, but I want you first to understand quite clearly my position here. I was at one time Commissioner of Police at Scotland Yard. I am now retired into private life. Your master sent for me when this tragedy occurred. He begged me to use my skill and experience in order to find out the truth.'

Sir Henry paused.

Edwards, his pale intelligent eyes on the other's face, inclined his head. He said:

'Quite so, Sir Henry.'

Clithering went on slowly and deliberately:

'In all police cases there is necessarily a lot of information that is held back. It is held back for various reasons—because it touches on a family skeleton, because it is considered to have no bearing on the case, because it would entail awkwardness and embarrassment to the parties concerned.'

Again Edwards said:

'Quite so, Sir Henry.'

'I expect, Edwards, that by now you appreciate quite clearly the main points of this business. The dead girl was on the point of becoming Mr. Jefferson's adopted daughter. Two people had a motive in seeing that this should not happen. Those two people are Mr. Gaskell and Mrs. Jefferson.'

The valet's eyes displayed a momentary gleam. He said: 'May I ask if they are under suspicion, sir?'

'They are in no danger of arrest, if that is what you mean. But the police are bound to be suspicious of them and will continue to be so *until the matter is cleared up*.'

'An unpleasant position for them, sir.'

'Very unpleasant. Now to get at the truth one must have *all* the facts of the case. A lot depends, *must* depend, on the reactions, the words and gestures, of Mr. Jefferson and his family. How did they feel, what did they show, what things were said? I am asking you, Edwards, for inside information—the kind of inside information that only you are likely to have. You know your master's moods. From observation of them you probably know what caused them. I am asking this, not as a policeman, but as a friend of Mr. Jefferson's. That is to say, if anything you tell me is not, in my opinion, relevant to the case, I shall not pass it on to the police.'

He paused. Edwards said quietly:

'I understand you, sir. You want me to speak quite frankly—to say things that in the ordinary course of events I should not say—and that, excuse me, sir, *you* wouldn't dream of listening to.'

Sir Henry said:

'You're a very intelligent fellow, Edwards. That's exactly what I *do* mean.'

Edwards was silent for a minute or two, then he began to speak.

'Of course I know Mr. Jefferson fairly well by now. I've been with him quite a number of years. And I see him in his 'off' moments, not only in his 'on' ones. Sometimes, sir, I've questioned in my own mind whether it's good for anyone to fight fate in the way Mr. Jefferson has fought. It's taken a terrible toll of him, sir. If, sometimes, he could have given way, been an unhappy, lonely, broken old man—well, it might have been better for him in the end. But he's too proud for that! He'll go down fighting—that's his motto.

'But that sort of thing leads, Sir Henry, to a lot of nervous reaction. He looks a good-tempered gentleman. I've seen him in violent rages when he could hardly speak for passion. And the one thing that roused him, sir, was deceit. . . .'

'Are you saying that for any particular reason, Edwards?'

'Yes, sir, I am. You asked me, sir, to speak quite frankly?'

'That is the idea.'

'Well, then, Sir Henry, in my opinion the young woman that Mr. Jefferson was so taken up with wasn't worth it. She was, to put it bluntly, a common little piece. And she didn't care tuppence for Mr. Jefferson. All that play of affection and gratitude was so much poppycock. I don't say there was any harm in her—but she wasn't, by a long way, what Mr. Jefferson thought her. It was funny, that, sir, for Mr. Jefferson was a shrewd gentleman; he wasn't often deceived over people. But there, a gentleman isn't himself in his judgment when it comes to a young woman being in question. Young Mrs. Jefferson, you see, whom he'd always depended upon a lot for sympathy, had changed a good deal this summer. He noticed it and he felt it badly. He was fond of her, you see. Mr. Mark he never liked much.'

Sir Henry interjected:

'And yet he had him with him constantly?'

'Yes, but that was for Miss Rosamund's sake. Mrs. Gaskell that was. She was the apple of his eye. He adored her. Mr. Mark was Miss Rosamund's husband. He always thought of him like that.'

'Supposing Mr. Mark had married someone else?'

'Mr. Jefferson, sir, would have been furious.'

Sir Henry raised his eyebrows. 'As much as that?'

'He wouldn't have shown it, but that's what it would have been.'

'And if Mrs. Jefferson had married again?'

'Mr. Jefferson wouldn't have liked that either, sir.'

'Please go on, Edwards.'

'I was saying, sir, that Mr. Jefferson fell for this young woman. I've often seen it happen with the gentlemen I've been with. Comes over them like a kind of disease. They want to protect the girl, and shield her, and shower benefits upon her—and nine times out of ten the girl is very well able to look after herself and has a good eye to the main chance.'

'So you think Ruby Keene was a schemer?'

'Well, Sir Henry, she was quite inexperienced, being so young, but she had the makings of a very fine schemer indeed when she'd once got well into her swing, so to speak! In another five years she'd have been an expert at the game!'

Sir Henry said:

'I'm glad to have your opinion of her. It's valuable. Now, do you recall any incident in which this matter was discussed between Mr. Jefferson and his family?'

'There was very little discussion, sir. Mr. Jefferson announced what he had in mind and stifled any protests. That is, he shut up Mr. Mark, who was a bit outspoken. Mrs. Jefferson didn't say much—she's a quiet lady—only urged him not to do anything in a great hurry.'

Sir Henry nodded.

'Anything else? What was the girl's attitude?'

With marked distaste the valet said:

'I should describe it, sir, as jubilant.'

'Ah—jubilant, you say? You had no reason to believe, Edwards, that'—he sought about for a phrase suitable to Edwards—'that—er—her affections were engaged elsewhere?'

'Mr. Jefferson was not proposing marriage, sir. He was going to adopt her.'

'Cut out the 'elsewhere' and let the question stand.'

The valet said slowly: 'There *was* one incident, sir. I happened to be a witness of it.'

'That is gratifying. Tell me.'

'There is probably nothing in it, sir. It was just that one day the young woman, chancing to open her handbag, a small snapshot fell out. Mr. Jefferson pounced on it and said: 'Hallo, Kitten, who's this, eh?'

'It was a snapshot, sir, of a young man, a dark young man with rather untidy hair and his tie very badly arranged.

'Miss Keene pretended that she didn't know anything about it. She said: "I've no idea, Jeffie. No idea at all. I don't know how it could have got into my bag. *I* didn't put it there!"

'Now, Mr. Jefferson, sir, wasn't quite a fool. That story wasn't good enough. He looked angry, his brows came down heavy, and his voice was gruff when he said:

'"Now then, Kitten, now then. *You* know who it is right enough."

'She changed her tactics quick, sir. Looked frightened. She said: "I do recognize him now. He comes here sometimes and I've danced with him. I don't know his name. The silly idiot must have stuffed his photo into my bag one day. These boys are too silly for anything!" She tossed her head and giggled and passed it off. But it wasn't a likely story, was it? And I don't think Mr. Jefferson quite believed it. He looked at her once or twice after that in a sharp way, and sometimes, if she'd been out, he asked her where she'd been.'

Sir Henry said: 'Have you ever seen the original of the photo about the hotel?'

'Not to my knowledge, sir. Of course, I am not much downstairs in the public apartments.'

Sir Henry nodded. He asked a few more questions, but Edwards could tell him nothing more.

2

In the police station at Danemouth, Superintendent Harper was interviewing Jessie Davis, Florence Small, Beatrice Henniker, Mary Price, and Lilian Ridgway.

They were girls much of an age, differing slightly in mentality. They ranged from 'county' to farmers' and shopkeepers' daughters. One and all they told the same story—Pamela Reeves had been just the same as usual, she had said nothing to any of them except that she was going to Woolworth's and would go home by a later bus.

In the corner of Superintendent Harper's office sat an elderly lady. The girls hardly noticed her. If they did, they may have wondered who she was. She was certainly no police matron. Possibly they assumed that she, like themselves, was a witness to be questioned.

The last girl was shown out. Superintendent Harper wiped his forehead and turned round to look at Miss Marple. His glance was inquiring, but not hopeful.

Miss Marple, however, spoke crisply.

'I'd like to speak to Florence Small.'

The Superintendent's eyebrows rose, but he nodded and touched a bell. A constable appeared.

Harper said: 'Florence Small.'

The girl reappeared, ushered in by the constable. She was the daughter of a well-to-do farmer—a tall girl with fair hair, a rather foolish mouth, and frightened brown eyes. She was twisting her hands and looked nervous.

Superintendent Harper looked at Miss Marple, who nodded.

The Superintendent got up. He said:

'This lady will ask you some questions.'

He went out, closing the door behind him.

Florence shot an uneasy glance at Miss Marple. Her eyes looked rather like one of her father's calves.

Miss Marple said: 'Sit down, Florence.'

Florence Small sat down obediently. Unrecognized by herself, she felt suddenly more at home, less uneasy. The unfamiliar and terrorizing atmosphere of a police station was replaced by something more familiar, the accustomed tone of command of somebody whose business it was to give orders. Miss Marple said:

'You understand, Florence, that it's of the utmost importance that everything about poor Pamela's doings on the day of her death should be known?'

Florence murmured that she quite understood.

'And I'm sure you want to do your best to help?'

Florence's eyes were wary as she said, of course she did.

'To keep back any piece of information is a very serious offence,' said Miss Marple.

The girl's fingers twisted nervously in her lap. She swallowed once or twice.

'I can make allowances,' went on Miss Marple, 'for the fact that you are naturally alarmed at being brought into contact with the police. You are afraid, too, that you may be blamed for not having spoken sooner. Possibly you are afraid that you may also be blamed for not stopping Pamela at the time. But you've got to be a brave girl and make a clean breast of things. If you refuse to tell what you know now, it will be a very serious matter indeed—*very* serious—practically *perjury*, and for that, as you know, you can be sent to prison.'

'I—I don't——'

Miss Marple said sharply:

'Now don't prevaricate, Florence! Tell me all about it at once! Pamela wasn't going to Woolworth's, was she?'

Florence licked her lips with a dry tongue and gazed imploringly at Miss Marple like a beast about to be slaughtered.

'Something to do with the films, wasn't it?' asked Miss Marple.

A look of intense relief mingled with awe passed over Florence's face. Her inhibitions left her. She gasped:

'Oh, *yes*!'

'I thought so,' said Miss Marple. 'Now I want all the details, please.'

Words poured from Florence in a gush.

'Oh! I've been ever so worried. I promised Pam, you see, I'd never say a word to a soul. And then when she was found all burnt up in that car—oh! it was horrible and I thought I should *die*—I felt it was all my fault. I ought to have stopped her. Only I never thought, not for a minute, that it wasn't all right. And then I was asked if she'd been quite as usual that day and I said "Yes" before I'd had time to think. And not having said anything then I didn't see how I could say anything later. And, after all, I didn't know anything—not really—only what Pam told me.'

'What did Pam tell you?'

'It was as we were walking up the lane to the bus—on the way to the rally. She asked me if I could keep a secret, and I said "Yes," and she made me swear not to tell. She was going into Danemouth for a film test after the rally! She'd met a film producer—just back from Hollywood, he was. He wanted a certain type, and he told Pam she was just what he was looking for. He warned her, though, not to build on it. You couldn't tell, he said, not until you saw how a person photographed. It might be no good at all. It was a kind of Bergner part, he said. You had to have someone quite young for it. A schoolgirl, it was, who changes places with a revue artist and has a wonderful career. Pam's acted in plays at school and she's awfully good. He said he could see she could act, but she'd have to have some intensive training. It wouldn't be all beer and skittles, he told her, it would be damned hard work. Did she think she could stick it?'

Florence Small stopped for breath. Miss Marple felt rather sick as she listened to the glib rehash of countless novels and screen stories. Pamela Reeves, like most other girls, would have been warned against talking to strangers—but the glamour of the films would obliterate all that.

'He was absolutely businesslike about it all,' continued Florence. 'Said if the test was successful she'd have a contract, and he said that as she was young and inexperienced she ought to let a lawyer look at it before she signed it. But she wasn't to pass on that *he'd* said that. He asked her if she'd have trouble with her parents, and Pam said she probably would, and he said: "Well, of course, that's always a difficulty with anyone as young as you are, but I think if it was put to them that this was a wonderful chance that wouldn't happen once in a million times, they'd see reason." But, anyway, he said, it wasn't any good going into that until they knew the result of the test. She mustn't be disappointed if it failed. He told her about Hollywood and about Vivien Leigh—how she'd suddenly taken London by storm—and how these sensational leaps into fame did happen. He himself had come back from America to work with the Lemville Studios and put some pep into the English film companies.'

Miss Marple nodded.

Florence went on:

'So it was all arranged. Pam was to go into Danemouth after the rally and meet him at his hotel and he'd take her along to the studios (they'd got a small testing studio in Danemouth, he told her). She'd have her test and she could catch the bus home afterwards. She could say she'd been shopping, and he'd let her know the result of the test in a few days, and if it was favourable Mr. Harmsteiter, the boss, would come along and talk to her parents.

'Well, of course, it sounded too wonderful! I was green with envy! Pam got through the rally without turning a hair—we always call her a regular poker face. Then, when she said she was going into Danemouth to Woolworth's she just winked at me.

'I saw her start off down the footpath.' Florence began to cry. 'I ought to have stopped her. I ought to have stopped her . . . I ought to have known a thing like that couldn't be true. I ought to have told someone. Oh dear, I wish I was *dead*!'

'There, there.' Miss Marple patted her on the shoulder. 'It's quite all right. No one will blame you. You've done the right thing in telling me.'

She devoted some minutes to cheering the child up.

Five minutes later she was telling the story to Superintendent Harper. The latter looked very grim.

'The clever devil!' he said. 'By God, I'll cook his goose for him. This puts rather a different aspect on things.'

'Yes, it does.'

Harper looked at her sideways.

'It doesn't surprise you?'

'I expected something of the kind.'

Superintendent Harper said curiously:

'What put you on to this particular girl? They all looked scared to death and there wasn't a pin to choose between them as far as I could see.'

Miss Marple said gently:

'You haven't had as much experience with girls telling lies as I have. Florence looked at you very straight, if you remember, and stood very rigid and just fidgeted with her feet like the others. But you didn't watch her as she went out of the door. I knew at once then that she'd got something to hide. They nearly always relax too soon. My little maid Janet always did. She'd explain quite convincinly that the mice had eaten the end of a cake and give herself away by smirking as she left the room.'

'I'm very grateful to you,' said Harper.

He added thoughtfully: 'Lemville Studios, eh?'

Miss Marple said nothing. She rose to her feet.

'I'm afraid,' she said, 'I must hurry away. So glad to have been able to help you.'

'Are you going back to the hotel?'

'Yes—to pack up. I must go back to St. Mary Mead as soon as possible. There's a lot for me to do there.'

CHAPTER XV

1

MISS MARPLE passed out through the french windows of her drawing-room, tripped down her neat garden path, through a garden gate, in through the vicarage garden gate, across the vicarage garden, and up to the drawing-room window, where she tapped gently on the pane.

The vicar was busy in his study composing his Sunday sermon, but the vicar's wife, who was young and pretty, was admiring the progress of her offspring across the hearthrug.

'Can I come in, Griselda?'

'Oh, do, Miss Marple. Just *look* at David! He gets so angry because he can only crawl in reverse. He wants to get to something and the more he tries the more he goes backwards into the coal-box!'

'He's looking very bonny, Griselda.'

'He's not bad, is he?' said the young mother, endeavouring to assume an indifferent manner. 'Of course I don't *bother* with him much. All the books say a child should be left alone as much as possible.'

'Very wise, dear,' said Miss Marple. 'Ahem, I came to ask if there was anything special you are collecting for at the moment?'

The vicar's wife turned somewhat astonished eyes upon her.

'Oh, heaps of things,' she said cheerfully. 'There always are.'

She ticked them off on her fingers.

'There's the Nave Restoration Fund, and St Giles's Mission, and our Sale of Work next Wednesday, and the Unmarried Mothers, and a Boy Scouts' Outing, and the Needlework Guild, and the Bishop's Appeal for Deep Sea Fishermen.'

'Any of them will do,' said Miss Marple. 'I thought I might make a little round—with a book, you know—if you would authorize me to do so?'

'Are you up to something? I believe you are. Of course I authorize you. Make it the Sale of Work; it would be lovely to get some real money instead of those awful sachets and comic pen-wipers and depressing children's frocks and dusters all done up to look like dolls.

'I suppose,' continued Griselda, accompanying her guest to the window, "you wouldn't like to tell me what it's all about?'

'Later, my dear,' said Miss Marple, hurrying off.

With a sigh the young mother returned to the hearthrug and, by way of carrying our her principles of stern neglect, butted her son three times in the stomach so that he caught hold of her hair and pulled it with gleeful yells. They then rolled over and over in a grand rough-and-tumble until the door opened and the vicarage maid announced to the most influential parishioner (who didn't like children):

'Missus is in here.'

Whereupon Griselda sat up and tried to look dignified and more what a vicar's wife should be.

2

Miss Marple, clasping a small black book with pencilled entries in it, walked briskly along the village street until she came to the crossroads. Here she turned to the left and walked past the *Blue Boar* until she came to Chatsworth, alias 'Mr. Booker's new house.'

She turned in at the gate, walked up to the front door and knocked briskly.

The door was opened by the blonde young woman named Dinah Lee. She was less carefully made up than usual, and in fact looked slightly dirty. She was wearing grey slacks and an emerald jumper.

'Good-morning,' said Miss Marple briskly and cheerfully. 'May I just come in for a minute?'

She pressed forward as she spoke, so that Dinah Lee, who was somewhat taken aback at the call, had no time to make up her mind.

'Thank you so much,' said Miss Marple, beaming amiably at her and sitting down rather gingerly on a 'period' bamboo chair.

'Quite warm for the time of year, is it not?' went on Miss Marple, still exuding geniality.

'Yes, rather. Oh, quite,' said Miss Lee.

At a loss how to deal with the situation, she opened a box and offered it to her guest. 'Er—have a cigarette?'

'Thank you so much, but I don't smoke. I just called, you know, to see if I could enlist your help for our Sale of Work next week.'

'Sale of Work?' said Dinah Lee, as one who repeats a phrase in a foreign language.

'At the vicarage,' said Miss Marple. 'Next Wednesday.'

'Oh!' Miss Lee's mouth fell open. 'I'm afraid I couldn't——'

'Not even a small subscription—half a crown perhaps?'

Miss Marple exhibited her little book.

'Oh—er—well, yes, I dare say I could manage that.'

The girl looked relieved and turned to hunt in her handbag.

Miss Marple's sharp eyes were looking round the room.

She said:

'I see you've no hearthrug in front of the fire.'

Dinah Lee turned round and stared at her. She could not but be aware of the very keen scrutiny the old lady was giving her, but it aroused in her no other emotion than slight annoyance. Miss Marple recognized that. She said:

'It's rather dangerous, you know. Sparks fly out and mark the carpet.'

'Funny old Tabby,' thought Dinah, but she said quite amiably if somewhat vaguely:

'There used to be one. I don't know where it's got to.'

'I suppose,' said Miss Marple, 'it was the fluffy, woolly kind?'

'Sheep,' said Dinah. 'That's what it looked like.'

She was amused now. An eccentric old bean, this.

She held out a half-crown. 'Here you are,' she said.

'Oh, thank you, my dear.'

Miss Marple took it and opened the little book.

'Er—what name shall I write down?'

Dinah's eyes grew suddenly hard and contemptuous.

'Nosey old cat,' she thought, 'that's all she came for—prying around for scandal!'

She said clearly and with malicious pleasure:

'Miss Dinah Lee.'

Miss Marple looked at her steadily.

She said:

'This is Mr. Basil Blake's cottage, isn't it?'

'Yes, and *I*'m Miss Dinah Lee!'

Her voice rang out challengingly, her head went back, her blue eyes flashed.

Very steadily Miss Marple looked at her. She said:

'Will you allow me to give you some advice, even though you may consider it impertinent?'

'I *shall* consider it impertinent. You had better say nothing.'

'Nevertheless,' said Miss Marple, 'I am going to speak. I want to advise you, very strongly, not to continue using your maiden name in the village.'

Dinah stared at her. She said:

'What—what do you mean?'

Miss Marple said earnestly:

'In a very short time you may need all the sympathy and goodwill you can find. It will be important to your husband, too, that he shall be thought well of. There is a prejudice in old-fashioned country districts against people living together who are not married. It has amused you both, I dare say, to pretend that that is what you are doing. It kept people away, so that you weren't bothered with what I expect you would call "old frumps." Nevertheless, old frumps have their uses.'

Dinah demanded:

'How did you know we are married?'

Miss Marple smiled a deprecating smile.

'Oh, my dear,' she said.

Dinah persisted.

'No, but how *did* you know? You didn't—you didn't go to Somerset House?'

A momentary flicker showed in Miss Marple's eyes.

'Somerset House? Oh, no. But it was quite easy to *guess*. Everything, you know, gets round in a village. The—er—the kind of quarrels you have—typical of early days of marriage. Quite—*quite* unlike an illicit relationship. It has been said, you know (and, I think, quite truly), that you can only really get under anybody's skin if you are married to them. When there is no—no *legal* bond, people are much more careful, they have to keep assuring themselves how happy and halcyon everything is. They have, you see, to *justify* themselves. They dare not quarrel! Married people, I have noticed, quite enjoy their battles and the—er—appropriate reconciliations.'

She paused, twinkling benignly.

'Well, I——' Dinah stopped and laughed. She sat down and lit a cigarette. 'You're absolutely marvellous!' she said.

Then she went on:

'But why do you want us to own up and admit to respectability?'

Miss Marple's face was grave. She said:

'Because, any minute now, *your husband may be arrested for murder*.'

3

For several moments Dinah stared at her. Then she said incredulously:

'Basil? Murder? Are you joking?'

'No, indeed. Haven't you seen the papers?'

Dinah caught her breath.

'You mean—that girl at the Majestic Hotel. Do you mean they suspect Basil of killing her?'

'Yes.'

'But it's nonsense.'

There was the whir of a car outside, and bang of a gate. Basil Blake flung open the door and came in, carrying some bottles. He said:

'Got the gin and the vermouth. Did you——'

He stopped and turned incredulous eyes on the prim, erect visitor.

Dinah burst out breathlessly:

'Is she mad? She says you're going to be arrested for the murder of that girl Ruby Keene.'

'Oh, God!' said Basil Blake. The bottles dropped from his arms on to the sofa. He reeled to a chair and dropped down in it and buried his face in his hands. He repeated: 'Oh, my God! Oh, my God!'

Dinah darted over to him. She caught his shoulders.

'Basil, look at me! It isn't true! I know it isn't true! I don't believe it for a moment!'

His hand went up and gripped hers.

'Bless you, darling.'

'But why should they think—— You didn't even *know* her, did you?'

'Oh, yes, he knew her,' said Miss Marple.

Basil said fiercely:

'Be quiet, you old hag. Listen, Dinah darling, I hardly knew her at all. Just ran across her once or twice at the Majestic. That's all, I swear that's all.'

Dinah said, bewildered:

'I don't understand. Why should anyone suspect you, then?'

Basil groaned. He put his hands over his eyes and rocked to and fro.

Miss Marple said:

'What did you do with the hearthrug?'

His reply came mechanically:

'I put it in the dustbin.'

Miss Marple clucked her tongue vexedly.

'That was stupid—very stupid. People don't put good hearthrugs in dustbins. It had spangles in it from her dress, I suppose?'

'Yes, I couldn't get them out.'

Dinah cried: 'But what are you both talking about?'

Basil said sullenly:

'Ask her. She seems to know all about it.'

'I'll tell you what I think happened, if you like,' said Miss Marple. 'You can correct me, Mr. Blake, if I go wrong. I think that after having had a violent quarrel with your wife at a party and after having had, perhaps, rather too much—er—to drink, you drove down here. I don't know what time you arrived——'

Basil Blake said sullenly:

'About two in the morning. I meant to go up to town first, then when I got to the suburbs I changed my mind. I thought Dinah might come down here after me. So I drove down here. The place was all dark. I opened the door and turned on the light and I saw—and I saw——'

He gulped and stopped. Miss Marple went on:

'You saw a girl lying on the hearthrug—a girl in a white evening dress—strangled. I don't know whether you recognized her then——'

Basil Blake shook his head violently.

'I couldn't look at her after the first glance—her face was all blue—

swollen. She'd been dead some time and she was *there*—in *my* room!'

He shuddered.

Miss Marple said gently:

"You weren't, of course, quite yourself. You were in a fuddled state and your nerves are not good. You were, I think, panic-stricken. You didn't know what to do——'

'I thought Dinah might turn up any minute. And she'd find me there with a dead body—a girl's dead body—and she'd think I'd killed her. Then I got an idea—it seemed, I don't know why, a good idea at the time—I thought: I'll put her in old Bantry's library. Damned pompous old stick, always looking down his nose, sneering at me as artistic and effeminate. Serve the pompous old brute right, I thought. He'll look a fool when a dead lovely is found on his hearthrug.' He added with a pathetic eagerness to explain: 'I was a bit drunk, you know, at the time. It really seemed positively *amusing* to me. Old Bantry with a dead blonde.'

'Yes, yes,' said Miss Marple. 'Little Tommy Bond had very much the same idea. Rather a sensitive boy with an inferiority complex, he said teacher was always picking on him. He put a frog in the clock and it jumped out at her.

'You were just the same,' went on Miss Marple, 'only, of course, bodies are more serious matters than frogs.'

Basil groaned again.

'By the morning I'd sobered up. I realized what I'd done. I was scared stiff. And then the police came here—another damned pompous ass of a Chief Constable. I was scared of him—and the only way I could hide it was by being abominably rude. In the middle of it all Dinah drove up.'

Dinah looked out of the window.

She said:

'There's a car driving up now . . . there are men in it.'

'The police, I think,' said Miss Marple.

Basil Blake got up. Suddenly he became quite calm and resolute. He even smiled. He said:

'So I'm for it, am I? All right, Dinah sweet, keep your head. Get on to old Sims—he's the family lawyer—and go to mother and tell her about our marriage. She won't bite. And don't worry. *I didn't do it.* So it's bound to be all right, see, sweetheart?'

There was a tap on the cottage door. Basil called 'Come in.' Inspector Slack entered with another man. He said:

'Mr. Basil Blake?'

'Yes.'

'I have a warrant here for your arrest on the charge of murdering Ruby Keene on the night of September 21st last. I warn you that anything you say may be used at your trial. You will please accompany me now. Full facilities will be given you for communicating with your solicitor.'

Basil nodded.

He looked at Dinah, but did not touch her. He said:

'So long, Dinah.'

'Cool customer,' thought Inspector Slack.

He acknowledged the presence of Miss Marple with a half bow and a 'Good-morning,' and thought to himself:

'Smart old Pussy, *she's* on to it! Good job we've got that hearthrug. That and finding out from the car-park man at the studio that he left that party at *eleven* instead of midnight. Don't think those friends of his meant to commit perjury. They were bottled and Blake told 'em firmly the next day it was twelve o'clock when he left and they believed him. Well, *his* goose is cooked good and proper! Mental, I expect! Broadmoor, not hanging. First the Reeves kid, probably strangled her, drove her out to the quarry, walked back into Danemouth, picked up his own car in some side lane, drove to this party, then back to Danemouth, brought Ruby Keene out here, strangled her, put her in old Bantry's library, then probably got the wind up about the car in the quarry, drove there, set it on fire, and got back here. Mad—sex and blood lust—lucky *this* girl's escaped. What they call recurring mania, I expect.'

Alone with Miss Marple, Dinah Blake turned to her. She said:

'I don't know who you are, but you've got to understand this—*Basil didn't do it.*"

Miss Marple said:

'I know he didn't. I know who *did* do it. But it's not going to be easy to prove. I've an idea that something you said—just now—may help. It gave me an idea—the *connection* I'd been trying to find—now what *was* it?'

CHAPTER XVI

1

'I'M HOME, ARTHUR!' declared Mrs. Bantry, announcing the fact like a Royal Proclamation as she flung open the study door.

Colonel Bantry immediately jumped up, kissed his wife, and declared heartily: 'Well, well, that's splendid!'

The words were unimpeachable, the manner very well done, but an affectionate wife of as many years' standing as Mrs. Bantry was not deceived. She said immediately:

'Is anything the matter?'

'No, of course not, Dolly. What should be the matter?'

'Oh, I don't know,' said Mrs. Bantry vaguely. 'Things are so queer, aren't they?'

She threw off her coat as she spoke and Colonel Bantry picked it up carefully and laid it across the back of the sofa.

All exactly as usual—yet not as usual. Her husband, Mrs. Bantry thought, seemed to have shrunk. He looked thinner, stooped more; there were pouches under his eyes and those eyes were not ready to meet hers.

He went on to say, still with that affectation of cheerfulness:

'Well, how did you enjoy your time at Danemouth?'

'Oh! it was great fun. You ought to have come, Arthur.'

'Couldn't get away, my dear. Lot of things to attend to here.'

'Still, I think the change would have done you good. And you like the Jeffersons?'

'Yes, yes, poor fellow. Nice chap. All very sad.'

'What have you been doing with yourself since I've been away?'

'Oh, nothing much. Been over the farms, you know. Agreed that Anderson shall have a new roof—can't patch it up any longer.'

'How did the Radfordshire Council meeting go?'

'I—well—as a matter of fact I didn't go.'

'Didn't *go*? But you were taking the chair?'

'Well, as a matter of fact, Dolly—seems there was some mistake about that. Asked me if I'd mind if Thompson took it instead.'

'I *see*,' said Mrs. Bantry.

She peeled off a glove and threw it deliberately into the waste-paper basket. Her husband went to retrieve it, and she stopped him, saying sharply:

'Leave it. I hate gloves.'

Colonel Bantry glanced at her uneasily.

Mrs. Bantry said sternly:

'Did you go to dinner with the Duffs on Thursday?'

'Oh, that! It was put off. Their cook was ill.'

'Stupid people,' said Mrs. Bantry. She went on: 'Did you go to the Naylors' yesterday?'

'I rang up and said I didn't feel up to it, hoped they'd excuse me. They quite understood.'

'They did, did they?' said Mrs. Bantry grimly.

She sat down by the desk and absent-mindedly picked up a pair of gardening scissors. With them she cut off the fingers, one by one, of her second glove.

'What *are* you doing, Dolly?'

'Feeling destructive,' said Mrs. Bantry.

She got up. 'Where shall we sit after dinner, Arthur? In the library?'

'Well—er—I don't think so—eh? Very nice in here—or the drawing-room.'

'I think,' said Mrs. Bantry, 'that we'll sit in the library!'

Her steady eye met his. Colonel Bantry drew himself up to his full height. A sparkle came into his eye.

He said:

'You're right, my dear. We'll sit in the library!'

2

Mrs. Bantry put down the telephone receiver with a sigh of annoyance. She had rung up twice, and each time the answer had been the same: Miss Marple was out.

Of a naturally impatient nature, Mrs. Bantry was never one to acquiesce in defeat. She rang up in rapid succession the vicarage, Mrs. Price Ridley, Miss Hartnell, Miss Wetherby, and, as a last resource, the fishmonger, who, by reason of his advantageous geographical position, usually knew where everybody was in the village.

The fishmonger was sorry, but he had not seen Miss Marple at all in the village that morning. She had not been her usual round.

'Where *can* the woman be?' demanded Mrs. Bantry impatiently aloud.

There was a deferential cough behind her. The discreet Lorrimer murmured:

'You were requiring Miss Marple, madam? I have just observed her approaching the house.'

Mrs. Bantry rushed to the front door, flung it open, and greeted Miss Marple breathlessly:

'I've been trying to get you *everywhere*. Where have you been?' She glanced over her shoulder. Lorrimer had discreetly vanished. 'Everything's *too* awful! People are beginning to cold-shoulder Arthur. He looks *years* older. We *must* do something, Jane. *You* must do something!'

Miss Marple said:

'You needn't worry, Dolly,' in a rather peculiar voice.

Colonel Bantry appeared from the study door.

'Ah, Miss Marple. Good-morning. Glad you've come. My wife's been ringing you up like a lunatic.'

'I thought I'd better bring you the news,' said Miss Marple, as she followed Mrs. Bantry into the study.

'News?'

'Basil Blake has just been arrested for the murder of Ruby Keene.'

'Basil Blake?' cried the Colonel.

'But he didn't do it,' said Miss Marple.

Colonel Bantry took no notice of this statement. It is doubtful if he even heard it.

'Do you mean to say he strangled that girl and then brought her along and put her in *my* library?'

'He put her in your library,' said Miss Marple. 'But he didn't kill her.'

'Nonsense! If he put her in my library, of course he killed her! The two things go together.'

'Not necessarily. He found her dead in his own cottage.'

'A likely story,' said the Colonel derisively. 'If you find a body, why, you ring up the police—naturally—if you're an honest man.'

'Ah,' said Miss Marple, 'but we haven't all got such iron nerves as you have, Colonel Bantry. You belong to the old school. This younger generation is different.'

'Got no stamina,' said the Colonel, repeating a well-worn opinion of his.

'Some of them,' said Miss Marple, 'have been through a bad time. I've heard a good deal about Basil. He did A.R.P. work, you know, when he was only eighteen. He went into a burning house and brought out four children, one after another. He went back for a dog, although they told him it wasn't safe. The building fell in on him. They got him out, but his chest was badly crushed and he had to lie in plaster for nearly a year and was ill for a long time after that. That's when he got interested in designing.'

'Oh!' The Colonel coughed and blew his nose. 'I—er—never knew that.'

'He doesn't talk about it,' said Miss Marple.

'Er—quite right. Proper spirit. Must be more in the young chap than I thought. Always thought he'd shirked the war, you know. Shows you ought to be careful in jumping to conclusions.'

Colonel Bantry looked ashamed.

'But, all the same'—his indignation revived—'what did he mean trying to fasten a murder on *me*?'

'I don't think he saw it like that,' said Miss Marple.

'He thought of it more as a—as a joke. You see, he was rather under the influence of alcohol at the time.'

'Bottled, was he?' said Colonel Bantry, with an Englishman's sympathy for alcoholic excess. 'Oh, well, can't judge a fellow by what he does when he's drunk. When I was at Cambridge, I remember I put a certain utensil—well, well, never mind. Deuce of a row there was about it.'

He chuckled, then checked himself sternly. He looked piercingly at Miss Marple with eyes that were shrewd and appraisingly. He said: '*You* don't think he did the murder, eh?'

'I'm sure he didn't.'

'And you think you know who did?'

Miss Marple nodded.

Mrs. Bantry, like an ecstatic Greek chorus, said: 'Isn't she wonderful?' to an unhearing world.

'Well, who was it?'

Miss Marple said:

'I was going to ask you to help me. I think, if we went up to Somerset House we should have a very good idea.'

CHAPTER XVII

1

SIR HENRY'S FACE was very grave.

He said:

'I don't like it.'

'I am aware,' said Miss Marple, 'that it isn't what you call orthodox. But it *is* so important, isn't it, to be quite *sure*—"to make assurance doubly sure," as Shakespeare has it. I think, if Mr. Jefferson would agree——'

'What about Harper? Is he to be in on this?'

'It might be awkward for him to know too much. But there might be a hint from you. To watch certain persons—have them trailed, you know.'

Sir Henry said slowly:

'Yes, that would meet the case. . . .'

2

Superintendent Harper looked piercingly at Sir Henry Clithering.

'Let's get this quite clear, sir. You're giving me a hint?'

Sir Henry said:

'I'm informing you of what my friend has just informed me—he didn't tell me in confidence—that he proposes to visit a solicitor in Danemouth to-morrow for the purpose of making a new will.'

The Superintendent's bushy eyebrows drew downwards over his steady eyes. He said:

'Does Mr. Conway Jefferson propose to inform his son-in-law and daughter-in-law of that fact?'

'He intends to tell them about it this evening.'

'I see.'

The Superintendent tapped his desk with a pen-holder.

He repeated again: 'I see. . . .'

Then the piercing eyes bored once more into the eyes of the other man. Harper said:

'So you're not satisfied with the case against Basil Blake?'

'Are you?'

The Superintendent's moustaches quivered. He said:

'Is Miss Marple?'

The two men looked at each other.

Then Harper said:

'You can leave it to me. I'll have men detailed. There will be no funny business, I can promise you that.'

Sir Henry said:

'There is one more thing. You'd better see this.'

He unfolded a slip of paper and pushed it across the table.

This time the Superintendent's calm deserted him. He whistled:

'So that's it, is it? That puts an entirely different complexion on the matter. How did you come to dig up this?'

'Women,' said Sir Henry, 'are eternally interested in marriages.'

'Especially,' said the Superintendent, 'elderly single women.'

3

Conway Jefferson looked up as his friend entered.

His grim face relaxed into a smile.

He said:

'Well, I told 'em. They took it very well.'

'What did you say?'

'Told 'em that, as Ruby was dead, I felt that the fifty thousand I'd originally left her should go to something that I could associate with her memory. It was to endow a hostel for young girls working as professional dancers in London. Damned silly way to leave your money—surprised they swallowed it. As though *I'd* do a thing like that!'

He added meditatively:

'You know, I made a fool of myself over that girl. Must be turning into a silly old man. I can see it now. She was a pretty kid—but most of what I saw in her I put there myself. I pretended she was another Rosamund. Same colouring, you know. But not the same heart or mind. Hand me that paper—rather an interesting bridge problem.'

4

Sir Henry went downstairs. He asked a question of the porter.

'Mr. Gaskell, sir? He's just gone off in his car. Had to go to London.'

'Oh! I see. Is Mrs. Jefferson about?'

'Mrs. Jefferson, sir, has just gone up to bed.'

Sir Henry looked into the lounge and through to the ballroom. In the lounge Hugo McLean was doing a crossword puzzle and frowning a good deal over it. In the ballroom Josie was smiling valiantly into the face of a stout, perspiring man as her nimble feet avoided his destructive tread. The stout man was clearly enjoying his dance. Raymond, graceful and weary, was dancing with an anæmic-looking girl with adenoids, dull brown hair, and an expensive and exceedingly unbecoming dress.

Sir Henry said under his breath:

'*And so to bed*,' and went upstairs.

5

It was three o'clock. The wind had fallen, the moon was shining over the quiet sea.

In Conway Jefferson's room there was no sound except his own heavy breathing as he lay, half propped up on pillows.

There was no breeze to stir the curtains at the window, but they stirred. . . . For a moment they parted, and a figure was silhouetted against the moonlight. Then they fell back into place. Everything was quiet again, but there was someone else inside the room.

Nearer and nearer to the bed the intruder stole. The deep breathing on the pillow did not relax.

There was no sound, or hardly any sound. A finger and thumb were ready to pick up a fold of skin, in the other hand the hypodermic was ready.

And then, suddenly, out of the shadows a hand came and closed over the hand that held the needle, the other arm held the figure in an iron grasp.

An unemotional voice, the voice of the law, said:

'No, you don't. I want that needle!'

The light switched on and from his pillows Conway Jefferson looked grimly at the murderer of Ruby Keene.

CHAPTER XVIII

1

SIR HENRY CLITHERING said:

'Speaking as Watson, I want to know your methods, Miss Marple.'

Superintendent Harper said:

'*I*'d like to know what put you on to it first.'

Colonel Melchett said:

'You've done it again, by Jove! I want to hear all about it from the beginning.

Miss Marple smoothed the puce silk of her best evening gown. She flushed and smiled and looked very self-conscious.

She said: 'I'm afraid you'll think my "methods," as Sir Henry calls them, are terribly amateurish. The truth is, you see, that most people —and I don't exclude policemen—are far too trusting for this wicked world. They believe what is told them. I never do. I'm afraid I always like to prove a thing for myself.'

'That is the scientific attitude,' said Sir Henry.

'In this case,' continued Miss Marple, 'certain things were taken for granted from the first—instead of just confining oneself to the facts. The facts, as I noted them, were that the victim was quite young and that she bit her nails and that her teeth stuck out a little—as young girls' so often do if not corrected in time with a plate—(and children are very naughty about their plates and taking them out when their elders aren't looking).

'But that is wandering from the point. Where was I? Oh, yes, looking down at the dead girl and feeling sorry, because it is always sad to see a young life cut short, and thinking that whoever had done it was a very wicked person. Of course it was all very confusing her being found in Colonel Bantry's library, altogether too like a book to be *true*. In fact, it made the wrong pattern. It wasn't, you see, *meant*, which confused us a lot. The *real* idea had been to plant the body on poor young Basil Blake (a *much* more likely person), and his action in putting it in the Colonel's library delayed things considerably, and must have been a source of great annoyance to the *real* murderer.

'Originally, you see, Mr. Blake would have been the first object of suspicion. They'd have made inquiries at Danemouth, found he knew the girl, then found he had tied himself up with another girl, and they'd have assumed that Ruby came to blackmail him, or something like that, and that he'd strangled her in a fit of rage. Just an ordinary, sordid, what I call *night-club* type of crime!

'But that, of course, *all went wrong*, and interest became focused much too soon on the Jefferson family—to the great annoyance of *a certain person*.

'As I've told you, I've got a very suspicious mind. My nephew Raymond tells me (in fun, of course, and quite affectionately) that I have a mind like a *sink*. He says that most Victorians have. All I can say is that the Victorians knew a good deal about human nature.

'As I say, having this rather insanitary—or surely *sanitary*?—mind, I looked at once at the *money* angle of it. Two people stood to benefit by this girl's death—you couldn't get away from that. Fifty thousand pounds is a lot of money—especially when you are in financial difficulties, as both these people were. Of course they both seemed very nice, agreeable people—they didn't seem *likely* people—but one never can tell, can one?

'Mrs. Jefferson, for instance—everyone liked her. But it did seem clear that she had become very restless that summer, and that she was tired of the life she led, completely dependent on her father-in-law. She knew, because the doctor had told her, that he couldn't live long—so *that* was all right—to put it callously—or it *would* have been all right if Ruby Keene hadn't come along. Mrs. Jefferson was passionately devoted to her son, and some women have a curious idea that crimes committed for the sake of their offspring are almost morally justified. I have come across that attitude once or twice in the village. "Well, 'twas all for Daisy, you see, miss," they say, and seem to think that that makes doubtful conduct quite all right. Very *lax* thinking.

'Mr. Mark Gaskell, of course, was a much more likely starter, if I may use such a sporting expression. He was a gambler and had not, I fancied, a very high moral code. But, for certain reasons, I was of the opinion that a *woman* was concerned in this crime.

'As I say, with my eye on motive, the money angle seemed *very* suggestive. It was annoying, therefore, to find that both these people had alibis for the time when Ruby Keene, according to the medical evidence, had met her death.

'But soon afterwards there came the discovery of the burnt-out car with Pamela Reeves' body in it, and then the whole thing leaped to the eye. The alibis, of course, were worthless.

'I now had two *halves* of the case, and both quite convincing, but they did not fit. There must *be* a connection, but I could not find it. The one person whom I *knew* to be concerned in the crime hadn't got a motive.

'It was stupid of me,' said Miss Marple meditatively. 'If it hadn't been for Dinah Lee I shouldn't have thought of it—the most obvious thing in the world. Somerset House! Marriage! It wasn't a question of only Mr. Gaskell or Mrs. Jefferson—there were the further possibilities of *marriage*. If either of those two was married, or even was *likely* to marry, *then the other party to the marriage contract was involved too.* Raymond, for instance, might think he had a pretty good chance of marrying a rich wife. He had been very assiduous to Mrs. Jefferson, and it was his charm, I think, that awoke her from her long widowhood. She had been quite content just being a daughter to Mr. Jefferson—like Ruth and Naomi—only Naomi, if you remember, took a lot of trouble to arrange a suitable marriage for Ruth.

'Besides Raymond there was Mr. McLean. She liked him very much and it seemed highly possible that she would marry him in the end. *He* wasn't well off—and he was not far from Danemouth on the night in question. So it seemed, didn't it,' said Miss Marple 'as though *anyone* might have done it?

'But, of course, really, in my own mind, I *knew*. You couldn't get away, could you, from those bitten nails?'

'Nails?' said Sir Henry. 'But she tore her nail and cut the others.'

'Nonsense,' said Miss Marple. '*Bitten* nails and close *cut* nails are quite different! Nobody could mistake them who knew anything about girls' nails—very ugly, bitten nails, as I always tell the girls in my class. Those nails, you see, were a *fact*. And they could only mean one thing. *The body in Colonel Bantry's library wasn't Ruby Keene at all.*

'And that brings you straight to the one person who must be concerned. *Josie!* Josie identified the body. She knew, she *must* have known, that it wasn't Ruby Keene's body. She said it was. She was puzzled, completely puzzled, at finding that body where it was. She practically betrayed that fact. Why? Because *she* knew, none better, where it ought to have been found! In Basil Blake's cottage. Who directed our attention to Basil? Josie, by saying to Raymond that Ruby might have been with the film man. And before that, by slipping a snapshot of him into Ruby's handbag. Who cherished such bitter anger against the dead girl that she couldn't hide it even when she looked down at her dead? Josie! Josie, who was shrewd, practical, hard as nails, and *all out for money*.

'That is what I meant about believing too readily. Nobody thought of disbelieving Josie's statement that the body was Ruby Keene's. Simply because it didn't seem at the time that she could have any motive for lying. Motive was always the difficulty—Josie was clearly involved, but Ruby's death seemed, if anything, contrary to her interests. It was not till Dinah Lee mentioned Somerset House that I got the connection.

'Marriage! If Josie and Mark Gaskell were actually married—then the whole thing was clear. As we know now, Mark and Josie were married a year ago. They were keeping it dark until Mr. Jefferson died.

'It was really quite interesting, you know, tracing out the course of events—seeing exactly how the plan had worked out. Complicated and yet simple. First of all the selection of the poor child, Pamela, the approach to her from the film angle. A screen test—of course the poor child couldn't resist it. Not when it was put up to her as plausibly as Mark Gaskell put it. She comes to the hotel, he is waiting for her, he takes her in by the side door and introduces her to Josie—one of their make-up experts! That poor child, it makes me quite sick to think of it! Sitting in Josie's bathroom while Josie bleaches her hair and makes up her face and varnishes her fingernails and toenails. During all this, the drug was given. In an ice-cream soda, very likely. She goes off into a coma. I imagine that they put her into one of the empty rooms opposite—they were only cleaned once a week, remember.

'After dinner Mark Gaskell went out in his car—to the sea-front, *he* said. That is when he took Pamela's body to the cottage dressed in one of Ruby's old dresses and arranged it on the hearthrug. She was still unconscious, but not dead, when he strangled her with the belt of the frock. . . . Not nice, no—but I hope and pray she knew nothing about it. Really, I feel quite pleased to think of him being hanged. . . . That must have been just after ten o'clock. Then he drove back at top speed and found the others in the lounge where Ruby Keene, *still alive*, was dancing her exhibition dance with Raymond.

'I should imagine that Josie had given Ruby instructions beforehand. Ruby was accustomed to doing what Josie told her. She was to change, go into Josie's room and wait. She, too, was drugged, probably in after-dinner coffee. She was yawning, remember, when she talked to young Bartlett.

'Josie came up later to "look for her"—*but nobody but Josie went into Josie's room.* She probably finished the girl off then—with an injection, perhaps, or a blow on the back of the head. She went down, danced with Raymond, debated with the Jeffersons where Ruby could be, and finally went up to bed. In the early hours of the morning she dressed the girl in Pamela's clothes, carried the body down the side stairs—she was a strong muscular young woman—fetched George Bartlett's car, drove two miles to the quarry, poured petrol over the car and set it alight. Then she walked back to the hotel, probably timing her arrival there for eight or nine o'clock—up early in her anxiety about Ruby!'

'An intricate plot,' said Colonel Melchett.

'Not more intricate than the steps of a dance,' said Miss Marple.

'I suppose not.'

'She was very thorough,' said Miss Marple. 'She even foresaw the discrepancy of the nails. That's why she managed to break one of Ruby's nails on her shawl. It made an excuse for pretending that Ruby had clipped her nails close.'

Harper said: 'Yes, she thought of everything. And the only real proof you had, Miss Marple, was a schoolgirl's bitten nails.'

'More than that,' said Miss Marple. 'People *will* talk too much. Mark Gaskell talked too much. He was speaking of Ruby and he said "her teeth ran down her throat." But the dead girl in Colonel Bantry's library had teeth that stuck *out*.'.

Conway Jefferson said rather grimly:

'And was the last dramatic *finale* your idea, Miss Marple?'

Miss Marple confessed. 'Well, it *was*, as a matter of fact. It's so nice to be *sure*, isn't it?'

'Sure is the word,' said Conway Jefferson grimly.

'You see,' said Miss Marple, 'once Mark and Josie knew that you were going to make a new will, they'd *have* to do something. They'd already committed *two* murders on account of the money. So they might as well commit a third. Mark, of course, must be absolutely clear, so he went off to London and established an alibi by dining at a restaurant with friends and going on to a night club. Josie was to do the work. They still wanted Ruby's death to be put down to Basil's account, so Mr. Jefferson's death must be thought due to his heart failing. There was digitalin, so the Superintendent tells me, in the syringe. Any doctor would think death from heart trouble quite natural in the circumstances. Josie had loosened one of the stone balls on the balcony and she was going to let it crash down afterwards. His death would be put down to the shock of the noise.'

Melchett said: 'Ingenious devil.'

Sir Henry said: 'So the third death you spoke of was to be Conway Jefferson?'

Miss Marple shook her head.

'Oh no—I meant Basil Blake. They'd have got him hanged if they could.'

'Or shut up in Broadmoor,' said Sir Henry.

Conway Jefferson grunted. He said:

'Always knew Rosamund had married a rotter. Tried not to admit it to myself. She was damned fond of him. Fond of a murderer! Well, he'll hang as well as the woman. I'm glad he went to pieces and gave the show away.'

Miss Marple said:

'She was always the strong character. It was her plan throughout. The irony of it is that she got the girl down here herself, never dreaming that she would take Mr. Jefferson's fancy and ruin all her own prospects.'

Jefferson said:

'Poor lass. Poor little Ruby. . . .'

Adelaide Jefferson and Hugo McLean came in. Adelaide looked almost beautiful to-night. She came up to Conway Jefferson and laid a hand on his shoulder. She said, with a little catch in her breath:

'I want to tell you something, Jeff. At once. I'm going to marry Hugo.'

Conway Jefferson looked up at her for a moment. He said gruffly:

'About time you married again. Congratulations to you both. By the way, Addie, I'm making a new will to-morrow.'

She nodded. 'Oh yes. I know.'

Jefferson said:

'No, you don't. I'm settling ten thousand pounds on you. Everything else I have goes to Peter when I die. How does that suit you, my girl?'

'Oh, *Jeff*!' Her voice broke. 'You're *wonderful*!'

'He's a nice lad. I'd like to see a good deal of him—in the time I've got left.'

'Oh, you shall!'

'Got a great feeling for crime, Peter has,' said Conway Jefferson meditatively. 'Not only has he got the fingernail of the murdered girl—one of the murdered girls, anyway—but he was lucky enough to have a bit of Josie's shawl caught in with the nail. So he's got a souvenir of the murderess too! That makes him *very* happy!'

2

Hugo and Adelaide passed by the ballroom. Raymond came up to them.

Adelaide said, rather quickly:

'I must tell you my news. We're going to be married.'

The smile on Raymond's face was perfect—a brave, pensive smile.

'I hope,' he said, ignoring Hugo and gazing into her eyes, 'that you will be very, very happy....'

They passed on and Raymond stood looking after them.

'A nice woman,' he said to himself. 'A very nice woman. And she would have had money too. The trouble I took to mug up that bit about the Devonshire Starrs. . . . Oh well, my luck's out. Dance, dance, little gentleman!'

And Raymond returned to the ballroom.

Hercule Poirot's Christmas

My dear James,

You have always been one of the most faithful and kindly of my readers, and I was therefore seriously perturbed when I received from you a word of criticism.

You complained that my murders were getting too refined—anaemic, in fact. You yearned for a 'good violent murder with lots of blood.' A murder where there was no doubt about its being murder!

So this is your special story—written for you. I hope it may please.

Your affectionate sister-in-law,
Agatha.

‘Yet who would have thought the old man to have had so much blood in him?’

Macbeth

PART ONE

December 22nd

I

STEPHEN pulled up the collar of his coat as he walked briskly along the platform. Overhead a dim fog clouded the station. Large engines hissed superbly, throwing off clouds of steam into the cold raw air. Everything was dirty and smoke-grimed.

Stephen thought with revulsion:

'What a foul country—what a foul city!'

His first excited reaction to London, its shops, its restaurants, its well-dressed, attractive women, had faded. He saw it now as a glittering rhinestone set in a dingy setting.

Supposing he were back in South Africa now. . . . He felt a quick pang of homesickness. Sunshine—blue skies—gardens of flowers—cool blue flowers—hedges of plumbago—blue convolvulus clinging to every little shanty.

And here—dirt, grime, and endless incessant crowds—moving, hurrying—jostling. Busy ants running industriously about their ant-hill.

For a moment he thought, 'I wish I hadn't come. . . .'

Then he remembered his purpose and his lips set back in a grim line. No, by hell, he'd go on with it! He'd planned this for years. He'd always meant to do—what he was going to do. Yes, he'd go on with it!

That momentary reluctance, that sudden questioning of himself: 'Why? Is it worth it? Why dwell on the past? Why not wipe out the whole thing?'—all that was only weakness. He was not a boy—to be turned this way and that by the whim of the moment. He was a man of forty, assured, purposeful. He would go on with it. He would do what he had come to England to do.

He got on the train and passed along the corridor looking for a place. He had waved aside a porter and was carrying his own raw-hide suitcase. He looked into carriage after carriage. The train was full. It was only three days before Christmas. Stephen Farr looked distastefully at the crowded carriages.

People! Incessant, innumerable people! And all so—so—what was the word—so *drab* looking! So alike, so horribly alike! Those that hadn't got faces like sheep had faces like rabbits, he thought. Some of them chattered and fussed. Some, heavily middle-aged men, grunted. More like pigs, those. Even the girls, slender, egg-faced, scarlet-lipped, were of a depressing uniformity.

He thought with a sudden longing of open veldt, sun-baked and lonely. . . .

And then, suddenly, he caught his breath, looking into a carriage. This girl was different. Black hair, rich creamy pallor—eyes with the depth and darkness of night in them. The sad proud eyes of the South. . . . It was all wrong that this girl should be sitting in this train among these dull, drab-looking people—all wrong that she should be going into the dreary midlands of England. She should have been on a balcony, a rose between her lips, a piece of black lace draping her proud head, and there should have been dust and heat and the smell of blood—the smell of the bull-ring—in the air. . . . She should be somewhere splendid, not squeezed into the corner of a third-class carriage.

He was an observant man. He did not fail to note the shabbiness of her little black coat and skirt, the cheap quality of her fabric gloves, the flimsy shoes and the defiant note of a flame-red handbag. Nevertheless splendour was the quality he associated with her. She *was* splendid, fine, exotic. . . .

What the hell was she doing in this country of fogs and chills and hurrying industrious ants?

He thought, 'I've got to know who she is and what she's doing here . . . I've got to know. . . .'

2

Pilar sat squeezed up against the window and thought how very odd the English smelt. . . . It was what had struck her so far most forcibly about England—the difference of smell. There was no garlic and no dust and very little perfume. In this carriage now there was a smell of cold stuffiness—the sulphur smell of the trains—the smell of soap and another very unpleasant smell—it came, she thought, from the fur collar of the stout woman sitting beside her. Pilar sniffed delicately, imbibing the odour of mothballs reluctantly. It was a funny scent to choose to put on yourself, she thought.

A whistle blew, a stentorian voice cried out something and the train jerked slowly out of the station. They had started. She was on her way. . . .

Her heart beat a little faster. Would it be all right? Would she be able to accomplish what she had set out to do? Surely—surely—she had thought it all out so carefully. . . . She was prepared for every eventuality. Oh, yes, she would succeed—she must succeed. . . .

The curve of Pilar's red mouth curved upwards. It was suddenly cruel, that mouth. Cruel and greedy—like the mouth of a child or a kitten—a mouth that knew only its own desires and that was as yet unaware of pity.

She looked round her with the frank curiosity of a child. All these people, seven of them—how funny they were, the English! They all seemed so rich, so prosperous—their clothes—their boots—Oh! undoubtedly England was a very rich country as she had always heard. But they were not at all gay—no, decidedly not gay.

That was a handsome man standing in the corridor. . . . Pilar thought he was very handsome. She liked his deeply bronzed face and his high bridged nose and his square shoulders. More quickly than any English girl, Pilar had seen that the man admired her. She had not looked at him once directly, but she knew perfectly how often he had looked at her and exactly how he had looked.

She registered the facts without much interest or emotion. She came from a country where men looked at women as a matter of course and did not disguise the fact unduly. She wondered if he was an Englishman and decided that he was not.

'He is too alive, too real, to be English,' Pilar decided. 'And yet he is fair. He may be perhaps Americano.' He was, she thought, rather like the actors she had seen in Wild West films.

An attendant pushed his way along the corridor.

'First lunch, please. First lunch. Take your seats for first lunch.'

The seven occupants of Pilar's carriage all held tickets for the first lunch. They rose in a body and the carriage was suddenly deserted and peaceful.

Pilar quickly pulled up the window which had been let down a couple of inches at the top by a militant-looking, grey-haired lady in the opposite corner. Then she sprawled comfortably back on her seat and peered out of the window at the northern suburbs of London. She did not turn her head at the sound of the door sliding back. It was the man from the corridor, and Pilar knew, of course, that he had entered the carriage on purpose to talk to her.

She continued to look pensively out of the window.

Stephen Farr said:

'Would you like the window down at all?'

Pilar replied demurely:

'On the contrary. I have just shut it.'

She spoke English perfectly, but with a slight accent.

During the pause that ensued, Stephen thought:

'A delicious voice. It has the sun in it. . . . It is warm like a summer night. . . .'

Pilar thought:

'I like his voice. It is big and strong. He is attractive—yes, he is attractive.'

Stephen said:

'The train is very full.'

'Oh, yes, indeed. The people go away from London, I suppose, because it is so black there.'

Pilar had not been brought up to believe that it was a crime to talk to strange men in trains. She could take care of herself as well as any girl, but she had no rigid taboos.

If Stephen had been brought up in England he might have felt ill at ease at entering into conversation with a young girl. But Stephen was a friendly soul who found it perfectly natural to talk to anyone if he felt like it.

He smiled without any self-consciousness and said:

'London's rather a terrible place, isn't it?'

'Oh, yes. I do not like it at all.'

'No more do I.'

Pilar said: 'You are not English, no?'

'I'm British, but I come from South Africa.'

'Oh, I see, that explains it.'

'Have you just come from abroad?'

Pilar nodded. 'I come from Spain.'

Stephen was interested.

'From Spain, do you? You're Spanish, then?'

'I am half Spanish. My mother was English. That is why I talk English so well.'

'What about this war business?' asked Stephen.

'It is very terrible, yes—very sad. There has been damage done, quite a lot—yes.'

'Which side are you on?'

Pilar's politics seemed to be rather vague. In the village where she came from, she explained, nobody had paid very much attention to the war. 'It has not been near us, you understand. The Mayor, he is, of course, an officer of the Government, so he is for the Government, and the priest is for General Franco—but most of the people are busy with the vines and the land, they have not time to go into these questions.'

'So there wasn't any fighting round you?'

Pilar said that there had not been. 'But then I drove in a car.' she explained, 'all across the country and there was much destruction. And I saw a bomb drop and it blew up a car—yes, and another destroyed a house. It was very exciting!'

Stephen Farr smiled a faintly twisted smile.

'So that's how it seemed to you?'

'It was a nuisance, too,' explained Pilar. 'Because I wanted to get on, and the driver of my car, he was killed.'

Stephen said, watching her:

'That didn't upset you?'

Pilar's great dark eyes opened very wide.

'Everyone must die! That is so, is it not? If it comes quickly from the sky—bouff—like that, it is as well as any other way. One is alive for a time—yes, and then one is dead. That is what happens in this world.'

Stephen Farr laughed.

'I don't think you are a pacifist.'

'You do not think I am what?' Pilar seemed puzzled by a word which had not previously entered her vocabulary.

'Do you forgive your enemies, señorita?'

Pilar shook her head.

'I have no enemies. But if I had——'

'Well?'

He was watching her, fascinated anew by the sweet, cruel upward-curving mouth.

Pilar said gravely:

'If I had an enemy—if anyone hated me and I hated them—then I would cut my enemy's throat like *this*. . . .'

She made a graphic gesture.

It was so swift and so crude that Stephen Farr was momentarily taken aback. He said:

'You're a bloodthirsty young woman!'

Pilar asked in a matter-of-fact tone:

'What would you do to your enemy?'

He started—stared at her, then laughed aloud.

'I wonder——' he said. 'I wonder!'

Pilar said disapprovingly:

'But surely—you know.'

He checked his laughter, drew in his breath and said in a low voice:

'Yes. I know. . . .'

Then, with a rapid change of manner, he asked:

'What made you come to England?'

Pilar replied with a certain demureness.

'I am going to stay with my relations—with my English relations.'

'I see.'

He leaned back in his seat, studying her—wondering what these English relations of whom she spoke were like—wondering what they would make of this Spanish stranger . . . trying to picture her in the midst of some sober British family at Christmas-time.

Pilar asked:

'It is nice, South Africa, yes?'

He began to talk to her about South Africa. She listened with the pleased attention of a child hearing a story. He enjoyed her naïve but shrewd questions and amused himself by making a kind of exaggerated fairy story of it all.

The return of the proper occupants of the carriage put an end to this diversion. He rose, smiled into her eyes, and made his way out again into the corridor.

As he stood back for a minute in the doorway, to allow an elderly lady to come in, his eyes fell on the label of Pilar's obviously foreign straw case. He read the name with interest—*Miss Pilar Estravados*—then as his eye caught the address, it widened to incredulity and some other feeling—*Gorston Hall, Longdale, Addlesfield*.

He half turned, staring at the girl with a new expression—puzzled, resentful, suspicious. . . . He went out into the corridor and stood there smoking a cigarette and frowning to himself. . . .

3

In the big blue and gold drawing-room at Gorston Hall Alfred Lee and Lydia, his wife, sat discussing their plans for Christmas. Alfred was a squarely-built man of middle-age with a gentle face and mild brown eyes. His voice when he spoke was quiet and precise with a very clear enunciation. His head was sunk into his shoulders and he gave a curious impression of inertia. Lydia, his wife, was an energetic, lean greyhound of a woman. She was amazingly thin, but all her movements had a swift, startled grace about them.

There was no beauty in her careless, haggard face, but it had distinction. Her voice was charming.

Alfred said:

'Father insists! There's nothing else for it.'

Lydia controlled a sudden impatient movement. She said:

'Must you always give in to him?'

'He's a very old man, my dear——'

'Oh, I know—I know!'

'He expects to have his own way.'

Lydia said dryly:

'Naturally, since he has always had it! But some time or other, Alfred, you will have to make a stand.'

'What do you mean, Lydia?'

He stared at her, so palpably upset and startled, that for a moment she bit her lip and seemed doubtful whether to go on.

Alfred Lee repeated:

'What do you mean, Lydia?'

She shrugged her thin, graceful shoulders.

She said, trying to choose her words cautiously:

'Your father is—inclined to be—tyrannical——'

'He's old.'

'And will grow older. And consequently more tyrannical. Where will it end? Already he dictates our lives to us completely. We can't make a plan of our own! If we do, it is always liable to be upset.'

Alfred said:

'Father expects to come first. He is very good to us, remember.'

'Oh! good to us!'

'*Very* good to us.'

Alfred spoke with a trace of sternness.

Lydia said calmly:

'You mean financially?'

'Yes. His own wants are very simple. But he never grudges us money. You can spend what you like on dress and on this house, and the bills are paid without a murmur. He gave us a new car only last week.'

'As far as money goes, your father is very generous, I admit,' said Lydia. 'But in return he expects us to behave like slaves.'

'Slaves?'

'That's the word I used. You *are* his slave, Alfred. If we have planned to go away and father suddenly wishes us not to go, you cancel the arrangements and remain without a murmur! If the whim takes him to send us away, we go. . . . We have no lives of our own—no independence.'

Her husband said distressfully:

'I wish you wouldn't talk like this, Lydia. It is very ungrateful. My father has done everything for us. . . .'

She bit off a retort that was on her lips. She shrugged those thin, graceful shoulders once more.

Alfred said:

'You know, Lydia, the old man is very fond of you——'

His wife said clearly and distinctly:

'I am not at all fond of him.'

'Lydia, it distresses me to hear you say things like that. It is so unkind——'

'Perhaps. But sometimes a compulsion comes over one to speak the truth.'

'If father guessed——'

'Your father knows perfectly well that I do not like him! It amuses him, I think.'

'Really, Lydia, I am sure you are wrong there. He has often told me how charming your manner to him is.'

'Naturally I've always been polite. I always shall be. I'm just letting you know what my real feelings are. I dislike your father, Alfred. I think he is a malicious and tyrannical old man. He bullies you and presumes on your affection for him. You ought to have stood up to him years ago.'

Alfred said sharply:

'That will do, Lydia. Please don't say any more.'

She sighed.

'I'm sorry. Perhaps I was wrong. . . . Let's talk of our Christmas arrangements. Do you think your brother David will really come?'

'Why not?'

She shook her head doubtfully.

'David is—queer. He's not been inside the house for years, remember. He was so devoted to your mother—he's got some feeling about this place.'

'David always got on father's nerves,' said Alfred, 'with his music and his dreamy ways. Father was, perhaps, a bit hard on him sometimes. But I think David and Hilda will come all right. Christmas time, you know.'

'Peace and goodwill,' said Lydia. Her delicate mouth curved ironically. 'I wonder! George and Magdalene are coming. They said they would probably arrive to-morrow. I'm afraid Magdalene will be frightfully bored.'

Alfred said with some slight annoyance:

'Why my brother George ever married a girl twenty years younger than himself I can't think! George was always a fool!'

'He's very successful in his career,' said Lydia. 'His constituents like him. I believe Magdalene works quite hard politically for him.'

Alfred said slowly:

'I don't think I like her very much. She is very good-looking—but I sometimes think she is like one of those beautiful pears one gets—they have a rosy flush and a rather waxen appearance——' He shook his head.

'And they're bad inside?' said Lydia. 'How funny you should say that, Alfred!'

'Why funny?'

She answered:

'Because—usually—you are such a gentle soul. You hardly ever say an unkind thing about anyone. I get annoyed with you sometimes because you're not sufficiently—oh, what shall I say?—sufficiently suspicious—not worldly enough!'

Her husband smiled.

'The world, I always think, is as you yourself make it.'

Lydia said harply:

'No! Evil is not only in one's mind. Evil exists! *You* seem to have no consciousness of the evil in the world. I have. I can feel it. I've always felt it—here in this house——' She bit her lip and turned away.

Alfred said, 'Lydia——'

But she raised a quick admonitory hand, her eyes looking past him at something over his shoulder. Alfred turned.

A dark man with a smooth face was standing there deferentially.

Lydia said sharply:

'What is it, Horbury?'

Horbury's voice was low, a mere deferential murmur.

'It's Mr. Lee, madam. He asked me to tell you that there would be two more guests arriving for Christmas, and would you have rooms prepared for them.'

Lydia said, 'Two more guests?'

Horbury said smoothly, 'Yes, madam, another gentleman and a young lady.'

Alfred said wonderingly:

'A young lady?'

'That's what Mr. Lee said, sir.'

Lydia said quickly:

'I will go up and see him——'

Horbury made one little step, it was a mere ghost of a movement but it stopped Lydia's rapid progress automatically.

'Excuse me, madam, but Mr. Lee is having his afternoon sleep. He asked specially that he should not be disturbed.'

'I see,' said Alfred. 'Of course we won't disturb him.'

'Thank you, sir.' Horbury withdrew.

Lydia said vehemently:

'How I dislike that man! He creeps about the house like a cat! One never hears him going or coming.'

'I don't like him very much either. But he knows his job. It's not so easy to get a good male nurse attendant. And father likes him, that's the main thing.'

'Yes, that's the main thing, as you say. Alfred, what is this about a young lady? What young lady?'

Her husband shook his head.

'I can't imagine. I can't even think of anyone it might be likely to be.'

They stared at each other. Then Lydia said, with a sudden twist of her expressive mouth:

'Do you know what I think, Alfred?'

'What?'

'I think your father has been bored lately. I think he is planning a little Christmas diversion for himself.'

'By introducing two strangers into a family gathering?'

'Oh! I don't know what the details are—but I do fancy that your father is preparing to—amuse himself.'

'I hope he *will* get some pleasure out of it,' said Alfred gravely. 'Poor old chap, tied by the leg, an invalid—after the adventurous life he has led.'

Lydia said slowly:

'After the—adventurous life he has led.'

The pause she made before the adjective gave it some special though obscure significance. Alfred seemed to feel it. He flushed and looked unhappy.

She cried out suddenly:

'How he ever had a son like you, I can't imagine! You two are poles apart. And he fascinates you—you simply worship him!'

Alfred said with a trace of vexation:

'Aren't you going a little far, Lydia? It's natural, I should say, for a son to love his father. It would be very unnatural not to do so.'

Lydia said:

'In that case, most of the members of this family are—unnatural! Oh, don't let's argue! I apologise. I've hurt your feelings, I know. Believe me, Alfred, I really didn't mean to do that. I admire you enormously for your—your—*fidelity*. Loyalty is such a rare virtue in these days. Let us say, shall we, that I am jealous? Women are supposed to be jealous of their mothers-in-law—why not, then, of their fathers-in-law?'

He put a gentle arm round her.

'Your tongue runs away with you, Lydia. There's no reason for you to be jealous.'

She gave him a quick remorseful kiss, a delicate caress on the tip of his ear.

'I know. All the same, Alfred, I don't believe I should have been in the least jealous of your mother. I wish I'd known her.'

He sighed.

'She was a poor creature,' he said.

His wife looked at him interestedly.

'So that's how she struck you . . . as a poor creature. . . . That's interesting.'

He said dreamily:

'I remember her as nearly always ill. . . . Often in tears . . .' He shook his head. 'She had no spirit.'

Still staring at him, she murmured very softly:

'How odd . . .'

But as he turned a questioning glance on her, she shook her head quickly and changed the subject.

'Since we are not allowed to know who our mysterious guests are I shall go out and finish my garden.'

'It's very cold, my dear, a biting wind.'

'I'll wrap up warmly.'

She left the room. Alfred Lee, left alone, stood for some minutes motionless, frowning a little to himself, then he walked over to the big window at the end of the room. Outside was a terrace running the whole length of the house. Here, after a minute or two, he saw Lydia emerge, carrying a flat basket. She was wearing a big blanket coat. She set down the basket and began to work at a square stone sink slightly raised above ground level.

Her husband watched for some time. At last he went out of the room, fetched himself a coat and muffler, and emerged on to the terrace by a side door. As he walked along he passed various other stone sinks arranged as miniature gardens, all the products of Lydia's agile fingers.

One represented a desert scene with smooth yellow sand, a little clump of green palm trees in coloured tin, and a procession of camels with one or two little Arab figures. Some primitive mud houses had been constructed of Plasticine. There was an Italian garden with terraces and formal beds with flowers in coloured sealing-wax. There was an arctic one, too, with lumps of green glass for icebergs, and a little cluster of penguins. Next came a Japanese garden with a couple of beautiful little stunted trees, looking-glass arranged for water, and bridges modelled out of Plasticine.

He came at last to stand beside her where she was at work. She had laid down blue paper and covered it over with glass. Round this were lumps of rock piled up. At the moment she was pouring out coarse pebbles from a little bag and forming them into a beach. Between the rocks were some small cacti.

Lydia was murmuring to herself:

'Yes, that's exactly right—exactly what I want.'

Alfred said:

'What's this latest work of art?'

She started, for she had not heard him come up.

'This? Oh, it's the Dead Sea, Alfred. Do you like it?'

He said, 'It's rather arid, isn't it? Oughtn't there to be more vegetation?'

She shook her head.

'It's my idea of the Dead Sea. It *is* dead, you see——'

'It's not so attractive as some of the others.'

'It's not meant to be specially attractive.'

Footsteps sounded on the terrace. An elderly butler, white-haired and slightly bowed, was coming towards them.

'Mrs. George Lee on the telephone, madam. She says will it be convenient if she and Mr. George arrive by the five-twenty tomorrow?'

'Yes, tell her that will be quite all right.'

'Thank you, madam.'

The butler hurried away. Lydia looked after him with a softened expression on her face.

'Dear old Tressilian. What a standby he is! I can't imagine what we should do without him.'

Alfred agreed.

'He's one of the old school. He's been with us nearly forty years. He's devoted to us all.'

Lydia nodded.

'Yes. He's like the faithful old retainers of fiction. I believe he'd lie himself blue in the face if it was necessary to protect one of the family!'

Alfred said:

'I believe he would. . . . Yes, I believe he would.'

Lydia smoothed over the last bit of her shingle.

'There,' she said. 'That's ready.'

'Ready?' Alfred looked puzzled.

She laughed.

'For Christmas, silly! For this sentimental family Christmas we're going to have.'

4

David was rereading the letter. Once he screwed it up into a ball and thrust it away from him. Then, reaching for it, he smoothed it out and read it again.

Quietly, without saying anything, his wife, Hilda, watched him. She noted the jerking muscle (or was it a nerve?) in his temple, the slight tremor of the long delicate hands, the nervous spasmodic movements of his whole body. When he pushed aside the lock of fair hair that always tended to stray down over his forehead and looked across at her with appealing blue eyes she was ready.

'Hilda, what shall we do about it?'

Hilda hesitated a minute before speaking. She had heard the appeal in his voice. She knew how dependent he was upon her—had always been ever since their marriage—knew that she could probably influence his decision finally and decisively. But for just that reason she was chary of pronouncing anything too final.

She said, and her voice had the calm, soothing quality that can be heard in the voice of an experienced nannie in a nursery:

'It depends on how you feel about it, David.'

A broad woman, Hilda, not beautiful, but with a certain magnetic quality. Something about her like a Dutch picture. Something warming and endearing in the sound of her voice. Something strong about her—the vital hidden strength that appeals to weakness. An over-stout dumpy middle-aged woman—not clever—not brilliant—but with *something* about her that you couldn't pass over. Force! Hilda Lee had force!

David got up and began pacing up and down. His hair was practically untouched by grey. He was strangely boyish-looking. His face had the mild quality of a Burne Jones knight. It was, somehow, not very real. . . .

He said, and his voice was wistful:

'You know how I feel about it, Hilda. You must.'

'I'm not sure.'

'But I've told you—I've told you again and again! How I hate it all—the house and the country round and everything! It brings back nothing but misery. I hated every moment that I spent there! When I think of it—of all that *she* suffered—my mother . . .'

His wife nodded sympathetically.

'She was so sweet, Hilda, and so patient. Lying there, often in pain, but bearing it—enduring everything. And when I think of my father'—his face darkened—'bringing all that misery into her life—humiliating her—boasting of his love affairs—constantly unfaithful to her and never troubling to conceal it.'

Hilda Lee said:

'She should not have put up with it. She should have left him.'

He said with a touch of reproof:

'She was too good to do that. She thought it was her duty to remain. Besides, it was her home—where else should she go?'

'She could have made a life of her own.'

David said fretfully:

'Not in those days! You don't understand. Women didn't behave like that. They put up with things. They endured patiently. She had us to consider. Even if she had divorced my father, what would have happened? He would probably have married again. There might have been a second family. *Our* interests might have gone to the wall. She had to think of all those considerations.'

Hilda did not answer.

David went on:

'No, she did right. She was a saint! She endured to the end—uncomplainingly.'

Hilda said, 'Not quite uncomplainingly or you would not know so much, David!'

He said softly, his face lighting up:

'Yes—she told me things. . . . She knew how I loved her. When she died——'

He stopped. He ran his hands through his hair.

'Hilda, it was awful—horrible! The desolation! She was quite young still, she *needn't* have died. *He* killed her—my father! He was responsible for her dying. He broke her heart. I decided then that I'd not go on living under his roof. I broke away—got away from it all.'

Hilda nodded.

'You were very wise,' she said. 'It was the right thing to do.'

David said:

'Father wanted me to go into the works. That would have meant living at home. I couldn't have stood that. I can't think how Alfred stands it—how he has stood it all these years.'

'Did he never rebel against it?' asked Hilda with some interest. 'I thought you told me something about his having given up some other career.'

David nodded.

'Alfred was going into the army. Father arranged it all. Alfred, the eldest, was to go into some cavalry regiment, Harry was to go into the works, so was I. George was to enter politics.'

'And it didn't work out like that?'

David shook his head.

'Harry broke all that up! He was always frightfully wild. Got into debt—and all sorts of other troubles. Finally he went off one day with several hundred pounds that didn't belong to him, leaving a note behind him saying an office stool didn't suit him and he was going to see the world.'

'And you never heard any more of him.'

'Oh, yes, we did!' David laughed. 'We heard quite often! He was always cabling for money from all over the world. He usually got it too!'

'And Alfred?'

'Father made him chuck up the army and come back and go into the works.'

'Did he mind?'

'Very much to begin with. He hated it. But father could always twist Alfred round his little finger. He's absolutely under father's thumb still, I believe.'

'And you—escaped!' said Hilda.

'Yes. I went to London and studied painting. Father told me plainly that if I went off on a fool's errand like that I'd get a small allowance from him during his lifetime and nothing when he died. I said I didn't care. He called me a young fool, and that was that! I've never seen him since.'

Hilda said gently:

'And you haven't regretted it?'

'No, indeed. I realise I shan't ever get anywhere with my art. I shall never be a great artist—but we're happy enough in this cottage—we've got everything we want—all the essentials. And if I die, well, my life's insured for you.'

He paused and then said:

'And now—*this*!'

He struck the letter with his open hand.

'I am sorry your father ever wrote that letter, if it upsets you so much,' said Hilda.

David went on as though he had not heard her.

'Asking me to bring my wife for Christmas, expressing a hope that we may be all together for Christmas; a united family! What can it mean?'

Hilda said:

'Need it mean anything more than it says?'

He looked at her questioningly.

'I mean,' she said, smiling, 'that your father is growing old. He's beginning to feel sentimental about family ties. That does happen, you know.'

'I suppose it does,' said David slowly.

'He's an old man and he's lonely.'

He gave her a quick look.

'You want me to go, don't you, Hilda?'

She said slowly:

'It seems a pity—not to answer an appeal. I'm old-fashioned, I dare say, but why not have peace and goodwill at Christmas-time?'

'After all I've told you?'

'I know, dear, I know. But all that's in the *past*. It's all done and finished with.'

'Not for me.'

'No, *because you won't let it die*. You keep the past alive in your own mind.'

'I can't forget.'

'You *won't* forget—that's what you mean, David.'

His mouth set in a firm line.

'We're like that, we Lees. We remember things for years—brood about them, keep memory green.'

Hilda said with a touch of impatience:

'Is that anything to be proud of? I do not think so!'

He looked thoughtfully at her, a touch of reserve in his manner.

He said: 'You don't attach much value to loyalty, then—loyalty to a memory?'

Hilda said:

'I believe the *present* matters—not the past! The past must go. If we seek to keep the past alive, we end, I think, by *distorting* it. We see it in exaggerated terms—a false perspective.

'I can remember every word and every incident of those days perfectly,' said David passionately.

'Yes, but you *shouldn't*, my dear! It isn't natural to do so! You're applying the judgment of a boy to those days instead of looking back on them with the more temperate outlook of a man.'

'What difference would that make?' demanded David.

Hilda hesitated. She was aware of unwisdom in going on, and yet there were things she badly wanted to say.

'I think,' she said, 'that you're seeing your father as a *bogy*! You're exalting him into a kind of personification of evil. Probably, if you were to see him now, you would realise that he was only a very ordinary man; a man, perhaps, whose passions ran away with him, a man whose life was far from blameless, but nevertheless merely a *man*—not a kind of inhuman monster!'

'You don't understand! His treatment of my mother——'

Hilda said gravely:

'There is a certain kind of meekness—of submission—that brings out the worst in a man—whereas that same man, faced by spirit and determination, might be a different creature!'

'So you say it was her fault——'

Hilda interrupted him.

'No, of course I don't! I've no doubt your father treated your mother very badly indeed, but marriage is an extraordinary thing—and I doubt if any outsider—even a child of the marriage—has the right to judge. Besides, all this resentment on your part now cannot help your mother. It is all *gone*—it is behind you! What is left now is an old man, in feeble health, asking his son to come home for Christmas.'

'And you want me to go?'

Hilda hesitated, then she suddenly made up her mind. 'Yes,' she said, 'I do. I want you to go and lay the bogy once and for all.'

5

George Lee, M.P. for Westeringham, was a somewhat corpulent gentleman of forty-one. His eyes were pale blue and slightly prominent with a suspicious expression, he had a heavy jowl, and a slow pedantic utterance.

He said now in a weighty manner:

'I have told you, Magdalene, that I think it my *duty* to go.'

His wife shrugged her shoulders impatiently.

She was a slender creature, a platinum blonde with plucked eyebrows and a smooth egg-like face. It could, on occasions, look quite blank and devoid of any expression whatever. She was looking like that now.

'Darling,' she said, 'it will be perfectly grim, I am sure of it.'

'Moreover,' said George Lee, and his face lit up as an attractive idea occurred to him, 'it will enable us to save considerably. Christmas is always an expensive time. We can put the servants on board wages.'

'Oh, well!' said Magdalene. 'After all, Christmas is pretty grim anywhere!'

'I suppose,' said George, pursuing his own line of thought, 'they will expect to have a Christmas dinner? A nice piece of beef, perhaps, instead of a turkey.'

'Who? The servants? Oh, George, don't fuss so. You're always worrying about money.'

'Somebody has to worry,' said George.

'Yes, but it's absurd to pinch and scrape in all these little ways. Why don't you make your father give you some more money?'

'He already gives me a very handsome allowance.'

'It's awful to be completely dependent on your father, as you are! He ought to settle some money on you outright.'

'That's not his way of doing things.'

Magdalene looked at him. Her hazel eyes were suddenly sharp and keen. The expressionless egg-like face showed sudden meaning.

'He's frightfully rich, isn't he, George? A kind of millionaire, isn't he?'

'A millionaire twice over, I believe.'

Magdalene gave an envious sigh.

'How did he make it all? South Africa, wasn't it?'

'Yes, he made a big fortune there in his early days. Mainly diamonds.'

'Thrilling!' said Magdalene.

'Then he came to England and started in business and his fortune has actually doubled or trebled itself, I believe.'

'What will happen when he dies?' asked Magdalene.

'Father's never said much on the subject. Of course one can't exactly *ask*. I should imagine that the bulk of his money will go to Alfred and myself. Alfred, of course, will get the larger share.'

'You've got other brothers, haven't you?'

'Yes, there's my brother David. I don't fancy *he* will get much. He went off to do art or some tomfoolery of that kind. I believe father warned him that he would cut him out of his will and David said he didn't care.'

'How silly,' said Magdalene with scorn.

'There was my sister Jennifer too. She went off with a foreigner—a Spanish artist—one of David's friends. But she died just over a year ago. She left a daughter, I believe. Father might leave a little money to her, but nothing much. And of course there's Harry——'

He stopped, slightly embarrassed.

'Harry?' said Magdalene, surprised. 'Who is Harry?'

'Ah—er—my brother.'

'I never knew you had another brother?'

'My dear, he wasn't a great—er—credit—to us. We don't mention him. His behaviour was disgraceful. We haven't heard anything of him for some years now. He's probably dead.'

Magdalene laughed suddenly.

'What is it? What are you laughing at?'

Magdalene said:

'I was only thinking how funny it was that you—*you*, George, should have a disreputable brother! You're so very respectable.'

'I should hope so,' said George coldly.

Her eyes narrowed.

'Your father isn't—very respectable, George?'

'Really, Magdalene!'

'Sometimes the things he says make me feel quite uncomfortable.'

George said: 'Really, Magdalene, you surprise me. Does—er—does Lydia feel the same?'

'He doesn't say the same kind of things to Lydia, said Magdalene. She added angrily. '*No*, he never says them to *her*. I can't think why not.'

George glanced at her quickly and then glanced away.

'Oh, well,' he said vaguely. 'One must make allowances. At father's age—and with his health being so bad——'

He paused. His wife asked:

'Is he really—pretty ill?'

'Oh, I wouldn't say *that*. He's remarkably tough. All the same, since he wants to have his family round him at Christmas, I think we are quite right to go. It may be his last Christmas.'

She said sharply: 'You *say* that, George, but really, I suppose, he may live for years?'

Slightly taken aback, her husband stammered:

'Yes—yes, of course he may.'

Magdalene turned away.

'Oh, well,' she said, 'I suppose we're doing the right thing by going.'

'I have no doubt about it.'

'But I hate it! Alfred's so dull, and Lydia snubs me."

'Nonsense.'

'She does. And I hate that beastly manservant.'

'Old Tressilian?'

'No, Horbury. Sneaking round like a cat and smirking.'

'Really Magdalene, I can't see that Horbury can affect you in any way!'

'He just gets on my nerves, that's all. But don't let's bother. We've got to go, I can see that. Won't do to offend the old man.

'No—no, that's just the point. About the servants' Christmas dinner——'

'Not now, George, some other time. I'll just ring up Lydia and tell her we'll come by the five-twenty to-morrow.'

Magdalene left the room precipitately. After telephoning she went up to her own room and sat down in front of the desk. She let down the flap and rummaged in its various pigeon-holes. Cascades of bills came tumbling out. Magdalene sorted through them, trying to arrange them in some kind of order. Finally, with an impatient sigh, she bundled them up and thrust them back whence they had come. She passed a hand over her smooth platinum head.

'What on earth am I to do?' she murmured.

6

On the first floor of Gorston Hall a long passage led to a big room overlooking the front drive. It was a room furnished in the more flamboyant of old-fashioned styles. It had heavy brocaded wall-paper, rich leather arm-chairs, large vases embossed with dragons, sculptures in bronze. . . . Everything in it was magnificent, costly and solid.

In a big grandfather arm-chair, the biggest and most imposing of all the chairs, sat the thin, shrivelled figure of an old man. His long clawlike hands rested on the arms of the chair. A gold-mounted stick was by his side. He wore an old shabby blue dressing-gown. On his feet were carpet slippers. His hair was white and the skin of his face was yellow.

A shabby insignificant figure, one might have thought. But the nose, aquiline and proud, and the eyes, dark and intensely alive, might cause an observer to alter his opinion. Here was fire and life and vigour.

Old Simeon Lee cackled to himself, a sudden, high cackle of amusement.

He said:

'You gave my message to Mrs. Alfred, hey?'

Horbury was standing beside his chair. He replied in his soft deferential voice.

'Yes, sir.'

'Exactly in the words I told you? Exactly, mind?'

'Yes, sir. I didn't make a mistake, sir.'

'No—you don't make mistakes. You'd better not make mistakes either—or you'll regret it! And what did she say, Horbury? What did Mr. Alfred say?'

Quietly, unemotionally, Horbury repeated what had passed. The old man cackled again and rubbed his hands together.

'Splendid . . . First rate . . . They'll have been thinking and wondering—all the afternoon! Splendid! I'll have 'em up now. Go and get them.'

'Yes, sir.'

Horbury walked noiselessly across the room and went out.

'And, Horbury——'

The old man looked round, then cursed to himself.

'Fellow moves like a cat. Never know where he is.'

He sat quite still in his chair, his fingers caressing his chin till there was a tap on the door, and Alfred and Lydia came in.

'Ah, there you are, there you are. Sit here, Lydia, my dear, by me. What a nice colour you've got.'

'I've been out in the cold. It makes one's cheeks burn afterwards.'

Alfred said:

'How are you, father, did you have a good rest this afternoon?'

'First rate—first rate. Dreamt about the old days! That was before I settled down and became a pillar of society.'

He cackled with sudden laughter.

His daughter-in-law sat silently smiling with polite attention.

Alfred said:

'What's this, father, about two extra being expected for Christmas?'

'Ah, that! Yes, I must tell you about that. It's going to be a grand Christmas for me this year—a grand Christmas. Let me see, George is coming and Magdalene——'

Lydia said:

'Yes, they are arriving to-morrow by the five-twenty.'

Old Simeon said:

'Poor stick, George! Nothing but a gasbag! Still, he *is* my son.'

Alfred said:

'His constituents like him.'

Simeon cackled again.

'They probably think he's honest. Honest! There never was a Lee who was honest yet.'

'Oh, come now, father.'

'I except you, my boy. I except you.'

'And David?' asked Lydia.

'David now. I'm curious to see the boy after all these years. He was a namby-pamby youngster. Wonder what his wife is like? At any rate *he* hasn't married a girl twenty years younger than himself, like that fool George!'

'Hilda wrote a very nice letter,' said Lydia. 'I've just had a wire from her confirming it and saying they are definitely arriving to-morrow.'

Her father-in-law looked at her, a keen, penetrating glance.

He laughed.

'I never get any change out of Lydia,' he said. 'I'll say this for you, Lydia, you're a well-bred woman. Breeding tells. I know that well enough. A funny thing, though, heredity. There's only one of you that's taken after me—only one out of all the litter.'

His eyes danced.

'Now guess who's coming for Christmas. I'll give you three guesses and I'll bet you a fiver you won't get the answer.'

He looked from one face to the other. Alfred said frowning:

'Horbury said you expected a young lady.'

'That intrigued you—yes, I dare say it did. Pilar will be arriving any minute now. I gave orders for the car to go and meet her.

Alfred said sharply:

'*Pilar?*'

Simeon said:

'Pilar Estravados. Jennifer's girl. My granddaughter. I wonder what she'll be like.'

Alfred cried out:

'Good heavens, father, you never told me . . .'

The old man was grinning.

'No, I thought I'd keep it a secret! Got Charlton to write out and fix things.'

Alfred repeated, his tone hurt and reproachful:

'You never told me. . . .'

His father said, still grinning wickedly:

'It would have spoilt the surprise! Wonder what it will be like to have young blood under this roof again? I never saw Estravados. Wonder which the girl takes after—her mother or her father?'

'Do you really think it's wise, father,' began Alfred. 'Taking everything into consideration——'

The old man interrupted him.

'Safety—safety—you play for safety too much, Alfred! Always have! That hasn't been my way! Do what you want and be damned to it! That's what I say! The girl's my granddaughter—the only grandchild in the family! I don't care what her father was or what he did! She's my flesh and blood! And she's coming to live here in my house.'

Lydia said sharply:

'She's coming to *live* here?'

He darted a quick look at her.

'Do you object?'

She shook her head. She said smiling:

'I couldn't very well object to your asking someone to your own house, could I? No, I was wondering about—her.'

'About her—what d'you mean?'

'Whether she would be happy here.'

Old Simeon flung up his head.

'She's not got a penny in the world. She ought to be thankful!'

Lydia shrugged her shoulders.

Simeon turned to Alfred:

'You see? It's going to be a grand Christmas! All my children round me. *All* my children! There, Alfred, there's your clue. Now guess who the other visitor is.'

Alfred stared at him.

'All my children! Guess, boy! *Harry*, of course! Your brother Harry!'

Alfred had gone very pale. He stammered:

'Harry—not Harry——'

'Harry himself!'

'But we thought he was dead!'

'Not he!'

'You—you are having him back here? After everything?'

'The prodigal son, eh? You're right! The fatted calf! We must kill the fatted calf, Alfred. We must give him a grand welcome.'

Alfred said:

'He treated you—all of us—disgracefully. He——'

'No need to recite his crimes! It's a long list. But Christmas, you'll remember, is the season of forgiveness! We'll welcome the prodigal home.'

Alfred rose. He murmured:

'This has been—rather a shock. I never dreamt that Harry would ever come inside these walls again.'

Simeon leaned forward.

'You never liked Harry, did you?' he said softly.

'After the way he behaved to you——'

Simeon cackled. He said:

'Ah, but bygones must be bygones. That's the spirit for Christmas, isn't it, Lydia?'

Lydia, too, had gone pale. She said dryly:

'I see that you have thought a good deal about Christmas this year.'

'I want my family round me. Peace and goodwill. I'm an old man. Are you going, my dear?'

Alfred had hurried out. Lydia paused a moment before following him.

Simeon nodded his head after the retreating figure.

'It's upset him. He and Harry never got on. Harry used to jeer at Alfred. Called him old Slow and Sure.'

Lydia's lips parted. She was about to speak, then, as she saw the old man's eager expression, she checked herself. Her self-control, she saw, disappointed him. The perception of that fact enabled her to say:

'The hare and the tortoise? Ah, well, the tortoise wins the race.'

'Not always,' said Simeon. 'Not always, my dear Lydia.'

She said, still smiling:

'Excuse me, I must go after Alfred. Sudden excitements always upset him.'

Simeon cackled.

'Yes, Alfred doesn't like changes. He always was a regular sobersides.'

Lydia said: 'Alfred is very devoted to *you*.'

'That seems odd to you, doesn't it?'

'Sometimes,' said Lydia, 'it does.'

She left the room. Simeon looked after her.

He chuckled softly and rubbed his palms together.

'Lots of fun,' he said. 'Lots of fun still. I'm going to enjoy this Christmas.'

With an effort he pulled himself upright, and with the help of his stick shuffled slowly across the room.

He went to a big safe that stood at the corner of the room. He twirled the handle of the combination. The door came open and with shaking fingers he felt inside.

He lifted out a small wash-leather bag, and opening it let a stream of uncut diamonds pass through his fingers.

'Well, my beauties, well. . . . Still the same—still my old friends. Those were good days—good days. . . . They shan't carve you and cut you about, my friends. *You* shan't hang round the necks of women or sit on their fingers or hang on their ears. You're *mine*! My old friends! We know a thing or two, you and I. I'm old, they say, and ill, but I'm not done for! Lots of life in the old dog yet. And there's still some fun to be got out of life. Still some fun——'

PART TWO

December 23rd

1

TRESSILIAN went to answer the doorbell. It had been an unusually aggressive peal, and now, before he could make his slow way across the hall, it pealed out again.

Tressilian flushed. An ill-mannered, impatient way of ringing the bell at a gentleman's house! If it was a fresh lot of those carol singers he'd give them a piece of his mind.

Through the frosted glass of the upper half of the door he saw a silhouette—a big man in a slouch hat. He opened the door. As he had thought—a cheap, flashy stranger—nasty pattern of suit he was wearing—loud! Some impudent begging fellow!

'Blessed if it isn't Tressilian,' said the stranger. 'How are you, Tressilian?'

Tressilian stared—took a deep breath—stared again. That bold arrogant jaw, the high bridged nose, the rollicking eye. Yes, they had all been there years ago. More subdued then. . . .

He said with a gasp:

'Mr. Harry!'

Harry Lee laughed.

'Looks as though I'd given you quite a shock. Why? I'm expected, aren't I?'

'Yes, indeed, sir. Certainly, sir.'

'Then why the surprise act?' Harry stepped back a foot or two and looked up at the house—a good solid mass of red brick, unimaginative but solid.

'Just the same ugly old mansion,' he remarked. 'Still standing, though, that's the main thing. How's my father, Tressilian?'

'He's somewhat of an invalid, sir. Keeps his room, and can't get about much. But he's wonderfully well, considering.'

'The old sinner!'

Harry Lee came inside, let Tressilian remove his scarf and take the somewhat theatrical hat.

'How's my dear brother Alfred, Tressilian?'

'He's very well, sir.'

Harry grinned.

'Looking forward to seeing me? Eh?'

'I expect so, sir.'

'I don't! Quite the contrary. I bet it's given him a nasty jolt, my turning up! Alfred and I never did get on. Ever read your Bible, Tressilian?'

'Why, yes, sir, sometimes, sir.'

'Remember the tale of the prodigal's return? The good brother didn't like it, remember? Didn't like it at all! Good old stay-at-home Alfred doesn't like it either, I bet.'

Tressilian remained silent looking down his nose. His stiffened back expressed protest. Harry clapped him on the shoulder.

'Lead on, old son,' he said. 'The fatted calf awaits me! Lead me right to it.'

Tressilian murmured:

'If you will come this way into the drawing-room, sir. I am not quite sure where everyone is. . . . They were unable to send to meet you, sir, not knowing the time of your arrival.'

Harry nodded. He followed Tressilian along the hall, turning his head to look about him as he went.

'All the old exhibits in their place, I see,' he remarked. 'I don't believe anything has changed since I went away twenty years ago.'

He followed Tressilian into the drawing-room. The old man murmured:

'I will see if I can find Mr. or Mrs. Alfred,' and hurried out.

Harry Lee had marched into the room and had then stopped, staring at the figure who was seated on one of the window-sills. His eyes roamed incredulously over the black hair and the creamy exotic pallor.

'Good Lord!' he said. 'Are you my father's seventh and most beautiful wife?'

Pilar slipped down and came towards him.

'I am Pilar Estravados,' she announced. 'And you must be my Uncle Harry, my mother's brother.'

Harry said, staring:

'So that's who you are! Jenny's daughter.'

Pilar said: 'Why did you ask me if I was your father's seventh wife? Has he really had six wives?'

Harry laughed.

'No, I believe he's only had one official one. Well—Pil—what's your name?'

'Pilar, yes.'

'Well, Pilar, it really gives me quite a turn to see something like you blooming in this mausoleum.'

'This—maus—please?'

'This museum of stuffed dummies! I always thought this house was lousy! Now I see it again I think it's lousier than ever!'

Pilar said in a shocked voice:

'Oh, no, it is very handsome here! The furniture is good and the carpets—thick carpets everywhere—and there are lots of ornaments. Everything is very good quality and very, very rich!'

'You're right there,' said Harry, grinning. He looked at her with amusement. 'You know, I can't help getting a kick out of seeing you in the midst——'

He broke off as Lydia came rapidly into the room.

She came straight to him.

'How d'you do, Harry? I'm Lydia—Alfred's wife.'

'How de do, Lydia.' He shook hands, examining her intelligent mobile face in a swift glance and approving mentally of the way she walked—very few women moved well.

Lydia in her turn took quick stock of him.

She thought: 'He looks a frightful tough—attractive, though. I wouldn't trust him an inch. . . .'

She said, smiling:

'How does it look after all these years? Quite different, or very much the same?'

'Pretty much the same.' He looked round him. 'This room's been done over.'

'Oh, many times.'

He said:

'I meant by you. You've made it—different.'

'Yes, I expect so. . . .'

He grinned at her, a sudden impish grin that reminded her with a start of the old man upstairs.

'It's got more class about it now! I remember hearing that old Alfred had married a girl whose people came over with the Conqueror.'

Lydia smiled. She said: 'I believe they did. But they've rather run to seed since those days.'

Harry said: 'How's old Alfred? Just the same blessed old stick-in-the-mud as ever?'

'I've no idea whether you will find him changed or not.'

'How are the others? Scattered all over England?'

'No—they're all here for Christmas, you know.'

Harry's eyes opened.

Regular Christmas family reunion? What's the matter with the old man? He used not to give a damn for sentiment. Don't remember his caring much for his family, either. He must have changed!'

'Perhaps.' Lydia's voice was dry.

Pilar was staring, her big eyes wide and interested.

Harry said: 'How's old George? Still the same skinflint? How he used to howl if he had to part with a halfpenny of his pocket-money!'

Lydia said: 'George is in Parliament. He's Member for Westeringham.'

'What? Popeye in Parliament? Lord, that's good.'

Harry threw back his head and laughed.

It was rich stentorian laughter—it sounded uncontrolled and brutal in the confined space of the room. Pilar drew in her breath with a gasp. Lydia flinched a little.

Then, at a movement behind him, Harry broke off his laugh and turned sharply. He had not heard anyone come in, but Alfred was standing there quietly. He was looking at Harry with an odd expression on his face.

Harry stood a minute, then a slow smile crept to his lips. He advanced a step.

'Why,' he said, 'it's Alfred!'

Alfred nodded.

'Hallo, Harry,' he said.

They stood staring at each other. Lydia caught her breath. She thought:

'How absurd! Like two dogs—looking at each other. . . .'

Pilar's gaze widened even further. She thought to herself:

'How silly they look standing there. . . . Why do they not embrace? No, of course the English do not do that. But they might *say* something. Why do they just *look*?'

Harry said at last:

'Well, well. Feels funny to be here again!'

'I expect so—yes. A good many years since you—got out.'

Harry threw up his head. He drew his finger along the line of his jaw. It was a gesture that was habitual with him. It expressed belligerence.

'Yes,' he said. 'I'm glad I have come'—he paused to bring out the word with greater significance—'*home*. . . .'

2

'I've been, I suppose, a very wicked man,' said Simeon Lee.

He was leaning back in his chair. His chin was raised and with one finger he was stroking his jaw reflectively. In front of him a big fire glowed and danced. Beside it sat Pilar, a little screen of papier-mâché held in her hand. With it she shielded her face from the blaze. Occasionally she fanned herself with it, using her wrist in a supple gesture. Simeon looked at her with satisfaction.

He went on talking, perhaps more to himself than to the girl, and yet stimulated by the fact of her presence.

'Yes,' he said. 'I've been a wicked man. What do you say to that, Pilar?'

Pilar shrugged her shoulders. She said:

'All men are wicked. The nuns say so. That is why one has to pray for them.'

'Ah, but I've been more wicked than most.' Simeon laughed. 'I don't regret it, you know. No, I don't regret anything. I've enjoyed myself . . . every minute! They say you repent when you get old. That's bunkum. I don't repent. And, as I tell you, I've done most things . . . all the good old sins! I've cheated and stolen and lied . . . Lord, yes! And women—always women! Someone told me the other day of an Arab chief who had a bodyguard of forty of his sons—all roughly the same age! Aha! Forty! I don't know about forty, but I bet I could produce a very fair bodyguard if I went about looking for the brats! Hey, Pilar, what do you think of that? Shocked?'

Pilar stared.

'No, why should I be shocked? Men always desire women. My father, too. That is why wives are so often unhappy and why they go to church and pray.'

Old Simeon was frowning.

'I made Adelaide unhappy,' he said. He spoke almost under his breath, to himself. 'Lord, what a woman! Pink and white and pretty as they make 'em when I married her! And afterwards? Always wailing and weeping. It rouses the devil in a man when his wife is always crying. . . . She'd no guts, that's what was the matter with Adelaide. If she'd stood up to me! But she never did—not once. I believed when I married her that I was going to be able to settle down—raise a family—cut loose from the old life. . . .'

His voice died away. He stared—stared into the glowing heart of the fire.

'Raise a family . . . God, what a family!' He gave a sudden shrill pipe of angry laughter. 'Look at 'em—look at 'em! Not a child among them—to carry on! What's the matter with them? Haven't they got any of my blood in their veins? Not a son among 'em, legitimate or illegitimate. Alfred, for instance—heavens above, how bored I get with Alfred! Looking at me with his dog's eyes. Ready to do anything I ask. Lord, what a fool! His wife, now—Lydia—I like Lydia. She's got spirit. She doesn't like me, though. No, she doesn't like me. But she has to put up with me for that nincompoop Alfred's sake.' He looked over at the girl by the fire. 'Pilar—remember—nothing is so boring as devotion.'

She smiled at him. He went on, warmed by the presence of youth and strong femininity.

'George? What's George? A stick! A stuffed codfish! A pompous windbag with no brains and no guts—and mean about money as well! David? David always was a fool—a fool and a dreamer. His mother's boy, that was always David. Only sensible thing he ever did was to marry that solid comfortable-looking woman.' He brought down his hand with a bang on the edge of his chair. 'Harry's the best of 'em! Poor old Harry, the wrong 'un! But at any rate he's *alive*!'

Pilar agreed.

'Yes, he is nice. He laughs—laughs out loud—and throws his head back. Oh, yes, I like him very much.'

The old man looked at her.

'You do, do you, Pilar? Harry always had a way with the girls. Takes after me there.' He began to laugh, a slow wheezy chuckle. 'I've had a good life—a very good life. Plenty of everything.'

Pilar said:

'In Spain we have a proverb. It is like this: "*Take what you like and pay for it, says God.*" '

Simeon beat an appreciative hand on the arm of his chair.

'That's good. That's the stuff. Take what you like. . . . I've done that—all my life—taken what I wanted. . . .'

Pilar said, her voice high and clear, and suddenly arresting:

'And have you paid for it?'

Simeon stopped laughing to himself. He sat up and stared at her. He said, 'What's that you say?'

'I said, have you paid for it, Grandfather?'

Simeon Lee said slowly:

'I—don't know. . . .'

Then, beating his fist on the arm of the chair, he cried out with sudden anger:

'What makes you say that, girl? What makes you say that?'

Pilar said: 'I—wondered.'

Her hand, holding the screen, was arrested. Her eyes were dark and mysterious. She sat, her head thrown back, conscious of herself, of her womanhood.

Simeon said: 'You devil's brat. . . .'

She said softly: 'But you like me, Grandfather. You like me to sit here with you.'

Simeon said: 'Yes, I like it. It's a long time since I've seen anything so young and beautiful. . . . It does me good, warms my old bones. . . . And you're my own flesh and blood. . . . Good for Jennifer, she turned out to be the best of the bunch after all!'

Pilar sat there smiling.

'Mind you, you don't fool me,' said Simeon. 'I know why you sit here so patiently and listen to me droning on. It's money—it's all money. . . . Or do you pretend you love your old grandfather?'

Pilar said: 'No, I do not love you. But I like you. I like you very much. You must believe that, for it is true. I think you have been wicked, but I like that too. You are more real than the other people in this house. And you have interesting things to say. You have travelled and you have led a life of adventure. If I were a man I would be like that, too.'

Simeon nodded.

'Yes, I believe you would. . . . We've gipsy blood in us, so it's always been said. It hasn't shown much in my children—except

Harry—but I think it's come out in you. I can be patient, mind you, when it's necessary. I waited once fifteen years to get even with a man who'd done me an injury. That's another characteristic of the Lees–they don't forget! They'll avenge a wrong if they have to wait years to do it. A man swindled me. I waited fifteen years till I saw my chance—and then I struck. I ruined him. Cleaned him right out!'

He laughed softly.

Pilar said: 'That was in South Africa?'

'Yes. A grand country.'

'You have been back there, yes?'

'I went back last five years after I married. That was the last time.'

'But before that? You were there for many years?'

'Yes.'

'Tell me about it.'

He began to talk. Pilar, shielding her face, listened.

His voice slowed, wearied. He said: 'Wait, I'll show you something.'

He pulled himself carefully to his feet. Then, with his stick, he limped slowly across the room. He opened the big safe. Turning, he beckoned her to him.

'There, look at these. Feel them, let them run through your fingers.'

He looked into her wondering face and laughed.

'Do you know what they are? Diamonds, child, diamonds.'

Pilar's eyes opened. She said as she bent over:

'But they are little pebbles, that is all.'

Simeon laughed.

'They are uncut diamonds. That is how they are found—like this.'

Pilar asked incredulously: 'And if they were cut they would be real diamonds?'

'Certainly.'

'They would flash and sparkle?'

'Flash and sparkle.'

Pilar said childishly: 'O-o-o, I cannot believe it!'

He was amused.

'It's quite true.'

'They are valuable?'

'Fairly valuable. Difficult to say before they are cut. Anyway, this little lot is worth several thousands of pounds.'

Pilar said with a space between each word:

'Several—thousands—of—pounds?'

'Say nine or ten thousand—they're biggish stones, you see.'

Pilar asked, her eyes opening:

'But why do you not sell them, then?'

'Because I like to have them here.'

'But all that money?'

'I don't need the money.'

'Oh—I see.' Pilar looked impressed.

She said: 'But why do you not have them cut and made beautiful?'

'Because I prefer them like this.' His face was set in a grim line. He turned away and began speaking to himself. 'They take me back—the touch of them, the feel of them through my fingers. . . . It all comes back to me, the sunshine, and the smell of the veldt, the oxen—old Eb—all the boys—the evenings. . . .'

There was a soft tap on the door.

Simeon said: 'Put 'em back in the safe and bang it to.'

Then he called: 'Come in.'

Horbury came in, soft and deferential.

He said: 'Tea is ready downstairs.'

3

Hilda said: 'So there you are, David. I've been looking for you everywhere. Don't let's stay in this room, it's so frightfully cold.'

David did not answer for a minute. He was standing looking at a chair, a low chair with faded satin upholstery. He said abruptly: 'That's her chair . . . the chair she always sat in . . . just the same—it's just the same. Only faded, of course.'

A little frown creased Hilda's forehead. She said:

'I see. Do let's come out of here, David. It's frightfully cold.'

David took no notice. Looking round, he said:

'She sat in here mostly. I remember sitting on that stool there while she read to me. *Jack the Giant Killer*—that was it—*Jack the Giant Killer*. I must have been six years old then.'

Hilda put a firm hand through his arm.

'Come back to the drawing-room, dear. There's no heating in this room.'

He turned obediently, but she felt a little shiver go through him.

'Just the same,' he murmured. 'Just the same. As though time had stood still.'

Hilda looked worried.

She said in a cheerful determined voice:

'I wonder where the others are? It must be nearly tea-time.'

David disengaged his arm and opened another door.

'There used to be a piano in here. . . . Oh, yes, here it is! I wonder if it's in tune.'

He sat down and opened the lid, running his hands lightly over the keys.

'Yes, it's evidently kept tuned.'

He began to play.

His touch was good, the melody flowed out from under his fingers.

Hilda asked: 'What is that? I seem to know it, and I can't quite remember.'

He said: 'I haven't played it for years. *She* used to play it. One of Mendelssohn's Songs Without Words.'

The sweet, over-sweet, melody filled the room.

Hilda said:

'Play some Mozart, do.'

David shook his head. He began another Mendelssohn.

Then suddenly he brought his hands down upon the keys in a harsh discord. He got up. He was trembling all over. Hilda went to him.

She said: 'David—David. . . .'

He said: 'It's nothing—it's nothing. . . .'

4

The bell pealed aggressively. Tressilian rose from his seat in the pantry and went slowly out and along to the door.

The bell pealed again. Tressilian frowned. Through the frosted glass of the door he saw the silhouette of a man wearing a slouch hat.

Tressilian passed a hand over his forehead. Something worried him. It was as though everything was happening twice.

Surely this had happened before. Surely——

He drew back the latch and opened the door.

Then the spell broke. The man standing there said:

'Is this where Mr. Simeon Lee lives?'

'Yes, sir.'

'I'd like to see him, please.'

A faint echo of memory awoke in Tressilian. It was an intonation of voice that he remembered from the old days when Mr. Lee was first in England.

Tressilian shook his head dubiously.

'Mr. Lee is an invalid, sir. He doesn't see many people now. If you——'

The stranger interrupted.

He drew out an envelope and handed it to the butler.

'Please give this to Mr. Lee.'

'Yes, sir.'

5

Simeon Lee took the envelope. He drew out the single sheet of paper it held. He looked surprised. His eyebrows rose, but he smiled.

'By all that's wonderful!' he said.

Then to the butler: 'Show Mr. Farr up here, Tressilian.'

'Yes, sir.'

Simeon said: 'I was just thinking of old Ebenezer Farr. He was my partner out there in Kimberley. Now here's his son come along!'

Tressilian reappeared. He announced:

'Mr. Farr.'

Stephen Farr came in with a trace of nervousness. He disguised it by putting on a little extra swagger. He said—and just for the moment his South African accent was more marked than usual: 'Mr. Lee?'

'I'm glad to see you. So you're Eb's boy?'

Stephen Farr grinned rather sheepishly.

He said: 'My first visit to the old country. Father always told me to look you up if I did come.'

'Quite right.' The old man looked round. 'This is my granddaughter, Pilar Estravados.'

'How do you do?' said Pilar demurely.

Stephen Farr thought with a touch of admiration:

'Cool little devil. She was surprised to see me, but it only showed for a flash.'

He said, rather heavily: 'I'm very pleased to make your acquaintance, Miss Estravados.'

'Thank you,' said Pilar.

Simeon Lee said: 'Sit down and tell me all about yourself. Are you in England for long?'

'Oh, I shan't hurry myself now I've really got here!'

He laughed, throwing his head back.

Simeon Lee said: 'Quite right. You must stay here with us for a while.'

'Oh, look here, sir. I can't butt in like that. It's only two days to Christmas.'

'You must spend Christmas with us—unless you've got other plans?'

'Well, no, I haven't, but I don't like——'

Simeon said: 'That's settled.' He turned his head. 'Pilar?'

'Yes, Grandfather.'

'Go and tell Lydia we shall have another guest. Ask her to come up here.'

Pilar left the room. Stephen's eyes followed her. Simeon noted the fact with amusement.

He said:

'You've come straight here from South Africa?'

'Pretty well.'

They began to talk of that country.

Lydia entered a few minutes later.

Simeon said: 'This is Stephen Farr, son of my old friend and partner, Ebenezer Farr. He's going to be with us for Christmas if you can find room for him.'

Lydia smiled.

'Of course.' Her eyes took in the stranger's appearance. His bronzed face and blue eyes and the easy backward tilt of his head.

'My daughter-in-law,' said Simeon.

Stephen said: 'I feel rather embarrassed—butting in on a family party like this.'

'You're one of the family, my boy,' said Simeon. 'Think of yourself as that.'

'You're too kind, sir.'

Pilar re-entered the room. She sat down quietly by the fire and picked up the hand screen. She used it as a fan, slowly tilting her wrist to and fro. Her eyes were demure and downcast.

PART THREE

December 24th

1

'DO YOU REALLY want me to stay on here, Father?' asked Harry. He tilted his head back. 'I'm stirring up rather a hornet's nest, you know?'

'What do you mean?' asked Simeon sharply.

'Brother Alfred,' said Harry. 'Good brother Alfred! He, if I may say so, resents my presence here.'

'The devil he does!' snapped Simeon. 'I'm master in this house.'

'All the same, sir, I expect you're pretty dependent on Alfred. I don't want to upset——'

'You'll do as I tell you,' snapped his father.

Harry yawned.

'Don't know that I shall be able to stick a stay-at-home life. Pretty stifling to a fellow who's knocked about the world.'

His father said: 'You'd better marry and settle down.'

Harry said: 'Who shall I marry? Pity one can't marry one's niece. Young Pilar is devilish attractive.'

'You've noticed that?'

'Talking of settling down, fat George has done well for himself as far as looks go. Who was she?'

Simeon shrugged his shoulders.

'How should I know? George picked her up at a mannequin parade, I believe. She says her father was a retired naval officer.'

Harry said: 'Probably a second mate of a coasting steamer. George will have a bit of trouble with her if he's not careful.'

'George,' said Simeon Lee, 'is a fool.'

Harry said: 'What did she marry him for—his money?'

Simeon shrugged his shoulders.

Harry said: 'Well, you think you can square Alfred all right?'

'We'll soon settle that,' said Simeon grimly.

He touched a bell that stood on a table near him.

Horbury appeared promptly. Simeon said:

'Ask Mr. Alfred to come here.'

Horbury went out and Harry drawled:

'That fellow listens at doors!'

Simeon shrugged his shoulders.

'Probably.'

Alfred hurried in. His face twitched when he saw his brother. Ignoring Harry, he said pointedly:

'You wanted me, Father?'

'Yes, sit down. I was just thinking we must reorganise things a bit now that we have two more people living in the house.'

'*Two?*'

'Pilar will make her home here, naturally. And Harry is home for good.'

Alfred said: 'Harry is coming to live here?'

'Why not, old boy?' said Harry.

Alfred turned sharply to him.

'I should think that you yourself would see that!'

'Well, sorry—but I don't.'

'After everything that has happened? The disgraceful way you behaved. The scandal——'

Harry waved an easy hand.

'All that's in the past, old boy.'

'You behaved abominably to Father, after all he'd done for you.'

'Look here, Alfred, it strikes me that's Father's business, not yours. If he's willing to forgive and forget——'

'I'm willing,' said Simeon. 'Harry's my son, after all, you know, Alfred.'

'Yes, but—I resent it—for Father's sake.'

Simeon said: 'Harry's coming here! I wish it.' He laid a hand gently on the latter's shoulder. 'I'm very fond of Harry.'

Alfred got up and left the room. His face was white. Harry rose too and went after him, laughing.

Simeon sat chuckling to himself. Then he started and looked round. 'Who the devil's that? Oh, it's you, Horbury. Don't creep about that way.'

'I beg your pardon, sir.'

'Never mind. Listen, I've got some orders for you. I want everybody to come up here after lunch—*everybody*.'

'Yes, sir.'

'There's something else. When they come, you come with them.

And when you get half-way along the passage *raise your voice, so that I can hear.* Any pretext will do. Understand?'

'Yes, sir.'

Horbury went downstairs. He said to Tressilian:

'If you ask me, we *are* going to have a Merry Christmas!'

Tressilian said sharply: 'What d'you mean?'

'You wait and see, Mr. Tressilian. It's Christmas Eve to-day, and a nice Christmas spirit abroad—I don't think!'

2

They came into the room and paused at the doorway.

Simeon was speaking into the telephone. He waved a hand to them.

'Sit down, all of you. I shan't be a minute.'

He went on speaking into the telephone.

'Is that Charlton, Hodgkins & Brace? Is that you, Charlton? Simeon Lee speaking. Yes, isn't it? . . . Yes. . . . No, I wanted you to make a new will for me. . . . Yes, it's some time since I made the other. . . . Circumstances have altered. . . . Oh no, no hurry. Don't want you to spoil your Christmas. Say Boxing Day or the day after. Come along and I'll tell you what I want done. No, that's quite all right. I shan't be dying just yet.'

He replaced the receiver, then looked round at the eight members of his family. He cackled and said:

'You're all looking very glum. What is the matter?'

Alfred said: 'You sent for us . . .'

Simeon said quickly: 'Oh, sorry—nothing portentous about it. Did you think it was a family council? No, I'm just rather tired to-day, that's all. None of you need come up after dinner. I shall go to bed. I want to be fresh for Christmas Day.'

He grinned at them. George said earnestly:

'Of course . . . of course . . .'

Simeon said: 'Grand old institution, Christmas! Promotes solidarity of family feeling. What do *you* think, Magdalene, my dear?'

Magdalene Lee jumped. Her rather silly little mouth flew open and then shut itself. She said:

'Oh—oh, *yes*!'

Simeon said: 'Let me see, you lived with a retired naval officer' —he paused—'your *father*. Don't suppose you made much of Christmas. It needs a big family for that!'

'Well—well—yes, perhaps it does.'

Simeon's eyes slid past her.

'Don't want to talk of anything unpleasant at this time of year, but you know, George, I'm afraid I'll have to cut down your allowance a bit. My establishment here is going to cost me a bit more to run in future.'

George got very red. 'But look here, Father, you can't do that!'

Simeon said softly: 'Oh, can't I?'

'My expenses are very heavy already. Very heavy. As it is, I don't know how I make both ends meet. It needs the most rigorous economy.'

'Let your wife do a bit more of it,' said Simeon. 'Women are good at that sort of thing. They often think of economies where a man would never have dreamt of them. And a clever woman can make her own clothes. My wife, I remember, was clever with her needle. About all she *was* clever with—a good woman, but deadly dull——'

David sprang up. His father said:

'Sit down, boy, you'll knock something over——'

David said: 'My mother——'

Simeon said: 'Your mother had the brains of a louse! And it seems to me she's transmitted those brains to her children.' He raised himself up suddenly. A red spot appeared in each cheek. His voice came high and shrill. 'You're not worth a penny piece, any of you! I'm sick of you all! You're not *men*! You're weaklings—a set of namby-pamby weaklings. Pilar's worth any two of you put together! I'll swear to heaven I've got a better son somewhere in the world than any of you, even if you are born the right side of the blanket!'

'Here, Father, hold hard,' cried Harry.

He had jumped up and stood there, a frown on his usually good-humoured face.

Simeon snapped:

'The same goes for *you*! What have *you* ever done? Whined to me for money from all over the world! I tell you I'm sick of the sight of you all! Get out!'

He leaned back in his chair, panting a little.

Slowly, one by one, his family went out. George was red and indignant, Magdalene looked frightened. David was pale and quivering. Harry blustered out of the room. Alfred went like a man in a dream. Lydia followed him with her head held high. Only Hilda paused in the doorway and came slowly back.

She stood over him, and he started when he opened his eyes and found her standing there. There was something menacing in the solid way she stood there quite immovably.

He said irritably: 'What is it?'

Hilda said: 'When your letter came I believed what you said—that you wanted your family round you for Christmas. I persuaded David to come.'

Simeon said, 'Well, what of it?'

Hilda said slowly: 'You *did* want your family round you—but not for the purpose you said! You wanted them there, didn't you, in order to set them all by the ears? God help you, it's your idea of *fun*!'

Simeon chuckled. He said 'I always had rather a specialised sense of humour. I don't expect anyone else to appreciate the joke. *I'm* enjoying it!'

She said nothing. A vague feeling of apprehension came over Simeon Lee.

He said sharply:

'What are you thinking about?'

Hilda Lee said slowly: 'I'm afraid . . .'

Simeon said: 'You're afraid—of me?'

Hilda said: 'Not *of* you. I'm afraid—*for* you!'

Like a judge who has delivered sentence, she turned away. She marched, slowly and heavily, out of the room. . . .

Simeon sat staring at the door.

Then he got to his feet and made his way over to the safe.

He murmured: 'Let's have a look at my beauties.'

3

The doorbell rang about a quarter to eight.

Tressilian went to answer it. He returned to his pantry to find

Horbury there, picking up the coffee-cups off the tray and looking at the mark on them.

'Who was it?' said Horbury.

'Superintendent of Police—Mr. Sugden—mind what you're doing!'

Horbury had dropped one of the cups with a crash.

'Look at that now,' lamented Tressilian. 'Eleven years I've had the washing up of those and never one broken, and now you come along touching things you've no business to touch, and look what happens!'

'I'm sorry, Mr. Tressilian. I am indeed,' the other apologised. His face was covered with perspiration. 'I don't know how it happened. Did you say a Superintendent of Police had called?'

'Yes—Mr. Sugden.'

The valet passed a tongue over pale lips.

'What—what did he want?'

'Collecting for the Police Orphanage.'

'Oh!' The valet straightened his shoulders. In a more natural voice he said:

'Did he get anything?'

'I took up the book to old Mr. Lee, and he told me to fetch the superintendent up and to put the sherry on the table.'

'Nothing but begging, this time of year,' said Horbury. 'The old devil's generous, I will say that for him, in spite of his other failings.'

Tressilian said with dignity:

'Mr. Lee has always been an open-handed gentleman.'

Horbury nodded.

'It's the best thing about him! Well, I'll be off now.'

'Going to the pictures?'

'I expect so. Ta-ta, Mr. Tressilian.'

He went through the door that led to the servants' hall.

Tressilian looked up at the clock hanging on the wall.

He went into the dining-room and laid the rolls in the napkins.

Then, after assuring himself that everything was as it should be, he sounded the gong in the hall.

As the last note died away the police superintendent came down the stairs. Superintendent Sugden was a large handsome man. He wore a tightly-buttoned blue suit and moved with a sense of his own importance.

He said affably: 'I rather think we shall have a frost to-night. Good thing; the weather's been very unseasonable lately.'

Tressilian said, shaking his head:

'The damp affects my rheumatism.'

The superintendent said that rheumatism was a painful complaint, and Tressilian let him out by the front door.

The old butler refastened the door and came back slowly into the hall. He passed his hand over his eyes and sighed. Then he straightened his back as he saw Lydia pass into the drawing-room. George Lee was just coming down the stairs.

Tressilian hovered ready. When the last guest, Magdalene, had entered the drawing-room, he made his own appearance, murmuring:

'Dinner is served.'

In his way Tressilian was a connoisseur of ladies' dress. He always noted and criticised the gowns of the ladies as he circled round the table, decanter in hand.

Mrs. Alfred, he noted, had got on her new flowered black and white taffeta. A bold design, very striking, but she could carry it off, though many ladies couldn't. The dress Mrs. George had on was a model, he was pretty sure of that. Must have cost a pretty penny. He wondered how Mr. George would like paying for it! Mr. George didn't like spending money—he never had. Mrs. David, now: a nice lady, but didn't have any idea of how to dress. For her figure, plain black velvet would have been the best. Figured velvet, and crimson at that, was a bad choice. Miss Pilar, now, it didn't matter what she wore, with her figure and her hair she looked well in anything. A flimsy cheap little white gown it was, though. Still, Mr. Lee would soon see to that! Taken to her wonderful, he had. Always was the same way when a gentleman was elderly. A young face could do anything with him!

'Hock or claret?' murmured Tressilian in a deferential whisper in Mrs. George's ear. Out of the tail of his eye he noted that Walter, the footman, was handing the vegetables before the gravy again—after all he had been told!

Tressilian went round with the soufflé. It struck him, now that his interest in the ladies' toilets and his misgivings over Walter's deficiencies were a thing of the past, that everyone was very silent to-night. At least, not exactly *silent*: Mr. Harry was talking enough for twenty—no, not Mr. Harry, the South African gentleman. And the others were talking too, but only, as it were, in spasms. There was something a little—queer about them.

Mr. Alfred, for instance, he looked downright ill. As though he had had a shock or something. Quite dazed he looked and just turning over the food on his plate without eating it. The mistress, she was worried about him. Tressilian could see that. Kept looking down the table towards him—not noticeably, of course, just quietly. Mr. George was very red in the face—gobbling his food, he was, without tasting it. He'd get a stroke one day if he wasn't careful. Mrs. George wasn't eating. Slimming, as likely as not. Miss Pilar seemed to be enjoying her food all right and talking and laughing up at the South African gentleman. Properly taken with her, he was. Didn't seem to be anything on *their* minds!

Mr. David? Tressilian felt worried about Mr. David. Just like his mother, he was, to look at. And remarkably young-looking still. But nervy; there, he'd knocked over his glass.

Tressilian whisked it away, mopped up the stream deftly. It was all over. Mr. David hardly seemed to notice what he had done; just sat staring in front of him with a white face.

Thinking of white faces, funny the way Horbury had looked in the pantry just now when he'd heard a police officer had come to the house . . . almost as though——.

Tressilian's mind stopped with a jerk. Walter had dropped a pear off the dish he was handing. Footmen were no good nowadays! They might be stable-boys, the way they went on!

He went round with the port. Mr. Harry seemed a bit distrait to-night. Kept looking at Mr. Alfred. Never had been any love lost between those two, not even as boys. Mr. Harry, of course, had always been his father's favourite, and that had rankled with Mr. Alfred. Mr. Lee had never cared for Mr. Alfred much. A pity, when Mr. Alfred always seemed so devoted to his father.

There, Mrs. Alfred was getting up now. She swept round the table. Very nice that design on the taffeta; that cape suited her. A very graceful lady.

He went out to the pantry, closing the dining-room door on the gentlemen with their port.

He took the coffee-tray into the drawing-room. The four ladies were sitting there rather uncomfortably, he thought. They were not talking. He handed round the coffee in silence.

He went out again. As he went into his pantry he heard the

dining-room door open. David Lee came out and went along the hall to the drawing-room.

Tressilian went back into his pantry. He read the riot act to Walter. Walter was nearly, if not quite, impertinent!

Tressilian, alone in his pantry, sat down rather wearily.

He had a feeling of depression. Christmas Eve, and all this strain and tension. . . . He didn't like it!

With an effort he roused himself. He went to the drawing-room and collected the coffee-cups. The room was empty except for Lydia, who was standing half concealed by the window curtain at the far end of the room. She was standing there looking out into the night.

From next door the piano sounded.

Mr. David playing. But why, Tressilian asked himself, did Mr. David play the 'Dead March'? For that's what it was. Oh, indeed things were very wrong.

He went slowly along the hall and back into his pantry.

It was then he first heard the noise from overhead: a crashing of china, the overthrowing of furniture, a series of cracks and bumps.

'Good gracious!' thought Tressilian. 'Whatever is the master doing? What's happening up there?'

And then, clear and high, came a scream—a horrible high wailing scream that died away in a choke or gurgle.

Tressilian stood there a moment paralysed, then he ran out into the hall and up the broad staircase. Others were with him. That scream had been heard all over the house.

They raced up the stairs and round the bend, past a recess with statues gleaming white and eerie, and along the straight passage to Simeon Lee's door. Mr. Farr was there already and Mrs. David. She was leaning back against the wall and he was twisting at the door handle.

'The door's locked,' he was saying. 'The door's locked!'

Harry Lee pushed past and wrested it from him. He, too, turned and twisted at the handle.

'Father,' he shouted. 'Father, let us in.'

He held up his hand and in the silence they all listened. There was no answer. No sound from inside the room.

The front door bell rang, but no one paid any attention to it.

Stephen Farr said:

'We've got to break the door down. It's the only way.'

Harry said: 'That's going to be a tough job. These doors are good solid stuff. Come on, Alfred.'

They heaved and strained. Finally they went and got an oak bench and used it as a battering-ram. The door gave at last. Its hinges splintered and the door sank shuddering from its frame.

For a minute they stood there huddled together looking in. What they saw was a sight that no one of them ever forgot. . . .

There had clearly been a terrific struggle. Heavy furniture was overturned. China vases lay splintered on the floor. In the middle of the hearthrug in front of the blazing fire lay Simeon Lee in a great pool of blood. . . . Blood was splashed all round. The place was like a shambles.

There was a long shuddering sigh, and then two voices spoke in turn. Strangely enough, the words they uttered were both quotations.

David Lee said:

'The mills of God grind slowly. . . .'

Lydia's voice came like a fluttering whisper:

'Who would have thought the old man to have had so much blood in him? . . .'

4

Superintendent Sugden had rung the bell three times. Finally, in desperation, he pounded on the knocker.

A scared Walter at length opened the door.

'Oo-er,' he said. A look of relief came over his face. 'I was just ringing up the police.'

'What for?' said Superintendent Sugden sharply. 'What's going on here?'

Walter whispered:

'It's old Mr. Lee. *He's been done in. . . .*'

The superintendent pushed past him and ran up the stairs. He came into the room without anyone being aware of his entrance. As he entered he saw Pilar bend forward and pick up something from the floor. He saw David Lee standing with his hands over his eyes.

He saw the others huddled into a little group. Alfred Lee alone had stepped near his father's body. He stood now quite close, looking down. His face was blank.

George Lee was saying importantly:

'Nothing must be touched—remember that—*nothing*—till the police arrive. That is *most* important!'

'Excuse me,' said Sugden.

He pushed his way forward, gently thrusting the ladies aside.

Alfred Lee recognised him.

'Ah,' he said. 'It's you, Superintendent Sugden. You've got here very quickly.'

'Yes, Mr. Lee.' Superintendent Sugden did not waste time on explanations. 'What's all this?'

'My father,' said Alfred Lee, 'has been killed—*murdered*. . . .'

His voice broke.

Magdalene began suddenly to sob hysterically.

Superintendent Sugden held up a large official hand.

He said authoritatively:

'Will everybody kindly leave the room except Mr. Lee and—er—Mr. George Lee? . . .'

They moved slowly towards the door, reluctantly, like sheep. Superintendent Sugden intercepted Pilar suddenly.

'Excuse me, miss,' he said pleasantly. 'Nothing must be touched or disturbed.'

She stared at him. Stephen Farr said impatiently:

'Of course not. She understands that.'

Superintendent Sugden said, still in the same pleasant manner: 'You picked up something from the floor just now?'

Pilar's eyes opened. She stared and said incredulously: '*I* did?'

Superintendent Sugden was still pleasant. His voice was just a little firmer.

'Yes, I saw you. . . .'

'Oh!'

'So please give it to me. It's in your hand now.'

Slowly Pilar unclosed her hand. There lay in it a wisp of rubber and a small object made of wood. Superintendent Sugden took them, enclosed them in an envelope and put them away in his breast pocket.

He said: 'Thank you.'

He turned away. Just for a minute Stephen Farr's eyes showed a startled respect. It was as though he had underestimated the large handsome superintendent.

They went slowly out of the room. Behind them they heard the superintendent's voice saying officially:

'And now, if you please . . .'

5

'Nothing like a wood fire,' said Colonel Johnson as he threw on an additional log and then drew his chair nearer to the blaze. 'Help yourself,' he added, hospitably calling attention to the tantalus and siphon that stood near his guest's elbow.

The guest raised a polite hand in negation. Cautiously he edged his own chair nearer to the blazing logs, though he was of the opinion that the opportunity for roasting the soles of one's feet (like some mediæval torture) did not offset the cold draught that swirled round the back of the shoulders.

Colonel Johnson, Chief Constable of Middleshire, might be of the opinion that nothing could beat a wood fire, but Hercule Poirot was of opinion that central heating could and did every time!

'Amazing business, that Cartwright case,' remarked the host reminiscently. 'Amazing man! Enormous charm of manner. Why, when he came here with you, he had us all eating out of his hand.'

He shook his head.

'We'll never have anything like that case!' he said. 'Nicotine poisoning is rare, fortunately.'

'There was a time when you would have considered all poisoning un-English,' suggested Hercule Poirot. 'A device of foreigners! Unsportsmanlike!'

'I hardly think we could say that,' said the chief constable. 'Plenty of poisoning by arsenic—probably a good deal more than has ever been suspected.'

'Possibly, yes.'

'Always an awkward business, a poisoning case,' said Johnson. 'Conflicting testimony of the experts—then doctors are usually so extremely cautious in what they say. Always a difficult case to take to a jury. No, if one *must* have murder (which heaven forbid!) give me a straightforward case. Something where there's no ambiguity about the cause of death.'

Poirot nodded.

'The bullet wound, the cut throat, the crushed-in skull? It is there your preference lies?'

'Oh, don't call it a preference, my dear fellow. Don't harbour the idea that I *like* murder cases! Hope I never have another. Anyway, we ought to be safe enough during your visit.'

Poirot began modestly:

'My reputation——'

But Johnson had gone on.

'Christmas time,' he said. 'Peace, goodwill—and all that kind of thing. Goodwill all round.'

Hercule Poirot leaned back in his chair. He joined his fingertips. He studied his host thoughtfully.

He murmured: 'It is, then, your opinion that Christmas time is an unlikely season for crime?'

'That's what I said.'

'Why?'

'Why?' Johnson was thrown slightly out of his stride. 'Well, as I've just said—season of good cheer, and all that!'

Hercule Poirot murmured:

'The British, they are so sentimental!'

Johnson said stoutly: 'What if we are? What if we do like the old ways, the old traditional festivities? What's the harm?'

'There is no harm. It is all most charming! But let us for a moment examine *facts*. You have said that Christmas is a season of good cheer. That means, does it not, a lot of eating and drinking? It means, in fact, the *over*eating! And with the overeating there comes the indigestion! And with the indigestion there comes the irritability!'

'Crimes,' said Colonel Johnson, 'are not committed from irritability.'

'I am not so sure! Take another point. There is, at Christmas, a spirit of goodwill. It is, as you say, "the thing to do." Old quarrels are patched up, those who have disagreed consent to agree once more, even if it is only temporarily.'

Johnson nodded.

'Bury the hatchet, that's right.'

Poirot pursued his theme:

'And families now, families who have been separated throughout the year, assemble once more together. Now under these conditions, my friend, you must admit that there will occur a great amount of *strain*. People who do not *feel* amiable are putting great pressure on themselves to *appear* amiable! There is at Christmas time a great deal of *hypocrisy*, honourable hypocrisy, hypocrisy undertaken *pour le bon motif, c'est entendu,* but nevertheless hypocrisy!'

'Well, I shouldn't put it quite like that myself,' said Colonel Johnson doubtfully.

Poirot beamed upon him.

'No, no. It is *I* who am putting it like that, not *you*! I am pointing out to you that under these conditions—mental strain, physical *malaise*—it is highly probable that dislikes that were before merely mild and disagreements that were trivial might suddenly assume a more serious character. The result of pretending to be a more amiable, a more forgiving, a more high-minded person than one really is, has sooner or later the effect of causing one to behave as a more disagreeable, a more ruthless and an altogether more unpleasant person than is actually the case! If you dam the stream of natural behaviour, *mon ami*, sooner or later the dam bursts and a cataclysm occurs!'

Colonel Johnson looked at him doubtfully.

'Never know when you're serious and when you're pulling my leg,' he grumbled.

Poirot smiled at him.

'I am not serious! Not in the least am I serious! But all the same, it is true what I say—artificial conditions bring about their natural reaction.'

Colonel Johnson's manservant entered the room.

'Superintendent Sugden on the phone, sir.'

'Right. I'll come.'

With a word of apology the chief constable left the room.

He returned some three minutes later. His face was grave and perturbed.

'Damn it all!' he said. 'Case of murder! On Christmas Eve, too!'

Poirot's eyebrows rose.

'It is that definitely—murder, I mean?'

'Eh? Oh, no other solution possible! Perfectly clear case. Murder—and a brutal murder at that!'

'Who is the victim?'

'Old Simeon Lee. One of the richest men we've got! Made his money in South Africa originally. Gold—no, diamonds, I believe. He sunk an immense fortune in manufacturing some particular gadget of mining machinery. His own invention, I believe. Anyway, it's paid him hand over fist! They say he's a millionaire twice over.'

Poirot said: 'He was well liked, yes?'

Johnson said slowly:

'Don't think anyone liked him. Queer sort of chap. He's been an invalid for some years now. I don't know very much about him myself. But of course he is one of the big figures of the county.'

'So this case, it will make a big stir?'

'Yes. I must get over to Longdale as fast as I can.'

He hesitated, looking at his guest. Poirot answered the unspoken question:

'You would like that I should accompany you?'

Johnson said awkwardly:

'Seems a shame to ask you. But, well, you know how it is! Superintendent Sugden is a good man, none better, painstaking, careful, thoroughly sound—but—well, he's not an *imaginative* chap in any way. Should like very much, as you are here, benefit of your advice.'

He halted a little over the end part of his speech, making it somewhat telegraphic in style. Poirot responded quickly.

'I shall be delighted. You can count on me to assist you in any way I can. We must not hurt the feelings of the good superintendent. It will be his case—not mine. I am only the unofficial consultant.'

Colonel Johnson said warmly:

'You're a good fellow, Poirot.'

With those words of commendation, the two men started out.

6

It was a constable who opened the front door to them and saluted. Behind him, Superintendent Sugden advanced down the hall and said:

'Glad you've got here, sir. Shall we come into this room here on the left—Mr. Lee's study? I'd like to run over the main outlines. The whole thing's a rum business.'

He ushered them into a small room on the left of the hall. There was a telephone there and a big desk covered with papers. The walls were lined with bookcases.

The chief constable said: 'Sugden, this is M. Hercule Poirot. You may have heard of him. Just happened to be staying with me. Superintendent Sugden.'

Poirot made a little bow and looked the other man over. He saw a tall man with square shoulders and a military bearing who had an aquiline nose, a pugnacious jaw and a large flourishing chestnut-coloured moustache. Sugden stared hard at Hercule Poirot after acknowledging the introduction. Hercule Poirot stared hard at Superintendent Sugden's moustache. Its luxuriance seemed to fascinate him.

The superintendent said:

'Of course I have heard of you, Mr. Poirot. You were in this part of the world some years ago, if I remember rightly. Death of Sir Bartholemew Strange. Poisoning case. Nicotine. Not my district, but of course I heard all about it.'

Colonel Johnson said impatiently:

'Now, then, Sugden, let's have the facts. A clear case, you said.'

'Yes, sir, it's murder right enough—not a doubt of that. Mr. Lee's throat was cut—jugular vein severed, I understand from the doctor. But there's something very odd about the whole matter.'

'You mean——?'

'I'd like you to hear my story first, sir. These are the circumstances: This afternoon, about five o'clock, I was rung up by Mr. Lee at Addlesfield police station. He sounded a bit odd over the phone—asked me to come and see him at eight o'clock this evening—made a special point of the time. Moreover, he instructed me to say to the butler that I was collecting subscriptions for some police charity.'

The chief constable looked up sharply.

'Wanted some plausible pretext to get you into the house?'

'That's right, sir. Well, naturally, Mr. Lee is an important person, and I acceded to his request. I got here a little before eight o'clock, and represented myself as seeking subscriptions for the Police Orphanage. The butler went away and returned to tell me that Mr. Lee would see me. Thereupon he showed me up to Mr. Lee's room, which is situated on the first floor, immediately over the dining-room.'

Superintendent Sugden paused, drew a breath and then proceeded in a somewhat official manner with his report.

'Mr. Lee was seated in a chair by the fireplace. He was wearing a dressing-gown. When the butler had left the room and closed the door, Mr. Lee asked me to sit near him. He then said rather hesitatingly that he wanted to give me particulars of a robbery. I asked him what had been taken. He replied that he had reason to believe that diamonds (uncut diamonds, I think he said) to the value of several thousand pounds had been stolen from his safe.'

'Diamonds, eh?' said the chief constable.

'Yes, sir. I asked him various routine questions, but his manner was very uncertain and his replies were somewhat vague in character. At last he said, "You must understand, Superintendent, that I may be mistaken in this matter." I said, "I do not quite understand, sir. Either the diamonds are missing or they are not missing—one or the other." He replied, "The diamonds are certainly missing, but it is just possible, Superintendent, that their disappearance may be simply a rather foolish kind of practical joke." Well, that seemed odd to me, but I said nothing. He went on: "It is difficult for me to explain in detail, but what it amounts to is this: So far as I can see only two persons can possibly have the stones. One of those persons might have done it as a joke. If the other person took them, then they have definitely been stolen." I said, "what exactly do you want me to do, sir?" He said quickly, "I want you, Superintendent, to return here in about an hour—no, make it a little more than that—say nine-fifteen. At that time I shall be able to tell you definitely whether I have been robbed or not." I was a little mystified, but I agreed and went away.'

Colonel Johnson commented:

'Curious—very curious. What do you say, Poirot?'

Hercule Poirot said:

'May I ask, Superintendent, what conclusions you yourself drew?'

The superintendent stroked his jaw as he replied carefully:

'Well, various ideas occurred to me, but on the whole I figured it out this way. There was no question of any practical joke. The diamonds had been stolen all right. But the old gentleman wasn't sure who'd done it. It's my opinion that he was speaking the truth when he said that it might have been one of two people—and of those two people one was a servant and the other was a *member of the family*.'

Poirot nodded appreciatively.

'*Très bien*. Yes, that explains his attitude very well.'

'Hence his desire that I should return later. In the interval he meant to have an interview with the person in question. He would tell them that he had already spoken of the matter to the police but that, if restitution were promptly made, he could hush the matter up.'

Colonel Johnson said:

'And if the suspect didn't respond?'

'In that case, he meant to place the investigation in our hands.'

Colonel Johnson frowned and twisted his moustache. He demurred.

'Why not take that course *before* calling you in?'

'No, no, sir.' The superintendent shook his head. 'Don't you see, if he had done that, it might have been bluff. It wouldn't have been half so convincing. The person might say to himself, "The old man won't call the police in, no matter what he suspects!" But if the old gentleman says to him, "I've *already spoken to the police*, the superintendent has only just left." Then the thief asks the butler, say, and the butler confirms that. He says, "Yes, the superintendent was here just before dinner." Then the thief is convinced the old gentleman means business and it's up to him to cough up the stones.'

'H'm, yes, I see that,' said Colonel Johnson. 'Any idea, Sugden, who this "member of the family" might be?'

'No, sir.'

'No indication whatsoever?'

'None.'

Johnson shook his head. Then he said:

'Well, let's get on with it.'

Superintendent Sugden resumed his official manner.

'I returned to the house, sir, at nine-fifteen precisely. Just as I was about to ring the front door bell, I heard a scream from inside the house, and then a confused sound of shouts and a general commotion. I rang several times and also used the knocker. It was three or four minutes before the door was answered. When the footman at last opened it I could see that something momentous had occurred. He was shaking all over and looked as though he was about to faint. He gasped out that Mr. Lee had been murdered. I ran hastily upstairs. I found Mr. Lee's room in a state of wild confusion. There had evidently been a severe struggle. Mr. Lee himself was lying in front of the fire with his throat cut, in a pool of blood.'

The chief constable said sharply:

'He couldn't have done it himself?'

Sugden shook his head.

'Impossible, sir. For one thing, there were the chairs and tables overturned, and the broken crockery and ornaments, and then there was no sign of the razor or knife with which the crime had been committed.'

The chief constable said thoughtfully:

'Yes, that seems conclusive. Anyone in the room?'

'Most of the family were there, sir. Just standing round.'

Colonel Johnson said sharply:

'Any ideas, Sugden?'

The superintendent said slowly:

'It's a bad business, sir. It looks to me as though one of them must have done it. I don't see how anyone from outside could have done it and got away in the time.'

'What about the window? Closed or open?'

'There are two windows in the room, sir. One was closed and locked. The other was open a few inches at the bottom—but it was fixed in that position by a burglar screw, and moreover, I've tried it and it's stuck fast—hasn't been opened for years, I should say. Also the wall outside is quite smooth and unbroken—no ivy or creepers. I don't see how anyone could have left that way.'

'How many doors in the room?'

'Just one. The room is at the end of a passage. That door was locked on the inside. When they heard the noise of the struggle and the old man's dying scream, and rushed upstairs, they had to break down the door to get in.'

Johnson said sharply:

'And who was in the room?'

Superintendent Sugden replied gravely:

'Nobody was in the room, sir, except the old man who had been killed not more than a few minutes previously.'

7

Colonel Johnson stared at Sugden for some minutes before he spluttered:

'Do you mean to tell me, Superintendent, that this is one of those damned cases you get in detective stories where a man is killed in a locked room by some apparently supernatural agency?'

A very faint smile agitated the superintendent's moustache as he replied gravely:

'I do not think it's quite as bad as that, sir.'

Colonel Johnson said:

'Suicide. It must be suicide!'

'Where's the weapon, if so? No, sir, suicide won't do.'

'Then how did the murderer escape? By the window?'

Sugden shook his head.

'I'll take my oath he didn't do that.'

'But the door was locked, you say, on the inside.'

The superintendent nodded. He drew a key from his pocket and laid it on the table.

'No fingerprints,' he announced. 'But just look at that key, sir. Take a look at it with that magnifying glass there.'

Poirot bent forward. He and Johnson examined the key together. The chief constable uttered an exclamation.

'By Jove, I get you. Those faint scratches on the end of the barrel. You see 'em, Poirot?'

'But yes, I see. That means, does it not, that the key was turned from outside the door—turned by means of a special implement that went through the keyhole and gripped the barrel—possibly an ordinary pair of pliers would do it.'

The superintendent nodded.

'It can be done all right.'

Poirot said: 'The idea being, then, that the death would be thought to be suicide, since the door was locked and no one was in the room?'

'That was the idea, Mr. Poirot, not a doubt of it, I should say.'

Poirot shook his head doubtfully.

'But the disorder in the room! As you say, that by itself wiped out the idea of suicide. Surely the murderer would first of all have set the room to rights.'

Superintendent Sugden said: 'But he hadn't *time*, Mr. Poirot. That's the whole point. He hadn't time. Let's say he counted on catching the old gentleman unawares. Well, that didn't come off. There was a struggle—a struggle heard plainly in the room underneath; and, what's more, the old gentleman called out for help. Everyone came rushing up. The murderer's only got time to nip out of the room and turn the key from the outside.'

'That is true,' Poirot admitted. 'Your murderer, he may have made the bungle. But why, oh why, did he not at least leave the weapon? For naturally, if there is no weapon, it cannot be suicide! That was an error most grave.'

Superintendent Sugden said stolidly:

'Criminals usually make mistakes. That's our experience.'

Poirot gave a slight sigh. He murmured:

'But all the same, in spite of his mistakes, he has escaped, this criminal.'

'I don't think he has exactly *escaped*.'

'You mean he is in the house still?'

'I don't see where else he can be. It was an inside job.'

'But, *tout de même*,' Poirot pointed out gently, 'he has escaped to this extent: *You do not know who he is*.'

Superintendent Sugden said gently but firmly:

'I rather fancy that we soon shall. We haven't done any questioning of the household yet.'

Colonel Johnson cut in:

'Look here, Sugden, one thing strikes me. Whoever turned that key from the outside must have had some knowledge of the job. That's to say he probably had had criminal experience. These sort of tools aren't easy to manage.'

'You mean it was a professional job, sir?'

'That's what I mean.'

'It does seem like it,' the other admitted. 'Following up that, it looks as though there were a professional thief among the servants. That would explain the diamonds being taken and the murder would follow on logically from that.'

'Well, anything wrong with that theory?'

'It's what I thought myself to begin with. But it's difficult. There are eight servants in the house; six of them are women, and of those six, five have been here for four years and more. Then there's the butler and the footman. The butler has been here for close on forty years—bit of a record that, I should say. The footman's local, son of the gardener, and brought up here. Don't see very well how he can be a professional. The only other person is Mr. Lee's valet attendant. He's comparatively new, but he was out of the house—still is—went out just before eight o'clock.'

Colonel Johnson said:

'Have you got a list of just who exactly was in the house?'

'Yes, sir. I got it from the butler.' He took out his note-book. 'Shall I read it to you?'

'Please, Sugden.'

'Mr. and Mrs. Alfred Lee. Mr. George Lee, M.P., and his wife. Mr. Harry Lee. Mr. and Mrs. David Lee. Miss'—the superintendent paused a little, taking the words carefully—'Pilar'—he pronounced it like a piece of architecture—'Estravados. Mr. Stephen Farr. Then for the servants: Edward Tressilian, butler. Walter Champion, footman. Emily Reeves, cook. Queenie Jones, kitchenmaid. Gladys Spent, head housemaid. Grace Best, second housemaid. Beatrice Moscombe, third housemaid. Joan Kench, betweenmaid. Sydney Horbury, valet attendant.'

'That's the lot, eh?'

'That's the lot, sir.'

'Any idea where everybody was at the time of the murder?'

'Only roughly. As I told you, I haven't questioned anybody yet. According to Tressilian, the gentlemen were in the dining-room still. The ladies had gone to the drawing-room. Tressilian had served coffee. According to his statement, he had just got back to his pantry when he heard a noise upstairs. It was followed by a scream. He ran out into the hall and upstairs in the wake of the others.'

Colonel Johnson said:

'How many of the family live in the house, and who are just staying here?'

'Mr. and Mrs. Alfred Lee live here. The others are just visiting.'

Johnson nodded.

'Where are they all?'

'I asked them to stay in the drawing-room until I was ready to take their statements.'

'I see. Well, we'd better go upstairs and take a look at the doings.'

The superintendent led the way up the broad stairs and along the passage.

As he entered the room where the crime had taken place Johnson drew a deep breath.

'Pretty horrible,' he commented.

He stood for a minute studying the overturned chairs, the smashed china and the blood-bespattered debris.

A thin elderly man stood up from where he had been kneeling by the body and gave a nod.

'Evening, Johnson,' he said. 'Bit of a shambles, eh?'

'I should say it was. Got anything for us, doctor?'

The doctor shrugged his shoulders. He grinned.

'I'll let you have the scientific language at the inquest! Nothing complicated about it. Throat cut like a pig. He bled to death in less than a minute. No sign of the weapon.'

Poirot went across the room to the windows. As the superintendent had said, one was shut and bolted. The other was open about four inches at the bottom. A thick patent screw of the kind known many years ago as an anti-burglar screw secured it in that position.

Sugden said: 'According to the butler, that window was never shut, wet or fine. There's a linoleum mat underneath it in case rain beat in, but it didn't much, as the overhanging roof protects it.'

Poirot nodded.

He came back to the body and stared down at the old man.

The lips were drawn back from the bloodless gums in something that looked like a snarl. The fingers were curved like claws.

Poirot said:

'He does not seem a strong man, no.'

The doctor said:

'He was pretty tough, I believe. He'd survived several pretty bad illnesses that would have killed most men.'

Poirot said: 'I do not mean that. I mean, he was not big, not strong physically.'

'No, he's frail enough.'

Poirot turned from the dead man. He bent to examine an overturned chair, a big chair of mahogany. Beside it was a round mahogany table and the fragments of a big china lamp. Two other smaller chairs lay nearby, also the smashed fragments of a decanter and two glasses, a heavy glass paperweight was unbroken, some miscellaneous books, a big Japanese vase smashed in pieces, and a bronze statuette of a naked girl completed the debris.

Poirot bent over all these exhibits, studying them gravely, but without touching them. He frowned to himself as though perplexed.

The chief constable said:

'Anything strike you, Poirot?'

Hercule Poirot sighed. He murmured:

'Such a frail shrunken old man—and yet—all this.'

Johnson looked puzzled. He turned away and said to the sergeant, who was busy at his work:

'What about prints?'

'Plenty of them, sir, all over the room.'

'What about the safe?'

'No good. Only prints on that are those of the old gentleman himself.'

Johnson turned to the doctor.

'What about bloodstains?' he asked. 'Surely whoever killed him must have got blood on him.'

The doctor said doubtfully:

'Not necessarily. Bleeding was almost entirely from the jugular vein. That wouldn't spout like an artery.'

'No, no. Still, there seems a lot of blood about.'

Poirot said:

'Yes, there is a lot of blood—it strikes one, that. A lot of blood.'

Superintendent Sugden said respectfully:

'Do you—er—does that suggest anything to you, Mr. Poirot?'

Poirot looked about him. He shook his head perplexedly.

He said:

'There is something here—some violence . . .' He stopped a minute, then went on: 'Yes, that is it—*violence*. . . . And blood—an insistence on *blood*. . . . There is—how shall I put it?—there is *too much blood*. Blood on the chairs, on the tables, on the carpet. . . . The blood ritual? Sacrificial blood? Is that it? Perhaps. Such a frail old man, so thin, so shrivelled, so dried up—and yet—in his death—*so much blood*. . . .'

His voice died away. Superintendent Sugden, staring at him with round, startled eyes, said in an awed voice:

'Funny—that's what she said—the lady. . . .'

Poirot said sharply:

'What lady? What was it she said?'

Sugden answered: 'Mrs. Lee—Mrs. Alfred. Stood over there by the door and half whispered it. It didn't make sense to me.'

'What did she say?'

'Something about who would have thought the old gentleman had so much blood in him. . . .'

Poirot said softly:

'"*Who would have thought the old man to have had so much blood in him?"* The words of Lady Macbeth. She said that. . . . Ah, that is interesting. . . .'

8

Alfred Lee and his wife came into the small study where Poirot, Sugden and the chief constable were standing waiting. Colonel Johnson came forward.

'How do you do, Mr. Lee? We've never actually met, but as you know, I'm chief constable of the county. Johnson's my name. I can't tell you how distressed I am by this.'

Alfred, his brown eyes like those of a suffering dog, said hoarsely:

'Thank you. It's terrible—quite terrible. I—this is my wife.'

Lydia said in her quiet voice:

'It has been a frightful shock to my husband—to all of us—but particularly to him.'

Her hand was on her husband's shoulder.

Colonel Johnson said:

'Won't you sit down, Mrs. Lee? Let me introduce M. Hercule Poirot.'

Hercule Poirot bowed. His eyes went interestedly from husband to wife.

Lydia's hand pressed gently on Alfred's shoulder.

'Sit down, Alfred.'

Alfred sat. He murmured:

'Hercule Poirot. Now, who—who—?'

He passed his hand in a dazed fashion over his forehead.

Lydia Lee said:

'Colonel Johnson will want to ask you a lot of questions, Alfred.'

The chief constable looked at her with approval. He was thankful that Mrs. Alfred Lee was turning out to be such a sensible and competent woman.

Alfred said:

'Of course. Of course. . . .'

Johnson said to himself:

'Shock seems to have knocked him out completely. Hope he can pull himself together a bit.'

Aloud he said:

'I've got a list here of everybody who was in the house to-night. Perhaps you'll tell me, Mr. Lee, if it is correct.'

He made a slight gesture to Sugden and the latter pulled out his note-book and once more recited the list of names.

The businesslike procedure seemed to restore Alfred Lee to something more like his usual self. He had regained command of himself, his eyes no longer looked dazed and staring. When Sugden finished, he nodded in agreement.

'That's quite right,' he said.

'Do you mind telling me a little more about your guests? Mr. and Mrs. George Lee and Mr. and Mrs. David Lee are, I gather, relatives.'

'They are my two younger brothers and their wives.'

'They are staying here only?'

'Yes, they came to us for Christmas.'

'Mr. Harry Lee is also a brother?'

'Yes.'

'And your two other guests? Miss Estravados and Mr. Farr?'

'Miss Estravados is my niece. Mr. Farr is the son of my father's one-time partner in South Africa.'

'Ah, an old friend.'

Lydia intervened.

'No, actually we have never seen him before.'

'I see. But you invited him to stay with you for Christmas?'

Alfred hesitated, then looked towards his wife. She said clearly:

'Mr. Farr turned up quite unexpectedly yesterday. He happened to be in the neighbourhood and came to call upon my father-in-law. When my father-in-law found he was the son of his old friend and partner, he insisted on his remaining with us for Christmas.'

Colonel Johnson said:

'I see. That explains the household. As regards the servants, Mrs. Lee, do you consider them all trustworthy?'

Lydia considered for a moment before replying. Then she said:

'Yes, I am quite sure they are all thoroughly reliable. They have mostly been with us for many years. Tressilian, the butler, has been here since my husband was a young child. The only newcomers are the betweenmaid, Joan, and the nurse-valet who attended on my father-in-law.'

'What about them?'

'Joan is rather a silly little thing. That is the worst that can be said of her. I know very little about Horbury. He has been here just over a year. He was quite competent at his job and my father-in-law seemed satisfied with him.'

Poirot said acutely:

'But you, Madame, were not so satisfied?'

Lydia shrugged her shoulders slightly.

'It was nothing to do with me.'

'But you are the mistress of the house, madame. The servants are your concern?'

'Oh yes, of course. But Horbury was my father-in-law's personal attendant. He did not come under my jurisdiction.'

'I see.'

Colonel Johnson said:

'We come now to the events of to-night. I'm afraid this will be painful for you, Mr. Lee, but I would like your account of what happened.'

Alfred said in a low voice: 'Of course.'

Colonel Johnson said, prompting him:

'When, for instance, did you last see your father?'

A slight spasm of pain crossed Alfred's face as he replied in a low voice:

'It was after tea. I was with him for a short time. Finally I said good-night to him and left him at—let me see—about a quarter to six.'

Poirot observed:

'You said good-night to him? You did not then expect to see him again that evening?'

'No. My father's supper, a light meal, was always brought to him at seven. After that he sometimes went to bed early or sometimes sat up in his chair, but he did not expect to see any members of the family again unless he specially sent for them.'

'Did he often send for them?'

'Sometimes. If he felt like it.'

'But it was not the ordinary procedure?'

'No.'

'Go on, please, Mr. Lee.'

Alfred continued:

'We had our dinner at eight o'clock. Dinner was over and my

wife and the other ladies had gone into the drawing-room.' His voice faltered. His eyes began to stare again. 'We were sitting there—at the table. . . . Suddenly there was the most astounding noise overhead. Chairs overturning, furniture crashing, breaking glass and china, and then—— Oh, God'—he shuddered—'I can hear it still—my father screamed—a horrible, long-drawn scream—the scream of a man in mortal agony. . . .'

He raised shaking hands to cover his face. Lydia stretched out her hand and touched his sleeve. Colonel Johnson said gently: 'And then?'

Alfred said in a broken voice:

'I think—just for a minute we were *stunned*. Then we sprang up and went out of the door and up the stairs to my father's room. The door was locked. We couldn't get in. It had to be broken open. Then, when we did get in, we saw——'

His voice died away.

Johnson said quickly:

'There's no need to go into that part of it, Mr. Lee. To go back a little, to the time you were in the dining-room. Who was there with you when you heard the cry?'

'Who was there? Why, we were all—— No, let me see. My brother was there—my brother Harry.'

'Nobody else?'

'No one else.'

'Where were the other gentlemen?'

Alfred sighed and frowned in an effort of remembrance.

'Let me see—it seems so long ago—yes, like years—what did happen? Oh, of course, George had gone to telephone. Then we began to talk of family matters, and Stephen Farr said something about seeing we wanted to discuss things, and he took himself off. He did it very nicely and tactfully.'

'And your brother David?'

Alfred frowned.

'David? Wasn't he there? No, of course he wasn't. I don't quite know when he slipped away.'

Poirot said gently:

'So you had the family matters to discuss?'

'Er—yes.'

'That is to say, you had matters to discuss with *one* member of your family?'

Lydia said:

'What do you mean, M. Poirot?'

He turned quickly to her.

'Madame, your husband says that Mr. Farr left them because he saw they had affairs of the family to discuss. But it was not a *conseil de famille*, since M. David was not there and M. George was not there. It was, then, a discussion between two members of the family only.'

Lydia said:

'My brother-in-law, Harry, had been abroad for a great number of years. It was natural that he and my husband should have things to talk over.'

'Ah! I see. It was like that.'

She shot him a quick glance, then turned her eyes away.

Johnson said:

'Well, that seems clear enough. Did you notice anyone else as you ran upstairs to your father's room?'

'I—really I don't know. I think so. We all came from different directions. But I'm afraid I didn't notice—I was so alarmed. That terrible cry. . . .'

Colonel Johnson passed quickly to another subject.

'Thank you, Mr. Lee. Now, there is another point. I understand that your father had some valuable diamonds in his possession.'

Alfred looked rather surprised.

'Yes,' he said. 'That is so.'

'Where did he keep them?'

'In the safe in his room.'

'Can you describe them at all?'

'They were rough diamonds—that is, uncut stones.'

'Why did your father have them there?'

'It was a whim of his. They were stones he had brought with him from South Africa. He never had them cut. He just liked keeping them in his possession. As I say, it was a whim of his.'

'I see,' said the chief constable.

From his tone it was plain that he did not see. He went on: 'Were they of much value?'

'My father estimated their value at about ten thousand pounds.'

'In fact they were very valuable stones?'

'Yes.'

'It seems a curious idea to keep such stones in a bedroom safe.'

Lydia interposed.

'My father-in-law, Colonel Johnson, was a somewhat curious man. His ideas were not the conventional ones. It definitely gave him pleasure to handle those stones.'

'They recalled, perhaps, the past to him,' said Poirot.

She gave him a quick appreciative look.

'Yes,' she said. 'I think they did.'

'Were they insured?' asked the chief constable.

'I think not.'

Johnson leaned forward. He asked quietly:

'Did you know, Mr. Lee, that those stones had been stolen?'

'What?' Alfred Lee stared at him.

'Your father said nothing to you of their disappearance?'

'Not a word.'

'You did not know that he had sent for Superintendent Sugden here and had reported the loss to him?'

'I hadn't the faintest idea of such a thing!'

The chief constable transferred his gaze.

'What about you, Mrs. Lee?'

Lydia shook her head.

'I heard nothing about it.'

'As far as you know, the stones were still in the safe?'

'Yes.'

She hesitated and then asked:

'Is that why he was killed? For the sake of those stones?'

Colonel Johnson said:

'That is what we are going to find out!'

He went on:

'Have you any idea, Mrs. Lee, who could have engineered such a theft?'

She shook her head.

'No, indeed. I am sure the servants are all honest. In any case, it would be very difficult for them to get at the safe. My father-in-law was always in his room. He never came downstairs.'

'Who attended to the room?'

'Horbury. He made the bed and dusted. The second housemaid went in to do the grate and lay the fire every morning, otherwise Horbury did everything.'

Poirot said:

'So Horbury would be the person with the best opportunity?'

'Yes.'

'Do you think that it was he who stole the diamonds, then?'

'It is possible, I suppose. . . . He had the best opportunity. Oh! I don't know what to think.'

Colonel Johnson said:

'Your husband has given us his account of the evening. Will you do the same, Mrs. Lee? When did you last see your father-in-law?'

'We were all up in his room this afternoon—before tea. That was the last time I saw him.'

'You did not see him later to bid him good-night?'

'No.'

Poirot said:

'Do you usually go and say good-night to him?'

Lydia said sharply:

'No.'

The chief constable went on:

'Where were you when the crime took place?'

'In the drawing-room.'

'You heard the noise of the struggle?'

'I think I heard something heavy fall. Of course my father-in-law's room is over the dining-room, not the drawing-room, so I shouldn't hear so much.'

'But you heard the cry?'

Lydia shuddered.

'Yes, I heard that. . . . It was horrible—like—like a soul in hell. I knew at once something dreadful had happened. I hurried out and followed my husband and Harry up the stairs.'

'Who else was in the drawing-room at the time?'

Lydia frowned.

'Really—I can't remember. David was next door in the music-room, playing Mendelssohn. I think Hilda had gone to join him.'

'And the other two ladies?'

Lydia said slowly:

'Magdalene went to telephone. I can't remember whether she had come back or not. I don't know where Pilar was.'

Poirot said gently:

'In fact you may have been quite alone in the drawing-room?'

'Yes—yes—as a matter of fact, I believe I was.'

Colonel Johnson said:

'About these diamonds. We ought, I think, to make quite sure about them. Do you know the combination of your father's safe, Mr. Lee? I see it is of a somewhat old-fashioned pattern.'

'You will find it written down in a small note-book he carried in the pocket of his dressing-gown.'

'Good. We will go and look presently. It will be better, perhaps, if we interview the other members of the house-party first. The ladies may want to get to bed.'

Lydia stood up.

'Come, Alfred.'

She turned to them. 'Shall I send them in to you?'

'One by one, if you wouldn't mind, Mrs. Lee.'

'Certainly.'

She moved towards the door. Alfred followed her.

Suddenly, at the last moment, he swung round.

'Of course,' he said. He came quickly back to Poirot. 'You are Hercule Poirot! I don't know where my wits have been. I should have realised at once.'

He spoke quickly, in a low, excited voice.

'It's an absolute godsend your being here! You must find out the truth, M. Poirot. Spare no expense! I will be responsible for any expense. *But find out* . . . My poor father—killed by some one—killed with the utmost brutality! You *must* find out, M. Poirot. My father has got to be avenged.'

Poirot answered quietly:

'I can assure you, M. Lee, that I am prepared to do my utmost to assist Colonel Johnson and Superintendent Sugden.'

Alfred Lee said:

'I want you to work for *me*. My father has got to be avenged.'

He began to tremble violently. Lydia had come back. She went up to him and drew his arm through hers.

'Come, Alfred,' she said. 'We must get the others.'

Her eyes met Poirot's. They were eyes that kept their own secrets. They did not waver.

Poirot said softly:

'*Who would have thought the old man——*'

She interrupted him:

'Stop! Don't say that!'

Poirot murmured:

'*You* said it, madame.'

She breathed softly:

'I know . . . I remember. . . . It was—so horrible.'

Then she went abruptly out of the room, her husband beside her.

9

George Lee was solemn and correct.

'A terrible business,' he said, shaking his head. 'A terrible, terrible business. I can only believe that it must—er—have been the work of a *lunatic!*'

Colonel Johnson said politely:

'That is your theory?'

'Yes. Yes, indeed. A homicidal maniac. Escaped, perhaps, from some mental home in the vicinity.'

Superintendent Sugden put in:

'And how do you suggest this—er—lunatic gained admittance to the house, Mr. Lee? And how did he leave it?'

George shook his head.

'That,' he said firmly, 'is for the police to discover.'

Sugden said:

'We made the round of the house at once. All windows were closed and barred. The side door was locked, so was the front door. Nobody could have left by the kitchen premises without being seen by the kitchen staff.'

George Lee cried:

'But that's absurd! You'll be saying next that my father was never murdered at all!'

'He was murdered all right,' said Superintendent Sugden. 'There's no doubt about that.'

The chief constable cleared his throat and took up the questioning.

'Just where were you, Mr. Lee, at the time of the crime?'

'I was in the dining-room. It was just after dinner. No, I was, I think, in this room. I had just finished telephoning.'

'You had been telephoning?'

'Yes. I had put a call through to the Conservative agent in Westeringham—my constituency. Some urgent matters.'

'And it was after that that you heard the scream?'

George Lee gave a slight shiver.

'Yes, very unpleasant. It—er—froze my marrow. It died away in a kind of choke or gurgle.'

He took out a handkerchief and wiped his forehead where the perspiration had broken out.

'Terrible business,' he muttered.

'And then you hurried upstairs?'

'Yes.'

'Did you see your brothers, Mr. Alfred and Mr. Harry Lee?'

'No, they must have gone up just ahead of me, I think.'

'When did you last see your father, Mr. Lee?'

'This afternoon. We were all up there.'

'You did not see him after that?'

'No.'

The chief constable paused, then he said:

'Were you aware that your father kept a quantity of valuable uncut diamonds in the safe in his bedroom?'

George Lee nodded.

'A most unwise procedure,' he said pompously. 'I often told him so. He might have been murdered for them—I mean—that is to say——'

Colonel Johnson cut in: 'Are you aware that these stones have disappeared?'

George's jaw dropped. His protuberant eyes stared.

'Then he *was* murdered for them?'

The chief constable said slowly:

'He was aware of their loss and reported it to the police some hours before his death.'

George said: 'But, then—I don't understand—I——'

Hercule Poirot said gently:

'We, too, do not understand. . . .''

10

Harry Lee came into the room with a swagger. For a moment Poirot stared at him, frowning. He had a feeling that somewhere he had seen this man before. He noted the features: the high-bridged nose, the arrogant poise of the head, the line of the jaw; and he realised that though Harry was a big man and his father had been a man of merely middle height, yet there had been a good deal of resemblance between them.

He noted something else, too. For all his swagger, Harry Lee was nervous. He was carrying it off with a swing, but the anxiety underneath was real enough.

'Well, gentlemen,' he said. 'What can I tell you?'

Colonel Johnson said:

'We shall be glad of any light you can throw on the events of this evening.'

Harry Lee shook his head.

'I don't know anything at all. It's all pretty horrible and utterly unexpected.'

Poirot said:

'You have recently returned from abroad, I think, Mr. Lee?'

Harry turned to him quickly.

'Yes. Landed in England a week ago.'

Poirot said:

'You had been away a long time?'

Harry Lee lifted up his chin and laughed.

'You might as well hear straight away—someone will soon tell you! I'm the prodigal son, gentlemen! It's nearly twenty years since I last set foot in this house.'

'But you returned—now. Will you tell us why?' asked Poirot.

With the same appearance of frankness Harry answered readily enough.

'It's the good old parable still. I got tired of the husks that the swine do eat—or don't eat, I forget which. I thought to myself that the fatted calf would be a welcome exchange. I had a letter from my father suggesting that I came home. I obeyed the summons and came. That's all.'

Poirot said:

'You came for a short visit—or a long one?'

Harry said:

'I came home—for good!'

'Your father was willing?'

'The old man was delighted.' He laughed again. The corners of his eyes crinkled engagingly. 'Pretty boring for the old man living here with Alfred! Alfred's a dull stick—very worthy and all that, but poor company. My father had been a bit of a rip in his time. He was looking forward to my company.'

'And your brother and his wife, were they pleased that you were to live here?'

Poirot asked the question with a slight lifting of his eyebrows.

'Alfred? Alfred was livid with rage. Don't know about Lydia. She was probably annoyed on Alfred's behalf. But I've no doubt she'd be quite pleased in the end. I like Lydia. She's a delightful woman. I should have got on with Lydia. But Alfred was quite another pair of shoes.' He laughed again. 'Alfred's always been as jealous as hell of me. He's always been the good dutiful stay-at home stick-in-the-mud son. And what was he going to get for it in the end?—what the good boy of the family always gets—a kick in the pants. Take it from me, gentlemen, virtue doesn't pay.' He looked from one face to another.

'Hope you're not shocked by my frankness. But, after all, it's the truth you're after. You'll drag out all the family dirty linen into the light of day in the end. I might as well display mine straight away. I'm not particularly broken-hearted by my father's death—after all, I hadn't seen the old devil since I was a boy—but nevertheless he was my father and he was murdered. I'm all out for revenge on the murderer.' He stroked his jawbone, watching them. 'We're rather hot on revenge in our family. None of the Lees forgets easily. I mean to make sure that my father's murderer is caught and hanged.'

'I think you can trust us to do our best in that line, Mr. Lee,' said Sugden.

'If you don't I shall take the law into my own hands,' said Harry Lee.

The chief constable said sharply:

'Have you any ideas on the subject of the murderer's identity, then, Mr. Lee?'

Harry shook his head.

'No,' he said slowly. 'No—I haven't. You know it's rather a jolt. Because I've been thinking about it—and I don't see that it can have been an outside job. . . .'

'Ah,' said Sugden, nodding his head.

'And if so,' said Harry Lee, 'then someone here in the house killed him. . . . But who the devil could have done it? Can't suspect the servants. Tressilian has been here since the year one. The half-witted footman? Not on your life. Horbury, now, he's a cool customer, but Tressilian tells me he was out at the pictures. So what do you come to? Passing over Stephen Farr (and why the devil should Stephen Farr come all the way from South Africa and murder a total stranger) there's only the family. And for the life of me I can't see one of us doing it. Alfred? He adored Father. George? He hasn't got the guts. David? David's always been a moon dreamer. He'd faint if he saw his own finger bleed. The wives? Women don't go and slit a man's throat in cold blood. So who did? Blessed if I know. But it's damned disturbing.'

Colonel Johnson cleared his throat—an official habit of his—and said:

'When did you last see your father this evening?'

'After tea. He'd just had a row with Alfred—about your humble servant. The old man was no end bucked with himself. He always liked stirring up trouble. In my opinion, that's why he kept my arrival dark from the others. Wanted to see the fur fly when I blew in unexpectedly! That's why he talked about altering his will, too.'

Poirot stirred softly. He murmured:

'So your father mentioned his will?'

'Yes—in front of the whole lot of us, watching us like a cat to see how we reacted. Just told the lawyer chap to come over and see him about it after Christmas.'

Poirot asked:

'What changes did he contemplate making?'

Harry Lee grinned:

'He didn't tell us that! Trust the old fox! I imagine—or shall we say I hoped—that the change was to the advantage of your humble servant! I should imagine I'd been cut out of any former wills. Now, I rather fancy, I was to go back. Nasty blow for the others. Pilar, too—he'd taken a fancy to her. She was in for something good, I should imagine. You haven't seen her yet? My Spanish niece. She's a beautiful creature, Pilar—with the lovely warmth of the South—and its cruelty. Wish I wasn't a mere uncle!'

'You say your father took to her?'

Harry nodded.

'She knew how to get round the old man. Sat up there with him a good deal. I bet she knew just what she was after! Well, he's dead now. No wills can be altered in Pilar's favour—nor mine either, worse luck.'

He frowned, paused a minute, and then went on with a change of tone.

'But I'm wandering from the point. You wanted to know what was the last time I saw my father? As I've told you, it was after tea—might have been a little past six. The old man was in good spirits then—a bit tired, perhaps. I went away and left him with Horbury. I never saw him again.'

'Where were you at the time of his death?'

'In the dining-room with brother Alfred. Not a very harmonious after-dinner session. We were in the middle of a pretty sharp argument when we heard the noise overhead. Sounded as though ten men were wrestling up there. And then poor old Father screamed. It was like killing a pig. The sound of it paralysed Alfred. He just sat there with his jaw dropping. I fairly shook him back to life, and we started off upstairs. The door was locked. Had to break it open. Took some doing, too. How the devil that door came to be locked, I can't imagine! There was no one in the room but Father, and I'm damned if anyone could have got away through the windows.'

Superintendent Sugden said:

'The door was locked from the outside.'

'What?' Harry stared. 'But I'll swear the key was on the *inside*.'

Poirot murmured:

'So you noticed that?'

Harry Lee said sharply:

'I do notice things. It's a habit of mine.'

He looked sharply from one face to the other.

'Is there anything more you want to know, gentlemen?'

Johnson shook his head.

'Thank you, Mr. Lee, not for the moment. Perhaps you will ask the next member of the family to come along?'

'Certainly I will.'

He walked to the door and went out without looking back.

The three men looked at each other.

Colonel Johnson said:

'What about it, Sugden?'

The superintendent shook his head doubtfully. He said:

'He's afraid of something. I wonder why? . . .'

11

Magdalene Lee paused effectively in the doorway. One long slender hand touched the burnished platinum sheen of her hair. The leaf-green velvet frock she wore clung to the delicate lines of her figure. She looked very young and a little frightened.

The three men were arrested for a moment looking at her. Johnson's eyes showed a sudden surprised admiration. Superintendent Sugden's showed no animation, merely the impatience of a man anxious to get on with his job. Hercule Poirot's eyes were deeply appreciative (as she saw), but the appreciation was not for her beauty, but for the effective use she made of it. She did not know that he was thinking to himself:

'Jolie mannequin, la petite. Mais elle a les yeux dures.'

Colonel Johnson was thinking:

'Damned good-looking girl. George Lee will have trouble with her if he doesn't look out. Got an eye for a man all right.'

Superintendent Sugden was thinking:

'Empty-headed vain piece of goods. Hope we get through with her quickly.'

'Will you sit down, Mrs. Lee? Let me see, you are——?'

'Mrs. George Lee.'

She accepted the chair with a warm smile of thanks. 'After all,' the glance seemed to say, 'although you *are* a man and a policeman, you are not so dreadful after all.'

The tail-end of the smile included Poirot. Foreigners were so susceptible where women were concerned. About Superintendent Sugden she did not bother.

She murmured, twisting her hands together in a pretty distress:

'It's all so terrible. I feel so frightened.'

'Come, come, Mrs. Lee,' said Colonel Johnson kindly but briskly. 'It's been a shock, I know, but it's all over now. We just want an account from you of what happened this evening.'

She cried out:

'But I don't know anything about it—I don't indeed.'

For a minute the chief constable's eyes narrowed. He said gently:

'No, of course not.'

'We only arrived here yesterday. George *would* make me come here for Christmas! I wish we hadn't. I'm sure I shall never feel the same again!'

'Very upsetting—yes.'

'I hardly know George's family, you see. I've only seen Mr. Lee once or twice—at our wedding and once since. Of course I've seen Alfred and Lydia more often, but they're really all quite strangers to me.'

Again the wide-eyed frightened child look. Again Hercule Poirot's eyes were appreciative—and again he thought to himself:

'Elle joue très bien la comédie, cette petite. . . .'

'Yes, yes,' said Colonel Johnson. 'Now just tell me about the last time you saw your father-in-law—Mr. Lee—alive.'

'Oh, *that*! That was this afternoon. It was dreadful!'

Johnson said quickly:

'Dreadful? Why?'

'They were so angry!'

'Who was angry?'

'Oh, all of them. . . . I don't mean George. His father didn't say anything to him. But all the others.'

'What happened exactly?'

'Well, when we got there—he asked for all of us—he was speaking into the telephone—to his lawyers about his will. And then he told Alfred he was looking very glum. I think that was because of Harry coming home to live. Alfred was very upset about that, I believe. You see, Harry did something quite dreadful. And then he said something about his wife—she's dead long ago—but she had the brains of a louse, he said, and David sprang up and looked as though he'd like to murder him—— Oh!' She stopped suddenly, her eyes alarmed. 'I didn't *mean* that—I didn't mean it at all!'

Colonel Johnson said soothingly:

'Quite—quite, figure of speech, that was all.'

'Hilda, that's David's wife, quieted him down and—well, I think that's all. Mr. Lee said he didn't want to see anyone again that evening. So we all went away.'

'And that was the last time you saw him?'

'Yes. Until—until——'

She shivered.

Colonel Johnson said:

'Yes, quite so. Now, where were you at the time of the crime?'

'Oh—let me see, I think I was in the drawing-room.'

'Aren't you sure?'

Magdalene's eyes flickered a little, the lids drooped over them. She said:

'Of course! How stupid of me. . . . I'd gone to telephone. One gets so mixed up.'

'You were telephoning, you say. In this room?'

'Yes, that's the only telephone except the one upstairs in my father-in-law's room.'

Superintendent Sugden said:

'Was anybody else in the room with you?'

Her eyes widened.

'Oh, no, I was quite alone.'

'Had you been here long?'

'Well—a little time. It takes some time to put a call through in the evening.'

'It was a trunk call, then?'

'Yes—to Westeringham.'

'I see.'

'And then?'

'And then there was that awful scream—and everybody running—and the door being locked and having to break it down. Oh! It was like a *nightmare*! I shall always, always remember it!'

'No, no,' Colonel Johnson's tone was mechanically kind. He went on:

'Did you know that your father-in-law kept a quantity of valuable diamonds in his safe?'

'No, did he?' Her tone was quite frankly thrilled. 'Real diamonds?'

Hercule Poirot said:

'Diamonds worth about ten thousand pounds.'

'Oh!' It was a soft gasping sound—holding in it the essence of feminine cupidity.

'Well,' said Colonel Johnson, 'I think that's all for the present. We needn't bother you any further, Mrs. Lee.'

'Oh, thank you.'

She stood up—smiled from Johnson to Poirot—the smile of a grateful little girl, then she went out walking with her head held high and her palms a little turned outwards.

Colonel Johnson called:

'Will you ask your brother-in-law, Mr. David Lee, to come here?'

Closing the door after her, he came back to the table.

'Well,' he said, 'what do you think? We're getting at some of it now! You notice one thing: George Lee was telephoning when he heard the scream! His wife was telephoning when she heard it! That doesn't fit–it doesn't fit at all.'

He added:

'What do you think, Sugden?'

The superintendent said slowly:

'I don't want to speak offensively of the lady, but I should say that though she's the kind who would be first class at getting money out of a gentleman, I don't think she's the kind who'd cut a gentleman's throat. That wouldn't be her line at all.'

'Ah, but one never knows, *mon vieux*,' murmured Poirot.

The chief constable turned round on him.

'And you, Poirot, what do you think?'

Hercule Poirot leaned forward. He straightened the blotter in front of him and flicked a minute speck of dust from a candlestick. He answered:

'I would say that the character of the late Mr. Simeon Lee begins to emerge for us. It is there, I think, that the whole importance of the case lies . . . in the character of the dead man.'

Superintendent Sugden turned a puzzled face to him.

'I don't quite get you, Mr. Poirot,' he said. 'What exactly has the character of the deceased got to do with his murder?'

Poirot said dreamily:

'The character of the victim has always something to do with his or her murder. The frank and unsuspicious mind of Desdemona was the direct cause of her death. A more suspicious woman would have seen Iago's machinations and circumvented them much earlier. The uncleanness of Marat directly invited his end in a bath. From the temper of Mercutio's mind came his death at the sword's point.'

Colonel Johnson pulled his moustache.

'What exactly are you getting at, Poirot?'

'I am telling you that because Simeon Lee was a certain kind of man, he set in motion certain forces, which forces in the end brought about his death.'

'You don't think the diamonds had anything to do with it, then?'

Poirot smiled at the honest perplexity in Johnson's face.

'*Mon cher*,' he said. 'It was because of Simeon Lee's peculiar character that he kept ten thousand pounds worth of uncut diamonds in his safe! You have not there the action of every man.'

'That's very true, Mr. Poirot,' said Superintendent Sugden, nodding his head with the air of a man who at last sees what a fellow-conversationalist is driving at. 'He was a queer one, Mr. Lee was. He kept those stones there so he could take them out and handle them and get the feeling of the past back. Depend upon it, that's why he never had them cut.'

Poirot nodded energetically.

'Precisely—precisely. I see you have great acumen, Superintendent.'

The superintendent looked a little doubtful at the compliment, but Colonel Johnson cut in:

'There's something else, Poirot. I don't know whether it has struck you——'

'*Mais oui*,' said Poirot. 'I know what you mean. Mrs. George Lee, she let the cat out of the bag more than she knew! She gave us a pretty impression of that last family meeting. She indicates—oh! so naïvely—that Alfred was angry with his father—and that David looked as "though he could murder him." Both those statements I think were true. But from them we can draw our own reconstruction. What did Simeon Lee assemble his family for? Why should they have arrived in time to hear him telephoning to his lawyer? *Parbleu*, it was no error, that. He *wanted* them to hear it! The poor old one, he sits in his chair and he has lost the diversions of his younger days. So he invents a new diversion for himself. He amuses himself by playing upon the cupidity and the greed of human nature—yes, and on its emotions and its passions, too! But from that arises one further deduction. In his game of rousing the greed and emotion of his children, he would not omit any one. He must, logically and necessarily, have had his dig at Mr. George Lee as well as at the others! His wife is carefully silent about that. At her, too, he may have shot a poisoned arrow or so. We shall find out, I think, from others what Simeon Lee had to say to George Lee and George Lee's wife——'

He broke off. The door opened and David Lee came in.

12

David Lee had himself well in hand. His demeanour was calm—almost unnaturally so. He came up to them, drew a chair forward and sat down, looking with grave interrogation at Colonel Johnson.

The electric light touched the fair peak of hair that grew on his forehead and showed up the sensitive modelling of the cheek bones. He looked absurdly young to be the son of that shrivelled old man who lay dead upstairs.

'Yes, gentlemen,' he said, 'what can I tell you?'

Colonel Johnson said:

'I understand, Mr. Lee, that there was a kind of family meeting held in your father's room this afternoon?'

'There was. But it was quite informal. I mean, it was not a family council or anything of that kind.'

'What took place there?'

David Lee answered calmly:

'My father was in a difficult mood. He was an old man and an invalid, of course, one had to make allowances for him. He seemed to have assembled us there in order to—well—vent his spite upon us.'

'Can you remember what he said?'

David said quietly:

'It was really all rather foolish. He said we were no use—any of us—that there wasn't a single man in the family! He said Pilar (that is my Spanish niece) was worth two of any of us. He said——'. David stopped.

Poirot said:

'Please, Mr. Lee, the exact words, if you can.'

David said reluctantly:

'He spoke rather coarsely—said he hoped that somewhere in the world he had better sons—even if they were born the wrong side of the blanket. . . .'

His sensitive face showed distaste for the words he was repeating. Superintendent Sugden looked up, suddenly alert. Leaning forward, he said:

'Did your father say anything in particular to your brother Mr. George Lee?'

'To George? I don't remember. Oh yes, I believe he told him he would have to cut down expenses in future; he'd have to reduce his allowance. George was very upset, got as red as a turkey cock. He spluttered and said he couldn't possibly manage with less. My father said quite coolly that he'd have to. He said he'd better get his wife to help him economise. Rather a nasty dig, that—George has always been the economical one—saves and stints on every penny. Magdalene, I fancy, is a bit of a spender—she has extravagant tastes.'

Poirot said:

'So that she, too, was annoyed?'

'Yes. Besides, my father worded something else rather crudely—mentioned her as having lived with a naval officer; of course he really meant her father, but it sounded rather dubious. Magdalene went scarlet. I don't blame her.'

Poirot said:

'Did your father mention his late wife, your mother?'

The red blood ran in waves up David's temples. His hands clenched themselves on the table in front of him, trembling slightly.

He said in a low choked voice:

'Yes, he did. He insulted her.'

Colonel Johnson said: 'What did he say?'

David said abruptly:

'I don't remember. Just some slighting reference.'

Poirot said softly:

'Your mother has been dead some years?'

David said shortly:

'She died when I was a boy.'

'She was not—perhaps—very happy in her life here?'

David gave a scornful laugh:

'Who could be happy with a man like my father? My mother was a saint. She died a broken-hearted woman.'

Poirot went on:

'Your father was, perhaps, distressed by her death?'

David said abruptly:

'I don't know. I left home.'

He paused and then said:

'Perhaps you may not be aware of the fact that when I came on this visit I had not seen my father for nearly twenty years. So you see I can't tell you very much about his habits or his enemies or what went on here.'

Colonel Johnson asked:

'Did you know that your father kept a lot of valuable diamonds in the safe in his bedroom?'

David said indifferently:

'Did he? Seems a foolish sort of thing to do.'

Johnson said:

'Will you describe briefly your own movements last night?'

'Mine? Oh, I went away from the dinner-table fairly quickly. It bores me, this sitting round over port. Besides, I could see that Alfred and Harry were working up for a quarrel. I hate rows. I slipped away and went to the music-room and played the piano.'

Poirot asked: 'The music-room, it is next to the drawing-room, is it not?'

'Yes. I played there for some time—till—till the thing happened.'

'What did you hear exactly?'

'Oh! A far-off noise of furniture being overturned somewhere upstairs. And then a pretty ghastly cry.' He clenched his hands again. 'Like a soul in hell. God, it was awful!'

Johnson said:

'Were you alone in the music-room?'

'Eh? No, my wife, Hilda, was there. She'd come in from the drawing-room. We—we went up with the others.'

He added quickly and nervously:

'You don't want me, do you, to describe what—what I saw there?'

Colonel Johnson said:

'No, quite unnecessary. Thank you, Mr. Lee, there's nothing more. You can't imagine, I suppose, who would be likely to want to murder your father?'

David Lee said recklessly:

'I should think—quite a lot of people! I don't know of anyone definite.'

He went out rapidly, shutting the door loudly behind him.

13

Colonel Johnson had had no time to do more than clear his throat when the door opened again and Hilda Lee came in.

Hercule Poirot looked at her with interest. He had to admit to himself that the wives these Lees had married were an interesting study. The swift intelligence and greyhound grace of Lydia, the meretricious airs and graces of Magdalene, and now the solid comfortable strength of Hilda. She was, he saw, younger than her rather dowdy style of hairdressing and unfashionable clothes made her appear. Her mouse-brown hair was unflecked with grey and her steady hazel eyes set in the rather podgy face shone out like beacons of kindliness. She was, he thought, a nice woman.

Colonel Johnson was talking in his kindliest tone.

'. . . A great strain on all of you,' he was saying. 'I gather from your husband, Mrs. Lee, that this is the first time you have been to Gorston Hall?'

She bowed her head.

'Were you previously acquainted with your father-in-law, Mr. Lee?'

Hilda replied in her pleasant voice:

'No. We were married soon after David left home. He always wanted to have nothing to do with his family. Until now we have not seen any of them.'

'How, then, did this visit come about?'

'My father-in-law wrote to David. He stressed his age and his desire that all his children should be with him this Christmas.'

'And your husband responded to this appeal?'

Hilda said:

'His acceptance was, I am afraid, all my doing. I—misunderstood the situation.'

Poirot interposed. He said:

'Will you be so kind as to explain yourself a little more clearly, madame? I think what you can tell us may be of value.'

She turned to him immediately.

She said:

'At that time I had never seen my father-in-law. I had no idea what his real motive was. I assumed that he was old and lonely and that he really wanted to be reconciled to all his children.'

'And what was his real motive, in your opinion, madame?'

Hilda hesitated a moment. Then she said slowly:

'I have no doubt—no doubt at all—that what my father-in-law really wanted was not to promote peace but to stir up strife.'

'In what way?'

Hilda said in a low voice:

'It amused him to—to appeal to the worst instincts in human nature. There was—how can I put it—a kind of diabolical impishness about him. He wished to set every member of the family at loggerheads with one another.'

Johnson said sharply:

'And did he succeed?'.

'Oh, yes,' said Hilda Lee. 'He succeeded.'

Poirot said:

'We have been told, madame, of a scene that took place this afternoon. It was, I think, rather a violent scene.'

She bowed her head.

'Will you describe it to us—as truthfully as possible, if you please.'

She reflected a minute.

'When we went in my father-in-law was telephoning.'

'To his lawyer, I understand?'

'Yes, he was suggesting that Mr.—was it Charlton?—I don't quite remember the name—should come over as he, my father-in-law, wanted to make a new will. His old one, he said, was quite out of date.'

Poirot said:

'Think carefully, madame, in your opinion did your father-in-law deliberately ensure that you should all overhear this conversation, or was it just by *chance* that you overheard it?'

Hilda Lee said:

'I am almost sure that he meant us to overhear.'

'With the object of fomenting doubt and suspicion among you?'

'Yes.'

'So that, really, he may not have meant to alter his will at all?'

She demurred.

'No, I think that part of it was quite genuine. He probably did wish to make a new will—but he enjoyed underlining the fact.'

'Madame,' said Poirot. 'I have no official standing and my questions, you understand, are not perhaps those that an English officer of the law would ask. But I have a great desire to know what form you think that new will would have taken. I am asking, you perceive, not for your knowledge, but simply for your opinion. *Les femmes*, they are never slow to form an opinion, *Dieu merci*.'

Hilda Lee smiled a little.

'I don't mind saying what I think. My husband's sister Jennifer married a Spaniard, Juan Estravados. Her daughter, Pilar, has just arrived here. She is a very lovely girl—and she is, of course, the only grandchild in the family. Old Mr. Lee was delighted with her. He took a tremendous fancy to her. In my opinion he wished to leave her a considerable sum in his new will. Probably he had only left her a small portion or even nothing at all in an old one.'

'Did you know your sister-in-law at all?'

'No, I never met her. Her Spanish husband died in tragic circumstances, I believe, soon after the marriage. Jennifer herself died a year ago. Pilar was left an orphan. This is why Mr. Lee sent for her to come and live with him in England.'

'And the other members of the family, did they welcome her coming?'

Hilda said quietly:

'I think they all liked her. It was very pleasant to have someone young and alive in the house.'

'And she, did she seem to like being here?'

Hilda said slowly:

'I don't know. It must seem cold and strange to a girl brought up in the South—in Spain.'

Johnson said:

'Can't be very pleasant being in Spain just at present. Now, Mrs. Lee, we'd like to hear your account of the conversation this afternoon.'

Poirot murmured:

'I apologise. I have made the digressions.'

Hilda Lee said:

'After my father-in-law finished telephoning, he looked round at us and laughed, and said we all looked very glum. Then he said that he was tired and should go to bed early. Nobody was to come up and see him this evening. He said he wanted to be in good form for Christmas Day. Something like that.

'Then——' Her brows knit in an effort of remembrance. 'I think he said something about its being necessary to be one of a large family to appreciate Christmas, and then he went on to speak of money. He said it would cost him more to run this house in future. He told George and Magdalene they would have to economise. Told her she ought to make her own clothes. Rather an old-fashioned idea, I'm afraid. I don't wonder it annoyed her. He said his own wife had been clever with her needle.'

Poirot said gently:

'Is that all that he said about her?'

Hilda flushed.

'He made a slighting reference to her brains. My husband was very devoted to his mother, and that upset him very much. And then, suddenly, Mr. Lee began shouting at us all. He worked himself up about it. I can understand, of course, how he felt——'

Poirot said gently, interrupting her:

'How did he feel?'

She turned her tranquil eyes upon him.

'He was disappointed, of course,' she said. 'Because there are no grandchildren—no boys, I mean—no Lees to carry on. I can see that that must have festered for a long time. And suddenly he couldn't keep it in any longer and vented his rage against his sons—saying they were a lot of namby-pamby old women—something like that. I felt sorry for him, then, because I realised how his pride was hurt by it.'

'And then?'

'And then,' said Hilda slowly, 'we all went away.'

'That was the last you saw of him?'

She bowed her head.

'Where were you at the time the crime occurred?'

'I was with my husband in the music-room. He was playing to me.'

'And then?'

'We heard tables and chairs overturned upstairs, and china being broken—some terrible struggle. And then that awful scream as his throat was cut. . . .'

Poirot said:

'Was it such an awful scream? Was it'—he paused—'*like a soul in hell?*'

Hilda Lee said:

'It was worse than that!'

'What do you mean, madame?'

'It was like someone *who had no soul.* . . . It was inhuman like a beast. . . .'

Poirot said gravely:

'So—you have judged him, madame?'

She raised a hand in sudden distress. Her eyes fell and she stared down at the floor.

14

Pilar came into the room with the wariness of an animal who suspects a trap. Her eyes went quickly from side to side. She looked not so much afraid as deeply suspicious.

Colonel Johnson rose and put a chair for her. Then he said:

'You understand English, I suppose, Miss Estravados?'

Pilar's eyes opened wide. She said:

'Of course. My mother was English. I am really very English indeed.'

A faint smile came to Colonel Johnson's lips, as his eyes took in the black gloss of her hair, the proud dark eyes and the curling red lips. Very English! An incongruous term to apply to Pilar Estravados.

He said:

'Mr. Lee was your grandfather. He sent for you to come from Spain. And you arrived a few days ago. Is that right?'

Pilar nodded.

'That is right. I had—oh! a lot of adventures getting out of Spain—there was a bomb from the air and the chauffeur he was killed—where his head had been there was all blood. And I could not drive a car, so for a long way I had to walk—and I do not like walking. I never walk. My feet were sore—but sore——'

Colonel Johnson smiled.

He said:

'At any rate you arrived here. Had your mother spoken to you of your grandfather much?'

Pilar nodded cheerfully.

'Oh, yes, she said he was an old devil.'

Hercule Poirot smiled. He said:

'And what did you think of him when you arrived, mademoiselle?'

Pilar said:

'Of course he was very, very old. He had to sit in a chair—and his face was all dried up. But I liked him all the same. I think that when he was a young man, he must have been handsome—very handsome, like you,' said Pilar to Superintendent Sugden. Her eyes dwelt with *naïve* pleasure on his handsome face, which had turned brick-red at the compliment.

Colonel Johnson stifled a chuckle. It was one of the few occasions when he had seen the stolid superintendent taken aback.

'But of course,' Pilar continued regretfully, 'he could never have been as big as you.'

Hercule Poirot sighed.

'You like, then, big men, señorita?' he inquired.

Pilar agreed enthusiastically.

'Oh, yes, I like a man to be very big, tall, and the shoulders broad, and very, very strong.'

Colonel Johnson said sharply.

'Did you see much of your grandfather when you arrived here?'

Pilar said:

'Oh, yes. I went to sit with him. He told me things—that he had been a very wicked man, and all the things he did in South Africa.'

'Did he ever tell you that he had diamonds in the safe in his room?'

'Yes, he showed them to me. But they were not like diamonds—they were just like pebbles—very ugly—very ugly indeed.'

Superintendent Sugden said shortly:

'So he showed them to you, did he?'

'Yes.'

'He didn't give you any of them?'

Pilar shook her head.

'No, he did not. I thought that perhaps one day he would—if I were very nice to him and came often to sit with him. Because old gentlemen they like very much young girls.'

Colonel Johnson said:

'Do you know that those diamonds have been stolen?'

Pilar opened her eyes very wide.

'Stolen?'

'Yes, have you any idea who might have taken them?'

Pilar nodded her head.

'Oh, yes,' she said. 'It would be Horbury.'

'Horbury? You mean the valet?'

'Yes.'

'Why do you think that?'

'Because he has the face of a thief. His eyes go so, from side to side, he walks softly and listens at doors. He is like a cat. And all cats are thieves.'

'H'm,' said Colonel Johnson. 'We'll leave it at that. Now I understand that all the family were up in your grandfather's room this afternoon, and that some—er—angry words passed.'

Pilar nodded and smiled.

'Yes,' she said. 'It was great fun. Grandfather made them oh! so angry!'

'Oh, you enjoyed it, did you?'

'Yes. I like to see people get angry. I like it very much. But here in England they do not get angry like they do in Spain. In Spain they take out their knives and they curse and shout. In England they do nothing, just get very red in the face and shut up their mouths tight.'

'Do you remember what was said?'

Pilar seemed rather doubtful.

'I am not sure. Grandfather said they were no good—that they had not got any children. He said I was better than any of them. He liked me, very much.'

'Did he say anything about money or a will?'

'A will—no, I don't think so. I don't remember.'

'What happened?'

'They all went away—except Hilda—the fat one, David's wife, she stayed behind.'

'Oh, she did, did she?'

'Yes. David looked very funny. He was all shaking and oh! so white. He looked as though he might be sick.'

'And what then?'

'Then I went and found Stephen. We danced to the gramophone.'

'Stephen Farr?'

'Yes. He is from South Africa—he is the son of grandfather's partner. He is very handsome too. Very brown and big, and he has nice eyes.'

Johnson asked:

'Where were you when the crime occurred?'

'You ask where I was?'

'Yes.'

'I had gone into the drawing-room with Lydia. And then I went up to my room and did my face. I was going to dance again with Stephen. And then, far away, I heard a scream and every one was running, so I went too. And they were trying to break down grandfather's door. Harry did it with Stephen, they are both big strong men.'

'Yes?'

'And then—crash—down it went—and we all looked in. Oh, such a sight—everything smashed and knocked over, and grandfather lying in a lot of blood, and his throat was cut like *this*'—she made a vivid dramatic gesture at her own neck—'right up under his ear.'

She paused, having obviously enjoyed her narrative.

Johnson said:

'The blood didn't make you feel ill?'

She stared.

'No, why should it? There is usually blood when people are killed. There was, oh! so much blood everywhere!'

Poirot said: 'Did anyone say anything?'

Pilar said:

'David said such a funny thing—what was it? Oh, yes. The mills of God—that is what he said'—she repeated it with emphasis on each word—'*The mills—of—God——* What does that mean? Mills are what make flour, are they not?'

Colonel Johnson said:

'Well, I don't think there is anything more just now, Miss Estravados.'

Pilar got up obediently. She flashed a quick charming smile at each man in turn.

'I will go now then.' She went out.

Colonel Johnson said:

'*The mills of God grind slowly, but they grind exceeding small.* And David Lee said that!'

15

As the door opened once more, Colonel Johnson looked up. For a moment he took the entering figure to be that of Harry Lee, but as Stephen Farr advanced into the room he saw his error.

'Sit down, Mr. Farr,' he said.

Stephen sat. His eyes, cool, intelligent eyes, went from one to the other of the three men. He said:

'I'm afraid I shan't be much use to you. But please ask me anything that you think may help. Perhaps I'd better explain to start with exactly who I am. My father, Ebenezer Farr, was Simeon

Lee's partner in South Africa in the old days. I'm talking of over forty years ago.'

He paused.

'My dad talked to me a lot about Simeon Lee—what a personality he was. He and dad cleaned up a good bit together. Simeon Lee went home with a fortune and my father didn't do badly either. My father always told me that when I came to this country I was to look up Mr. Lee. I said once that is was a long time ago and that he'd probably not know who I was, but dad scoffed at the idea. He said, "When two men have been through what Simeon and I went through, they don't forget." Well, my father died a couple of years ago. This year I came over to England for the first time, and I thought I'd act on dad's advice and look up Mr. Lee.'

With a slight smile he went on:

'I was just a little nervous when I came along here, but I needn't have been. Mr. Lee gave me a warm welcome and absolutely insisted that I should stay with the family over Christmas. I was afraid I was butting in, but he wouldn't hear of a refusal.'

He added rather shyly:

'They were all very nice to me—Mr. and Mrs. Alfred Lee couldn't have been nicer. I'm terribly sorry for them that all this should come upon them'

'How long have you been here, Mr. Farr?'

'Since yesterday.'

'Did you see Mr. Lee today at all?'

'Yes, I had a chat with him this morning. He was in good spirits then and anxious to hear about a lot of people and places.'

'That was the last time you saw him?'

'Yes.'

'Did he mention to you that he kept a quantity of uncut diamonds in his safe?'

'No.'

He added before the other could speak:

'Do you mean that this business was murder and robbery?'

'We're not sure yet,' said Johnson. 'Now to come to the events of this evening, will you tell me in your own words what you were doing?'

'Certainly. After the ladies left the dining-room I stayed and had a glass of port. Then I realised that the Lees had family business they wanted to discuss and that my being there was hampering them so I excused myself and left them.'

'And what did you do then?'

Stephen Farr leaned back in his chair. His forefinger caressed his jaw. He said rather woodenly:

'I—er—went along to a big room with a parquet floor—kind of ballroom, I fancy. There's a gramophone there and dance records. I put some records on.'

Poirot said: 'It was possible, perhaps, that someone might join you there?'

A very faint smile curved Stephen Farr's lips. He answered:

'It was possible, yes. One always hopes.'

And he grinned outright.

Poirot said:

'Señorita Estravados is very beautiful.'

Stephen answered:

'She's easily the best thing to look at that I've seen since I came to England.'

'Did Miss Estravados join you?' asked Colonel Johnson.

Stephen shook his head.

'I was still there when I heard the rumpus. I came out into the hall and ran hell for leather to see what was the matter. I helped Harry Lee to break the door down.'

'And that's all you have to tell us?'

'Absolutely all, I'm afraid.'

Hercule Poirot leaned forward. He said softly:

'But I think, Monsieur Farr, that you could tell us a good deal if you liked.'

Farr said sharply:

'What d'you mean?'

'You can tell us of something that is very important in this case—the character of Mr. Lee. You say that your father talked much of him to you. What manner of a man was it that he described to you?'

Stephen Farr said slowly:

'I think I see what you're driving at. What was Simeon Lee like in his young days? Well—you want me to be frank, I suppose?'

'If you please.'

'Well, to begin with, I don't think that Simeon Lee was a highly moral member of society. I don't mean that he was exactly a crook, but he sailed pretty near the wind. His morals were nothing to boast about anyway. He had charm, though, a good deal of it. And he was fantastically generous. No one with a hard-luck story ever appealed to him in vain. He drank a bit, but not over-much, was attractive to women and had a sense of humour. All the same, he had a queer revengeful streak in him. Talk of the elephant never forgets and you talk of Simeon Lee. My father told me of several cases where Lee waited years to get even with someone who'd done him a nasty turn.'

Superintendent Sugden said:

'Two might play at that game. You've no knowledge, I suppose, Mr. Farr, of anyone who Simeon Lee had done a bad turn to out there? Nothing out of the past that could explain the crime committed here this evening?'

Stephen Farr shook his head.

'He had enemies, of course, must have had, being the man he was. But I know of no specific case. Besides,' his eyes narrowed, 'I understand (as a matter of fact, I've been questioning Tressilian) there have been no strangers in or near the house this evening.'

Hercule Poirot said:

'With the exception of yourself, M. Farr.'

Stephen Farr swung round upon him.

'Oh, so that's it? Suspicious stranger within the gates! Well, you won't find anything of that kind. No back history of Simeon Lee doing Ebenezer Farr down, and Eb's son coming over to revenge his dad! No,' he shook his head, 'Simeon and Ebenezer had nothing against each other. I came here, as I've told you, out of sheer curiosity. And moreover, I should imagine a gramophone is as good an alibi as anything else. I never stopped putting on records—somebody must have heard them. One record wouldn't give me time to race away upstairs—these passages are a mile long, anyway—slit an old man's throat, wash off the blood and get back again before the others came rushing up. The idea's farcical!'

Colonel Johnson said:

'We're not making any insinuations against you, Mr. Farr.'

Stephen Farr said:

'I didn't care much for the tone of Mr. Hercule Poirot's voice.'

'That,' said Hercule Poirot, 'is unfortunate!'

He smiled benignly at the other.

Stephen Farr looked angrily at him.

Colonel Johnson interposed quickly:

'Thank you, Mr. Farr. That will be all for the present. You will, of course, not leave this house.'

Stephen Farr nodded. He got up and left the room, walking with a freely swinging stride.

As the door closed behind him, Johnson said:

'There goes X, the unknown quantity. His story seems straightforward enough. All the same, he's the dark horse. He *might* have pinched those diamonds—might have come here with a bogus story just to gain admittance. You'd better get his fingerprints, Sugden, and see if he's known.'

'I've already got them,' said the superintendent with a dry smile.

'Good man. You don't overlook much. I suppose you're on to all the obvious lines?'

Superintendent Sugden checked off on his fingers.

'Check up on those telephone calls—times, etc. Check up on Horbury. What time he left, who saw him go. Check up all entrances and exits. Check up on staff generally. Check up financial position of members of family. Get on to the lawyers and check up on will. Search house for the weapon and for bloodstains on clothing—also possibly diamonds hidden somewhere.'

'That covers everything, I think,' said Colonel Johnson approvingly. 'Can you suggest anything, M. Poirot?'

Poirot shook his head.

He said:

'I find the superintendent admirably thorough.'

Sugden said gloomily:

'It won't be any joke looking through this house for the missing diamonds. Never saw so many ornaments and knick-knacks in my life.'

'The hiding-places are certainly abundant,' Poirot agreed.

'And there's really nothing you would suggest, Poirot?'

The Chief Constable looked a little disappointed—rather like a man whose dog has refused to do its trick.

Poirot said:

'You will permit that I take a line of my own?'

'Certainly—certainly,' said Johnson at the same moment as Superintendent Sugden said rather suspiciously:

'What line?'

'I would like,' said Hercule Poirot, 'to converse—very often—very frequently—with members of the family.'

'You mean you'd like to have another shot at questioning them?' asked the colonel a little puzzled.

'No, no, not to question—to converse!'

'Why?' asked Sugden.

Hercule Poirot waved an emphatic hand.

'In conversation, points arise! If a human being converses much, it is impossible for him to avoid the truth!'

Sugden said: 'Then you think someone is lying?'

Poirot sighed.

'*Mon cher*, everyone lies—in parts like the egg of the English curate. It is profitable to separate the harmless lies from the vital ones.'

Colonel Johnson said sharply:

'All the same, it's incredible, you know. Here's a particularly crude and brutal murder—and whom have we as suspects? Alfred Lee and his wife—both charming, well-bred, quiet people. George Lee, who's a Member of Parliament and the essence of respectability. His wife? She's just an ordinary modern lovely. David Lee seems a gentle creature and we've got his brother Harry's word for it that he can't stand the sight of blood. His wife seems a nice sensible woman—quite commonplace. Remains the Spanish niece and the man from South Africa. Spanish beauties have hot tempers but I don't see that attractive creature slitting the old man's neck in cold blood, especially as from what has come out she had every reason to keep him alive—at any rate until he had signed a new will. Stephen Farr's a possibility—that is to say he may be a professional crook and have come here after the diamonds. The old man discovered the loss and Farr slit his throat to keep him quiet. That could have been so—that gramophone *alibi* isn't too good.'

Poirot shook his head.

'My dear friend,' he said. 'Compare the physique of M. Stephen Farr and old Simeon Lee. If Farr decided to kill the old man he could have done it in a minute—Simeon Lee couldn't possibly have put up that fight against him. Can one believe that that frail old man and that magnificent specimen of humanity struggled for some minutes over-turning chairs and breaking china? To imagine such a thing is fantastic!'

Colonel Johnson's eyes narrowed.

'You mean,' he said, 'that it was a *weak* man who killed Simeon Lee?'

'Or a woman!' said the superintendent.

16

Colonel Johnson looked at his watch.

'Nothing much more that I can do here. You've got things well in hand, Sugden. Oh, just one thing. We ought to see the butler fellow. I know you've questioned him, but we know a bit more about things now. It's important to get confirmation of just where everybody says he was at the time of the murder.'

Tressilian came in slowly. The Chief Constable told him to sit down.

'Thank you, sir. I will, if you don't mind. I've been feeling very queer—very queer indeed. My legs, sir, and my head.'

Poirot said gently: 'You have had the shock, yes.'

The butler shuddered. 'Such—such a violent thing to happen. In this house! Where everything has always gone on so quietly.'

Poirot said:

'It was a well-ordered house, yes? But not a happy one?'

'I wouldn't like to say that, sir.'

'In the old days when all the family was at home, was it happy then?'

Tressilian said slowly:

'It wasn't perhaps what one would call very harmonious, sir.'

'The late Mrs. Lee was somewhat of an invalid, was she not?'

'Yes, sir, very poorly she was.'

'Were her children fond of her?'

'Mr. David, he was devoted to her. More like a daughter than a son. And after she died he broke away, couldn't face living here any longer.'

Poirot said:

'And Mr. Harry? What was he like?'

'Always rather a wild young gentleman, sir, but good-hearted. Oh, dear, gave me quite a turn, it did, when the bell rang—and then again, so impatient like, and I opened the door and there was a strange man, and then Mr. Harry's voice said, 'Hallo, Tressilian. Still here, eh?' Just the same as ever.'

Poirot said sympathetically:

'It must have been the strange feeling, yes, indeed.'

Tressilian said, a little pink flush showing in his cheek:

'It seems sometimes, sir, as though the past isn't the past! I believe there's been a play on in London about something like that. There's something in it, sir—there really is. There's a feeling comes over you—as though you'd done everything before. It just seems to me as though the bell rings and I go to answer it and there's Mr. Harry—even if it should be Mr. Farr or some other person—I'm just saying to myself—*but I've done this before. . . .*'

Poirot said:

'That is very interesting—very interesting.'

Tressilian looked at him gratefully.

Johnson, somewhat impatient, cleared his throat and took charge of the conversation.

'Just want to get various times checked correctly,' he said. 'Now, when the noise upstairs started, I understand that only Mr. Alfred Lee and Mr. Harry Lee were in the dining-room. Is that so?'

'I really couldn't tell you, sir. All the gentlemen were there when I served coffee to them—but that would be about a quarter of an hour earlier.'

'Mr. George Lee was telephoning. Can you confirm that?'

'I think somebody did telephone, sir. The bell rings in my pantry, and when anybody takes off the receiver to call a number, there's just a faint noise on the bell. I do remember hearing that, but I didn't pay attention to it.'

'You don't know exactly when it was?'

'I couldn't say, sir. It was after I had taken coffee to the gentleman, that is all I can say.'

'Do you know where any of the ladies were at the time I mentioned?'

'Mrs. Alfred was in the drawing-room, sir, when I went for the coffee tray. That was just a minute or two before I heard the cry upstairs.'

Poirot asked:

'What was she doing?'

'She was standing by the far window, sir. She was holding the curtain a little back and looking out.'

'And none of the other ladies were in the room?'

'No, sir.'

'Do you know where they were?'

'I couldn't say at all, sir.'

'You don't know where anyone else was?'

'Mr. David, I think, was playing in the music-room next door to the drawing-room.'

'You heard him playing?'

'Yes, sir.' Again the old man shivered. 'It was like a sign, sir, so I felt afterwards. It was the "Dead March" he was playing. Even at the time, I remember, it gave me the creeps.'

'It is curious, yes,' said Poirot.

'Now about this fellow, Horbury, the valet,' said the chief constable. 'Are you definitely prepared to swear that he was out of the house by eight o'clock?'

'Oh yes, sir. It was just after Mr. Sugden here arrived. I remember particular because he broke a coffee-cup.'

Poirot said:

'Horbury broke a coffee-cup?'

'Yes, sir—one of the old Worcester ones. Eleven years I've washed them up and never one broken till this evening.'

Poirot said:

'What was Horbury doing with the coffee-cups?'

'Well, of course, sir, he'd no business to have been handling them at all. He was just holding one up, admiring it like, and I happened to mention that Mr. Sugden had called, and he dropped it.'

Poirot said:

'Did you say "Mr. Sugden" or did you mention the word police?'

Tressilian looked a little startled.

'Now I come to think of it, sir, I mentioned that the police superintendent had called.'

'And Horbury dropped the coffee-cup,' said Poirot.

'Seems suggestive, that,' said the chief constable. 'Did Horbury ask any questions about the superintendent's visit?'

'Yes, sir, asked what he wanted here. I said he'd come collecting for the Police Orphanage and had gone up to Mr. Lee.'

'Did Horbury seem relieved when you said that?'

'Do you know, sir, now you mention it, he certainly did. His manner changed at once. Said Mr. Lee was a good old chap and free with his money—rather disrespectfully he spoke—and then he went off.'

'Which way?'

'Out through the door to the servants' hall.'

Sugden interposed:

'All that's O.K., sir. He passed through the kitchen, where the cook and the kitchenmaid saw him, and out through the back door.'

'Now listen, Tressilian, and think carefully. Is there any means by which Horbury could return to the house without anyone seeing him?'

The old man shook his head.

'I don't see how he could have done so, sir. All the doors are locked on the inside.'

'Supposing he had had a key?'

'The doors are bolted as well.'

'How does he get in when he comes?'

'He has a key of the back door, sir. All the servants come in that way.'

'He *could* have returned that way, then?'

'Not without passing through the kitchen, sir. And the kitchen would be occupied till well after half-past nine or a quarter to ten.'

Colonel Johnson said:

'That seems conclusive. Thank you, Tressilian.'

The old man got up and with a bow left the room. He returned, however, a minute or two later.

'Horbury has just returned, sir. Would you like to see him now?'

'Yes, please, send him in at once.'

17

Sydney Horbury did not present a very prepossessing appearance. He came into the room and stood rubbing his hands together and darting quick looks from one person to another. His manner was unctuous.

Johnson said:

'You're Sydney Horbury?'

'Yes, sir.'

'Valet attendant to the late Mr. Lee?'

'Yes, sir. It's terrible, sir, isn't it? You could have knocked me down with a feather when I heard from Gladys. Poor old gentleman——'

Johnson cut him short.

'Just answer my questions, please.'

'Yes, sir, certainly, sir.'

'What time did you go out to-night, and where have you been?'

'I left the house just before eight, sir. I went to the Superb, sir, just five minutes' walk away. *Love in Old Seville* was the picture, sir.'

'Anyone who saw you there?'

'The young lady in the box office, sir, she knows me. And the commissionaire at the door, he knows me too. And—er—as a matter of fact, I was with a young lady, sir. I met her there by appointment.'

'Oh, you did, did you? What's her name?'

'Doris Buckle, sir. She works in the Combined Dairies, sir, 23, Markham Road.'

'Good. We'll look into that. Did you come straight home?'

'I saw my young lady home first, sir. Then I came straight back. You'll find it's quite all right, sir. I didn't have anything to do with this. I was——'

Colonel Johnson said curtly:

'Nobody's accusing you of having anything to do with it.'

'No, sir, of course not, sir. But it's not very pleasant when a murder happens in a house.'

'Nobody said it was. Now, then, how long had you been in Mr. Lee's service?'

'Just over a year, sir.'

'Did you like your place here?'

'Yes, sir. I was quite satisfied. The pay was good. Mr. Lee was rather difficult sometimes, but of course I'm used to attending on invalids.'

'You've had previous experience?'

'Oh, yes, sir. I was with Major West and with the Honourable Jasper Finch——'

'You can give all those particulars to Sugden later. What I want to know is this: At what time did you last see Mr. Lee this evening?'

'It was about half-past seven, sir. Mr. Lee had a light supper brought to him every evening at seven o'clock. I then prepared him for bed. After that he would sit in front of the fire in his dressing-gown till he felt like going to bed.'

'What time was that usually?'

'It varied, sir. Sometimes he would go to bed as early as

eight o'clock—that's if he felt tired. Sometimes he would sit up till eleven or after.'

'What did he do when he did want to go to bed?'

'Usually he rang for me, sir.'

'And you assisted him to bed?'

'Yes, sir.'

'But this was your evening out. Did you always have Fridays?'

'Yes, sir. Friday was my regular day.'

'What happened then when Mr. Lee wanted to go to bed?'

'He would ring his bell and either Tressilian or Walter would see to him.'

'He was not helpless? He could move about?'

'Yes, sir, but not very easily. Rheumatoid arthritis was what he suffered from, sir. He was worse some days than others.'

'Did he never go into another room in the daytime?'

'No, sir. He preferred to be in just the one room. Mr. Lee wasn't luxurious in his tastes. It was a big room with pleny of air and light in it.'

'Mr. Lee had his supper at seven, you say?'

'Yes, sir. I took the tray away and put out the sherry and two glasses on the bureau.'

'Why did you do that?'

'Mr. Lee's orders.'

'Was that usual?'

'Sometimes. It was the rule that none of the family came to see Mr. Lee in the evening unless he invited them. Some evenings he liked to be alone. Other evenings he'd send down and ask Mr. Alfred, or Mrs. Alfred, or both of them, to come up after dinner.'

'But, as far as you know, he had not done so on this occasion? That is, he had not sent a message to any member of the family requesting their presence?'

'He hadn't sent any message by *me*, sir.'

'So that he wasn't expecting any of the family?'

'He might have asked one of them personally, sir.'

'Of course.'

Horbury continued:

'I saw that everything was in order, wished Mr. Lee good-night and left the room.'

Poirot asked:

'Did you make up the fire before you left the room?'

The valet hesitated.

'It wasn't necessary, sir. It was well built up.'

'Could Mr. Lee have done that himself?'

'Oh no, sir. I expect Mr. Harry Lee had done it.'

'Mr. Harry Lee was with him when you came in before supper?'

'Yes, sir. He went away when I came.'

'What was the relationship between the two as far as you could judge?'

'Mr. Harry Lee seemed in very good spirits, sir. Throwing back his head and laughing a good deal.'

'And Mr. Lee?'

'He was quiet and rather thoughtful.'

'I see. Now there's something more I want to know, Horbury: What can you tell us about the diamonds Mr. Lee kept in his safe?'

'Diamonds, sir? I never saw any diamonds.'

'Mr. Lee kept a quantity of uncut stones there. You must have seen him handling them.'

'Those funny little pebbles, sir? Yes, I did see him with them once or twice. But I didn't know they were diamonds. He was showing them to the foreign young lady only yesterday—or was it the day before?'

Colonel Johnson said abruptly:

'These stones have been stolen.'

Horbury cried out:

'I hope you don't think, sir, that *I* had anything to do with it!'

'I'm not making any accusations,' said Johnson. 'Now then, is there anything you can tell us that has any bearing on this matter?'

'The diamonds, sir? Or the murder?'

'Both.'

Horbury considered. He passed his tongue over his pale lips. At last he looked up with eyes that were a shade furtive.

'I don't think there's anything, sir.'

Poirot said softly:

'Nothing you've overheard, say, in the course of your duties, which might be helpful?'

The valet's eyelids flickered a little.

'No, sir, I don't think so, sir. There was a little awkwardness between Mr. Lee and—and some members of his family.'

'Which members?'

'I gathered there was a little trouble over Mr. Harry Lee's return.

Mr. Alfred Lee resented it. I understand he and his father had a few words about it—but that was all there was to it. Mr. Lee didn't accuse him for a minute of having taken any diamonds. And I'm sure Mr. Alfred wouldn't do such a thing.'

Poirot said quickly:

'His interview with Mr. Alfred was *after* he had discovered the loss of the diamonds, was it not, though?'

'Yes, sir.'

Poirot leaned forward.

'I thought, Horbury,' he said softly, '*that you did not know of the theft of the diamonds until we informed you of it just now.* How, then, do you know that Mr. Lee had discovered his loss *before* he had this conversation with his son?'

Horbury turned brick red.

'No use lying. Out with it,' said Sugden. 'When did you know?'

Horbury said sullenly:

'I heard him telephoning to someone about it.'

'You weren't in the room?'

'No, outside the door. Couldn't hear much—only a word or two.'

'What did you hear exactly?' asked Poirot sweetly.

'I heard the words robbery and diamonds, and I heard him say, "I don't know who to suspect"—and I heard him say something about this evening at eight o'clock.'

Superintendent Sugden nodded.

'That was to me he was speaking, my lad. About five-ten, was it?'

'That's right, sir.'

'And when you went into his room afterwards, did he look upset?'

'Just a bit, sir. Seemed absent-minded and worried.'

'So much so that you got the wind up—eh?'

'Look here, Mr. Sugden, I won't have you saying things like that. Never touched any diamonds, I didn't, and you can't prove I did. I'm not a thief.'

Superintendent Sugden, unimpressed, said:

'That remains to be seen.' He glanced questioningly at the chief constable, received a nod and went on: 'That'll do for you, my lad. Shan't want you again to-night.'

Horbury went out gratefully in haste. Sugden said appreciatively:

'Pretty bit of work, M. Poirot. You trapped him as neatly as I've ever seen it done. He may be a thief or he may not, but he's certainly a first-class liar!'

'An unprepossessing person,' said Poirot.

'Nasty bit of goods,' agreed Johnson. 'Question is, what do we think of his evidence?'

Sugden summarised the position neatly.

'Seems to me there are three possibilities: 1. Horbury's a thief *and* a murderer. 2. Horbury's a thief, but *not* a murderer. 3. Horbury's an innocent man. Certain amount of evidence for 1. He overheard telephone call and knew the theft had been discovered. Gathered from old man's manner that he was suspected. Made his plans accordingly. Went out ostentatiously at eight o'clock and cooked up an *alibi*. Easy enough to slip out of a cinema and return there unnoticed. He'd have to be pretty sure of the girl, though, that she wouldn't give him away. I'll see what I can get out of her to-morrow.'

'How, then, did he manage to re-enter the house?' asked Poirot.

'That's more difficult,' Sugden admitted. 'But there might be ways. Say one of the women servants unlocked a side door for him.'

Poirot raised his eyebrows quizzically.

'He places, then, his life at the mercy of two women? With *one* woman it would be taking a big risk; with *two—eh bien*, I find the risk fantastic!'

Sugden said:

'Some criminals think they can get away with anything!'

He went on:

'Let's take 2. Horbury pinched those diamonds. He took 'em out of the house to-night and has possibly passed them on to some accomplice. That's quite easy going and highly probable. Now we've got to admit that somebody else chose this night to murder Mr. Lee. That somebody being quite unaware of the diamond complication. It's possible, of course, but it's a bit of a coincidence.

'Possibility 3—Horbury's innocent. Somebody else both took the diamonds and murdered the old gentleman. There it is; it's up to us to get at the truth.'

Colonel Johnson yawned. He looked again at his watch and got up.

'Well,' he said, 'I think we'll call it a night, eh? Better just have a look in the safe before we go. Odd thing if those wretched diamonds were there all the time.'

But the diamonds were not in the safe. They found the

combination where Alfred Lee had told them, in the small notebook taken from the dressing-gown pocket of the dead man. In the safe they found an empty chamois leather bag. Among the papers the safe contained only one was of interest.

It was a will dated some fifteen years previously. After various legacies and bequests, the provisions were simple enough. Half Simeon Lee's fortune went to Alfred Lee. The other half was to be divided in equal shares between his remaining children: Harry, George, David and Jennifer.

PART FOUR

December 25th

1

IN THE BRIGHT SUN of Christmas noon, Poirot walked in the gardens of Gorston Hall. The Hall itself was a large solidly built house with no special architectural pretensions.

Here, on the south side, was a broad terrace flanked with a hedge of clipped yew. Little plants grew in the interstices of the stone flags and at intervals along the terrace there were stone sinks arranged as miniature gardens.

Poirot surveyed them with benign approval. He murmured to himself:

'C'est bien imaginé, ça!'

In the distance he caught sight of two figures going towards an ornamental sheet of water some three hundred yards away. Pilar was easily recognisable as one of the figures, and he thought at first the other was Stephen Farr, then he saw that the man with Pilar was Harry Lee. Harry seemed very attentive to his attractive niece. At intervals he flung his head back and laughed, then bent once more attentively towards her.

'Assuredly, there is one who does not mourn,' Poirot murmured to himself.

A soft sound behind him made him turn. Magdalene Lee was standing there. She, too, was looking at the retreating figures of the man and girl. She turned her head and smiled enchantingly at Poirot.

She said:

'It's such a glorious sunny day! One can hardly believe in all the horrors of last night, can one, M. Poirot?'

'It is difficult, truly, madame.'

Magdalene sighed.

'I've never been mixed up in tragedy before. I've—I've really only just grown up. I stayed a child too long, I think. . . . That's not a good thing to do.'

Again she sighed. She said:

'Pilar, now, seems so extraordinarily self-possessed. . . . I suppose it's the Spanish blood. It's all very odd, isn't it?'

'What is odd, madame?'

'The way she turned up here, out of the blue!'

Poirot said:

'I have learned that Mr. Lee had been searching for her for some time. He had been in correspondence with the Consulate in Madrid and with the vice-consul at Aliquara, where her mother died.'

'He was very secretive about it all,' said Magdalene. 'Alfred knew nothing about it. No more did Lydia.'

'Ah!' said Poirot.

Magdalene came a little nearer to him. He could smell the delicate perfume she used.

'You know, M. Poirot, there's some story connected with Jennifer's husband, Estravados. He died quite soon after the marriage, and there's some mystery about it. Alfred and Lydia know. I believe it was something—rather disgraceful. . . .'

'That,' said Poirot, 'is indeed sad.'

Magdalene said:

'My husband feels—and I agree with him—that the family ought to have been told more about the girl's antecedents. After all, if her father was a *criminal*——'

She paused, but Hercule Poirot said nothing. He seemed to be admiring such beauties of nature as could be seen in the winter season in the grounds of Gorston Hall.

Magdalene said:

'I can't help feeling that the manner of my father-in-law's death was somehow *significant*. It—it was so very *un-English*.'

Hercule Poirot turned slowly. His grave eyes met hers in innocent inquiry.

'Ah,' he said. 'The Spanish touch, you think?'

'Well, they *are* cruel, aren't they?' Magdalene spoke with an effect of childish appeal. 'All those bull fights and things!'

Hercule Poirot said pleasantly:

'You are saying that in your opinion Señorita Estravados cut her grandfather's throat?'

'Oh no, M. Poirot!' Magdalene was vehement. She was shocked. 'I never said anything of the kind! Indeed, I didn't!'

'Well,' said Poirot. 'Perhaps you did not.'

'But I *do* think that she is—well, a suspicious person. The furtive way she picked up something from the floor of that room last night, for instance.'

A different note crept into Hercule Poirot's voice. He said sharply:

'She picked up something from the floor last night?'

Magdalene nodded. Her childish mouth curved spitefully.

'Yes, as soon as we got into the room. She gave a quick glance round to see if anyone was looking, and then pounced on it. But the superintendent man saw her, I'm glad to say, and made her give it up.'

'What was it that she picked up, do you know, madame?'

'No. I wasn't near enough to see.' Magdalene's voice held regret. 'It was something quite small.'

Poirot frowned to himself.

'It is interesting, that,' he murmured to himself.

Magdalene said quickly:

'Yes, I thought you ought to know about it. After all, we don't know *anything* about Pilar's upbringing and what her life has been like. Alfred is always so unsuspicious and dear Lydia is so casual.' Then she murmured: 'Perhaps I'd better go and see if I can help Lydia in any way. There may be letters to write.'

She left him with a smile of satisfied malice on her lips.

Poirot remained lost in thought on the terrace.

2

To him there came Superintendent Sugden. The police superintendent looked gloomy. He said:

'Good-morning, Mr. Poirot. Doesn't seem quite the right thing to say Merry Christmas, does it?'

'*Mon cher collègue*, I certainly do not observe any traces of merriment on your countenance. If you had said Merry Christmas I should not have replied "Many of them!"'

'I don't want another one like this one, and that's a fact,' said Sugden.

'You have made the progress, yes?'

'I've checked up on a good many points. Horbury's alibi is

holding water all right. The commissionaire at the cinema saw him go in with the girl, and saw him come out with her at the end of the performance, and seems pretty positive he didn't leave, and couldn't have left and returned during the performance. The girl swears quite definitely he was with her in the cinema all the time.'

Poirot's eyebrows rose.

'I hardly see, then, what more there is to say.'

The cynical Sugden said:

'Well, one never knows with girls! Lie themselves black in the face for the sake of a man.'

'That does credit to their hearts,' said Hercule Poirot.

Sugden growled:

'That's a foreign way of looking at it. It's defeating the ends of justice.'

Hercule Poirot said:

'Justice is a very strange thing. Have you ever reflected on it?'

Sugden stared at him.

He said:

'You're a queer one, Mr. Poirot.'

'Not at all. I follow a logical train of thought. But we will not enter into a dispute on the question. It is your belief, then, that this demoiselle from the milk shop is not speaking the truth?'

Sugden shook his head.

'No,' he said, 'it's not like that at all. As a matter of fact, I think she *is* telling the truth. She's a simple kind of girl, and I think if she was telling me a pack of lies I'd spot it.'

Poirot said:

'You have the experience, yes.'

'That's just it, Mr. Poirot. One does know, more or less, after a lifetime of taking down statements, when a person's lying and when they're not. No, I think the girl's evidence is genuine, and if so Horbury *couldn't* have murdered old Mr. Lee, and that brings us right back to the people in the house.'

He drew a deep breath.

'One of 'em did it, Mr. Poirot. One of 'em did it. But *which*?'

'You have no new data?'

'Yes, I've had a certain amount of luck over the telephone calls. Mr. George Lee put through a call to Westeringham at two minutes to nine. That call lasted under six minutes.'

'Aha!'

'As you say! Moreover, *no other call* was put through—to Westeringham or anywhere else.'

'Very interesting,' said Poirot, with approval. 'M. George Lee says he has just finished telephoning when he hears the noise overhead—but actually he had finished telephoning nearly *ten minutes before that*. Where was he in those ten minutes? Mrs. George Lee says that *she* was telephoning—but actually she never put through a call at all. Where was *she*?'

Sugden said: 'I saw you talking to her, M. Poirot?'

His voice held a question, but Poirot replied:

'You are in error!'

'Eh?'

'*I* was not talking to *her*—she was talking to *me*!'

'Oh——' Sugden seemed to be about to brush the distinction aside impatiently; then, as its significance sank in, he said:

'*She* was talking to *you*, you say?'

'Most definitely. She came out here for that purpose.'

'What did she have to say?'

'She wished to stress certain points: the un-English character of the crime—the possibly undesirable antecedents of Miss Estravados on the paternal side—the fact that Miss Estravados had furtively picked up something from the floor last night.'

'She told you that, did she?' said Sugden with interest.

'Yes. What was it that the Señorita picked up?'

Sugden sighed.

'I could give you three hundred guesses! I'll show it to you. It's the sort of thing that solves the whole mystery in detective stories! If you can make anything out of it, I'll retire from the police force!'

'Show it me.'

Sugden took an envelope from his pocket and tilted its contents on to the palm of his hand. A faint grin showed on his face.

'There you are. What do you make of it?'

On the superintendent's broad palm lay a little triangular piece of pink rubber and a small wooden peg.

His grin broadened as Poirot picked up the articles and frowned over them.

'Make anything of them, Mr. Poirot?'

'This little piece of stuff might have been cut from a sponge-bag?'

'It was. It comes from a sponge-bag in Mr. Lee's room. Somebody with sharp scissors just cut a small triangular piece out of it.

Mr. Lee may have done it himself, for all I know. But it beats me *why* he should do it. Horbury can't throw any light on the matter. As for the peg, it's about the size of a cribbage peg, but they're usually made of ivory. This is just rough wood—whittled out of a bit of deal, I should say.'

'Most remarkable,' murmured Poirot.

'Keep 'em if you like,' said Sugden kindly. '*I* don't want them.'

'*Mon ami*, I would not deprive you of them!'

'They don't mean anything at all to you?'

'I must confess—nothing whatever!'

'Splendid!' said Sugden with heavy sarcasm, returning them to his pocket. 'We *are* getting on!'

Poirot said:

'Mrs. George Lee, she recounts that the young lady stooped and picked these bagatelles up in a furtive manner. Should you say that that was true?'

Sugden considered the point.

'N-o,' he said hesitatingly. 'I shouldn't quite go as far as that. She didn't look guilty—nothing of that kind—but she did set about it rather—well, quickly and quietly—if you know what I mean. *And she didn't know I'd seen her do it!* That I'm sure of. She jumped when I rounded on her.'

Poirot said thoughtfully:

'Then there *was* a reason? But what conceivable reason could there have been? That little piece of rubber is quite fresh. It has not been used for anything. It can have no meaning whatsoever; and yet——'

Sugden said impatiently:

'Well, you can worry about it if you like, Mr. Poirot. I've got other things to think about.'

Poirot asked:

'The case stands—where, in your opinion?'

Sugden took out his note-book.

'Let's get down to *facts*. To begin with, there are the people who *couldn't* have done it. Let's get them out of the way first——'

'They are?'

'Alfred and Harry Lee. They've got a definite *alibi*. Also Mrs. Alfred Lee, since Tressilian saw her in the drawing-room only about a minute before the row started upstairs. Those three are clear. Now for the others. Here's a list. I've put it this way for clearness.'

He handed the book to Poirot.

At the time of the crime

George Lee	*was*	*?*
Mrs. George Lee	*was*	*?*
David Lee	*was*	*playing piano in music-room (confirmed by his wife)*
Mrs. David Lee	*was*	*in music-room (confirmed by husband)*
Miss Estravados	*was*	*in her bedroom (no confirmation)*
Stephen Farr	*was*	*in ballroom playing gramophone (confirmed by three of staff who could hear the music in servants' hall).*

Poirot said, handing back the list:

'And therefore?'

'And therefore,' said Sugden, 'George Lee could have killed the old man. Mrs. George Lee could have killed him. Pilar Estravados could have killed him; and *either Mr. or Mrs. David Lee could have killed him,* but not *both*.'

'You do not, then, accept that alibi?'

Superintendent Sugden shook his head emphatically.

'Not on your life! Husband and wife—devoted to each other! They may be in it together, or if one of them did it, the other is ready to swear to an *alibi*. I look at it this way: *Someone* was in the music-room playing the piano. It *may* have been David Lee. It probably *was*, since he was an acknowledged musician, but there's nothing to say his wife was there too *except her word and his*. In the same way, it *may* have been Hilda Lee who was playing that piano while David Lee crept upstairs and killed his father! No, it's an absolutely different case from the two brothers in the dining-room. Alfred Lee and Harry Lee don't love each other. Neither of them would perjure himself for the other's sake.'

'What about Stephen Farr?'

'He's a possible suspect because that gramophone *alibi* is a bit thin. On the other hand, it's the sort of alibi that's really sounder than a good cast-iron dyed-in-the-wool alibi which ten to one has been faked up beforehand!'

Poirot bowed his head thoughtfully.

'I know what you mean. It is the alibi of a man *who did not know that he would be called upon to provide such a thing.*'

'Exactly! And anyway, somehow, I don't believe a stranger was mixed up in this thing.'

Poirot said quickly: 'I agree with you. It is here a *family* affair. It is a poison that works in the blood—it is intimate—it is deep-seated. There is here, I think, *hate* and *knowledge*. . . .'

He waved his hands.

'I do not know—it is difficult!'

Superintendent Sugden had waited respectfully, but without being much impressed.

He said:

'Quite so, Mr. Poirot. But we'll get at it, never fear, with elimination and logic. We've got the *possibilities* now—the people with *opportunity*. George Lee, Magdalene Lee, David Lee, Hilda Lee, Pilar Estravados, and I'll add Stephen Farr. Now we come to *motive*. Who had a *motive* for putting old Mr. Lee out of the way? There again we can wash out certain people. Miss Estravados, for one. I gather that as the will stands now, she doesn't get anything at all. If Simeon Lee had died before her mother, her mother's share would have come down to her (unless her mother willed it otherwise), but as Jennifer Estravados predeceased Simeon Lee, that particular legacy reverts to the other members of the family. So it was definitely to Miss Estravados' interests to keep the old man alive. He'd taken a fancy to her; it's pretty certain he'd have left her a good slice of money when he made a new will. She had everything to lose and nothing to gain by his murder. You agree to that?'

'Perfectly.'

'There remains, of course, the possibility that she cut his throat in the heat of a quarrel, but that seems extremely unlikely to me. To begin with, they were on the best of terms, and she hadn't been here long enough to bear him a grudge about anything. It therefore seems highly unlikely that Miss Estravados has anything to do with the crime—except that you might argue that to cut a man's throat is an un-English sort of thing to do, as your friend Mrs. George put it.'

'Do not call her *my* friend,' said Poirot hastily. 'Or I shall speak of *your* friend Miss Estravados, who finds you such a handsome man!'

He had the pleasure of seeing the superintendent's official poise upset again. The police officer turned crimson. Poirot looked at him with malicious amusement.

He said, and there was a wistful note in his voice:

'It is true that your moustache is superb. . . . Tell me, do you use for it a special *pomade?*'

'Pomade? Good Lord, no!'

'What do you use?'

'Use? Nothing at all. It—it just *grows*.'

Poirot sighed.

'You are favoured by nature.' He caressed his own luxuriant black moustache, then sighed. 'However expensive the preparation,' he murmured, 'to restore the natural colour does somewhat impoverish the quality of the hair.'

Superintendent Sugden, uninterested in hairdressing problems, was continuing in a stolid manner:

'Considering the *motive* for the crime, I should say that we can probably wash out Mr. Stephen Farr. It's just *possible* that there was some hanky-panky between his father and Mr. Lee and the former suffered, but I doubt it. Farr's manner was too easy and assured when he mentioned that subject. He was quite confident—and I don't think he was acting. No, I don't think we'll find anything there.'

'I do not think you will,' said Poirot.

'And there's one other person with a motive for keeping old Mr. Lee alive—his son Harry. It's true that he benefits under the will, but I don't believe *he was aware of the fact*. Certainly couldn't have been *sure* of it! The general impression seemed to be that Harry had been definitely cut out of his share of the inheritance at the time he cut loose. But now he was on the point of coming back into favour! It was all to his advantage that his father should make a new will. He wouldn't be such a fool as to kill him now. Actually, as we know, he *couldn't* have done it. You see, we're getting on; we're clearing quite a lot of people out of the way.'

'How true. Very soon there will be nobody left!'

Sugden grinned.

'We're not going as far as that! We've got George Lee and his wife, and David Lee and Mrs. David. They all benefit by the death, and George Lee, from all I can make out, is grasping about money. Moreover, his father was threatening to cut down supplies. So we've George Lee with motive *and* opportunity!'

'Continue,' said Poirot.

'And we've got Mrs. George! As fond of money as a cat is fond of cream; and I'd be prepared to bet she's heavily in debt at the minute! She was jealous of the Spanish girl. She was quick to spot that the other was gaining an ascendancy over the old man. She'd heard him say that he was sending for the lawyer. So she struck quickly. You could make out a case.'

'Possibly.'

'Then there's David Lee and his wife. They inherit under the present will, but I don't believe, somehow, that the money motive would be particularly strong in their case.'

'No?'

'No. David Lee seems to be a bit of a dreamer—not a mercenary type. But he's—well, he's *odd.* As I see it, there are three possible motives for this murder: There's the diamond complication, there's the will, and there's—well—just plain *hate.*'

'Ah, you see that, do you?'

Sugden said:

'Naturally. It's been present in my mind all along. *If* David Lee killed his father, I don't think it was for money. And if he was the criminal it might explain the—well, the blood-letting!'

Poirot looked at him appreciatively.

'Yes, I wondered when you would take that into consideration. *So much blood*—that is what Mrs. Alfred said. It takes one back to ancient rituals—to blood sacrifice, to the anointing with the blood of the sacrifice. . . .'

Sugden said, frowning:

'You mean whoever did it was mad?'

'*Mon cher*—there are all sorts of deep instincts in man of which he himself is unaware. The craving for blood—the demand for sacrifice!'

Sugden said doubtfully:

'David Lee looks a quiet, harmless fellow.'

Poirot said:

'You do not understand the psychology. David Lee is a man who lives in the past—a man in whom the memory of his mother is still very much alive. He kept away from his father for many years because he could not forgive his father's treatment of his mother. He came here, let us suppose, to forgive. *But he may not have been able to forgive*. . . . We do know one thing—that when David Lee stood by his father's dead body, some part of him was appeased and satisfied: *"The mills of God grind slowly, yet they grind exceeding small."* Retribution! Payment! The wrong wiped out by expiation!'

Sugden gave a sudden shudder. He said:

'Don't talk like that, Mr. Poirot. You give me quite a turn. It may be that it's as you say. If so, Mrs. David knows—and means to shield him all she knows how. I can imagine her doing that. On the other hand, I can't imagine her being a murderess. She's such a comfortable commonplace sort of woman.'

Poirot looked at him curiously.

'So she strikes you like that?' he murmured.

'Well, yes—a homely body, if you know what I mean!'

'Oh, I know what you mean perfectly!'

Sugden looked at him.

'Come, now, Mr. Poirot, you've got ideas about the case. Let's have them.'

Poirot said slowly:

'I have ideas, yes, but they are rather nebulous. Let me first hear your summing-up of the case.'

'Well, it's as I said—three possible motives: hate, gain, and this diamond complication. Take the facts chronologically.

'3.30. Family gathering. Telephone conversation to lawyer overheard by all the family. Then the old man lets loose on his family, tells them where they all get off. They slink out like a lot of scared rabbits.'

'Hilda Lee remained behind,' said Poirot.

'So she did. But not for long. Then about six Alfred has an interview with his father—unpleasant interview. Harry is to be reinstated. Alfred isn't pleased. Alfred, of course, *ought* to be our principal suspect. He had by far the strongest motive. However, to get on, Harry comes along next. Is in boisterous spirits. Has got the old man just where he wants him. But *before* those two interviews Simeon Lee has discovered the loss of the diamonds and has telephoned to me. He doesn't mention his loss to either of his two sons. Why? In my opinion because he was quite sure neither of them had anything to do with it. Neither of them was under suspicion. I believe, as I've said all along, that the old man suspected Horbury and *one other person*. And I'm pretty sure of what he meant to do. Remember, he said definitely he didn't want anyone to come and sit with him that evening. Why? Because he was preparing the way for two things: First my visit; and second, the visit of that other *suspected person*. He did ask *someone* to come and see him immediately after dinner. Now who was that person likely to be? Might have been George Lee. Much more likely to have been his wife. And there's another person who comes back into the picture here—Pilar Estravados. He's shown her the diamonds. He'd told her their value. How do we know that girl isn't a thief? Remember those mysterious hints about the disgraceful behaviour of her father? Perhaps *he* was a professional thief and finally went to prison for it.'

Poirot said slowly:

'And so, as you say, Pilar Estravados comes back into the picture. . . .'

'Yes—as a *thief*. No other way. She *may* have lost her head when she was found out. She *may* have flown at her grandfather and attacked him.'

Poirot said slowly: 'It is possible—yes. . . .'

Superintendent Sugden looked at him keenly.

'But that's not *your* idea? Come, Mr. Poirot, what *is* your idea?'

Poirot said:

'I go back always to the same thing: *the character of the dead man*. What manner of a man was Simeon Lee?'

'There isn't much mystery about that,' said Sugden, staring.

'Tell me, then. That is to say, tell me from the local point of view what was known of the man.'

Superintendent Sugden drew a doubtful finger along his jawbone. He looked perplexed. He said:

'I'm not a local man myself. I come from Reeveshire, over the border—next county. But of course old Mr. Lee was a well-known figure in these parts. I know all about him by hearsay.'

'Yes? And that hearsay was—what?'

Sugden said:

'Well, he was a sharp customer; there weren't many who could get the better of him. But he was generous with his money. Open-handed as they make 'em. Beats me how Mr. George Lee can be the exact opposite, and he his father's son.'

'Ah! But there are two distinct strains in the family. Alfred, George and David resemble—superficially at least—their mother's side of the family. I have been looking at some portraits in the gallery this morning.'

'He was hot-tempered,' continued Superintendent Sugden, 'and of course he had a bad reputation with women—that was in his younger days. He's been an invalid for many years now. But even there he always behaved generously. If there was trouble, he always paid up handsomely and got the girl married off as often as not. He may have been a bad lot, but he wasn't mean. He treated his wife badly, ran after other women, and neglected her. She died of a broken heart, so they say. It's a convenient term, but I believe she was really very unhappy, poor lady. She was always sickly and never went about much. There's no doubt that Mr. Lee was an odd character. Had a revengeful streak in him, too. If anyone did him a nasty turn he always paid it back, so they say, and didn't mind how long he had to wait to do it.'

'The mills of God grind slowly, yet they grind exceeding small,' murmured Poirot.

Superintendent Sugden said heavily.

'Mills of the devil, more likely! Nothing saintly about Simeon Lee. The kind of man you might say had sold his soul to the devil and enjoyed the bargain! And he was proud, too, proud as Lucifer.'

'Proud as Lucifer!' said Poirot. 'It is suggestive, what you say there.'

Superintendent Sugden said, looking puzzled:

'You don't mean that he was murdered because he was proud?'

'I mean,' said Poirot, 'that there is such a thing as inheritance. Simeon Lee transmitted that pride to his sons——'

He broke off. Hilda Lee had come out of the house and was standing looking along the terrace.

3

'I wanted to find you, M. Poirot.'

Superintendent Sugden had excused himself and gone back into the house. Looking after him, Hilda said:

'I didn't know he was with you. I thought he was with Pilar. He seems a nice man, quite considerate.'

Her voice was pleasant, a low, soothing cadence to it.

Poirot asked:

'You wanted to see me, you say?'

She inclined her head.

'Yes. I think you can help me.'

'I shall be delighted to do so, madame.'

She said:

'You are a very intelligent man, M. Poirot. I saw that last night. There are things which you will, I think, find out quite easily. I want you to understand my husband.'

'Yes, madame?'

'I shouldn't talk like this to Superintendent Sugden. He wouldn't understand. But you will.'

Poirot bowed. 'You honour me, madame.'

Hilda went calmly on:

'My husband, for many years, ever since I married him, has been what I can only describe as a mental cripple.'

'Ah!'

'When one suffers some great hurt physically, it causes shock and pain, but slowly it mends, the flesh heals, the bone knits. There may be, perhaps, a little weakness, a slight scar, but nothing more. My husband, M. Poirot, suffered a great hurt *mentally* at his most susceptible age. He adored his mother and he saw her die. He believed that his father was morally responsible for that death. From that shock he has never quite recovered. His resentment against his father never died down. It was I who persuaded David to come here this Christmas, to be reconciled to his father. I wanted it—for *his* sake—I wanted that mental wound to heal. I realise now that coming here was a mistake. Simeon Lee amused himself by probing into that old wound. It was—a very dangerous thing to do. . . .'

Poirot said:

'Are you telling me, madame, that your husband killed his father?'

'I am telling you, M. Poirot, that he easily *might* have done so. . . . And I will also tell you this—that he did *not*! When Simeon Lee was killed, his son was playing the "Dead March." The wish to kill was in his heart. It passed out through his fingers and died in waves of sound—that is the truth.'

Poirot was silent for a minute or two, then he said:

'And you, madame, what is your verdict on that past drama?'

'You mean the death of Simeon Lee's wife?'

'Yes.'

Hilda said slowly:

'I know enough of life to know that you can never judge any case on its outside merits. To all seeming, Simeon Lee was entirely to blame and his wife was abominably treated. At the same time, I honestly believe that there is a kind of meekness, a predisposition to martyrdom which does arouse the worst instincts in men of a certain type. Simeon Lee would have admired, I think, spirit and force of character. He was merely irritated by patience and tears.'

Poirot nodded. He said:

'Your husband said last night: "My mother never complained." Is that true?'

Hilda Lee said impatiently:

'Of course it isn't! She complained the whole time to David! She laid the whole burden of her unhappiness on his shoulders. He was too young—far too young to bear all she gave him to bear!'

Poirot looked thoughtfully at her. She flushed under his gaze and bit her lip.

He said:

'I see.'

She said sharply:

'What do you see?'

He answered:

'I see that you have had to be a mother to your husband when you would have preferred to be a wife.'

She turned away.

At that moment David Lee came out of the house and along the terrace towards them. He said, and his voice had a clear joyful note in it:

'Hilda, isn't it a glorious day? Almost like spring instead of winter.'

He came nearer. His head was thrown back, a lock of fair hair fell across his forehead, his blue eyes shone. He looked amazingly young and boyish. There was about him a youthful eagerness, a carefree radiance. Hercule Poirot caught his breath. . . .

David said:

'Let's go down to the lake, Hilda.'

She smiled, put her arm through his, and they moved off together.

As Poirot watched them go, he saw her turn and give him a rapid glance. He caught a momentary glimpse of swift anxiety—or was it, he wondered, fear?

Slowly Hercule Poirot walked to the other end of the terrace.

He murmured to himself:

'As I have always said, me, I am the father confessor! And since women come to confession more frequently than men, it is women who have come to me this morning. Will there, I wonder, be another very shortly?'

As he turned at the end of the terrace and paced back again, he knew that his question was answered. Lydia Lee was coming towards him.

4

Lydia said:

'Good-morning, M. Poirot. Tressilian told me I should find you out here with Harry; but I am glad to find you alone. My husband has been speaking about you. I know he is very anxious to talk to you.'

'Ah! Yes? Shall I go and see him now?'

'Not just yet. He got hardly any sleep last night. In the end I gave him a strong sleeping draught. He is still asleep, and I don't want to disturb him.'

'I quite understand. That was very wise. I could see last night that the shock had been very great.'

She said seriously:

'You see, M. Poirot, he really *cared*—much more than the others.'

'I understand.'

She asked:

'Have you—has the superintendent—any idea of who can have done this awful thing?'

Poirot said deliberately:

'We have certain ideas, madame, as to who did *not* do it.'

Lydia said, almost impatiently:

'It's like a nightmare—so fantastic—I can't believe it's *real*!'

She added:

'What about Horbury? Was he really at the cinema, as he said?'

'Yes, madame, his story has been checked. He was speaking the truth.'

Lydia stopped and plucked at a bit of yew. Her face went a little paler. She said:

'But that's *awful*! It only leaves—the family!'

'Exactly.'

'M. Poirot, I *can't* believe it!'

'Madame, you *can* and you *do* believe it!'

She seemed about to protest. Then suddenly she smiled ruefully. She said: 'What a hypocrite one is!'

He nodded.

'If you were to be frank with me, madame,' he said, 'you would admit that to you it seems quite natural that one of his family should murder your father-in-law.'

Lydia said sharply:

'That's really a fantastic thing to say, M. Poirot!'

'Yes, it is. But your father-in-law was a fantastic person!'

Lydia said:

'Poor old man. I can feel sorry for him now. When he was alive, he just annoyed me unspeakably!'

Poirot said:

'So I should imagine!'

He bent over one of the stone sinks.

'They are very ingenious, these. Very pleasing.'

'I'm glad you like them. It's one of my hobbies. Do you like this Arctic one with the penguins and the ice?'

'Charming. And this—what is this?'

'Oh, that's the Dead Sea—or going to be. It isn't finished yet. You mustn't look at it. Now this one is supposed to be Piana in Corsica. The rocks there, you know, are quite pink and too lovely where they go down into the blue sea. This desert scene is rather fun, don't you think?'

She led him along. When they had reached the farther end she glanced at her wrist-watch.

'I must go and see if Alfred is awake.'

When she had gone Poirot went slowly back again to the garden representing the Dead Sea. He looked at it with a good deal of interest. Then he scooped up a few of the pebbles and let them run through his fingers.

Suddenly his face changed. He held up the pebbles close to his face.

'Sapristi!' he said. 'This is a surprise! Now what exactly does this mean?'

PART FIVE

December 26th

1

THE CHIEF CONSTABLE and Superintendent Sugden stared at Poirot incredulously. The latter returned a stream of small pebbles carefully into a small cardboard box and pushed it across to the chief constable.

'Oh, yes,' he said. 'It is the diamonds all right.'

'And you found them where, did you say? In the garden?'

'In one of the small gardens constructed by Madame Alfred Lee.'

'Mrs. Alfred?' Sugden shook his head. 'Doesn't seem likely.'

Poirot said:

'You mean, I presume, that you do not consider it likely that Mrs. Alfred cut her father-in-law's throat?'

Sugden said quickly:

'We know she didn't do that. I meant it seemed unlikely that she pinched these diamonds.'

Poirot said:

'One would not easily believe her a thief—no.'

Sugden said:

'Anybody could have hidden them there.'

'That is true. It was convenient that in that particular garden—the Dead Sea as it represents—there happened to be pebbles very similar in shape and appearance.'

Sugden said:

'You mean she fixed it like that beforehand? Ready?'

Colonel Johnson said warmly:

'I don't believe it for a moment. Not for a moment. Why should she take the diamonds in the first place?'

'Well, as to that——' Sugden said slowly.

Poirot nipped in quickly:

'There is a possible answer to that. She took the diamonds to suggest a motive for the murder. That is to say she knew that murder was going to be done though she herself took no active part in it.'

Johnson frowned.

'That won't hold water for a minute. You're making her out to be an accomplice—but whose accomplice would she be likely to be? Only her husband's. But as we know that he, too, had nothing to do with the murder, the whole theory falls to the ground.'

Sugden stroked his jaw reflectively.

'Yes,' he said, 'that's so. No, if Mrs. Lee took the diamonds—and it's a big if—it was just plain robbery, and it's true she might have prepared that garden specially as a hiding-place for them till the hue and cry had died down. Another possibility is that of *coincidence*. That garden, with its similarity of pebbles, struck the thief, whoever he or she was, as an ideal hiding-place.'

Poirot said:

'That is quite possible. I am always prepared to admit *one* coincidence.'

Superintendent Sugden shook his head dubiously.

Poirot said:

'What is your opinion, Superintendent?'

The superintendent said cautiously:

'Mrs. Lee's a very nice lady. Doesn't seem likely that she'd be mixed up in any business that was fishy. But, of course, one never knows.'

Colonel Johnson said testily:

'In any case, whatever the truth is about the diamonds, her being mixed up in the murder is out of the question. The butler saw her in the drawing-room at the actual time of the crime. You remember that, Poirot?'

Poirot said:

'I had not forgotten that.'

The chief constable turned to his subordinate.

'We'd better get on. What have you got to report? Anything fresh?'

'Yes, sir. I've got hold of some new information. To start with—Horbury. There's a reason why he might be scared of the police.'

'Robbery? Eh?'

'No, sir. Extorting money under threats. Modified blackmail. The case couldn't be proved so he got off, but I rather fancy he's got away with a thing or two in that line. Having a guilty conscience, he probably thought we were on to something of that kind when Tressilian mentioned a police officer last night and it made him get the wind up.'

The chief constable said:

'H'm! So much for Horbury. What else?'

The superintendent coughed.

'Er—Mrs. George Lee, sir. We've got a line on her before her marriage. Was living with a Commander Jones. Passed as his daughter—but she *wasn't* his daughter. . . . I think from what we've been told, that old Mr. Lee summed her up pretty correctly—he was smart where women were concerned, knew a bad lot when he saw one—and was just amusing himself by taking a shot in the dark. *And* he got her on the raw!'

Colonel Johnson said thoughtfully:

'That gives her another possible motive—apart from the money angle. She may have thought he knew something definite and was going to give her away to her husband. That telephone story of hers is pretty fishy. She *didn't* telephone.'

Sugden suggested:

'Why not have them in together, sir, and get at that telephone business straight? See what we get.'

Colonel Johnson said:

'Good idea.'

He rang the bell. Tressilian answered it.

'Ask Mr. and Mrs. George Lee to come here.'

'Very good, sir.'

As the old man turned away, Poirot said:

'The date on that wall calendar, has it remained like it is since the murder?'

Tressilian turned back.

'Which calendar, sir?'

'The one on the wall over there.'

The three men were sitting once more in Alfred Lee's small sitting-room. The calendar in question was a large one with tear-off leaves, a bold date on each leaf.

Tressilian peered across the room, then shuffled slowly across till he was a foot or two away.

He said:

'Excuse me, sir, it has been torn off. It's the twenty-sixth to-day.'

'Ah, pardon. Who would have been the person to tear it off?'

'Mr. Lee does, sir, every morning. Mr. Alfred, he's a very methodical gentleman.'

'I see. Thank you.'

Tressilian went out. Sugden said, puzzled:

'Is there anything fishy about that calendar, Mr. Poirot? Have I missed something there?'

With a shrug of his shoulders Poirot said:

'The calendar is of no importance. It was just a little experiment I was making.'

Colonel Johnson said:

'Inquest to-morrow. There'll be an adjournment, of course.'

Sugden said:

'Yes, sir, I've seen the Coroner and it's all arranged for.'

2

George Lee came into the room, accompanied by his wife.

Colonel Johnson said:

'Good-morning. Sit down, will you? There are a few questions I want to ask you both. Something I'm not quite clear about.'

'I shall be glad to give you any assistance I can,' said George somewhat pompously.

Magdalene said faintly: 'Of course!'

The chief constable gave a slight nod to Sugden. The latter said:

'About those telephone calls on the night of the crime. You put through a call to Westeringham, I think you said, Mr. Lee?'

George said coldly:

'Yes, I did. To my agent in the constituency. I can refer you to him and——'

Superintendent Sugden held up his hand to stem the flow.

'Quite so—quite so, Mr. Lee. We're not disputing that point. Your call went through at 8.59 exactly.'

'Well—I—er—couldn't say as to the exact time.'

'Ah,' said Sugden. 'But we can! We always check up on these things very carefully. Very carefully indeed. The call was put through at 8.59 and it was terminated at 9.4. Your father, Mr. Lee, was killed about 9.15. I must ask you once more for an account of your movements.'

'I've told you—I was telephoning!'

'No, Mr. Lee, you weren't.'

'Nonsense—you must have made a mistake! Well, I may, perhaps, have just finished telephoning—I think I debated making another call—was just considering whether it was—er—worth—the expense—when I heard the noise upstairs.'

'You would hardly debate whether or not to make a telephone call for ten minutes.'

George went purple. He began to splutter.

'What do you mean? What the devil do you mean? Damned impudence! Are you doubting my word? Doubting the word of a man of my position. I—er—why should I have to account for every minute of my time?'

Superintendent Sugden said with a stolidness that Poirot admired:

'It's usual.'

George turned angrily on the chief constable.

'Colonel Johnson. Do you countenance this—this unprecedented attitude?'

The chief constable said crisply:

'In a murder case, Mr. Lee, these questions must be asked—*and answered.*'

'I have answered them! I had finished telephoning and was—er—deliberating a further call.'

'You were in this room when the alarm was raised upstairs?'

'I was—yes, I was.'

Johnson turned to Magdalene.

'I think, Mrs. Lee,' he said, 'that you stated that *you* were telephoning when the alarm broke out, and that at the time you were alone in this room?'

Magdalene was flustered. She caught her breath, looked sideways at George—at Sugden, then appealingly at Colonel Johnson. She said:

'Oh, really—I don't know—I don't remember what I said . . . I was so *upset* . . .'

Sugden said:

'We've got it all written down, you know.'

She turned her batteries on him—wide appealing eyes—quivering mouth. But she met in return the rigid aloofness of a man of stern respectability who didn't approve of her type.

She said uncertainly:

'I—I—of course I telephoned. I can't be quite sure just *when*——'

She stopped.

George said:

'What's all this? Where did you telephone from? Not in here.'

Superintendent Sugden said:

'I suggest, Mrs. Lee, that *you didn't telephone at all.* In that case, where were you and what were you doing?'

Magdalene glanced distractedly about her and burst into tears. She sobbed:

'George, don't let them bully me! You know that if anyone frightens me and thunders questions at me, I can't remember anything *at all*! I—I didn't know *what* I was saying that night—it was all so horrible—and I was so upset—and they're being so beastly to me. . . .'

She jumped up and ran sobbing out of the room.

Springing up, George Lee blustered:

'What d'you mean? I won't have my wife bullied and frightened out of her life! She's very sensitive. It's disgraceful! I shall have a question asked in the House about the disgraceful bullying methods of the police. It's absolutely disgraceful!'

He strode out of the room and banged the door.

Superintendent Sugden threw his head back and laughed.

He said:

'We've got them going properly! Now we'll see!'

Johnson said frowning:

'Extraordinary business! Looks fishy. We must get a further statement out of her.'

Sugden said easily:

'Oh! she'll be back in a minute or two. When she's decided what to say. Eh, Mr. Poirot?'

Poirot, who had been sitting in a dream, gave a start.

'*Pardon?*'

'I said she'll be back.'

'Probably—yes, possibly—oh, yes!'

Sugden said, staring at him:

'What's the matter, Mr. Poirot? Seen a ghost?'

Poirot said slowly:

'You know—I am not sure that I have not done *just exactly that*.'

Colonel Johnson said impatiently:

'Well, Sugden, anything else?'

Sugden said:

'I've been trying to check up on the order in which everyone arrived on the scene of the murder. It's quite clear what must have happened. After the murder when the victim's dying cry had given the alarm, the murderer slipped out, locked the door with pliers, or something of that kind, and a moment or two later became one of the people hurrying *to* the scene of the crime. Unfortunately it's not easy to check exactly whom everyone has seen because people's memories aren't very accurate on a point like that. Tressilian says he saw Harry and Alfred Lee cross the hall from the dining-room and race upstairs. That lets them out, but we don't suspect them anyway. As far as I can make out, Miss Estravados got there late—one of the last. The general idea seems to be that Farr, Mrs. George and Mrs. David were the first. Each of those three says one of the others was just ahead of them. That's what's so difficult, you can't distinguish between a deliberate lie and a genuine haziness of recollection. Everybody ran there—that's agreed, but in what order they ran isn't so easy to get at.'

Poirot said slowly:

'You think that important?'

Sugden said:

'It's the time element. The time, remember, was incredibly short.'

Poirot said:

'I agree with you that the time element is very important in this case.'

Sugden went on:

'What makes it more difficult is that there are two staircases. There's the main one in the hall here about equidistant from the dining-room and the drawing-room doors. Then there's one the other end of the house. Stephen Farr came up by the latter. Miss Estravados came along the upper landing from that end of the house (her room is right the other end). The others say they went up by this one.'

Poirot said:

'It is a confusion, yes.'

The door opened and Magdalene came quickly in. She was breathing fast and had a bright spot of colour in each cheek. She came up to the table and said quietly:

'My husband thinks I'm lying down. I slipped out of my room

quietly. Colonel Johnson,' she appealed to him with wide, distressed eyes, 'if I tell you the truth you *will* keep quiet about it, won't you? I mean you don't have to make *everything* public?'

Colonel Johnson said:

'You mean, I take it, Mrs. Lee, something that has no connection with the crime?'

'Yes, no connection at all. Just something in my—my private life.'

The chief constable said:

'You'd better make a clean breast of it, Mrs. Lee, and leave us to judge.'

Magdalene said, her eyes swimming:

'Yes, I will trust you. I know I can. You look so kind. You see, it's like this. There's somebody——' She stopped.

'Yes, Mrs. Lee?'

'I wanted to telephone to somebody last night—a man—a friend of mine, and I didn't want George to know about it. I know it was very wrong of me—but well, it was like that. So I went to telephone after dinner when I thought George would be safely in the dining-room. But when I got here I heard him telephoning, so I waited.'

'Where did you wait, madame?' asked Poirot.

'There's a place for coats and things behind the stairs. It's dark there. I slipped back there, where I could see George come out from this room. But he didn't come out, and then all the noise happened and Mr. Lee screamed, and I ran upstairs.'

'So your husband did not leave this room until the moment of the murder?'

'No.'

The chief constable said:

'And you yourself from nine o'clock to nine-fifteen were waiting in the recess behind the stairs?'

'Yes, but I couldn't *say* so, you see! They'd want to know what I was doing there. It's been very, very awkward for me, you *do* see that, *don't* you?'

Johnson said dryly: 'It was certainly awkward.'

She smiled at him sweetly.

'I'm *so* relieved to have told you the truth. And you *won't* tell my husband, will you? No, I'm sure you won't! I can trust you, all of you.'

She included them all in her final pleading look, then she slipped quickly out of the room.

Colonel Johnson drew a deep breath.

'Well,' he said. 'It *might* be like that! It's a perfectly plausible story. On the other hand——'

'It might not,' finished Sugden. 'That's just it. We don't know.'

3

Lydia Lee stood by the far window of the drawing-room looking out. Her figure was half hidden by the heavy window curtains. A sound in the room made her turn with a start to see Hercule Poirot standing by the door.

She said: 'You startled me, M. Poirot.'

'I apologise, madame. I walk softly.'

She said:

'I thought it was Horbury.'

Hercule Poirot nodded.

'It is true, he steps softly, that one—like a cat—or a *thief*.'

He paused a minute, watching her.

Her face showed nothing, but she made a slight grimace of distaste as she said:

'I have never cared for that man. I shall be glad to get rid of him.'

'I think you will be wise to do so, madame.'

She looked at him quickly. She said:

'What do you mean? Do you know anything against him?'

Poirot said:

'He is a man who collects secrets—and uses them to his advantage.'

She said sharply:

'Do you think he knows anything—about the murder?'

Poirot shrugged his shoulders.

He said:

'He has quiet feet and long ears. He may have overheard something that he is keeping to himself.'

Lydia said clearly:

'Do you mean that he may try to blackmail one of us?'

'It is within the bounds of possibility. But that is not what I came here to say."

'What did you come to say?'

Poirot said slowly:

'I have been talking with M. Alfred Lee. He has made to me a proposition, and I wished to discuss it with you before accepting or declining it. But I was so struck by the picture you made—the charming pattern of your jumper against the deep red of the curtains, that I paused to admire.'

Lydia said sharply:

'Really, M. Poirot, must we waste time in compliments?'

'I beg your pardon, madame. So few English ladies understand *la toilette*. The dress you were wearing the first night I saw you, its bold but simple pattern, it had grace—distinction.'

Lydia said impatiently:

'What was it you wanted to see me about?'

Poirot became grave.

'Just this, madame. Your husband, he wishes me to take up the investigation very seriously. He demands that I stay here, in the house, and do my utmost to get to the bottom of the matter.'

Lydia said sharply:

'Well?'

Poirot said slowly:

'I would not wish to accept an invitation that was not endorsed by the lady of the house.'

She said coldly:

'Naturally I endorse my husband's invitation.'

'Yes, madame, but I need more than that. Do you really *want* me to come here?'

'Why not?'

'Let us be more frank. What I ask you is this: do you want the truth to come out, or not?'

'Naturally.'

Poirot sighed.

'Must you return me these conventional replies?'

Lydia said:

'I am a conventional woman.'

Then she bit her lip, hesitated, and said:

'Perhaps it is better to speak frankly. Of course I understand you! The position is not a pleasant one. My father-in-law has been brutally murdered, and unless a case can be made out against the most likely suspect—Horbury—for robbery and murder—and it seems that it cannot—then it comes to this—*one of his own family killed him*. To bring that person to justice will mean bringing shame and disgrace on us all. . . . If I am to speak honestly I must say that I do *not* want this to happen.'

Poirot said:

'You are content for the murderer to escape unpunished?'

'There are probably several undiscovered murderers at large in the world.'

'That, I grant you.'

'Does one more matter, then?'

Poirot said:

'And what about the other members of the family? The innocent?'

She stared.

'What about them?'

'Do you realise that if it turns out as you hope, *no one will ever know*. The shadow will remain on all alike. . . .'

She said uncertainly:

'I hadn't thought of that.'

Poirot said:

'*No one will ever know who the guilty person is. . . .*'

He added softly:

'Unless *you* already know, madame?'

She cried out:

'You have no business to say that! It's not true! Oh! If only it could be a stranger—not a member of the family.'

Poirot said:

'It might be both.'

She stared at him.

'What do you mean?'

'It might be a member of the family—and at the same time a stranger. . . . You do not see what I mean? *Eh bien*, it is an idea that has occurred to the mind of Hercule Poirot.'

He looked at her.

'Well, madame, what am I to say to Mr. Lee?'

Lydia raised her hands and let them fall in a sudden helpless gesture.

She said:

'Of course—you must accept.'

4

Pilar stood in the centre of the music-room. She stood very straight, her eyes darting from side to side like an animal who fears an attack.

She said:

'I want to get away from here!'

Stephen Farr said gently:

'You're not the only one who feels like that. But they won't let us go, my dear.'

'You mean—the police?'

'Yes.'

Pilar said very seriously:

'It is not nice to be mixed up with the police. It is a thing that should not happen to respectable people.'

Stephen said with a faint smile:

'Meaning yourself?'

Pilar said:

'No, I mean Alfred and Lydia and David and George and Hilda and—yes—Magdalene, too.'

Stephen lit a cigarette. He puffed at it for a moment or two before saying:

'Why the exception?'

'What is that, please?'

Stephen said:

'Why leave out brother Harry?'

Pilar laughed, her teeth showing white and even.

'Oh, Harry is different! I think he knows very well what it is to be mixed up with the police.'

'Perhaps you are right. He certainly is a little too picturesque to blend well into the domestic picture.'

He went on:

'Do you like your English relations, Pilar?'

Pilar said doubtfully:

'They are kind—they are all very kind. But they do not laugh much, they are not gay.'

'My dear girl, there's just been a murder in the house!'

'Y—es,' said Pilar doubtfully.

'A murder,' said Stephen instructively, 'is not such an everyday occurrence as your nonchalance seems to imply. In England they take their murders seriously whatever they may do in Spain.'

Pilar said:

'You are laughing at me. . . .'

Stephen said:

'You're wrong. I'm not in a laughing mood.'

Pilar looked at him and said:

'Because you, too, wish to get away from here?'

'Yes.'

'And the big, handsome policeman will not let you go?'

'I haven't asked him. But if I did, I've no doubt he'd say no. I've got to watch my step, Pilar, and be very, very careful.'

'That is tiresome,' said Pilar, nodding her head.

'It's just a little bit more than tiresome, my dear. Then there's that lunatic foreigner prowling about. I don't suppose he's any good but he makes me feel jumpy.'

Pilar was frowning. She said:

'My grandfather was very, very rich, was he not?'

'I should imagine so.'

'Where does his money go to now? To Alfred and the others?'

'Depends on his will.'

Pilar said thoughtfully:

'He might have left me some money, but I am afraid that perhaps he did not.'

Stephen said kindly:

'You'll be all right. After all, you're one of the family. You belong here. They'll have to look after you.'

Pilar said with a sigh:

'I—belong here. It is very funny, that. And yet it is not funny at all.'

'I can see that you mightn't find it very humorous.'

Pilar sighed again. She said:

'Do you think if we put on the gramophone, we could dance?'

Stephen said dubiously:

'It wouldn't look any too good. This is a house of mourning, you callous Spanish baggage.'

Pilar said, her big eyes opening very wide:

'But I do not feel sad at all. Because I did not really know my grandfather, and though I liked to talk to him, I do not want to cry and be unhappy because he is dead. It is very silly to pretend.'

Stephen said:

'You're adorable!'

Pilar said coaxingly:

'We could put some stockings and some gloves in the gramophone, and then it would not make much noise, and no one would hear.'

'Come along then, temptress.'

She laughed happily and ran out of the room, going along towards the ballroom at the far end of the house.

Then, as she reached the side passage which led to the garden door, she stopped dead. Stephen caught up with her and stopped also.

Hercule Poirot had unhooked a portrait from the wall and was studying it by the light from the terrace. He looked up and saw them.

'Aha!' he said. 'You arrive at an opportune moment.'

Pilar said: 'What are you doing?'

She came and stood beside him.

Poirot said gravely:

'I am studying something very important, the face of Simeon Lee when he was a young man.'

'Oh, is that my grandfather?'

'Yes, mademoiselle.'

She stared at the painted face. She said slowly:

'How different—how very different. . . . He was so old, so shrivelled up. Here he is like Harry, like Harry might have been ten years ago.'

Hercule Poirot nodded.

'Yes, mademoiselle. Harry Lee is very much the son of his father. Now here——' He led her a little way along the gallery. 'Here is madame, your grandmother—a long gentle face, very blonde hair, mild blue eyes.'

Pilar said:

'Like David.'

Stephen said:

'Just a look of Alfred too.'

Poirot said:

'The heredity, it is very interesting. Mr. Lee and his wife were diametrically opposite types. On the whole the children of the marriage took after the mother. See here, mademoiselle.'

He pointed to a picture of a girl of nineteen or so, with hair like spun gold and wide, laughing blue eyes. The colouring was that of Simeon Lee's wife, but there was a spirit, a vivacity that those mild blue eyes and placid features had never known.

'Oh!' said Pilar.

The colour came up in her face.

Her hand went to her neck. She drew out a locket on a long gold chain. She pressed the catch and it flew open. The same laughing face looked up at Poirot.

'My mother,' said Pilar.

Poirot nodded. On the opposite side of the locket was the portrait of a man. He was young and handsome, with black hair and dark blue eyes.

Poirot said:

'Your father?'

Pilar said:

'Yes, my father. He is very beautiful, is he not?'

'Yes, indeed. Few Spaniards have blue eyes, have they, señorita?'

'Sometimes, in the North. Besides, my father's mother was Irish.'

Poirot said thoughtfully:

'So you have Spanish blood, and Irish and English, and a touch of gipsy too. Do you know what I think, mademoiselle? With that inheritance, you should make a bad enemy.'

Stephen said, laughing:

'Remember what you said in the train, Pilar? That your way of dealing with your enemies would be to cut their throats. Oh!'

He stopped—suddenly realising the import of his words.

Hercule Poirot was quick to lead the conversation away. He said:

'Ah, yes, there was something, señorita, I had to ask you. Your passport. It is needed by my friend the superintendent. There are, you know, police regulations—very stupid, very tiresome, but necessary—for a foreigner in this country. And of course, by law you are a foreigner.'

Pilar's eyebrows rose.

'My passport? Yes, I will get it. It is in my room.'

Poirot said apologetically as he walked by her side.

'I am most sorry to trouble you. I am indeed.'

They had reached the end of the long gallery. Here was a flight of stairs. Pilar ran up and Poirot followed. Stephen came too. Pilar's bedroom was just at the head of the stairs.

She said as she reached the door.

'I will get it for you.'

She went in. Poirot and Stephen Farr remained waiting outside.

Stephen said remorsefully:

'Damn' silly of me to say a thing like that. I don't think she noticed, though, do you?'

Poirot did not answer. He held his head a little on one side as though listening.

He said:

'The English are extraordinarily fond of fresh air. Miss Estravados must have inherited that characteristic.'

Stephen said staring:

'Why?'

Poirot said softly:

'Because though it is to-day extremely cold—the black frost you call it (not like yesterday so mild and sunny) Miss Estravados has just flung up her lower window-sash. Amazing to love so much the fresh air.'

Suddenly there was an exclamation in Spanish from inside the room and Pilar reappeared laughingly dismayed.

'Ah!' she cried. 'But I am stupid—and clumsy. My little case it was on the window-sill, and I was sorting through it so quickly and very stupidly I knock my passport out of the window. It is down on the flower-bed below. I will get it.'

'I'll get it,' said Stephen, but Pilar had flown past him and cried back over her shoulder:

'No, it was my stupidity. You go to the drawing-room with M. Poirot and I will bring it to you there.'

Stephen Farr seemed inclined to go after her, but Poirot's hand fell gently on his arm and Poirot's voice said:

'Let us go this way.'

They went along the first floor corridor towards the other end of the house until they got to the head of the main staircase. Here Poirot said:

'Let us not go down for a minute. If you will come with me to the room of the crime there is something I want to ask you.'

They went along the corridor which led to Simeon Lee's room. On their left they passed an alcove which contained two marble statues, stalwart nymphs clasping their draperies in an agony of Victorian propriety.

Stephen Farr glanced at them and murmured:

'Pretty frightful by daylight. I thought there were three of them when I came along the other night, but thank goodness there are only two!'

'They are not what is admired nowadays,' admitted Poirot. 'But no doubt they cost much money in their time. They look better by night, I think.'

'Yes, one sees only a white glimmering figure.'

Poirot murmured:

'All cats are grey in the dark!'

They found Superintendent Sugden in the room. He was kneeling by the safe and examining it with a magnifying-glass. He looked up as they entered.

'This was opened with the key all right,' he said. 'By someone who knew the combination. No sign of anything else.'

Poirot went up to him, drew him aside and whispered something. The superintendent nodded and left the room.

Poirot turned to Stephen Farr, who was standing staring at the arm-chair in which Simeon Lee always sat. His brows were drawn together and the veins showed in his forehead. Poirot looked at him for a minute or two in silence, then he said:

'You have the memories—yes?'

Stephen said slowly:

'Two days ago he sat there alive—and now . . .'

Then, shaking off his absorption, he said:

'Yes, M. Poirot, you brought me here to ask me something?'

'Ah yes. You were, I think, the first person to arrive on the scene that night?'

'Was I? I don't remember. No, I think one of the ladies was here before me.'

'Which lady?'

'One of the wives—George's wife or David's—I know they were both here pretty soon.'

'You did not hear the scream, I think you said?'

'I don't think I did. I can't quite remember. Somebody did cry out but that may have been someone downstairs.'

Poirot said:

'You did not hear a noise like this?'

He threw his head back and suddenly gave vent to a piercing yell.

It was so unexpected that Stephen started backwards and nearly fell over. He said angrily:

'For the Lord's sake, do you want to scare the whole house? No, I didn't hear anything in the least like that! You'll have the whole place by the ears again! They'll think another murder has happened!'

Poirot looked crestfallen. He murmured:

'True . . . it was foolish . . . We must go at once.'

He hurried out of the room. Lydia and Alfred were at the foot of the stairs peering up—George came out of the library to join them, and Pilar came running, a passport held in her hand.

Poirot cried:

'It is nothing—nothing. Do not be alarmed. A little experiment that I make. That was all.'

Alfred looked annoyed and George indignant. Poirot left Stephen to explain and he hurriedly slipped away along the passage to the other end of the house.

At the end of the passage Superintendent Sugden came quietly out of Pilar's door and met Poirot.

'*Eh bien?*' asked Poirot.

The superintendent shook his head.

'Not a sound.'

His eyes met Poirot's appreciatively and he nodded.

5

Alfred Lee said:

'Then you accept, M. Poirot?'

His hand, as it went to his mouth, shook slightly. His mild brown eyes were alight with a new and feverish expression. He stammered slightly in his speech. Lydia, standing silently by, looked at him with some anxiety.

Alfred said:

'You don't know—you c-c-can't imagine—what it m-m-means to me. . . . My father's murderer *must* be f-f-found.'

Poirot said:

'Since you have assured me that you have reflected long and carefully—yes, I accept. But you comprehend, Mr. Lee, there can be no drawing back. I am not the dog one sets on to hunt and then recalls because you do not like the game he puts up!'

'Of course . . . of course. . . . Everything is ready. Your bedroom is prepared. Stay as long as you like——'

Poirot said gravely:

'It will not be long.'

'Eh? What's that?'

'I said it will not be long. There is in this crime such a restricted circle that it cannot possibly take long to arrive at the truth. Already, I think, the end draws near.'

Alfred stared at him.

'Impossible!' he said.

'Not at all. The facts all point more or less clearly in one direction. There is just some irrelevant matter to be cleared out of the way. When that is done the truth will appear.'

Alfred said incredulously:

'You mean you *know*?'

Poirot smiled.

'Oh, yes,' he said. 'I know.'

Alfred said:

'My father—my father——' He turned away.

Poirot said briskly:

'There are, M. Lee, two requests that I have to make.'

Alfred said in a muffled voice:

'Anything—anything.'

'Then, in the first place, I would like the portrait of M. Lee as a young man placed in the bedroom you are good enough to allot to me.'

Alfred and Lydia stared at him.

The former said:

'My father's portrait—but why?'

Poirot said with a wave of the hand:

'It will—how shall I say—inspire me?'

Lydia said sharply:

'Do you propose, M. Poirot, to solve a crime by clairvoyance?'

'Let us say, madame, that I intend to use not only the eyes of the body, but the eyes of the mind.'

She shrugged her shoulders.

Poirot continued:

'Next, M. Lee, I should like to know of the true circumstances attending the death of your sister's husband, Juan Estravados.'

Lydia said:

'Is that necessary?'

'I want all the facts, madame.'

Alfred said:

'Juan Estravados, as the result of a quarrel about a woman, killed another man in a café.'

'How did he kill him?'

Alfred looked appealingly at Lydia. She said evenly:

'He stabbed him. Juan Estravados was not condemned to death, as there had been provocation. He was sentenced to a term of imprisonment and died in prison.'

'Does his daughter know about her father?'

'I think not.'

Alfred said:

'No, Jennifer never told her.'

'Thank you.'

Lydia said:

'You don't think that Pilar—— Oh, it's absurd!'

Poirot said:

'Now, M. Lee, will you give me some facts about your brother, M. Harry Lee?'

'What do you want to know?'

'I understand that he was considered somewhat of a disgrace to the family. Why?'

Lydia said:

'It is so long ago . . .'

Alfred said, the colour coming up in his face:

'If you want to know, M. Poirot, he stole a large sum of money by forging my father's name to a cheque. Naturally my father didn't prosecute. Harry's always been crooked. He's been in trouble all over the world. Always cabling for money to get out of a scrape. He's been in and out of gaol here, there and everywhere.'

Lydia said:

'You don't really *know* all this, Alfred.'

Alfred said angrily, his hands shaking:

'Harry's no good—no good whatever! He never has been!'

Poirot said:

'There is, I see, no love lost between you?'

Alfred said:

'He victimised my father—victimised him shamefully!'

Lydia sighed—a quick, impatient sigh. Poirot heard it and gave her a sharp glance.

She said:

'If only those diamonds could be found. I'm sure the solution lies there.'

Poirot said:

'*They have been found,* madame.'

'What?'

Poirot said gently:

'They were found in your little garden of the Dead Sea. . . .'

Lydia cried:

'In my garden? How—how extraordinary!'

Poirot said softly:

'Is it not, madame?'

PART SIX

December 27th

1

ALFRED LEE said with a sigh:

'That was better than I feared!'

They had just returned from the inquest.

Mr. Charlton, an old-fashioned type of solicitor with a cautious blue eye, had been present and had returned with them. He said:

'Ah—I told you the proceedings would be purely formal—purely formal—there was bound to be an adjournment—to enable the police to gather up additional evidence.'

George Lee said vexedly:

'It is all most unpleasant—really *most* unpleasant—a terrible position in which to be placed! I myself am quite convinced that this crime was done by a maniac who somehow or other gained admittance to the house. That man Sugden is as obstinate as a mule. Colonel Johnson should enlist the aid of Scotland Yard. These local police are no good. Thick-headed. What about this man Horbury, for instance? I hear his past is definitely unsatisfactory but the police do nothing whatever about it.'

Mr. Charlton said:

'Ah—I believe the man Horbury has a satisfactory alibi covering the period of time in question. The police have accepted it.'

'Why should they?' George fumed. 'If I were they, I should accept such an alibi with reserve—with great reserve. Naturally a criminal always provides himself with an alibi! It is the duty of the police to break down the alibi—that is, if they know their job.'

'Well, well,' said Mr. Charlton. 'I don't think it's quite our business to teach the police their jobs, eh? Pretty competent body of men on the whole.'

George shook his head darkly.

'Scotland Yard should be called in. I'm not at all satisfied with Superintendent Sugden—he may be painstaking—but he is certainly far from brilliant.'

Mr. Charlton said:

'I don't agree with you, you know. Sugden's a good man. Doesn't throw his weight about, but he gets there.'

Lydia said:

'I'm sure the police are doing their best. Mr. Charlton, will you have a glass of sherry?'

Mr. Charlton thanked her politely, but declined. Then, clearing his throat, he proceeded to the reading of the will, all members of the family being assembled.

He read it with a certain relish, lingering over its more obscure phraseology, and savouring its legal technicalities.

He came to the end, took off his glasses, wiped them and looked round on the assembled company inquiringly.

Harry Lee said:

'All this legal stuff's a bit hard to follow. Give us the bare bones of it, will you?'

'Really,' said Mr. Charlton. 'It's a perfectly simple will.'

Harry said:

'My God, what's a difficult will like, then?'

Mr. Charlton rebuked him with a cold glance. He said:

'The main provisions of the will are quite simple. Half Mr. Lee's property goes to his son, Mr. Alfred Lee, the remainder is divided between his other children.'

Harry laughed unpleasantly. He said:

'As usual, Alfred's struck lucky! Half my father's fortune! Lucky dog, aren't you, Alfred?'

Alfred flushed. Lydia said sharply:

'Alfred was a loyal and devoted son to his father. He's managed the works for years and has had all the responsibility.'

Harry said:

'Oh, yes, Alfred was always the good boy.'

Alfred said sharply:

'You may consider *yourself* lucky, I think, Harry, that my father left you anything at all!'

Harry laughed, throwing his head back. He said:

'You'd have liked it better if he'd cut me right out, wouldn't you? You've always disliked me.'

Mr. Charlton coughed. He was used—only too well used—to the painful scenes that succeeded the reading of a will. He was anxious to get away before the usual family quarrel got too well under way.

He murmured:

'I think—er—that that is all that I need—er——'

Harry said sharply:

'What about Pilar?'

Mr. Charlton coughed again, this time apologetically.

'Er—Miss Estravados is not mentioned in the will.'

Harry said:

'Doesn't she get her mother's share?'

Mr. Charlton explained.

'Señora Estravados, if she had lived, would of course have received an equal share with the rest of you, but as she is dead, the portion that would have been hers goes back into the estate to be shared out between you.'

Pilar said slowly in her rich Southern voice:

'Then—I—have—nothing?'

Lydia said quickly:

'My dear, the family will see to that, of course.'

George Lee said:

'You will be able to make your home here with Alfred—eh, Alfred? We—er—you are our niece—it is our duty to look after you.'

Hilda said:

'We shall always be glad to have Pilar with us.'

Harry said:

'She ought to have her proper share. She ought to have Jennifer's whack.'

Mr. Charlton murmured:

'Must really—er—be going. Good-bye, Mrs. Lee—anything I can do—er—consult me at any time. . . .'

He escaped quickly. His experience enabled him to predict that all the ingredients for a family row were present.

As the door shut behind him Lydia said in her clear voice:

'I agree with Harry. I think Pilar is entitled to a definite share. This will was made many years before Jennifer's death.'

'Nonsense,' said George. 'Very slipshod and illegal way of thinking, Lydia. The law's the law. We must abide by it.'

Magdalene said:

'It's hard luck, of course, and we're all very sorry for Pilar, but George is right. As he says, the law is the law.'

Lydia got up. She took Pilar by the hand.

'My dear,' she said. 'This must be very unpleasant for you. Will you please leave us while we discuss the question?'

She led the girl to the door.

'Don't worry, Pilar, dear,' she said. 'Leave it to me.'

Pilar went slowly out of the room. Lydia shut the door behind her and turned back.

There was a moment's pause while everyone drew breath and in another moment the battle was in full swing.

Harry said: 'You've always been a damned skinflint, George.'

George retorted:

'At any rate, I've not been a sponge and a rotter!'

'You've been just as much of a sponge as I have! You've battened on father all these years.'

'You seem to forget that I hold a responsible and arduous position which——'

Harry said:

'Responsible and arduous my foot! You're only an inflated gasbag!'

Magdalene screamed.

'How dare you?'

Hilda's calm voice, slightly raised, said:

'Couldn't we just discuss this *quietly*?'

Lydia threw her a grateful glance.

David said with sudden violence:

'Must we have all this disgraceful fuss over *money*!'

Magdalene said venomously to him:

'It's all very well to be so high-minded. You're not going to refuse your legacy, are you? *You* want money just as much as the rest of us do! All this unworldliness is just a pose!'

David said in a strangled voice:

'You think I ought to refuse it? I wonder——'

Hilda said sharply:

'Of course you oughtn't. Must we all behave like children? Alfred, you're the head of the family——'

Alfred seemed to wake out of a dream. He said:

'I beg your pardon. All of you shouting at once. It—it confuses me.'

Lydia said:

'As Hilda has just pointed out, why must we behave like greedy children? Let us discuss this thing quietly and sanely and'—she added this quickly—'one at a time. Alfred shall speak first because he is the eldest. What do you think, Alfred, we should do about Pilar?'

He said slowly:

'She must make her home here, certainly. And we should make her an allowance. I do not see that she has any legal claim to the money which would have gone to her mother. She's not a Lee, remember. She's a Spanish subject.'

'No legal claim, no,' said Lydia. 'But I think she has a *moral* claim. As I see it, your father, although his daughter had married a Spaniard against his wishes, recognised her to have an equal claim upon him. George, Harry, David and Jennifer were to share equally. Jennifer only died last year. I am sure that when he sent for Mr. Charlton, he meant to make ample provision for Pilar in a new will. He would have allotted her at least her mother's share. It is possible that he might have done much more than that. She was the only grandchild, remember. I think the least *we* can do is to endeavour to remedy an injustice that your father himself was preparing to remedy.'

Alfred said warmly:

'Well put, Lydia! I was wrong. I agree with you that Pilar must be given Jennifer's share of my father's fortune.'

Lydia said:

'Your turn, Harry.'

Harry said:

'As you know, I agree. I think Lydia has put the case very well, and I'd like to say I admire her for it.'

Lydia said:

'George?'

George was red in the face. He spluttered:

'Certainly not! Whole thing's preposterous! Give her a home and a decent dress allowance. Quite enough for her!'

'Then you refuse to co-operate?' asked Alfred.

'Yes, I do.'

'And he's quite right,' said Magdalene. 'It's disgraceful to suggest he should do anything of the kind! Considering that George is the *only* member of the family who has done *anything* in the world, I think it's a shame his father left him so little!'

Lydia said:

'David?'

David said vaguely:

'Oh, I think you're right. It's a pity there's got to be so much ugliness and disputing about it all.'

Hilda said:

'You're quite right, Lydia. It's only justice!'

Harry looked round.

He said:

'Well, that's clear. Of the family, Alfred, myself and David are in favour of the motion. George is against it. The ayes have it.'

George said sharply:

'There is no question of ayes or noes. My share of my father's estate is mine absolutely. I shall not part with a penny of it.'

'No, indeed,' said Magdalene.

Lydia said sharply:

'If you like to stand out, that is your business. The rest of us will make up your share of the total.'

She looked round for assent and the others nodded.

Harry said:

'Alfred's got the lion's share. He ought to stand most of the racket.'

Alfred said:

'I see that your original disinterested suggestion will soon break down.'

Hilda said firmly:

'Don't let's start again! Lydia shall tell Pilar what we've decided. We can settle details later.' She added in the hope of making a diversion, 'I wonder where Mr. Farr is, and M. Poirot?'

Alfred said:

'We dropped Poirot in the village on our way to the inquest. He said he had an important purchase to make.'

Harry said:

'Why didn't *he* go to the inquest? Surely he ought to have done!'

Lydia said:

'Perhaps he knew it was not going to be important. Who's that out there in the garden? Superintendent Sugden, or Mr. Farr?'

The efforts of the two women were successful. The family conclave broke up.

Lydia said to Hilda privately:

'Thank you, Hilda. It was nice of you to back me up. You know, you really *have* been a comfort in all this.'

Hilda said thoughtfully:

'Queer how money upsets people.'

The others had all left the room. The two women were alone.

Lydia said:

'Yes—even Harry—although it was his suggestion! And my poor

Alfred—he is so British—he doesn't really like Lee money going to a Spanish subject.'

Hilda said, smiling:

'Do you think we women are more unworldly?'

Lydia said with a shrug of her graceful shoulders:

'Well, you know, it isn't really our money—not our *own*! That may make a difference.'

Hilda said thoughtfully:

'She is a strange child—Pilar, I mean. I wonder what will become of her?'

Lydia sighed.

'I'm glad that she will be independent. To live here, to be given a home and a dress allowance, would not, I think, be very satisfactory to her. She's too proud and, I think, too—too—alien.'

She added musingly:

'I once brought some beautiful blue lapis home from Egypt. Out there, against the sun and the sand, it was a glorious colour—a brilliant warm blue. But when I got it home, the blue of it hardly showed any more. It was just a dull, darkish string of beads.'

Hilda said:

'Yes, I see. . . .'

Lydia said gently:

'I am so glad to come to know you and David at last. I'm glad you both came here.'

Hilda sighed:

'How often I've wished in the last few days that we hadn't!'

'I know. You must have done. . . . But you know, Hilda, the shock hasn't affected David nearly as badly as it might have done. I mean, he is so sensitive that it might have upset him completely. Actually, since the murder, he's seemed ever so much better——'

Hilda looked slightly disturbed. She said:

'So you've noticed that? It's rather dreadful in a way. . . . But oh! Lydia, it's undoubtedly so!'

She was silent a minute recollecting words that her husband had spoken only the night before. He had said to her, eagerly, his fair hair tossed back from his forehead:

'Hilda, you remember in Tosca—when Scarpia is dead and Tosca lights the candles at his head and feet? Do you remember what she says: "*Now* I can forgive him. . . ." That is what I feel—about father. I see now that all these years I couldn't forgive him, and yet I really wanted to. . . . But now—*now*—there's no rancour any more. It's all wiped away. And I feel—oh, I feel as though a great load had been lifted from my back.'

She had said, striving to fight back a sudden fear:

'Because he's dead?'

He had answered quickly, stammering in his eagerness:

'No, no, you don't understand. Not because *he is* dead, but because my childish stupid hate of him is dead. . . .'

Hilda thought of those words now.

She would have liked to repeat them to the woman at her side, but she felt instinctively that it was wiser not.

She followed Lydia out of the drawing-room into the hall.

Magdalene was there, standing by the hall table with a little parcel in her hand. She jumped when she saw them. She said:

'Oh, this must be M. Poirot's important purchase. I saw him put it down here just now. I wonder what it is?'

She looked from one to the other of them, giggling a little, but her eyes were sharp and anxious, belying the affected gaiety of her words.

Lydia's eyebrows rose. She said:

'I must go and wash before lunch.'

Magdalene said, still with that affectation of childishness, but unable to keep the desperate note out of her voice:

'I must just *peep!*'

She unrolled the piece of paper and gave a sharp exclamation. She stared at the thing in her hand.

Lydia stopped and Hilda too. Both women stared.

Magdalene said in a puzzled voice:

'It's a false moustache. But—but—why——?'

Hilda said doubtfully:

'Disguise? But——'

Lydia finished the sentence for her.

'But M. Poirot has a very fine moustache of his own!'

Magdalene was wrapping the parcel up again. She said:

'I don't understand. It's—it's *mad*. *Why* does M. Poirot buy a false moustache?'

2

When Pilar left the drawing-room she walked slowly along the hall. Stephen Farr was coming in through the garden door. He said:

'Well? Is the family conclave over? Has the will been read?'

Pilar said, her breath coming fast:

'I have got nothing—nothing at all! It was a will made many years ago. My grandfather left money to my mother, but because she is dead it does not go to me but goes back to *them*.'

Stephen said:

'That seems rather hard lines.'

Pilar said:

'If that old man had lived, he would have made another will. He would have left money to *me*—a lot of money! Perhaps in time he would have left me *all* the money!'

Stephen said, smiling:

'That wouldn't have been very fair either, would it?'

'Why not? He would have liked me best, that is all.'

Stephen said:

'What a greedy child you are. A real little gold-digger.'

Pilar said soberly:

'The world is very cruel to women. They must do what they can for themselves—while they are young. When they are old and ugly no one will help them."

Stephen said slowly:

'That's more true than I like to think. But it isn't *quite* true. Alfred Lee, for instance, was genuinely fond of his father in spite of the old man being thoroughly trying and exacting.'

Pilar's chin went up.

'Alfred,' she said, 'is rather a fool.'

Stephen laughed.

Then he said:

'Well, don't worry, lovely Pilar. The Lees are bound to look after you, you know.'

Pilar said disconsolately:

'It will not be very amusing, that.'

Stephen said slowly:

'No, I'm afraid it won't. I can't see you living here, Pilar. Would you like to come to South Africa?'

Pilar nodded.

Stephen said:

'There's sun there, and space. There's hard work too. Are you good at work, Pilar?'

Pilar said doubtfully:

'I do not know.'

He said:

'You'd rather sit on a balcony and eat sweets all day long? And grow enormously fat and have three double chins?'

Pilar laughed and Stephen said:

'That's better. I've made you laugh.'

Pilar said:

'I thought I should laugh this Christmas! In books I have read that an English Christmas is very gay, that one eats burning raisins and there is a plum pudding all in flames, and something that is called a Yule log.'

Stephen said:

'Ah, but you must have a Christmas uncomplicated by murder. Come in here a minute. Lydia took me in here yesterday. It's her store-room.'

He led her into a small room little bigger than a cupboard.

'Look, Pilar, boxes and boxes of crackers, and preserved fruits and oranges and dates and nuts. And here——'

'Oh!' Pilar clasped her hands. 'They are pretty, these gold and silver balls.'

'Those were to hang on a tree, with presents for the servants. And here are little snowmen all glittering with frost to put on the dinner table. And here are balloons of every colour all ready to blow up!'

'Oh!' Pilar's eyes shone. 'Oh! can we blow one up? Lydia would not mind. I do love balloons.'

Stephen said:

'Baby! Here, which will you have?'

Pilar said: 'I will have a red one.'

They selected their balloons and blew, their cheeks distended. Pilar stopped blowing to laugh, and her balloon went down again.

She said:

'You look so funny—blowing—with your cheeks puffed out.'

Her laugh rang out. Then she fell to, blowing industriously. They tied up their balloons carefully and began to play with them, patting them upwards, sending them to and fro.

Pilar said:

'Out in the hall there would be more room.'

They were sending the balloons to each other, and laughing, when Poirot came along the hall. He regarded them indulgently.

'So you play *les jeux d'enfants*? It is pretty, that!'

Pilar said breathlessly:

'Mine is the red one. It is bigger than his. Much bigger. If we took it outside it would go right up in the sky.'

'Let's send them up and wish,' said Stephen.

'Oh, yes, that is a good idea.'

Pilar ran to the garden door, Stephen followed. Poirot came behind, still looking indulgent.

'I will wish for a great deal of money,' announced Pilar.

She stood on tiptoe, holding the string of the balloon. It tugged gently as a puff of wind came. Pilar let go and it floated along, taken by the breeze.

Stephen laughed.

'You mustn't tell your wish.'

'No, why not?'

'Because it doesn't come true. Now, I'm going to wish.'

He released his balloon. But he was not so lucky. It floated sideways, caught on a holly bush and expired with a bang.

Pilar ran to it.

She announced tragically:

'It is gone . . .'

Then, as she stirred the little limp wisp of rubber with her toe, she said:

'So that was what I picked up in grandfather's room. He, too, had had a balloon, only his was a pink one.'

Poirot gave a sharp exclamation. Pilar turned inquiringly. Poirot said:

'It is nothing. I stabbed—no stubbed—the toe.'

He wheeled round and looked at the house.

He said:

'So many windows! A house, mademoiselle, has its eyes—and its ears. It is indeed regrettable that the English are so fond of open windows.'

Lydia came out on the terrace.

She said:

'Lunch is just ready. Pilar, my dear, everything has been settled quite satisfactorily. Alfred will explain the exact details to you after lunch. Shall we come in?'

They went into the house. Poirot came last. He was looking grave.

3

Lunch was over.

As they came out of the dining-room, Alfred said to Pilar:

'Will you come into my room? There is something I want to talk over with you.'

He led her across the hall and into his study, shutting the door after him. The others went on into the drawing-room. Only Hercule Poirot remained in the hall looking thoughtfully at the closed study door.

He was aware suddenly of the old butler hovering uneasily near him.

Poirot said:

'Yes, Tressilian, what is it?'

The old man seemed troubled. He said:

'I wanted to speak to Mr. Lee. But I don't like to disturb him now.'

Poirot said: 'Something has occurred?'

Tressilian said slowly:

'It's such a queer thing. It doesn't make sense.'

'Tell me,' said Hercule Poirot.

Tressilian hesitated. Then he said:

'Well, it's this, sir. You may have noticed that each side of the front door there was a cannon ball. Big heavy stone things. Well, sir, *one of them's gone*.'

Hercule Poirot's eyebrows rose. He said:

'Since when?'

'They were both there this morning, sir. I'll take my oath on that.'

'Let us see.'

Together they went outside the front door. Poirot bent and examined the remaining cannon ball. When he straightened himself, his face was very grave.

Tressilian quavered:

'Who'd want to steal a thing like that, sir? It doesn't make *sense*.'

Poirot said:

'I do not like it. I do not like it at all. . . .'

Tressilian was watching him anxiously. He said slowly:

'What's come to the house, sir? Ever since the master was murdered it doesn't seem like the same place. I feel the whole time as though I was going about in a dream. I mix things up, and I sometimes feel I can't trust my own eyes.'

Hercule Poirot shook his head. He said:

'You are wrong. Your own eyes are just what you must trust.'

Tressilian said, shaking his head:

'My sight's bad—I can't see like I used to do. I get things mixed up—and people. I'm getting too old for my work.'

Hercule Poirot clapped him on the shoulder and said:

'Courage.'

'Thank you, sir. You mean it kindly, I know. But there it is, I am too old. I'm always going back to the old days and the old faces. Miss Jenny and Master David and Master Alfred. I'm always seeing them as young gentlemen and ladies. Ever since that night when Mr. Harry came home——'

Poirot nodded.

'Yes,' he said, 'that is what I thought. You said just now "Ever since the master was murdered"—but it began before that. *It is ever since Mr. Harry came home*, is it not, that things have altered and seemed unreal?'

The butler said:

'You're quite right, sir. It was then. Mr. Harry always brought trouble into the house, even in the old days.'

His eyes wandered back to the empty stone base.

'Who can have taken it, sir?' he whispered. 'And why? It's—it's like a madhouse.'

Hercule Poirot said:

'It is not madness I am afraid of. It is sanity! Somebody, Tressilian, is in great danger.'

He turned and re-entered the house.

At that moment Pilar came out from the study. A red spot shone on either cheek. She held her head high and her eyes glittered.

As Poirot came up to her, she suddenly stamped her foot and said:

'I will not take it.'

Poirot raised his eyebrows. He said:

'What is this that you will not take, mademoiselle?'

Pilar said:

'Alfred has just told me that I am to have my mother's share of the money my grandfather left.'

'Well?'

'I could not get it by law, he said. But he and Lydia and the others consider it should be mine. They say it is a matter of justice. And so they will hand it over to me.'

Poirot said again:

'Well?'

Pilar stamped once more with her foot.

'Do you not understand? They are giving it to me—*giving* it to me.'

'Need that hurt your pride? Since what they say is true—that it should in justice be yours?'

Pilar said:

'You do not understand. . . .'

Poirot said:

'On the contrary—I understand very well.'

'Oh! . . .'She turned away pettishly.

There was a ring at the bell. Poirot glanced over his shoulder. He saw the silhouette of Superintendent Sugden outside the door. He said hurriedly to Pilar:

'Where are you going?'

She said sulkily:

'To the drawing-room. To the others.'

Poirot said quickly:

'Good. Stay with them there. Do not wander about the house alone, especially after dark. Be on your guard. You are in great danger, mademoiselle. You will never be in greater danger than yo are to-day.'

He turned away from her and went to meet Sugden.

The latter waited till Tressilian had gone back into his pantry.

Then he shoved a cable form under Poirot's nose.

'Now we've got it!' he said. 'Read that. It's from the South African Police.'

The cable said:

'*Ebenezer Farr's only son died two years ago.*'

Sugden said:

'So now we know! Funny—I was on a different tack altogether. . . .'

4

Pilar marched into the drawing-room, her head held high.

She went straight up to Lydia, who was sitting in the window with some knitting.

Pilar said:

'Lydia, I have come to tell you that I will not take that money. I am going away—at once. . . .'

Lydia looked astonished. She laid down her knitting. She said:

'My dear child, Alfred must have explained very badly! It is not in the least a matter of charity, if that is what you feel. Really, it is not a question of kindness or generosity on our part. It is a plain matter of right and wrong. In the ordinary course of events your mother would have inherited this money, and you would have come into it from her. It is your right—your blood right. It is a matter, not of charity, but of *justice!*'

Pilar said fiercely:

'And that is why I cannot do it—not when you speak like that—not when you are like that! I enjoyed coming here. It was fun! It was an adventure, but now you have spoilt it all! I am going away now, at once—you will never be bothered by me again. . . .'

Tears choked her voice. She turned and ran blindly out of the room.

Lydia stared. She said helplessly:

'I'd no idea she would take it like that!'

Hilda said:

'The child seems quite upset.'

George cleared his throat and said portentously:

'Er—as I pointed out this morning—the principle involved is wrong. Pilar has the wit to see that for herself. She refuses to accept charity——'

Lydia said sharply:

'It is *not* charity. It is her right!'

George said:

'She does not seem to think so!'

Superintendent Sugden and Hercule Poirot came in. The former looked round and asked:

'Where's Mr. Farr? I want a word with him.'

Before anyone had time to answer, Hercule Poirot said sharply:

'Where is the Señorita Estravados?'

George Lee said with a trace of malicious satisfaction:

'Going to clear out, so she says. Apparently she has had enough of her English relations.'

Poirot wheeled round.

He said to Sugden:

'Come!'

As the two men emerged into the hall, there was the sound of a heavy crash and a far-away shriek.

Poirot cried:

'Quick . . . Come . . .'

They raced along the hall and up the far staircase. The door of Pilar's room was open and a man stood in the doorway. He turned his head as they ran up. It was Stephen Farr.

He said:

'She's alive . . .'

Pilar stood crouched against the wall of her room. She was staring at the floor where a big stone cannon ball was lying.

She said breathlessly:

'It was on top of my door, balanced there. It would have crashed down on my head when I came in, but my skirt caught on a nail and jerked me back just as I was coming in.'

Poirot knelt down and examined the nail. On it was a thread of purple tweed. He looked up and nodded gravely.

'That nail, mademoiselle,' he said, 'saved your life.'

The superintendent said bewildered:

'Look here, what's the meaning of all this?'

Pilar said:

'Someone tried to kill me!'

She nodded her head several times.

Superintendent Sugden glanced up at the door.

'Booby trap,' he said. 'An old-fashioned booby trap—and its purpose was murder! That's the second murder planned in this house. But this time it didn't come off!'

Stephen Farr said huskily:

'Thank God you're safe.'

Pilar flung out her hands in a wide, appealing gesture.

'*Madre de Dios*,' she cried. 'Why should anyone wish to kill *me*? What have I done?'

Hercule Poirot said slowly:

'You should rather ask, mademoiselle, *what do I know?*'

She stared.

'Know? I do not know anything.'

Hercule Poirot said:

'That is where you are wrong. Tell me, Mademoiselle Pilar, where were you at the time of the murder? You were not in this room.'

'I was. I have told you so!'

Superintendent Sugden said with deceptive mildness:

'Yes, but you weren't speaking the truth when you said that, you know. You told us you heard your grandfather scream—you couldn't have heard that if you were in here—Mr. Poirot and I tested that yesterday.'

'Oh!' Pilar caught her breath.

Poirot said:

'You were somewhere very much nearer his room. I will tell you where I think you were, mademoiselle. You were in the recess with the statues quite close to your grandfather's door.'

Pilar said, startled:

'Oh. . . . How did you know?'

Poirot said with a faint smile:

'Mr. Farr saw you there.'

Stephen said sharply:

'I did not. That's an absolute lie!'

Poirot said:

'I ask your pardon, Mr. Farr, but you *did* see her. Remember your impression that there were *three* statues in that recess, not *two*. Only one person wore a white dress that night. Mademoiselle Estravados. *She* was the third white figure you saw. That is so, is it not, mademoiselle?'

Pilar said after a moment's hesitation:

'Yes, it is true.'

Poirot said gently:

'Now tell us, mademoiselle, the whole truth. *Why* were you there?'

Pilar said:

'I left the drawing-room after dinner and I thought I would go and see my grandfather. I thought he would be pleased. But when I turned into the passage I saw someone else was there at his door. I did not want to be seen because I knew my grandfather had said he did not want to see anyone that night. I slipped into the recess in case the person at the door turned round.

'Then, all at once, I heard the most terrible sounds, tables—chairs'—she waved her hands—'everything falling and crashing. I did not move. I do not know why. I was frightened. And then there was a terrible scream'—she crossed herself—'and my heart it stopped beating, and I said, "*Someone is dead. . . .*"'

'And then?'

'And then people began coming running along the passage and I came out at the end and joined them.'

Superintendent Sugden said sharply:

'You said nothing of all this when we first questioned you. Why not?'

Pilar shook her head. She said with an air of wisdom:

'It is not good to tell too much to the police. I thought, you see, that if I said I was near there you might think that *I* had killed him. So I said I was in my room.'

Sugden said sharply:

'If you tell deliberate lies all that it ends in is that you're bound to come under suspicion.'

Stephen Farr said:

'Pilar?'

'Yes?'

'*Who did you see standing at the door* when you turned into the passage? Tell us.'

Sugden said:

'Yes, tell us.'

For a moment the girl hesitated. Her eyes opened, then narrowed. She said slowly:

'I don't know who it was. It was too dimly lit to see. *But it was a woman. . . .*'

5

Superintendent Sugden looked round at the circle of faces. He said with something as near irritation as he had yet shown:

'This is very irregular, Mr. Poirot.'

Poirot said:

'It is a little idea of mine. I wish to share with everyone the knowledge that I have acquired. I shall then invite their co-operation, and so we shall get at the truth.'

Sugden murmured under his breath:

'Monkey tricks.'

He leaned back in his chair.

Poirot said:

'To begin with, you have, I think, an explanation to ask of Mr. Farr.'

Sugden's mouth tightened.

'I should have chosen a less public moment,' he said. 'However, I've no objection.' He handed the cable to Stephen Farr. 'Now, Mr. *Farr*, as you call yourself, perhaps you can explain *this*?'

Stephen Farr took it. Raising his eyebrows, he read it slowly out loud. Then, with a bow, he handed it back to the superintendent.

'Yes,' he said. 'It's pretty damning, isn't it?'

Sugden said:

'Is that all you've got to say about it? You quite understand there is no obligation on you to make a statement——'

Stephen Farr interrupted. He said:

'You needn't caution me, Superintendent. I can see it trembling on your tongue! Yes, I'll give you an explanation. It's not a very good one, but it's the truth.'

He paused. Then he began:

'I'm not Ebenezer Farr's son. But I knew both father and son quite well. Now try and put yourself in my place. (My name is Stephen Grant, by the way.) I arrived in this country for the first time in my life. I was disappointed. Everything and everybody seemed drab and lifeless. Then I was travelling by train and I saw a girl. I've got to say it straight out: I fell for that girl! She was the loveliest and most unlikely creature in the world! I talked to her for a while in the train and I made up my mind then and there not to lose sight of her. As I was leaving the compartment I caught sight of the label on her suitcase. Her name meant nothing to me, but the address to which she was travelling did. I'd heard of Gorston Hall, and I knew all about its owner. He was Ebenezer Farr's one-time partner and old Eb often talked about him and said what a personality he was.

'Well, the idea came to me to go to Gorston Hall and pretend I was Eb's son. He had died, as this cable says, two years ago, but

I remembered old Eb saying that he had not heard from Simeon Lee now for many years, and I judged that Lee would not know of the death of Eb's son. Anyway, I felt it was worth trying.'

Sugden said:

'You didn't try it on at once, though. You stayed in the King's Arms at Addlesfield for two days.'

Stephen said:

'I was thinking it over—whether to try it or not. At last I made up my mind I would. It appealed to me as a bit of an adventure. Well, it worked like a charm! The old man greeted me in the friendliest manner and at once asked me to come and stay in the house. I accepted. There you are, Superintendent, there's my explanation. If you don't fancy it, cast your mind back to your courting days and see if you don't remember some bit of foolishness you indulged in then. As for my real name, as I say, it's Stephen Grant. You can cable to South Africa and check up on me, but I'll tell you this: you'll find I'm a perfectly respectable citizen. I'm not a crook or a jewel thief.'

Poirot said softly:

'I never believed you were.'

Superintendent Sugden stroked his jaw cautiously.

He said:

'I'll have to check up on that story. What I'd like to know is this: Why didn't you come clean after the murder instead of telling us a pack of lies?'

Stephen said disarmingly:

'Because I was a fool! I thought I could get away with it! I thought it would look fishy if I admitted to being here under a false name. If I hadn't been a complete idiot I would have realised you were bound to cable to Jo'burg.'

Sugden said:

'Well, Mr. Farr—er—Grant—I'm not saying I disbelieve your story. It will be proved or disproved soon enough.'

He looked across inquiringly at Poirot. The latter said:

'I think Miss Estravados has something to say.'

Pilar had gone very white. She said in a breathless voice:

'It is true. I would never have told you, but for Lydia and the money. To come here and pretend and cheat and act—that was fun, but when Lydia said the money was mine and that it was only justice, that was different; it was not fun any longer.'

Alfred Lee said with a puzzled face:

'I do not understand, my dear, what you are talking about?'

Pilar said:

'You think I am your niece, Pilar Estravados? But that is not so! Pilar was killed when I was travelling with her in a car in Spain. A bomb came and it hit the car and she was killed, but I was not touched. I did not know her very well, but she had told me all about herself and how her grandfather had sent for her from England and that he was very rich. I had no money at all and I did not know where to go or what to do. And I thought suddenly: "Why should not I take Pilar's passport and go to England and become very rich?"' Her face lit up with its sudden wide smile. 'Oh, it was fun wondering if I could get away with it! Our faces on the photograph were not unlike. But when they wanted my passport here I opened the window and threw it out and ran down to get it, and then I rubbed some earth just over the face a little because at a barrier travelling they do not look very closely, but here they might——'

Alfred Lee said angrily:

'Do you mean to say that you represented yourself to my father as his granddaughter, and played on his affection for you?'

Pilar nodded. She said complacently:

'Yes, I saw at once I could make him like me very much.'

George Lee broke out:

'Preposterous!' he spluttered. 'Criminal! Attempting to get money by false pretences.'

Harry Lee said:

'She didn't get any from *you*, old boy! Pilar, I'm on your side! I've got a profound admiration for your daring. And thank goodness I'm not your uncle any more! That gives me a much freer hand.'

Pilar said to Poirot:

'*You* knew? When did you know?'

Poirot smiled:

'Mademoiselle, if you have studied the laws of Mendel you would know that two blue-eyed people are not likely to have a brown-eyed child. Your mother was, I was sure, a most chaste and respectable lady. It followed, then, that you were not Pilar Estravados at all. When you did your trick with the passport, I was quite sure of it. It was ingenious, but not, you understand, quite ingenious enough.'

Superintendent's Sugden said unpleasantly:

'The whole thing's not quite ingenious enough.'

Pilar stared at him. She said:

'I don't understand. . . .'

Sugden said:

'You've told us a story—but I think there's a good deal more you haven't told.'

Stephen said:

'You leave her alone!'

Superintendent Sugden took no notice. He went on:

'You've told us that you went up to your grandfather's room after dinner. You said it was an impulse on your part. I'm going to suggest something else. It was you who stole those diamonds. You'd handled them. On occasion, perhaps, you'd put them away in the safe and the old man hadn't watched you do it! When he found the stones were missing, he saw at once that only two people could have taken them. One was Horbury, who might have got to know the combination and have crept in and stolen them during the night. The other person was *you*.

'Well, Mr. Lee at once took measures. He rang me up and had me come to see him. Then he sent word to you to come and see him immediately after dinner. You did so and he accused you of the theft. You denied it; he pressed the charge. I don't know what happened next—perhaps he tumbled to the fact that you weren't his granddaughter, but a very clever little professional thief. Anyway, the game was up, exposure loomed over you and you slashed at him with a knife. There was a struggle and he screamed. You were properly up against it then. You hurried out of the room, turned the key from the outside and then, knowing you could not get away, before the others came, *you slipped into the recess by the statues*.'

Pilar cried shrilly:

'It is not true! It is not true! I did not steal the diamonds! I did not kill him. I swear it by the Blessed Virgin.'

Sugden said sharply:

'*Then who did?* You say you saw a figure standing outside Mr. Lee's door. According to your story, *that person must have been the murderer. No one else* passed the recess! But we've only *your* word for it *that there was a figure there at all*. In other words, *you made that up* to exculpate yourself!'

George Lee said sharply:

'Of course she's guilty! It's all clear enough! I always *said* an outsider killed my father! Preposterous nonsense to pretend one of his family would do a thing like that! It—it wouldn't be natural!'

Poirot stirred in his seat. He said:

'I disagree with you. Taking into consideration the character of Simeon Lee, it would be a very natural thing to happen.'

'Eh?' George's jaw dropped. He stared at Poirot.

Poirot went on:

'And in my opinion that very thing *did* happen. Simeon Lee was killed by his own flesh and blood, for what seemed to the murderer a very good and sufficient reason.'

George cried:

'One of us? I deny——'

Poirot's voice broke in hard as steel.

'There is a case against every person here. We will, Mr. George Lee, begin with the case against *you*. *You* had no love for your father! You kept on good terms with him for the sake of money. On the day of his death *he threatened to cut down your allowance*. You knew that on his death you would probably inherit a very substantial sum. There is the motive. After dinner you went, as you say, to telephone. You *did* telephone—but the call lasted only *five minutes*. After that you could easily have gone to your father's room, chatted with him and then attacked him and killed him. You left the room and turned the key from outside, for you hoped the affair would be put down to a burglar. You omitted, in your panic, to make sure that the window was fully open so as to support the burglar theory. That was stupid; but you are, if you will pardon my saying so, rather a stupid man!

'However,' said Poirot, after a brief pause during which George tried to speak and failed, 'many stupid men have been criminals!'

He turned his eyes on Magdalene.

'Madame, too, she also had a motive. She is, I think, in debt, and the tone of certain of your father's remarks may—have caused her uneasiness. She, too, has no alibi. She went to telephone, but she did *not* telephone, and we have *only her word* for what she did do. . . .

'Then,' he paused, 'there is Mr. David Lee. We have heard, not once but many times, of the revengeful tempers and long memories that went with the Lee blood. Mr. David Lee did not forget or forgive the way his father had treated his mother. A final jibe directed at the dead lady may have been the last straw. David Lee is said to have been playing the piano at the time of the murder. By a coincidence he was playing the "Dead March." But suppose *somebody else* was playing that "Dead March," somebody who knew what he was going to do, and who approved his action?'

Hilda Lee said quietly:

'That is an infamous suggestion.'

Poirot turned to her. 'I will offer you another, madame. It was *your* hand that did the deed. It was *you* who crept upstairs to execute judgment on a man you considered beyond human forgiveness. You are of those, madame, who can be terrible in anger. . . .'

Hilda said:

'I did not kill him.'

Superintendent Sugden said brusquely:

'Mr. Poirot's quite right. There is a possible case against everyone except Mr. Alfred Lee, Mr. Harry Lee and Mrs. Alfred Lee.'

Poirot said gently:

'I should not even except those three. . . .'

The superintendent protested:

'Oh, come now, Mr. Poirot!'

Lydia Lee said:

'And what is the case against me, M. Poirot?'

She smiled a little as she spoke, her brows raised ironically.

Poirot bowed. He said:

'Your motive, madame, I pass over. It is sufficiently obvious. As to the rest, you were wearing last night a flowered taffeta dress of a very distinctive pattern with a cape. I will remind you of the fact that Tressilian, the butler, is short-sighted. Objects at a distance are dim and vague to him. I will also point out that your drawing-room is big and lighted by heavily-shaded lamps. On that night, a minute or two before the cries were heard, Tressilian came into the drawing-room to take away the coffee-cups. He saw you, *as he thought*, in a familiar attitude by the far window half concealed by the heavy curtains."

Lydia Lee said:

'He did see me.'

Poirot went on:

'I suggest that it is possible that *what Tressilian saw was the cape of your dress*, arranged to show by the window curtain, as though you yourself were standing there.'

Lydia said:

'I was standing there. . . .'

Alfred said:

'How dare you suggest——'

Harry interrupted him.

'Let him go on, Alfred. It's our turn next. How do you suggest that dear Alfred killed his beloved father since we were both together in the dining-room at the time?'

Poirot beamed at him.

'That,' he said, 'is very simple. An alibi gains in force accordingly as it is unwillingly given. You and your brother are on bad terms. It is well known. *You* jibe at *him* in public. *He* has not a good word to say for *you*! But *supposing that were all part of a very clever plot*. Supposing that Alfred Lee is tired of dancing attendance upon an exacting task-master. Supposing that you and he have got together some time ago. Your plan is laid. You come home. Alfred appears to resent your presence. He shows jealousy and dislike of you. You show contempt for him. And then comes the night of the murder you have so cleverly planned together. One of you remains in the dining-room, talking and perhaps quarrelling aloud as though two people were there. *The other goes upstairs and commits the crime*....'

Alfred sprang to his feet.

'You devil!' He said. His voice was inarticulate. 'You inhuman devil....'

Sugden was staring at Poirot. He said:

'Do you really mean——?'

Poirot said, with a sudden ring of authority in his voice:

'I have had to show you the *possibilities*! These are the things that *might* have happened! Which of them actually *did* happen we can only tell by passing from the outside appearance to the inside reality....'

He paused and then said slowly:

'We must come back, as I said before, to the character of Simeon Lee himself....'

6

There was a momentary pause. Strangely enough, all indignation and all rancour had died down. Hercule Poirot held his audience under the spell of his personality. They watched him, fascinated, as he began slowly to speak.

'It is all there, you see. The dead man is the focus and centre of the mystery! We must probe deep into the heart and mind of Simeon Lee and see what we find there. For a man does not live and die to himself alone. That which he has, he hands on—to those who come after him....

'What had Simeon Lee to bequeath to his sons and daughter? Pride, to begin with—a pride which in the old man was frustrated in his disappointment over his children. Then there was the quality of patience. We have been told that Simeon Lee waited patiently for years in order to revenge himself upon someone who had done him an injury. We see that that aspect of his temperament was inherited by the son who resembled him least in face. David Lee also could remember and continue to harbour resentment through long years. In *face*, Harry Lee was the only one of his children who closely resembled him. That resemblance is quite striking when we examine the portrait of Simeon Lee as a young man. There is the same high-bridged aquiline nose, the long sharp line of the jaw, the backward poise of the head. I think, too, that Harry inherited many of his father's mannerisms—that habit, for instance, of throwing back his head and laughing, and another habit of drawing his finger along the line of his jaw.

'Bearing all these things in mind, and being convinced that the murder was committed by a person closely connected with the dead man, I studied the family from the psychological standpoint. That is, I tried to decide which of them were *psychologically possible criminals*. And in my judgment only two persons qualified in that respect. They were Alfred Lee and Hilda Lee, David's wife. David himself I rejected as a possible murderer. I do not think a person of his delicate susceptibilities could have faced the actual bloodshed of a cut throat. George Lee and his wife I likewise rejected. Whatever their desires, I did not think they had the temperament to take a *risk*. They were both essentially cautious. Mrs. Alfred Lee I felt sure was quite incapable of an act of violence. She has too much irony in her nature. About Harry Lee I hesitated. He had a certain coarse truculence of aspect, but I was nearly sure that Harry Lee, in spite of his bluff and his bluster, was essentially a weakling. That, I now know, was also his father's opinion. Harry, he said, was worth no more than the rest. That left me with the two people I have already mentioned. Alfred Lee was a person capable of a great deal of selfless devotion. He was a man who had controlled and subordinated himself to the will of another for many long years. It is always possible under these conditions for something to snap. Moreover, he might quite possibly have harboured a secret grudge against his father which might gradually have grown in force through never being expressed in any way. It is the quietest and meekest people who are often capable of the most sudden and unexpected violences for the reason that when their control does snap, it does entirely! The other person I considered was capable of the crime was Hilda Lee. She is the kind of individual who is capable on occasions of taking the law into her own hands—though never through selfish motives. Such people judge and also execute. Many Old Testament characters are of this type. Jael and Judith, for example.

'And now having got so far I examined the circumstances of the crime itself. And the first thing that arises—that strikes one in the face, as it were—is the extraordinary conditions under which that crime took place! Take your minds back to that room where Simeon Lee lay dead. If you remember, there was both a heavy table and a heavy chair overturned, a lamp, crockery, glasses, etc. But the chair and the table were especially surprising. They were of solid mahogany. It was hard to see how *any* struggle between that frail old man and his opponent could result in so much solid furniture being overturned and knocked down. The whole thing seemed *unreal*. And yet surely no one in their senses would stage such an effect if it had not really occurred—unless possibly Simeon Lee had been killed by a powerful man and the idea was to suggest that the assailant was a woman or somebody of weak physique.

'But such an idea was unconvincing in the extreme, since the noise of the furniture falling would give the alarm and the murderer would thereby have very little time to make his exit. It would surely be to *anyone's* advantage to cut Simeon Lee's throat as *quietly* as possible.

'Another extraordinary point was the turning of the key in the lock from the outside. Again, there seemed no *reason* for such a proceeding. It could not suggest suicide, since nothing in the death itself accorded with suicide. It was not to suggest escape through the windows—for those windows were so arranged that escape that way was impossible! Moreover, once again, it involved *time*. Time which *must* be precious to the murderer!

'There was one other incomprehensible thing—a piece of rubber cut from Simeon Lee's spongebag and a small wooden peg shown to me by Superintendent Sugden. These had been picked up from the floor by one of the persons who first entered that room. There again—*these things did not make sense!* They meant exactly nothing at all! Yet they had been there.

'The crime, you perceive, is becoming increasingly incomprehensible. It has no order, no method—*enfin*, it is not *reasonable*.

'And now we come to a further difficulty. Superintendent Sugden was sent for by the dead man; a robbery was reported to him and he was asked to return an hour and a half later. *Why?* If it is because Simeon Lee suspected his granddaughter or some other member of the family, why does he not ask Superintendent Sugden to wait downstairs while he has his interview straightaway with the suspected party? With the superintendent actually in the house, his lever over the guilty person would have been much stronger.

'So now we arrive at the point where not only the behaviour of the murderer is extraordinary, but the behaviour of Simeon Lee also is extraordinary!

'And I say to myself: "This thing is all wrong!" Why? Because we are looking at it *from the angle that the murderer wants us to look at it*. . . .

'We have three things that do not make sense: the struggle, the turned key, and the snip of rubber. But there *must* be some way of looking at those three things which *would* make sense! And I empty my mind blank and forget the circumstances of the crime and take these things *on their own merits*. I say—a *struggle*. What does *that* suggest? Violence—breakage—noise. . . . The *key? Why* does one turn a key? So that no one shall enter? But the key did not prevent that, since the door was broken down almost immediately. To keep someone *in?* To keep someone *out?* A snip of rubber? I say to myself: "A little piece of a spongebag is a little piece of a spongebag, and that is all!"

'So you would say there is nothing there—and yet that is not strictly true, for three impressions remain: noise—seclusion—blankness. . . .

'Do they fit with either of my two possibles? No, they do not. To both Alfred Lee and Hilda Lee a *quiet* murder would have been infinitely preferable, to have wasted time in locking the door from the outside is absurd, and the little piece of spongebag means yet once more—nothing at all!

'And yet I have very strongly the feeling that there is nothing absurd about this crime—that it is on the contrary very well planned and admirably executed. That it has, in fact, *succeeded*! Therefore that everything that has happened was *meant*. . . .

'And then, going over it again, I got my first glimmer of light. . . .

'Blood—*so much blood*—blood everywhere. . . . An insistence on blood—fresh, wet, gleaming blood. . . . So much blood—*too much blood*. . . .

'And a second thought comes with that. This is a crime of *blood*—it is *in* the blood. *It is Simeon Lee's own blood that rises up against him*. . . .'

Hercule Poirot leaned forward.

'The two most valuable clues in this case were uttered quite unconsciously by two different people. The first was when Mrs. Alfred Lee quoted a line from *Macbeth*: *"Who would have thought the old man to have had so much blood in him?"* The other was a phrase uttered by Tressilian, the butler. He described how he felt dazed and things seemed to be happening that had happened before. It was a very simple occurrence that gave him that strange feeling. He heard a ring at the bell and went to open the door to Harry Lee, and the next day he did the same thing to Stephen Farr.

'Now *why* did he have that feeling? Look at Harry Lee and Stephen Farr *and you will see why*. They are astoundingly alike! *That* was why *opening the door to Stephen Farr was just like opening the door to Harry Lee*. It might almost have been the same man standing there. And then, only to-day, Tressilian mentioned that he was always getting muddled between people. No wonder! Stephen Farr has a high-bridged nose, a habit of throwing his head back when he laughs, and a trick of stroking his jaw with his forefinger. Look long and earnestly at the portrait of Simeon Lee as a young man and you see *not only Harry Lee, but Stephen Farr....*'

Stephen moved. His chair creaked.

Poirot said:

'Remember that outburst of Simeon Lee's, his tirade against his family. He said, if you remember, that he would swear he had better sons *born the wrong side of the blanket*. We are back again at the character of Simeon Lee. Simeon Lee, who was successful with women and who broke his wife's heart! Simeon Lee, who boasted to Pilar that he might have a bodyguard of sons almost the same age! So I came to this conclusion: Simeon Lee had not only his legitimate family in the house, *but an unacknowledged and unrecognised son of his own blood*.'

Stephen got to his feet.

Poirot said:

'That was your real reason, wasn't it? Not that pretty romance of the girl you met in the train! You were coming here *before you met her*. Coming to see *what kind of a man your father was....*'

Stephen had gone dead white. He said, and his voice was broken and husky:

'Yes, I've always wondered.... Mother spoke about him sometimes. It grew into a kind of obsession with me—to see what he was like! I made a bit of money and I came to England. I wasn't going to let him know who I was. I pretended to be old Eb's son. I came here for one reason only—to see the man who was my father....'

Superintendent Sugden said in almost a whisper:

'Lord, I've been blind. . . . I can see it now. Twice I've taken you for Mr. Harry Lee and then seen my mistake, and yet I never guessed!'

He turned to Pilar.

'That was it, wasn't it? It was Stephen Farr you saw standing outside that door? You hesitated, I remember, and looked at him before you said it was a woman. It was Farr you saw, *and you weren't going to give him away.*'

There was a gentle rustle.

Hilda Lee's deep voice spoke:

'No,' she said. 'You're wrong. It was *I* whom Pilar saw. . . .'

Poirot said:

'You, Madame? Yes, I thought so. . . .'

Hilda said quietly:

'Self-preservation is a curious thing. I wouldn't believe I could be such a coward. To keep silence just because I was afraid!'

Poirot said:

'You will tell us now?'

She nodded.

'I was with David in the music-room. He was playing. He was in a very queer mood. I was a little frightened and I felt my responsibility very keenly because it was I who had insisted on coming here. David began to play the "Dead March," and suddenly I made up my mind. However odd it might seem, I determined that we would both leave at once—that night. I went quietly out of the music-room and upstairs. I meant to go to old Mr. Lee and tell him quite plainly why we were going. I went along the corridor to his room and knocked on the door. There was no answer. I knocked again a little louder. There was still no answer. Then I tried the doorhandle. The door was locked. And then, as I stood hesitating, *I heard a sound inside the room*——'

She stopped.

'You won't believe me, but it's true! *Some one was in there*—assaulting Mr. Lee. I heard tables and chairs overturned and the crash of glass and china, and then I heard that one last horrible cry that died away to nothing—and then silence.

'I stood there paralysed! I couldn't move! And then Mr. Farr came running along and Magdalene and all the others and Mr. Farr and Harry began to batter on the door. It went down and we saw the room, *and there was no one in it*—except Mr. Lee lying dead in all that blood.'

Her quiet voice rose higher. She cried:

'*There was no one else there—no one*, you understand! And *no one had come out of the room. . . .*'

7

Superintendent Sugden drew a deep breath.

He said:

'Either I'm going mad or everybody else is! What you've said, Mrs. Lee, is just plumb impossible. It's crazy!'

Hilda Lee cried:

'I tell you I heard them fighting in there, and I heard the old man scream when his throat was cut—and no one came out and no one was in the room!'

Hercule Poirot said:

'And all this time you have said nothing.'

Hilda Lee's face was white, but she said steadily:

'No, because if I told you what had happened, there's only one thing you could say or think—that it was *I* who killed him. . . .'

Poirot shook his head.

'No,' he said. 'You did not kill him. His son killed him.'

Stephen Farr said:

'I swear before God I never touched him!'

'Not you,' said Poirot. 'He had other sons!'

Harry said:

'What the hell——'

George stared. David drew his hands across his eyes. Alfred blinked twice.

Poirot said:

'The very first night I was here—the night of the murder—I saw a ghost. *It was the ghost of the dead man.* When I first saw Harry Lee I was puzzled. I felt I had seen him before. Then I noted his features carefully and I realised how like his father he was, and I told myself that that was what caused the feeling of familiarity.

'But yesterday a man sitting opposite me threw back his head and laughed—*and I knew who it was Harry Lee reminded me of.* And I traced again, in another face, the features of the dead man.

'No wonder poor old Tressilian felt confused when he had answered the door not to two, but to *three* men who resembled each other closely. No wonder he confessed to getting muddled about people when there were three men in the house who, at a little distance, could pass for each other! The same build, the same gestures (one in particular, a trick of stroking the jaw), the same habit of laughing with the head thrown back, the same distinctive high-bridged nose. Yet the similarity was not always easy to see—*for the third man had a moustache*.'

He leaned forward.

'One forgets sometimes that police officers are men, that they have wives and children, mothers'—he paused—'and *fathers*. . . . Remember Simeon Lee's local reputation: a man who broke his wife's heart because of his affairs with women. A son born the wrong side of the blanket may inherit many things. He may inherit his pride and his patience and his revengeful spirit!'

His voice rose.

'All your life, Sugden, you've resented the wrong your father did you. I think you determined long ago to kill him. You come from the next county, not very far away. Doubtless your mother, with the money Simeon Lee so generously gave her, was able to find a husband who would stand father to her child. Easy for you to enter the Middleshire Police Force and wait your opportunity. A police superintendent has a grand opportunity of committing a murder and getting away with it.'

Sugden's face had gone white as paper.

He said:

'You're mad! I was outside the house when he was killed.'

Poirot shook his head.

'No, you killed him before you left the house the first time. No one saw him alive after you left. It was all so easy for you. Simeon Lee expected you, yes, *but he never sent for you*. It was *you* who rang him up and spoke vaguely about an attempt at robbery. You said you would call upon him just before eight that night and would pretend to be collecting for a police charity. Simeon Lee had no suspicions. He did not know you were his son. You came and told him a tale of substituted diamonds. He opened the safe to show you that the real diamonds were safe in his possession. You apologised, came back to the hearth with him and, catching him unawares, you cut his throat, holding your hand over his mouth so that he shouldn't cry out. Child's play to a man of your powerful physique.

'Then you set the scene. You took the diamonds. You piled up tables and chairs, lamps and glasses, and twined a very thin rope or cord which you had brought in coiled round your body, in and out between them. You had with you a bottle of some freshly killed animal's blood to which you had added a quantity of sodium citrate. You sprinkled this about freely and added more sodium citrate to the pool of blood which flowed from Simeon Lee's wound. You made up the fire so that the body should keep its warmth. Then you passed the two ends of the cord out through the narrow slit at the bottom of the window and let them hang down the wall. You left the room and turned the key from the outside. That was vital, *since no one must by any chance enter that room.*

'Then you went out and hid the diamonds in the stone sink garden. If, sooner, or later, they were discovered there, they would only focus suspicion more strongly where you wanted it: on the members of Simeon Lee's legitimate family. A little before nine-fifteen you returned and, going up to the wall underneath the window, you pulled on the cord. That dislodged the carefully-piled-up structure you had arranged. Furniture and china fell with a crash. You pulled on one end of the cord and re-wound it round your body under your coat and waistcoat.

'You had one further device!'

He turned to the others.

'Do you remember, all of you, how each of you described the dying scream of Mr. Lee in a different way? You, Mr. Lee, described it as the cry of a man in mortal agony. Your wife and David Lee both used the expression: a soul in hell. Mrs. David Lee, on the contrary, said it was the cry of someone who had *no* soul. She said it was inhuman like a beast. It was Harry Lee who came nearest to the truth. He said it sounded like killing a pig.

'Do you know those long pink bladders that are sold at fairs with faces painted on them called "Dying Pigs"? As the air rushes out they give forth an inhuman wail. That, Sugden, was your final touch. You arranged one of those in the room. The mouth of it was stopped up with a peg, but that peg was connected to the cord. When you pulled on the cord the peg came out and the pig began to deflate. On top of the falling furniture came the scream of the "Dying Pig."'

He turned once more to the others.

'You see now what it was that Pilar Estravados picked up? The superintendent had hoped to get there in time to retrieve that little wisp of rubber before any one noticed it. However, he took it from Pilar quickly enough in his most official manner. But remember *he never mentioned that incident to anyone*. In itself that was a singularly suspicious fact. I heard of it from Magdalene Lee and tackled him about it. He was prepared for that eventuality. He had snipped a piece from Mr. Lee's rubber sponge-bag and produced that together with a wooden peg. Superficially it answered to the same description—a fragment of rubber and a piece of wood. It meant, as I realised at the time, absolutely nothing! But, fool that I was, I did not at once say: "This means nothing, *so it cannot have been there, and Superintendent Sugden is lying. . . .*" No, I foolishly went on trying to find an explanation for it. It was not until Mademoiselle Estravados was playing with a balloon that burst, and she cried out that it must have been a burst balloon she picked up in Simeon Lee's room, that I saw the truth.

'You see now how everything fits in? The improbable struggle, *which is necessary to establish a false time of death*; the locked door—so that nobody shall find the body too soon; the dying man's scream. The crime is now logical and reasonable.

'But from the moment that Pilar Estravados cried aloud her discovery about the balloon, she was a source of danger to the murderer. And if that remark had been heard by him from the house (which it well might, for her voice was high and clear and the windows were open), she herself was in considerable danger. Already she had given the murderer one very nasty moment. She had said, speaking of old Mr. Lee, "He must have been very good-looking when he was young." And had added, speaking directly to Sugden: "*Like you.*" She meant that literally, and Sugden knew it. No wonder Sugden went purple in the face and nearly choked. It was so unexpected and so deadly dangerous. He hoped after that to fix the guilt on her, but it proved unexpectedly difficult, since as the old man's portionless granddaughter she had obviously no motive for the crime. Later, when he overhead from the house her clear, high voice calling out its remark about the balloon, he decided on desperate measures. He set that booby trap when we were at lunch. Luckily, almost by a miracle, it failed. . . .'

There was dead silence.

Then Sugden said quietly:

'When were you sure?'

Poirot said:

'I was not quite sure till I brought home a false moustache and tried it on Simeon Lee's picture. Then—the face that looked at me was yours.'

Sugden said:

'God rot his soul in hell! I'm glad I did it!'

PART SEVEN

December 28th

1

LYDIA LEE said:

'Pilar, I think you had better stay with us until we can arrange something definite for you.'

Pilar said meekly:

'You are very good, Lydia. You are nice. You forgive people quite easily without making a fuss about it.'

Lydia said, smiling:

'I still call you Pilar, though I suppose your name is something else.'

'Yes, I am really Conchita Lopez.'

'Conchita is a pretty name too.'

'You are really almost too nice, Lydia. But you don't need to be bothered by me. I am going to marry Stephen, and we are going to South Africa.'

Lydia said, smiling:

'Well, that rounds off things very nicely.'

Pilar said timidly:

'Since you have been so kind, do you think, Lydia, that one day we might come back and stay with you—perhaps for Christmas—and then we could have the crackers and the burning raisins and those shiny things on a tree and the little snowmen?'

'Certainly, you shall come and have a real English Christmas.'

'That will be lovely. You see, Lydia, I feel that this year it was not a nice Christmas at all.'

Lydia caught her breath. She said:

'No, it was not a nice Christmas. . . .'

2

Harry said:

'Well, good-bye, Alfred. Don't suppose you'll be troubled by seeing much of me. I'm off to Hawaii. Always meant to live there if I had a bit of money.'

Alfred said:

'Good-bye, Harry. I expect you'll enjoy yourself. I hope so.'

Harry said rather awkwardly:

'Sorry I riled you so much, old man. Rotten sense of humour I've got. Can't help trying to pull a fellow's leg.'

Alfred said with an effort:

'Suppose I must learn to take a joke.'

Harry said with relief:

'Well—so-long.'

3

Alfred said:

'David, Lydia and I have decided to sell up this place. I thought perhaps you'd like some of the things that were our mother's—her chair and that footstool. You were always her favourite.'

David hesitated a minute. Then he said slowly:

'Thanks for the thought, Alfred, but do you know, I don't think I will. I don't want anything out of the house. I feel it's better to break with the past altogether.'

Alfred said:

'Yes, I understand. Maybe you're right.'

4

George said:

'Well, good-bye, Alfred. Good-bye, Lydia. What a terrible time we have been through. There's the trial coming on, too. I suppose the whole disgraceful story is bound to come out—Sugden being—er—my father's son. One couldn't arrange for it to be put to him, I suppose, that it would be better if he pleaded advanced Communist views and dislike of my father as a Capitalist—something of that kind?'

Lydia said:

'My dear George, do you really imagine that a man like Sugden would tell lies to soothe *our* feelings?'

George said:

'Er—perhaps not. No, I see your point. All the same, the man must be mad. Well, good-bye again.'

Magdalene said:

'*Good*-bye. Next year do let's all go to the Riviera or somewhere for Christmas and be really gay.'

George said:

'Depends on the Exchange.'

Magdalene said:

'Darling, don't be *mean*.'

5

Alfred came out on the terrace. Lydia was bending over a stone sink. She straightened up when she saw him.

He said with a sigh:

'Well—they've all gone.'

Lydia said:

'Yes—what a blessing.'

'It is rather.'

Alfred said:

'You'll be glad to leave here.'

She asked:

'Will you mind very much?'

'No, I shall be glad. There are so many interesting things we can do together. To live on here would be to be constantly reminded of that nightmare. Thank God it's all over!'

Lydia said:

'Thanks to Hercule Poirot.'

'Yes. You know, it was really amazing the way everything fell into place when he explained it.'

'I know. Like when you finish a jig-saw puzzle and all the queer-shaped bits you swear won't fit in anywhere find their places quite naturally.'

Alfred said:

'There's one little thing that never fitted in. What *was* George doing *after* he telephoned. Why wouldn't he say?'

'Don't you know? I knew all the time. He was having a look through your papers on your desk.'

'Oh! No, Lydia, no one would do a thing like that!'

'George would. He's frightfully curious about money matters. But of course he couldn't say so. He'd have had to be actually in the dock before he'd have owned up to that.'

Alfred said:

'Are you making another garden?'

'Yes.'

'What is it this time?'

'I think,' said Lydia, 'it's an attempt at the Garden of Eden. A new version—without any serpent—and Adam and Eve are definitely middle-aged.'

Alfred said gently:

'Dear Lydia, how patient you have been all these years. You have been very good to me.'

Lydia said:

'But, you see, Alfred, I love you. . . .'

6

Colonel Johnson said:

'God bless my soul!' Then he said: 'Upon my word!' And finally once more: 'God bless my soul!'

He leaned back in his chair and stared at Poirot. He said plaintively:

'My best man! What's the police coming to?'

Poirot said:

'Even policemen have private lives! Sugden was a very proud man.'

Colonel Johnson shook his head.

To relieve his feelings he kicked at the logs in the grate. He said jerkily:

'I always say—nothing like a wood fire.'

Hercule Poirot, conscious of the draughts round his neck, thought to himself:

'*Pour moi*, every time the central heating. . . .'